Nolyn

MICHAEL J. SULLIVAN

Nolyn © 2021 by Michael J. Sullivan
Cover illustration © 2020 by Marc Simonetti
Cover design © 2021 Shawn T. King
Map © 2021 by Michael J. Sullivan
Interior design © 2021 Robin Sullivan
978-1-943363-63-6
All rights reserved.

Published in the United States by Riyria Enterprises, LLC
Learn more about Michael's writings at michael-j-sullivan.com
To contact Michael, email him at michael@michael-j-sullivan.com

First Edition
Printed in the USA

1   3   5   7   9   8   6   4   2

RIYRIA
ENTERPRISES

Praise for Nolyn

"*Nolyn* is masterfully executed and the disparate storylines are equally intriguing as they are spun beautifully together into an ending full of gnarled twists and grim surprises that will leave you clamoring for more. For true fans of epic fantasy, Michael J. Sullivan's The Rise and the Fall series is not one to miss."
– David Estes, Amazon #1 bestselling author of *Fatemarked*

"Breathtakingly epic in scope, yet the characters are infused with the breath of genuine humanity that makes Sullivan's work utterly unique."
– Andy Peloquin, bestselling author of The Silent Champions series

"Vengeance and love test the boundaries of honor in this phenomenal epic fantasy by Michael J. Sullivan. Heart-wrenching and powerful, you can't help but root for Nolyn and Sephryn as they struggle to unravel the plots against them before the final trap is sprung. I loved every minute and can't wait to see what happens next!"
– Megan Haskell, award-winning author of The Sanyare Chronicles

"With *Nolyn*, a true master of epic fantasy shines even brighter. Sullivan has an amazing ability to craft a brilliant ensemble of characters and lead readers on an adventure that keeps them wide-eyed and begging for more with each expertly written page."
– Dyrk Ashton, author of The Paternus Trilogy

"*Nolyn* was yet another well-crafted and enthralling tale from a masterful storyteller, who never fails to give me what I craved from the world of Elan."
– TS Chan, Novel Notions

Works by Michael J. Sullivan

THE LEGENDS OF THE FIRST EMPIRE
Age of Myth • *Age of Swords* • *Age of War*
Age of Legend • *Age of Death* • *Age of Empyre*

THE RISE AND FALL TRILOGY
Nolyn • *Farilane* • *Esrahaddon*

THE RIYRIA CHRONICLES
The Crown Tower • *The Rose and the Thorn*
The Death of Dulgath • *The Disappearance of Winter's Daughter*
Drumindor (Summer 2024)

THE RIYRIA REVELATIONS
Theft of Swords (*The Crown Conspiracy* • *Avempartha*)
Rise of Empire (*Nyphron Rising* • *The Emerald Storm*)
Heir of Novron (*Wintertide* • *Percepliquis*)

STANDALONE TALES
Hollow World (Sci-fi Thriller Novel)
Pile of Bones (Legends of the First Empire Short Story)

SHORT STORIES IN ANTHOLOGIES
When Swords Fall Silent: "May Luck Be With You" (Riyria Chronicles)
Heroes Wanted: "The Ashmoore Affair" (Riyria Chronicles)
Blackguards: "Professional Integrity" (Riyria Chronicles)
Unfettered: "The Jester" (Riyria Chronicles)
Unbound: "The Game" (Fantasy: LitRpg)
Unfettered II: "Little Wren and the Big Forest" (Legends of the First Empire)
The End: Visions of the Apocalypse: "Burning Alexandria" (Dystopian Sci-fi)
Triumph Over Tragedy: "Traditions" (Fantasy: Tales from Elan)
The Fantasy Faction Anthology: "Autumn Mist" (Fantasy: Contemporary)

This book is dedicated to everyone who has dared to dream the impossible.

Always remember that the only way to guarantee failure is to stop trying.

Contents

Author's Note   *xiii*
World Map   *xvii*

Chapter 01: The Arrow of Death   1
Chapter 02: The Monk   18
Chapter 03: The Gathering   37
Chapter 04: The Voice   56
Chapter 05: One of Them   76
Chapter 06: Divine Providence   87
Chapter 07: The Thief and the Poker   97
Chapter 08: Escape from Urlineus   120
Chapter 09: Inside the Gem Fortress   134
Chapter 10: Death Pays a Visit   153
Chapter 11: The Orinfar   162
Chapter 12: Crossroads   180
Chapter 13: Vernes   193
Chapter 14: A Gem of Great Worth   215
Chapter 15: Teshlor Nights   226
Chapter 16: Hail, Prymus   237
Chapter 17: Cries in the Dark   246
Chapter 18: Six Toes In   253
Chapter 19: Father and Son   265

Contents

Chapter 20: Children of Legends   277
Chapter 21: A Cup of Wine   294
Chapter 22: Founder's Day   305
Chapter 23: Miralyith   317
Chapter 24: The Horn   330
Chapter 25: The Invisible Hand Moves   338
Chapter 26: Telling the Truth   351
Chapter 27: The Last Galantian   357
Chapter 28: Finding the Way Home   372

Farilane Sneak Peek   *383*
Afterword   *405*
Acknowledgments   *409*
About the Author   *411*
About the Type   *412*

Author's Note

Hello! I'm Michael J. Sullivan, the author of *Nolyn*. This book is the first in my latest series, The Rise and Fall, and I'm pleased to announce that it became a *New York Times* Bestseller! If you had told me twenty-five years ago that I'd become a bestselling author with twenty published novels, I would have concluded you were insane. You see, as a young man, I spent more than a decade trying to get published. By October of 1995, when none of the thirteen books I had written went anywhere, I quit and vowed never to do anything creative again. So, I started an advertising agency.

A decade later, I had proven to myself that I wasn't a complete failure because my wife, Robin, and I had built a successful business. At just thirty-four years of age, I'd accomplished most of my life's goals: I had a beautiful and intelligent wife, wonderful children, a house, and financial stability. Times were good, but there was a problem. Both my wife and I had reached the top of the mountain and felt like Alexander with no more worlds to conquer . . . except one—the one that got away.

In the early 2000s, I picked up the first Harry Potter book for my daughter, who was struggling with dyslexia. Reading it, I remembered the joy of stepping between the covers of a book and tumbling into an immersive world and meeting people I wished were real-life friends. In my quest for publication by studying award-winning novels, I'd lost the fun. I'd forgotten the whole reason I started writing in the first place. I had refused to put pen to paper for over a decade, but that hadn't stopped the stories. In particular, there were two insistent characters beating on the door to my consciousness, demanding to be let in.

In 2004, I sat down to write the first novel set in the world of Elan about an idealistic ex-mercenary and a cynical thief. But what made writing these books so truly crazy is that I had no intention to publish. That way led to the dark side—to the depression of waiting for a call that would never come. I abandoned the dream, and with that decision came the freedom to enjoy writing again.

I won't bore you with the details of how the books eventually made it "into the world." The short version is that my wife, who came to believe in the dream I had given up, willed them into existence using a combination of small press publishers, self-publishing, and finally, the "Big Five." After finishing the Riyria Revelations, I never expected to return to the world of Elan. But then, Robin became depressed by the absence of her favorite duo (and so did many of my readers). So I created the Riyria Chronicles to provide some standalone tales exploring how Royce and Hadrian had met and started working together.

Being a fantasy author, I had created thousands of years of history while building the world of Elan, but only a small fraction of my universe had made it onto the page. Having studied history, I know there is a significant difference between how people remember the past and what actually happened. Therefore, the Elan I created consisted of two realities: the truth and a web of lies intertwined with various myths and legends.

And that's how The Legends of the First Empire series came into being. While Riyria centered on a pair of rogues with complementary skills, Legends focused on an unlikely group of ordinary people born in extraordinary times. Their ability to rise to the occasion ended up steering Elan's future, even if many of their deeds would become lost to antiquity.

Unlike when I first finished Riyria, I knew that I would return to the world of Elan. In Legends, we begin in what would have been Elan's Bronze Age, and we see the early formation of the First Great Empire.

Having done that, it only made sense to show its eventual fall, which brings us to this series.

The three books are titled *Nolyn*, *Farilane*, and *Esrahaddon*. For those who have read my other stories, two of these names may be familiar. Nolyn is born in *Age of War*, the son of two of Elan's most famous historical figures. Esrahaddon makes his rather mysterious appearance in Riyria during *Theft of Swords*. Truth be told, Farilane is briefly mentioned in both series, although I suspect many won't remember her. She's a scholar who is obsessed with history. Like Brin, who wrote the famed *Book of Brin*, Farilane pens *The Migration of Peoples*, a foundational historical record about my little invented world.

Now, if you are worried because you've never read any of my previous books, please don't be. I write each of my series to stand independently, and no knowledge of the others is required. That said, if you finish this book and decide to venture further into the world of Elan, you'll find yourself on an Easter egg hunt where there are various "winks and nods" for people in the know.

Okay, so what is *Nolyn* about? Well, it begins about eight hundred and fifty years after the Great War and the founding of the First Empire. Humanity is trending away from its barbaric roots and embracing a more sophisticated civilization. But Nolyn's militaristic father still rules, and who is best suited to lead this emerging culture to its next evolutionary stage is in question.

Like both the Riyria Revelations and Legends of the First Empire, I penned this entire series before releasing the first book. I do this so I can ensure that the story wraps up in a satisfying way. Plus, I have the freedom to go back and add foundations in earlier books when a great idea comes to me later on. Also, writing in this manner means people won't have to wait years (or decades) for the next installment. The plan is to release the books in the summer at one-year intervals. But for those who want the tales sooner, each title will have a pre-launch using

Kickstarter. People who pre-order that way will get the books three to four months before their official retail release.

Before I go, I would like to discuss how I structured this series because it's not conventional. In most fantasy tales, you follow the same group of characters across multiple books, but The Rise and Fall books are more akin to three standalone novels. As indicated by the titular names, each one focuses on an important figure who lives at a pivotal point in the First Empire's 2,000-year history.

And with all that said, I'll take my leave and let you dive into the first book. I want to extend my gratitude to you for giving *Nolyn* a try. If you haven't read any of my other stories, I hope that reading this one opens the door to more tales from the world of Elan, of which there are many: six Riyria Revelations, four Riyria Chronicles, and six Legends of the First Empire books. As for reading order, I suggest starting with *Age of Myth*, since The Legends of the First Empire series and The Rise and Fall have some character cross-over. While you're doing that, Robin and I will continue to edit and polish the remaining two books. You see, writing the book is only half the battle. There is plenty of work yet to do to ensure that you receive the best stories possible. Hopefully, I'll see you again in the summer of 2022 for the release of *Farilane*.

Now, turn the page, tap the screen, or adjust the volume, a new era in Elan awaits.

Michael J. Sullivan

Nolyn

BOOK ONE OF

The Rise and Fall

MICHAEL J. SULLIVAN

CHAPTER ONE

The Arrow of Death

Nolyn Nyphronian stood in unrelenting heat and a cloud of biting flies, contemplating philosophy—no small achievement in a rain forest where hot, moist air made breathing a labor, and all things frantically rushed to become dirt. Clothes rotted and metal rusted at baffling speeds. Leather turned green in days; all else picked up a spotted black taint—jungle grime, they called it. Everything everywhere returned to that from whence it came.

But in the Erbon Forest, the race to dirt is absolutely absurd. If the enemy doesn't kill us, the jungle will.

That reminded him of the popular, albeit fatalistic, adage among the imperial legions that "The Arrow of Death is never seen." Despite this theory, Nolyn had always believed that when his time came, he would know. Now he had proof. The scout he'd dispatched was returning, and far too soon to be bringing good news.

Nolyn couldn't remember the scout's name. He'd met a lot of people since transferring to the Seventh Legion. Three days traveling with a group of twenty men hadn't been enough time to learn much of anything, much less everyone's name. While the scout had been gone, the remainder of the squadron had waited where a rare shaft of sunlight reached the forest floor. None of them had spoken, moved, or so much as coughed. They were deep inside the enemy's territory—silence their only protection.

Cutting his way out of the brush, the scout was slick with sweat and breathing heavily. The kid's eyes were wide with worry, but no blood coated his blade. *The fear isn't from having been attacked—not yet, at least.*

"No outpost?" Nolyn assumed but wanted to make it official.

"Not just that, sir," the scout said, then took a breath. "There's no pass. Cliffs just come together." He looked back into the dense cluster of wagon-wheel-sized leaves that had closed up, erasing all evidence of his passage. "This is a box canyon, sir. There's no way out 'cept the way we come in. We're trapped."

That explains his quick return. Nolyn calmly nodded as if he received such news every day. "Thank you," was all he said.

I was right, Sephryn. We aren't meant for each other. Never before had he hated winning an argument. *First Bran, now me. She'll be alone—the last of us.*

Touching the braided leather strap around his wrist, a gift from Sephryn, he wondered how long it would take for news of his death to reach Percepliquis, and who would be the one to tell her. *Maybe my father.* That brought a miserable smile to Nolyn's lips. *No—that's what a real father would do; that's what a human being would do. Nyphron has never been either.*

Nolyn walked over to Acer, the only animal they had. Because squadron commanders were expected to look down on their troops, the horse was fitted with a saddle. Even so, Nolyn hadn't ridden her. He held out the reins to the scout. "Here."

The kid looked at the animal, puzzled. "I don't understand."

Nolyn thrust the reins into the young man's hands. "Ride back to Urlineus. Report what happened. Tell them to send help."

The light of purpose and understanding ignited in the young man's eyes. He nodded. "Yes, sir. Right away, sir."

"Go, lad. Hurry. We're counting on you."

The scout mounted, and with a last look back, he spurred the horse and thundered away, crashing through the broad leafy plants lining the rough trail they had only recently cut. The squadron watched until the sounds of the horse faded, then they stared at Nolyn. He wondered if The Arrow of Death was now visible to everyone.

Just as he didn't know their names, they didn't know him. They were facing their first crisis, and likely their last. He could lie and offer hope to shore up their courage, but he doubted it would matter.

Everything returns to dirt. All that remains is theater.

"My apologies, gentlemen." Nolyn tried to sound as gallant as possible. "It appears you are to be sacrificed along with me, and for that, I'm sincerely sorry."

"What do you mean, Your Highness?" Jerel DeMardefeld asked. Nolyn remembered *his* name because it sounded as absurdly dignified as the man looked. DeMardefeld stood out from the rest by virtue of his exceptional plate armor and polished weapons, making even Nolyn appear a pauper. At that moment, the impeccably bedecked soldier stared incredulously, as if Nolyn had just declared the sun was but a lie.

Nolyn took a breath. "I'm about to be assassinated, and because someone wants my death to be seen as a casualty of war, all of you will have the misfortune of joining me." He frowned, felt the need to say more, and added, "You deserve better."

They didn't break, which surprised Nolyn. Legions were held together by discipline and faith in the infallibility of their leaders, even unfamiliar ones. By admitting defeat, he had cut those invisible bonds. They were free to run, to panic, or, if nothing else, at least to complain. Instead, they remained silent, though their eyes shifted to the ground.

They're all thinking the same thing: dirt. This day has forced everyone to become a philosopher.

"I don't understand," the First Spear said. "If that's true, why didn't you take the horse? Why send the scout? It'll take days for any help to arrive, and we only have hours. You've thrown away your only hope of escape."

"Did I? What a fool I am." Nolyn moved to a fallen tree and began breaking off dead branches. "What's your name, First Spear?"

"Amicus, sir."

"Well, Amicus, you're a bright fellow." Nolyn snapped another stick. "Which is why I'm turning command of this squadron over to you."

"Me? But *you're* the prymus, sir."

"Not anymore. You're going to do your best to lead these men to safety. I'm going to stay here and build a nice fire."

"Oh, no, sir!" one of the others said. Nolyn didn't know his name, either, but the spike on his helmet declared he was the squadron's Second Spear. "You can't do that, sir. You'll bring the ghazel for sure. Building a fire is like hanging a lantern in a swamp. You'll draw in a cloud of them, but these pests have four-inch claws and fangs."

"That's what he wants," Jerel said with absolute conviction. "He plans to distract the ghazel to help us escape."

Nolyn picked up another branch and snapped it in half, tossing both pieces onto a small pile. As he did, Jerel DeMardefeld took out his hatchet and started chopping wood.

"You don't have to do that," Nolyn said.

Jerel only smiled at him and then at Amicus.

In reply, Amicus frowned, set his shield on the ground, then scratched the bristle on his neck. He addressed Nolyn, "Are you certain you're the emperor's son? Because . . ." He looked down the narrow trail where the scout had gone. "It's not normal for the likes of you to sacrifice yourself for people like us. It's always the other way around."

"Not normal at all," Jerel added as he cleaved a thick branch in half.

"Oh, really?" Nolyn said. "You're both such experts. As I'm the *only* child of Nyphron, who are you comparing me with?"

"I just meant . . ." Amicus apparently didn't know what he meant and concluded his absent thought by folding his arms.

"You're wasting time. Sun's going down." That was merely a guess. Nolyn wasn't certain how late it was. In Calynia's jungle region, time was difficult to gauge. Except for the one diminishing shaft of sunlight, the leafy canopy blocked the sky.

"You honestly want us to abandon you? So we"—Amicus gestured to the others—"can get away?"

Nolyn shrugged. "Look, it's not like I'm loving the idea, but it's your best chance. So yeah, that's pretty much it. I stay, build a big fire, make a lot of noise, and invite as many unwanted guests as I can. Might help, certainly can't hurt."

"Wait a minute." Amicus looked down the trail once more, then whirled back on Nolyn. "Everett's the youngest. Is that why you sent him on the horse?"

Everett—is that his name? Nolyn thought. *By Mar, I'm terrible with names. Faces I do okay with, not bad at numbers, but names . . .*

"That'd be my guess," Jerel said. His smile turned into a grin, which was still directed at Amicus.

The First Spear glared back. "Oh, shut up. This has nothing to do with you and your delusions."

Jerel shrugged and returned to chopping wood.

Amicus started shaking his head. "No, I'm not buying it. None of it." His voice picked up an edge of anger. "You don't even know us. Besides, you're the prince, an officer, and a—" He stopped.

Nolyn lifted his sight from the woodpile to look at the First Spear. "Yes? Go on."

The soldier refused to reply. He stared, his face a grim shield.

"Well, say it, First Spear. What am I?"

Amicus remained silent.

"We're all likely to die," Nolyn continued. "And although I'm new to Calynia, I've fought the ghazel for far longer than you can imagine. I suspect we both know what they do to their enemies. I can't punish you any more than they. So go on, speak your mind. Tell me. What am I?"

"One of *them*," Amicus said. "An Instarya."

"Ah." Nolyn presented a judicial smile and nodded. "Honestly, I didn't know which way you were going to go with that. Could have been elf, or Fhrey, or privileged—none of which is true, by the way, and that includes Instarya."

"Your father is Emperor Nyphron, leader of the Fhrey warrior clan. That makes you one, too."

"You're forgetting Persephone." He paused, still holding two sticks destined for the fire. "It's been over eight hundred years since my mother died, so I suppose your mistake is understandable—depressing but expected. A lot of people have forgotten her." He threw the sticks into the pile. "She was the one who named me. Do you know what *Nolyn* means?"

"I know it's Fhrey."

"It means 'no-land.' It means I don't belong anywhere. My father is Fhrey, but my mother was human, which makes me . . . what? Both? Neither? Something else entirely?" His voice was raised. "You're pointing the finger. You tell me, First Spear, what *am* I? I'd honestly like to know."

That shut Amicus up. He sighed, and with one more look at Jerel, he removed his helmet.

Nolyn saw doubt cut grooves across his brow, but . . .

He looks familiar. Is this the first time I've seen him without the helm?

Studying the soldier's unobscured face, Nolyn was convinced he'd seen the First Spear of the Seventh Legion's Sikaria Auxiliary Squadron before. But Nolyn couldn't place where. The memory was as elusive as names had always proven to be.

"Amicus? We going?" the Second Spear asked.

For a moment, the First Spear didn't answer. His sight tracked to Nolyn with an irritated, almost hateful, glare. "No. We're staying."

Nolyn shook his head in disbelief. "This is ridiculous. You're all going to die because of what? Honor? Decency? Duty?"

"You started it."

Nolyn sighed. "Stupid is what it is." He looked down the trail. "I doubt even Everett will escape. They know we can't get out any other way, so the ghazel will come at us from upriver, corking our way out."

Amicus nodded. "In the dark, they'll expect us to run blindly and become separated. Easy pickings is what they're hoping for." He looked down at the little pile of wood Nolyn had assembled. "But with a *big* fire to help us *see* . . ."

Nolyn considered this. "The Durat Ran ghazel from the north hate bright lights. Living in mountain caves makes their big eyes overly sensitive. How is it here?"

Amicus gestured at the jungle canopy. "Same way with the Gur Um Ran. Jungles are dark, too."

Nolyn nodded. "And I suppose if we put our backs to the cliff and had the river in front . . ."

"Then we would narrow their access," Amicus finished. "Reduce the benefit of their numbers, negate their advantage."

Nolyn looked around. "They'll send—what do you think? A hundred daku?"

"They aren't called that here," the Second Spear said. "The Gur Um Ran call their veteran warriors zaphers. And it will be more like two hundred."

Nolyn looked at the man. "I swear I have the worst memory for names. Have you told me yours?"

"Yes, sir. Back in Urlineus, sir."

"Tell me again, will you?"

"Riley Glot, sir."

"Thank you, Riley. And two hundred, you say? Since there are twenty of us, we'll *only* need to kill ten each," he said sarcastically, then regretted it. Now wasn't the time to weaken morale. "I mean, that shouldn't be a problem, right?" he added with as much enthusiasm as he could muster.

"Oh, absolutely, sir," Riley said, with more sincerity than Nolyn expected. "With Amicus, we ought to—"

The First Spear coughed.

"Ought to what?" Nolyn asked.

Riley didn't offer any more.

"Is there something I should know?" Nolyn pressed. "I only ask because, well, since you aren't abandoning me, I remain the commander of this squadron. Our chance of survival is somewhere between nonexistent and iffy, so if there's something that could help, perhaps you'd like to share?"

Again, Riley stared at Amicus. They all did.

"The squad appears to be tossing the ball to you, First Spear," Nolyn said. "What's your play?"

Amicus glared back at the men around him but offered no explanation.

I saw him in a crowd, Nolyn realized, *a big one, an event of some kind.*

Nolyn studied the annoyingly familiar man. Like the rest, the First Spear was laden with armor, a javelin, dagger, and survival gear weighing nearly sixty pounds. That was a heavy load to bear through a sweltering jungle, so it struck Nolyn as odd that Amicus chose to carry additional weight. The man wore three swords: one on each hip and a third—a giant one—strapped to his back. First Spears were responsible for the men of their squadron. As such, they often carried extra bandages, food, or liquor, which they handed out as needed. Packing two extra swords was an odd choice, particularly the big one, which could be of little use in the dense jungle.

Three swords! The thought finally registered. *Of course! That's what he's famous for.*

"What is your full name, Amicus?"

The First Spear's frown increased. He shot pointed looks at his fellow soldiers.

"You have one, don't you? A family name?" Nolyn chuckled at the man's reluctance. "Come now, The Arrow of Death is hurtling our way. What tale will any of us tell?"

After a deep sigh, Amicus said, "Killian."

Amicus was a common name, but *Killian* was not, and *everyone* knew Amicus Killian.

"What are you doing here?"

The First Spear glared once more at his fellows. "I *was* hiding."

Nolyn had fought the Fir Ran, Fen Ran, and Durat Ran ghazel in the forests, swamps, and mountains of Avrlyn, but even after centuries, he still wasn't certain if the goblins were truly nocturnal. Ghazel attacked at night because they saw better than men in the dark. But even when the legions attacked in daylight, the battles were never easy. The ghazel's homes and camps were always located in dim, gloomy places where they had the advantage. Light was usually an ally of the legion, but on this day, the Seventh Sikaria Auxiliary Squadron struggled in the fading dusk to build a fire.

The wet wood was stubborn. Gleefully eager to become dirt, it had no desire to turn to ash.

Three teams labored with bow, spindle, drill, and fire board. Two other groups scraped knife blades against flint files. The rest had cut and dragged logs to the base of a V-shaped fissure in the cliff. The crevice provided the walls for their makeshift fortress, which would hopefully have a fire for its moat.

As darkness descended, the men worked by feel, and even Nolyn could barely see his own hands. Full-blooded Fhrey saw almost as well as goblins in the dark, and Nolyn's improved eyesight was one of the few gifts he had inherited from his father. But the triple canopy of the jungle lessened even his vision, so his men had to be blind. The squadron was deathly silent while drilling and scraping argued with wood. A communal sigh was released when the flicker of an infant flame cast back the darkness. A drilling team had beaten the flint scrapers.

Sometimes the old ways work best.

As that baby flame was raised to a toddler by a community of well-wishers, Nolyn took the time he had left to get to know his men. He shook hands with each, asking who they were. Names remained slippery fish that his mind couldn't hold onto. Instead, he focused on *who* they were: a runaway slave, a murderer fleeing the gallows, a fourth-generation soldier, a part-time thief and full-time gambler, an idealist, a drought-suffering farmer, and a young son of a poor Calynian woman who struggled to feed her family.

Many called the nearby provinces home, but some came from as far away as western Warica. Most were there because the military was their best option to make money and obtain status. Shiny Jerel DeMardefeld remained unique in his lack of need, and if Nolyn were to guess, he would suspect Jerel had joined the legion out of boredom. The Second Spear, Riley Glot, *whose name rhymes with dryly rot,* had previously mentioned that Jerel was *different* but then declined to say more. In addition to Amicus Killian, Jerel DeMardefeld, and Riley Glot, *whose name also rhymes with wily plot,* Nolyn managed to commit to memory the names of Paladeious and Greig, two giant-sized men whom Amicus had suggested should be stationed on the right and left flanks. Amicus, Riley, and a dark-tanned bear of a man called Azuriah Myth would form up in the center. Nolyn remembered Myth's name because it bordered on comical and sounded entirely made up.

"I've never been to Percepliquis," a young Calynian lamented. He was the destitute one who sent his pay to his mother living in a hovel somewhere outside Dagastan. Although Nolyn wasn't personally acquainted with the eastern coastal city, he knew enough that the term *city* was more than generous; it was wishful. And a *hovel* in that neighborhood must be an extremely humble home. The soldier admitted he was only nineteen, but he looked to be thirty. His black curly hair and matching beard hid his youth, but his eyes seemed weary—they had seen too much too soon. Like most people from that region, his name was complicated and difficult to pronounce. Knowing a lost cause when he saw one, Nolyn didn't bother trying. Instead, he mentally designated him *the Poor Calynian.*

"Is the city as incredible as they say?" the lad continued. "I've heard the roads are perfectly straight and don't get muddy, and that water, clean and clear, can be summoned into people's houses at will. It must be wonderful."

"Yes, it is," Nolyn replied because he knew that from the Poor Calynian's viewpoint it would be seen that way. But Nolyn knew the empyre's capital was something else entirely.

"I thought one day I might see it. You know, as part of a victory parade or something. But this war . . ."

"Never ends?" Nolyn finished for him, then nodded. "We've been fighting it for over four hundred years."

"That long?" The soldier scratched his beard. "I'll never see Percepliquis, then."

The first volley of arrows came without warning, clattering off nearby rocks. An arm's length from Nolyn, a man died instantly as an arrow pierced his eye and punched out the back of his skull. Paladeious, that mountain of a man, grunted as a wooden shaft hit him in the thigh. He stayed on his feet, and with an angry growl, he snapped the black-feathered end off.

"Shields!" Amicus shouted. The men responded, and the second volley thundered against a wall of wood.

Only then did Nolyn notice the Poor Calynian on the ground. The young man had been struck in the first volley. An arrow had hit him in the face while he was scratching his beard. The shaft had pierced his hand before continuing through both cheeks. The arrow remained in his mouth like a bit on a horse. He rocked on his knees; his hand pinned to his cheek.

"Don't move," Nolyn ordered. Pulling his dagger, he cut the feathered end from the arrow. Then he gripped the youth's head and jerked the shaft out. The soldier's face and mouth were slick with blood but not as much as Nolyn had expected. Incredibly, the arrow had missed the man's tongue, jaw, and teeth—a miracle wound: *all flesh and no bone,* as the saying went. The Poor Calynian kept his wits and quickly wrapped a strip of cloth around his face.

These men are well trained. Nolyn looked at Amicus Killian, who stood directly before him. *That's because he taught them.*

The shrieks of their enemy came next—a high-pitched, jagged set of cries. The sound was all too familiar, and like teeth scraping metal, the noise set Nolyn on edge. The foul creatures flooded out of the darkness like a swarm of wasps. They skittered from the dense maw of the jungle, their talons clicking. A sickly yellow glow rose behind oval pupils. Their hunched backs, powerful arms, and mouths filled with row upon row of needle-sharp teeth were the shared nightmare of all legionnaires, the unwanted souvenir that survivors brought home.

The standard battle maneuver employed by the legion was the Triple Line, a combat system whose evolution Nolyn had personally witnessed. The ancient phalanx, with its rigid devotion to straight lines and long spears, had given way to the more flexible javelin assault followed by a shoulder-to-shoulder wall of shields defended by short swords. Each row had a commander. The first line was designated for fodder—the inexperienced and ill equipped. The second group usually consisted of the strong and young, and veterans comprised the third. The standard station for a prymus was on his horse in the rear, giving him a clear view of the battle. But with only enough men for two lines, Amicus commanded the first and Nolyn the second.

The First Spear positioned himself at the center, becoming the prow of their little ship that braced against an angry sea. Making the commander the focal point of the attack was unconventional, and while brave, doing so was also ill advised. Nolyn considered intervening, but experience had taught him not to second-guess a First Spear's instincts—especially when the prymus was new to the region.

Nolyn ordered an initial flight of javelins, the effectiveness of which was difficult to gauge in the dark. Then the men closed ranks. Trapped as they were, the first line's unenviable task was to become an impenetrable wall, denying the enemy all opportunities. As the goblins advanced, Amicus inexplicably dropped his shield and broke the line. He stepped forward while drawing two swords. If it had been anyone else, Nolyn would have ordered him back, concluding that the soldier had panicked. But this wasn't the first time the prymus had seen Amicus Killian fight.

That had been years before when everyone in Percepliquis had crowded into the Imperial Arena to witness the Battle of the Century, as it had been promoted throughout the city—the day a lowly human fought an Instarya, one of the best fighters of the invincible Fhrey warrior tribe. Nolyn had attended the spectacle with Sephryn. As prince, he could have sat in the High Box, but the two had chosen to stand in the Common Field. The view was limited but the energy amazing. During a competition that was as much an act of rebellion as entertainment, everyone saw where the heir and the councilwoman stood—shoulder to shoulder with humans.

The fight became the stuff of legend.

Amicus Killian had fought Abryll Orphe, son of Plymerath, the legendary hero from the Great War. Abryll, dressed in shimmering bronze armor, danced about the arena, his blue cloak and long, blond hair flowing. Amicus didn't move. Dressed in only a leather skirt, bracers, and simple sandals, he waited—a sword in each hand and that huge one on his back. He'd used them in every arena battle where, over the course of three short years, he had become the most famous warrior in the world. Holding Sephryn's hand on that day, Nolyn had learned why.

Now, while trapped in a dead-end canyon facing a horde of ghazel in the light of a fully grown fire, he witnessed the inconceivable again.

The enemy spotted Amicus and the door he held open in the ranks. They rushed him, coming two at a time. Caught in the narrow cleft and blocked by the fire, there wasn't room for more. With an economy of movement, Amicus wasted no step, swing, glance, or even breath. Every action was purposeful, as if he performed a practiced-to-perfection choreography. Watching him, seeing how the fighter was two steps ahead of his opponents in each encounter, Nolyn recalled the man's famous nickname—the one the crowds had chanted in the arena, *"PRO-PHET! PRO-PHET! PRO-PHET!"*

He sees the future, Nolyn thought. *Nothing else can explain it.*

Never off-balance or in doubt, the man moved with simple grace: thrust, slice, block, jab. All of it looked so easy. The ghazel appeared as trivial as children with sticks. But Nolyn had faced their kind in numerous battles in a different war. He knew all too well their strength, speed, and cunning. And yet, they fell in pairs before Amicus's twin blades. Two, four, six . . . the carcasses piled up.

"That's ten," Riley called back. "He's already met *his* quota."

Why the goblins kept charging puzzled Nolyn. Maybe they thought Amicus would tire? Or perhaps slaying the one who had killed so many would elevate the victor? The most likely answer was that the warrior's lack of shield, and his unprotected position ahead of the line, was too tempting to resist. Whatever the reason, they continued to come, two by two, left and right. And they died in sets. It took a surprisingly long time for their mass slaughter to abate. By then, a wall of bodies had stacked up, impeding their forward advance. The ghazel finally found a solution to their problem, and another hail of arrows flew past the fire.

That was where the tide ought to have turned. With his shield buried beneath the bodies, Amicus had no defense, or so Nolyn thought. When the man ducked behind the pile of corpses, Nolyn realized the full extent of the unfathomable martial genius of Amicus Killian. The man hadn't merely defended his life against waves of powerful enemies; he had planned where each body needed to fall. He'd killed every goblin in the precise place to build a defense against the assault of arrows that he knew would eventually come. The man wasn't just *two steps* ahead of his enemies; he was *miles beyond* them.

"PRO-PHET! PRO-PHET! PRO-PHET!"

After two fruitless volleys, the battle paused. The fire blazed, and from the darkness of the far side, the ominous clicking drone of frustration rose.

Stalemate. Although it'll be short-lived.

Being trapped and unable to feed the fire, they would see their only source of light die. But it was full-grown now, a proper bonfire fed by the logs Paladeious and Greig had added. It might last until dawn, but daylight wouldn't save them. Even with Amicus's amazing feat, they were still significantly outnumbered.

No one spoke. All eyes peered through the dancing flames, struggling to spot what the shifting shadows were up to.

Amicus remained in his gruesome fortress of death, swords in hand. *He doesn't even look winded.*

Nolyn checked on the Poor Calynian. The lad's bandage, which made him look like a gagged prisoner, was soaked with blood, but it didn't drip. Nolyn pulled a cloth from his belt pouch and wrapped the boy's wounded hand.

"T'anks," the Poor Calynian managed to say around his bandaged mouth. "Gonna 'ave to fight left-'anded."

"Can you?"

The kid shrugged. "Find out soon, eh?"

Nolyn was hoping they wouldn't. If Amicus could maintain his amazing performance, there was a chance they would see sunlight at least one more time—and with it, a clear picture of their foes. In the Erbon Forest, it was tempting to think of the ghazel as animals: mindless beasts that could be stymied by the complexities of doors, fires, and a single-man slaughterhouse.

Nolyn knew better.

Ghazel were as cunning as men—more so—and once again, they proved it. From the far side of the fire came the unmistakable sound of chanting. The moment the Seventh Sikaria Auxiliary heard that, the entire squadron cursed. Everyone knew what that meant: oberdaza.

The goblins had a witch doctor, one of the crazed little wretches dressed in feathers and beads who danced and summoned dark magic. Their presence was never welcomed. No one knew exactly what to expect—that was part of their terror. The squadron might be swallowed by the ground they stood on or struck dead by lightning. They had to wait for the chant to end to discover their fate.

The answer came in the form of a rumble, a deep growl as if the jungle had grown angry. Loud and powerful, the noise shook the ground.

No, it's the ground's movement making the sounds. Nolyn felt shards of rock strike him, and he turned. Behind them, the cliff's face quivered. Pebbles became rocks as the wall cracked and splintered. Then the fire suddenly went out, as if a giant had blown on a candle.

Choices became simple.

"Legionnaires!" Nolyn shouted while raising his sword. "Charge!"

He had no idea if anyone listened or if they could hear him in that crash of rock and drone of clacking claws. All he saw were shadows and vague rushing shapes. Nolyn sprinted straight ahead over hot coals, hoping to avoid death by a rockslide. The crash shook the ground. A blast of powdered rock and a hail of stones followed.

Ahead, the darkness was filled with glowing sets of yellow eyes that darted like fireflies. A pair flashed directly before Nolyn. He instinctively ducked and stabbed. Claws breezed overhead as his blade punched into flesh. Pulling it free, Nolyn ran on. Faint moonlight dribbled in, revealing outlines of leaves and hunched shoulders. Hundreds of years of battle granted Nolyn his own sixth sense, and he blindly dodged, swung, and killed as he advanced. Without warning, a stunning blow rang his helm and threw Nolyn to the ground. Remaining motionless was suicide, so while he was still working out which way was up, he log-rolled into a tree. Scrambling to the far side, he heard something hit the trunk. With an even chance of success, Nolyn thrust to the left and was rewarded with a cry.

Clearheaded once more, he sprinted into the darkness, but he'd lost all sense of direction. He might be running back to the cleft or out into the canyon. Neither mattered; moving was the important thing. Listening for voices, telltale sounds that could help him regroup, he heard screams from every direction. His men were scattered, the battle lost.

Striking an unseen log with his knee, Nolyn went down again. His teeth clamped against a cry. He rolled beneath the fallen tree and waited for the pain to subside. Cries cut the night, but they were distant and fading until . . .

Nothing.

Around him, stillness reigned.

I'm alone.

Nolyn pulled himself deeper beneath the massive log and waited. He was dug in, partially buried, and filling his nostrils was the overwhelming smell of dirt.

CHAPTER TWO

The Monk

The marketplace was alive with evening shoppers, mostly women looking to buy something cheap for dinner. Sephryn was one of those. She'd already gotten a good deal on a quatra of walnuts and thought she might try to pick up some eggs once the crowd thinned at Helena's Poultry. Eggs were relatively cheap but approaching a merchant when there was a line of eager customers was the very definition of stupid. As the sun lowered in the western sky, so, too, did merchants' prices. Sephryn didn't splurge on meat or fish for herself, but eggs were something that she—

"Sephryn!" Arvis Dyer raced through the little square. Her wild, matted hair was decorated with bits of straw, and the old soldier's tunic she always wore made her easy to spot. With one knee-high sandal and the other foot bare, the woman ran with a lopsided gait.

Arvis stopped short, her face frantic. "Hurry!" She waved for Sephryn to follow.

"What is it this time, Arvis?" Sephryn asked, studying the line to Helena's stand.

Arvis had a habit of coming to Sephryn with all sorts of problems. One autumn, she accused a group of children of raising a demon in Imperial Square. When Sephryn got there, she found that four kids had carved a scary face on a pumpkin and put a candle inside. Arvis also insisted there were sharks in the sewers, that the clacking sound wagon wheels made on the cobblestone roads was a secret language, and that Pestilence took the shape of a man named Manny and walked the streets when it rained. Still, she was a friend. And for all her manic ravings, she had proven valuable as Sephryn's eyes and ears in neighborhoods where most were loath to walk.

"What's wrong?"

"He's dying!"

"Who?" Sephryn asked, but it was no use. The woman was charging back the way she had come, screaming at people to clear the way, which they did. When crazy came, people scattered.

Clutching her little bag of newly purchased nuts, Sephryn sighed and chased after. Arvis's declaration would likely turn out to be another fantasy, but she couldn't take the chance. Together they shared the stares of irritation from those they passed. Arvis elicited scorn. Wearing men's clothing was odd, but dressing in the remnants of a tattered military uniform was disrespectful. She was clearly courageous, but like most of the city dwellers, Sephryn also suspected Arvis might well be insane.

They raced down the hill past the bathhouses until Arvis reached the intersection at the end of Barber's Row. In the street, a small crowd had gathered.

"What's going on?" Sephryn asked.

Seeing her, or more likely Arvis, charging at them, several people stepped aside. On the ground, a young man lay in a pool of blood, his left hand severed, and dark red blood spilled from a stomach wound. The moment she realized she didn't know him, Sephryn felt relief, which led to guilt, and guilt was an all-too-familiar terminus. The man seemed to be in his mid-twenties. He wore a simple undyed linen tunic, a rope belt, and sandals. Nothing fancy, but not rags, either.

Kneeling down, she touched his still-warm neck. Sephryn was no physician, but she knew what to feel for and didn't find it. He was dead. Looking up at the circle of people, she saw the faces of men and a few women staring back. Farther away stood two Instarya. From their pristine white palliums edged in purple and studded with gold pins, she deduced they were both young—at least by Fhrey standards. An older Instarya wouldn't wear the long robes that resembled a Fhrey asica. The younger generation had developed a taste for the old-world Fhrey culture that sickened their fathers.

"He's dead," she declared. "Who killed him?" She spoke to the crowd, who said nothing, but several eyes shifted toward the Fhrey. Sephryn recognized the pair, who were known troublemakers, but she hadn't suspected they were capable of going so far.

"I did," the left one of the pair replied. His name was Fryln, and his tone was as lighthearted as his smile.

Though she always tried to be fair and impartial, Sephryn found it difficult when dealing with the Instarya. All the imperial Fhrey possessed a destructive level of superiority, but the warrior tribe was the worst. The emperor was Instarya, and he unerringly filled every high office with his brethren. Although the empyre was overwhelmingly human, nearly all the high-ranking administrators, generals, and magistrates were Instarya, or at least Fhrey. And each spoke with the same dialect: arrogance.

"Why?" she asked, reminding herself not to jump to conclusions, which was difficult as she'd seen similar crimes too many times before. No two were exactly alike, but all were close enough to warrant a certain expectation.

"He tried to steal from me, so I cut off his hand. That's what we do to thieves. Then he attacked me, so I gutted him. That's the emperor's law—is it not?"

"Liar!" Arvis shouted. "Kendel just bumped into them. I saw it. He wasn't looking where he was going—"

"I felt a distinct tug on my purse," Fryln said. "I turned and saw this creature with his hand on me. So I—"

"Liar! Liar! Liar! Liar!" Arvis screamed manically. She had a tendency to do that, which never helped her case.

The Fhrey pulled his blood-soaked dagger. The crowd gasped and shuffled back like a herd of startled cows. Two stumbled; one fell. Arvis didn't move. She glared defiantly with a mad look in her eyes, daring the attack.

"Put that away, Fryln!" Sephryn ordered.

He turned toward her, that mocking grin still on his face.

He's enjoying this.

"Or what?" he challenged, raising his chin and looking down his nose. That, too, was one of the Instarya idiosyncrasies, the habitually learned behavior of the dominant minority. Sephryn could write a book on the topic, if writing was legal.

She was on one knee, still in a pool of Kendel's blood.

Not the best place to confront a pair of belligerents, particularly one who's just killed. They're like sharks — blood and fear make them aggressive.

Sephryn stood up. "Or I'll have you arrested and tried for murder." She was firm but kept her tone calm. She didn't want to escalate the situation.

The Fhrey relaxed his stance, but the blade remained drawn. "I told you, he tried to rob me. I defended myself. Are you going to rely on the opinion of a lunatic? No one else will. You can arrest me if you like, but I'll be free in minutes. Besides, he was just a Rhune."

The crowd rustled. The term was an old one, rarely heard these days. It dated back to a time when the Fhrey were believed to be gods and humans were thought of as no better than animals.

That crossed a line for Sephryn. Try as she did to be civil, she wasn't without a temper. Her family was actually famous for it. And while the hereditary trait was something she fought to quell, controlling her anger was still a work in progress. "And you're just an *elf*," she replied.

The smile of the Instarya vanished, and once more, the crowd gasped.

"What did you call him?" the other Fhrey asked.

Sephryn didn't move or take her eyes off Fryln, the one with the dagger, whose pallium wasn't quite as pristine as she'd first thought.

Small dots of blood stained the edge. "Odd," she began, her hot temper not yet run its course, "elves are famous for their exceptional hearing. What's the matter? Do you have a head cold?"

Fryln took a step toward her.

"What are you going to do, kill me, too?" Sephryn asked. "Do you suppose stabbing the Imperial Council Director will make things better?"

"You think too much of yourself, Sephryn. The Imperial Council is a joke, and so are you. It's been hundreds of years and you haven't accomplished a thing. Can't even get an audience with the emperor, can you?"

"Maybe not, but I'm surprised you've forgotten that most of the city guards are human. *They* don't agree with your sentiment about the council." She looked down at the dead man. "And I doubt they share your feelings about humans. Kendel was well liked. He had a lot of friends and family. So maybe you won't stay locked up for more than a few minutes, but what about after? If I recall correctly, he has a brother or two serving. What if one of them decides to repay you by cutting off *your* hand and letting you bleed out in some dark alley?"

"If that happened, they'd be executed." There was that haughty, imperious tone.

"Maybe," she replied. "But it'd be little comfort to your parents as they bury you, don't you think? What a loss, trading potentially thousands of your years for Kendel's few dozen. But go ahead. Push me further."

The Fhrey didn't move, eyes blazing as he held the blade tightly.

"She's not worth it," his friend said. "Don't forget Ferrol's Law. You can't kill another Fhrey."

"But she's—"

"Even a single drop of Fhrey blood is enough. It's not worth sacrificing your immortal spirit. You'll be forever barred from entering the afterlife."

"Maybe Ferrol doesn't care about half-breeds."

"Do you want to take that chance?" his friend asked.

Fryln pointed the dagger at Sephryn. "Fine. But you watch yourself, mongrel. That's a thin line to hide behind. Maybe killing half-a-Fhrey *would* prevent my entrance to Phyre, but there's nothing against inflicting *pain*."

"Mongrel?" Arvis said, outraged. "Be sure to repeat that when Prince Nolyn sits on the throne."

The two Fhrey laughed. "That'll never happen," Fryln said as he sheathed his dagger. Then the two walked away from her, the crowd, and the man they had murdered.

"Fryln, Fryln, Fryln, Fryln," Arvis quietly recited, her eyes closed in concentration.

"What are you doing, Arvis?"

"Keeping a list to tell Nolyn. I want to see them punished when he's crowned. I wish I knew who the other one was."

"Eril Orphe, and Fryln's last name is Ronelle. But I don't think you'll get the chance. Emperor Nyphron is just a little over seventeen hundred. He'll likely live another five hundred years."

Arvis thought a moment, her mouth twitching. "But *you'll* still be around. Maybe you could think of me when they get what's coming. Or perhaps we should go get Kendel's brothers after all. Do you know where they live?"

"No, let's not do that. Your first idea was better. I'll make sure Nolyn knows, and we'll let him take care of it. Agreed?"

Arvis reluctantly nodded.

Crisis averted.

Truth was, Sephryn didn't know Kendel. She stopped short of labeling her comments to Fryln lies because the dead man probably *did* have friends and family, and though less likely, *some* might be city guards. Truthfully, Sephryn had her doubts about an arrest. The Orphes and Ronelles were powerful families, and what Fryln had said about Sephryn's position wasn't completely wrong.

She had led protests and practiced civil disobedience for centuries, which finally resulted in the creation of the Imperial Council. Humans now had a voice in the palace, albeit a weak one.

Still, Sephryn took exception to the charge that the council hadn't accomplished *anything*. They had improved the lives of thousands of humans, though more in the provinces than in the capital. Fryln was right about one thing, though. After many years of trying, the Imperial Council still hadn't been able to coax the emperor to attend a single meeting, and nothing truly significant could be accomplished without his say-so.

The crowd shuffled abruptly as an older woman entered the square. Sephryn didn't know her, but the look of anguish made her identity an easy guess. The woman fell on the body and cried. She shouted, but no one could understand what she said. They weren't words in the usual sense, but rather the sound of primal suffering. Perhaps they were what the old mystic Suri used to refer to as the language of creation. The sounds that emanated from every living thing on the face of Elan.

Others arrived, marked as family by wailing and tears.

"Why can't you stop this?" the mother sobbed at her. "You've been our hope. We've believed in you. Trusted you. Why couldn't you have . . ." She fell back into the language of creation that was too painful for Sephryn to hear.

Arvis reached out a hand of support, but Sephryn swatted it away. She didn't want sympathy, didn't deserve it. She had no answers, just excuses, and that wasn't enough.

Thinking she might cry and not wanting anyone to see, Sephryn found a quiet doorstep in a dim alley. The fact that she hadn't known Kendel didn't matter. His was another life taken. One more that didn't need to die. She sat, face in her hands, between a rain barrel and a near-empty woodpile, but the tears didn't come.

Have I grown so callous?

That was one of her fears, insanity was another.

Only someone truly nuts would keep trying after so long. Maybe that's why I'm friends with Arvis. Perhaps I'm not far behind her on the road to Crazy Town. It's been—she did the math—*seven hundred and ninety-six years. I've spent the better part of my first millennium fighting to make things better.*

Everything had been so hopeful, so full of possibilities, back in the year Fifty-Two. What a wonderful year that had been. The Northern Goblin Wars had yet to break out, so Nolyn was by her side. Bran was, too. All three of them had such grand plans for the future. Bran had always been the most fearless, the instigator. He found it impossible to ignore the cruelties of the Fhrey. He provoked the Instarya, called them out, shamed them.

No, that belittles his deeds. He was terrified, but that didn't stop him.

He had made his parents proud.

At least one of us did.

The year Fifty-Two had been the best of her life—days so golden she gleefully revisited the memories. She had lived more than eight times the life span of a human, but only that one year had been great.

She shook her head and chided herself. *This self-pity is pointless. I've had other good years. I've won a few battles. I have a son—a wonderful, perfect boy. And, of course, my childhood was a delight.*

As she thought about it, Sephryn realized that was part of the problem. The glories of her youth had ruined her adulthood. Nothing in the centuries since had ever compared to the wonders of her first few decades. How could they? Back then, there had been magic.

A man with a partially bald head and wearing an ugly brown frock passed the opening of the alley.

Bran?

The thought just popped into her head—an utterly irrational notion. Bran had left Percepliquis centuries ago, and she hadn't heard from him again. Although she didn't know for certain, Bran had to be dead. No human had ever lived longer than a hundred years, which made it utterly impossible for her to have seen him walk by.

But it looked so much like him . . .

Bran always dressed in the worst clothes, having had no interest in better ones. He would have gone naked if not for modesty and the weather. And the last time she saw him, Bran had been going bald, but only at the very top of his head—a bizarre sight, all that wild hair wreathed around a bare patch of pink. In over eight hundred years, she'd never seen anyone else with that peculiarity.

Until now.

Did I really just see him walk by?

Bran had been an old man by human standards, but Sephryn and Nolyn appeared no different from the days of their youth. Bran's hair had gone gray, his face sagged, and wrinkles ran like a rash across his skin. But his eyes remained unchanged. Whenever she had looked into them, she recognized her childhood friend. He was still in there, even though the shell was rotting.

Bran was human. It can't be him, she thought even as she rushed to the end of the alley and peered out at the street.

Percepliquis wasn't just the capital of the empyre and the center of the world. The city was also the largest and most populous. A vast variety of people flooded its streets, arriving from nine of the eleven provinces. No one came from Erivania, the Fhrey homeland, or Ryin Contita, which wasn't really a province at all, just a buffer between humans and the Fhrey whom Nyphron had defeated. Everyone else came to the city, or at least it felt that way to Sephryn as she frantically searched the crowds and currents of humanity, looking for a single person: a man that couldn't—according to the laws of nature—be there.

But I've witnessed magic before. Bran and Suri were so close. Is it possible that . . .

When she spotted him again, she realized he actually wasn't difficult to find. The slender, disheveled man in the ugly brown robe with the telltale bald spot moved up the crowded thoroughfare exactly where he ought to be. He wove through the massive evening migration of workers and stepped around the pilgrims who made roadblocks as they stared up at the towering height of the buildings.

She ran after him. "Bran!" she shouted. "Bran, wait!"

He didn't hear. Sephryn closed the distance quickly, her heart pounding with hope, the first she'd had in years. "Bran!"

The man finally heard and turned.

It's not him.

The disappointment was devastating. She stopped, halted by dashed hopes.

The man stared, puzzled. "Were you calling me?"

For a moment, Sephryn didn't reply; she couldn't. Then, as he watched her with eyes that were not at all Bran's, she said, "I'm sorry. I thought you were someone else."

Rather than turn away, or even show annoyance at the interruption, the man's expression grew intense. He looked as if she had said something wholly different, as if she had posed a brilliantly cunning question, and he was struggling to find the answer. In that lingering moment, Sephryn had time to plumb the depths of her mistake. The man was nothing like Bran. His face was pleasant, might even be considered cute, like a gerbil endowed with a large nose and an unsettlingly passionate stare.

"I'm sorry to have bothered you." She turned away, embarrassed and more than a little angry with herself.

I'm such an idiot. How could I have thought it was him? I've spent too much time with Arvis. Before long, I'll start understanding the language of wagon wheels.

The street they stood on was Ebonydale, named after the market to which it led. She thought to go back for the eggs now that it was —

"Dammit!" She lifted her empty hands, glaring at them as if the two fists had betrayed her.

The nuts were gone.

I must have put them down when I was examining Kendel's body. She noticed the stains on her skirt, a reminder of the man she had failed to save.

I'm going home, she concluded and turned away.

"Wait!" the man in the frock called. "Tell me. Who did you think I was?"

She looked back only to cast a dismissive wave of her hand. "Nobody. You're not him, so, again, my apologies."

No eggs and no nuts meant next to no dinner. Mica would be angry with her, but that was nothing new. The old woman was so—

"You called me *Bran.*" The man was following her, and his tone picked up a tinge of accusation.

What's with this guy? I said I was sorry. "Yeah, that was my friend's name."

"And you thought I was him . . . why?"

"Look, it was a mistake, okay? I'm sorry I bothered you. Have a nice evening. Goodbye."

"Did he dress like me? And wear his hair this way?" He patted the top of his head. "Is that why you thought—"

Sephryn stopped and turned. "You know him?"

The man's mouth hung open as he stared at her. "Who . . . who *are* you?"

"I'm Sephryn. What is your name?"

The man looked flummoxed beyond the ability to speak but managed to say, "I'm—ah—I'm Brother Seymour."

Sephryn gave him a wry smile and shook her head. "You're lying; I don't have a brother."

He laughed then. "Oh, no. Ah—my name is Seymour Destone. I'm a member of the Monks of Maribor. We call one another—well, that is to say, our titles are—"

"How do you know Bran?"

"I don't—I mean, Bran, the founder of our order, lived eight centuries ago. I couldn't *know* him . . . no one could. I only know *of* him. We follow his teachings and emulate his appearance, right down to how he dressed." He tugged on his frock. "We shave the tops of our heads for the same reason."

"Bran didn't do that."

"I beg to differ. All portraits of him clearly show a —"

"He looked that way because he was going bald."

Seymour stared back in shock, then pointed at her. "How do you know such things? Have you been to the Dibben Monastery?"

"Never heard of it."

"I'll take that as a no. So how is it that you are familiar with Bran the Beloved?"

"The *Beloved*?"

Seymour grinned and nodded rapidly. "Yes. Did he come to you in a vision? Did he speak to you in a dream? How do you know of him?"

Sephryn shrugged. "We grew up together. As kids, we used to play tag."

After that, Sephryn couldn't get rid of the man who had called himself her brother, and then explained the assertion away in a manner that didn't make any sense. She'd told the truth about growing up with Bran, and it was fun watching those oh-so-serious eyes nearly fall out of his head. People — humans — guessed she was in her late twenties, early thirties at most. The truth always shocked, but the monk's reaction made her rethink the wisdom of such a cheeky reply. For whatever reason, he revered Bran. A little more forethought might have tempered her reply. After all, she had no idea who this guy was. He could be unstable or dangerous. That idea didn't bother her as much as it might others. Small men in dingy robes just didn't worry her the way Instarya in palliums or soldiers in armor did.

She continued to walk, cutting the distance to the safety of her home. Seymour followed like a dog she'd foolishly fed.

"What do you mean you *grew up* with Bran the Beloved?"

"I mean what I said." She spoke without looking at him, her eyes focused on the street ahead. She hoped her body language and a curt reply would end the whole affair.

"You can't leave it at that." He continued to dog her.

Why does that never work with men?

"Of course I can," she snapped. "Look, I don't know who you are. You could be a criminal, trying to lure me somewhere, so you can—"

"You were the one who approached me! You *chased* me. Remember? You tapped my shoulder and—"

"I didn't touch you!"

He rolled his eyes. "I was speaking metaphorically." He sighed. "And I can't be luring you to your doom since I'm *literally* following you to . . . I honestly don't know where. I'm not even sure where we are at this moment. I'm new to the city. Just got here today. Percepliquis is *not* an easy place to navigate. I had no idea there were this many people in the whole world. It's like a massive rabbit warren, streets upon streets, bridges, avenues, alleys. It's magnificent, of course, but also bewildering."

"Where are you from?"

"Rodencia, a small town northwest of here. The place is a disaster, a muddy mess. When I was last there, they'd dug up the streets to put in a hideous sewer system that made—oh never mind. Most recently, I hail from Dibben Monastery, just to the east of the Bern River."

"The Bern? Did you pass near the Mystic Wood?"

His gerbil eyes brightened. "Yes. Do you know the area?"

"My mother used to take me there when I was a child. She was born nearby on a high hill, a place called Dahl Rhen, which was nestled in the crook of the forest."

"What is your mother's name?" he asked tentatively, as if uncertain about hearing the answer.

"No, no, no, this isn't about me. We're talking about you right now. Remember? I'm trying to determine if you're a vicious murderer of women." Sephryn cut through the basket shop near a little bridge, saving time, and they reentered the crowds on Ishim's Way, the tiny lane where she owned a narrow brick building.

She used to rent the second floor from an old woman, but her landlady had died ten years later and left the building to her grandson, who in turn died forty years after that. His daughter didn't have the money to pay taxes on the place, so Sephryn helped the girl by purchasing a permanent lease on her room. Two more generations of poor management passed, and Sephryn ended up acquiring the whole building. She migrated her quarters down to the nicer, first floor, and let out her original room to Mica.

"You mentioned the Monks of Maribor. What does that mean exactly?"

"It's, ah . . . well, we're a group of men who try to follow the teachings of Bran by worshiping Maribor, the god of Man."

"There is no such thing as *Maribor*."

"You're only saying that because it's illegal to believe in any god other than Ferrol."

"I don't care about that. But you're wrong. The *goddess* of the humans is *Mari*."

"What makes you say that?"

"Because she is," Sephryn replied, baffled by the man's ignorance.

"And where did you get such a notion?"

"From my parents, and trust me, they ought to know."

"Who are they?"

"Not about me. Remember?" They skirted the big urn fountain in the little square where Sephryn and Mica drew their water. She recognized half a dozen of the women filling jugs, and she didn't want anyone asking about the blood on her clothing—something Seymour either didn't notice or didn't care about. That, along with his gerbil-like face, made it difficult to hate him. "Can you tell me what happened to Bran? He left here centuries ago, and I hadn't heard a word since."

"Teachings say that he went to a little village in the south named Dulgath. That's where he founded his first monastery."

"And what precisely is that? I've heard the word, but I don't know what it means."

"I'm surprised you've heard of it at all. In the whole world, there are only seven, and most are in remote locations. A monastery is a place where we practice asceticism. In other words, by separating ourselves from the distractions of the world, we can completely focus on our devotional doctrines. We seek to better understand the wisdom of our Lord Maribor."

"Yeah, okay, whatever. Then what?"

"Then what, what?"

"What happened to Bran?"

"Oh. Well, then he went into the far east."

"Was he being chased?"

"Chased? No. Why would you ask that?"

"Why else would he run off into the wilderness?"

"He didn't *run off*. Bran was in search of *The Book of Brin*."

Sephryn laughed. Seymour was at it again. First, he lied about being her brother, now he was telling her that—

"Why is that funny?"

"Because it makes no sense. Bran *has The Book of Brin*. His mother gave it to him on his thirteenth birthday. She used it to teach him to read and write—we all learned from it."

"Not *that Book of Brin*, I know that tome well. The members of my order have dedicated our lives to learning its every word. What I'm referring to is the *second Book of Brin*."

"There's no such thing."

They reached the stone steps that led to the front door of Sephryn's building, a slender, tapering, ancient structure of pockmarked blond brick and creeping moss. At that moment, she recalled it was Bran who had found the place for her. Sephryn had just returned to Percepliquis from Merredydd after her mother's death. Bran was waiting for her, and the two spent the day searching for a place she could afford. Back then, she had few resources and was too proud to ask her father for help.

Little had changed. As Director of the Imperial Council, she earned a good salary but gave most of the money away. Sephryn found it difficult to reconcile living well while those she was paid to help struggled in poverty. With her most recent income donated, she had nothing to offer this odd monk from the countryside, except . . .

No. I can't. Mica will kill me.

The old woman was intensely religious, which was strange since so few humans worshiped the Fhrey god, Ferrol. Whether for religious reasons or just because she liked to nag, Mica disapproved of Sephryn's decisions. The most fervent complaints stemmed from Sephryn living alone, working too late at council meetings, not staying home with her child, and why Nurgya's father wasn't providing for them.

Sephryn took hold of the door's latch and paused.

Don't do it, she told herself. *Don't take in another stray.* Over the years, Sephryn had opened her home to hundreds, all of them destitute and unable to pay. Although most moved on after getting back on their feet, Mica had remained.

"Do you have a place to stay?" Sephryn asked the monk, who lingered on the steps with one foot up and the other still on the street.

"Ah, no. I don't. You seem familiar with the city. Do you have any suggestions?"

"How much money do you have?" Realizing that might be too intrusive, she reworded the query. "How much can you afford to spend on a room?" Sephryn bit her lip, waiting for the answer, knowing what it would be.

Seymour looked pained and shook his head. "We don't have much need for coins in Dibben."

"You have no money at all? You really did learn from Bran, didn't you?" She noticed he had only one small bag that couldn't hold more than a meal. "What were you planning on doing?"

"Well, I came here to start a church. The brotherhood decided it was time for us to open the doors of truth to the wider world, and what better place than the capital to do that? After all, this is the city where Bran started preaching."

"I meant how were you expecting to survive without any money?"

Again, the pained look, as if she'd slapped him. "Um, I was, ah — we have a saying at the monastery: *Maribor will provide.*"

"That's your plan?"

He nodded. "Granted, it could use some work." He smiled.

The expression melted her heart, not merely because it was ridiculously cute in a puppy-begging-for-a-treat sort of way, but because Bran had often done the same thing, in the exact same way.

"I guess I'll find a stable or maybe a dry spot under a bridge," Seymour said. "The city is full of bridges. I've never seen so many in one place. Don't have a blanket, but it shouldn't be so cold tonight, right? Maybe a little chilly by morning, but—"

"You can stay here," she said, regretting the words even as they came out.

Turning, she opened the door and braced for the onslaught that was Mica.

"Are you sure? Because I could—"

"Yes, I'm sure."

Maybe having him with me will temper Mica's tirade.

Sephryn entered the home and was surprised by the silence. Usually, Mica spotted her from the window and charged down the stairs, spouting a barrage of reprimands.

She's probably putting Nurgya to sleep.

There was a loud *thud* from behind Sephryn, and she spun.

The monk was on the floor. He had fallen to his knees, his face turned upward, his eyes fixed on the wall above the fireplace mantel. "By the holy beard of Maribor, can that be what I think it is?"

"What I think is that you hurt my floor." Sephryn pulled off her head wrap and threw it on the hook near the door.

The ground level of the building was made up of two rooms, a bedroom and a kitchen that flowed into a sitting area, all of which centered on the fireplace. Mica kept the place clean, which was good because Sephryn wasn't a tidy person. She once asserted that mold was a viable means of cleaning a plate—albeit significantly slower than letting a dog lick it. The problem was never having enough dishes for the time required. Mica went to the ridiculous trouble of using soap and water. At least it had seemed absurd until Sephryn had had Nurgya. Since then, she'd rethought her mold-cleaning approach.

Seymour remained on the floor, staring up at the mantel above the hearth where no fire had been lit—that, too, was odd. Spring was taking its time, and the building was chilly.

"Oh, stop it, will you," Sephryn chided Seymour. "It's just a bow—my mother's. Damn thing is too big to fit anywhere else."

"The length, color, that unique bend, and the mark near the top, I've seen paintings of it." Seymour spoke in a quavering voice that was barely above a whisper. "That's *Audrey*." He said the name with so much emotion she thought he might cry or possibly faint. "You're the daughter of . . . of . . . Moya the Magnificent?"

"Moya the *Magnificent*? Oh, Dear Mari! How my mother would have loved that." Sephryn rolled her eyes.

"Then your father . . ." Seymour put the pieces together, as anyone who had read *The Book of Brin* would. "He must have been Tekchin—a Galantian! That's how it's possible for you to have met Bran! You're half Fhrey!"

"The green eyes didn't tip you off? And for the record, my father is still alive, which reminds me, I really should plan a trip to Merredydd. I sent a message about his grandson and asked him to visit. I would go there, but I don't like traveling, and there's so much to do here. Every day brings a new problem."

"You have a child?"

"Yes, and I don't have a husband, so don't bother asking about him."

"I wasn't going to."

"Really? Everyone else does. Speaking of which . . ." She moved to the stairs, looking up and listening. "Mica?" she called.

No answer.

"Who is that?"

"My son's nursemaid, who, like you, has a way of making me go against my better judgment. She works for me, and not the other way around, which is one of those things she conveniently forgets." Raising her voice, she called again, "Mica!"

Still no answer.

Did she fall asleep? Or has something happened to Nurgya?

Sephryn charged up the first flight of stairs and barged onto Mica's floor. The place looked like it always did, with two notable exceptions: The little table near the stairs had been toppled, and Nurgya's wooden teething ring lay on the floor. Seeing them, Sephryn's heart crawled into her throat, trying to escape, making it difficult to breathe.

Nurgya!

She raced up the wooden stairs to the nursery. Climbing the final steps, Sephryn didn't know what to expect. Something awful, certainly. It had been that sort of day, and for Mica to be gone was more than strange. But what she found was beyond imagining.

Blood was everywhere, as if a dog had swum in a lake of it and then stood in the center of the nursery and shook. The curtains, the crib, the ceiling and walls—everything was stained. The rocking chair was splattered, as was the hope chest, the pillows, and the blankets. One wall had a radiant spray as if someone had burst a wineskin against it. At the base of that mark was Mica's dress, the material entirely soaked. The one thing she didn't see was Nurgya.

She couldn't breathe, needed air. Turning around, Sephryn reached for and found the wall.

Breathe. Breathe, stupid. Breathe for Nurgya's sake.

For an instant, she thought the house was shaking, rumbling, vibrating wildly, then she realized it was her legs. They were giving out.

"What happened in here?" Seymour asked as he cautiously inched up the steps.

Sephryn turned and grabbed him, hugging the monk as she sobbed. That's when she saw it, and in that horrible moment, her tears, and perhaps even her heart, stopped. Written in blood on the wall above the stairwell were the words:

CHILD STILL ALIVE.
TELL ANYONE AND HE DIES.
WILL CONTACT YOU.

CHAPTER THREE

The Gathering

Sunlight, faint and hazy, trickled down through the jungle canopy to illuminate Nolyn's world of misty green. He'd slept a little, an hour or maybe two taken in brief naps—none of which were intentional. With the advent of light, he decided to move, and crawling from beneath the log, he found his muscles stiff. If any ghazel lingered nearby, he'd present an easy target, but Nolyn hadn't heard anything except insects, dripping water, and wind in leaves. The sound of water got him going. The Erbon Forest made everything sweat: the trees, the plants, the air itself, and most certainly men. He was desperate for a drink.

Nolyn moved through the jungle brush, holding his sword up like a talisman against evil. He swore to clean the dried blood from the blade, right after drinking his fill at the river. Nolyn hated seeing the metal soiled. He'd taken exacting care of the weapon for centuries. It had been a present from Bran's mother, a gift for Nolyn's twenty-second birthday. As far as Nolyn knew, it was the last sword that Roan of Rhen had ever forged—a holy relic from a lost era, an age of myth and legend.

Dew on the plants soaked his clothes, torturing him to the point that he sucked some water from the stem of a flower that acted like a cup. Not nearly enough, and he hoped it wasn't poisonous. He wouldn't put anything past the jungle, as it, more than the goblins, had stymied the empyre's legions for the last four centuries. Reports had leaked west about the increased casualties as the imperial forces pushed east. Plagued by heat, rain, and insect-borne diseases, entire companies of men were lost, but none of those hardships bothered the ghazel. Nolyn had avoided most of the second war with the goblins, but his fate may have only been delayed.

Following the sound of gurgling water, he carefully approached the river, which was small and angry in that area of the ravine. Water frothed over moss-covered rocks that were nestled among massive boulders and crisscrossed by rotting logs draped with stringy vines.

Most of Nolyn's life had been spent in the northwestern imperial provinces along the Bern and Urum rivers, areas with temperate climates, maple trees, rolling hills, stone walls, and four seasons. The southeastern world of unbearable heat and humidity was an alien place, and he soon discovered that this jungle world was home to many peculiarities. He'd been in the province of Calynia for less than a week, and he'd already seen cats the size of deer, beetles as large as apples, and hairy spiders bigger than his hand. Nolyn hated arachnids and was absolutely certain the horrors with eight legs shouldn't be capable of growing beards.

Surveying the leafy glade cut by the headwater, Nolyn knew his peril. *If I were hunting me, I'd stake out this river. Everything needs water to survive.*

That didn't change his thirst, a condition made all the more intolerable by the closeness of the river. Nolyn crept through the undergrowth, searching for a place where the plants came closest to the stream. He avoided stepping into the open. Instead, he inched his way through the dense leaves of the jungo plants, which were the size and shape of elephant ears. That was another thing that defied reason. Everyone else in Urlineus acted like the giant, long-nosed animals were unexceptional.

What is with this place and all the gigantism?

Still several feet from the salvation of running water, Nolyn heard a rustle just to his left. Nothing so obvious as a snapping branch or the hideous clacking of claws, but something moved—something big. He crouched lower, then froze.

Breathing.

There's either a water buffalo ten feet away or a ghazel. His mind, which couldn't remember a name, was prone to devolve into silliness when he was on edge, so it added *or an elephant.*

Nolyn waited, listening to the deep breaths.

It's just beyond this curtain of leaves. If I move, it will hear me.

Nolyn struggled to remain still. He was little more than an arm's length from the rushing river. He could hear its spray hitting the broad-faced leaves, which sounded like rain on a tent's roof. Being so close to the ecstasy of drinking was maddening.

Leave, you dumb elephant!

It did move, but not away. Nolyn heard the shift of weight and the scrape of a foot as whatever was over there settled in.

What if it's only an animal? I could be sitting here for no good reason. Even if it's a goblin, I could kill just one.

During the First Goblin War, he'd killed hundreds, but not a single one had been easy, and no victory was certain. On too many occasions, he'd nearly died. Some battles left him terrified by how close he'd come; other fights left him seriously wounded.

In this jungle, even a light wound would be fatal.

Nolyn continued to wait, trying to find reasons to remain hidden. Then Thirst came up with ideas of its own: *You're running out of time. The only hope is to use the daylight to get back past the front lines. Your muscles will stiffen again, and you're already severely dehydrated from sweating. You'll grow weaker the longer you wait. You might even go mad.*

That last one was flimsy. Nolyn figured he was already a bit insane, and being a little crazy might actually give him an advantage. In the end, he simply couldn't take waiting anymore. Gripping his blade tightly and clenching his teeth, he took a deep breath and crashed through the curtain of green. He slashed his way forward until his blade struck against metal.

He found himself face-to-face with Amicus.

With the swords still locked over their heads, Nolyn pulled back in surprise. Amicus glared at him.

"Sorry," Nolyn said. "Couldn't see who it was through the leaves."

"Scared a year out of me." Amicus lowered his blade. "I didn't hear a thing, just noticed the leaves quiver an instant before—you're lucky I didn't take your head off . . . sir." His voice was angry, shaken, and the honorific perfunctory.

Nolyn smiled. "I was thinking the same about you."

Amicus smirked.

"I only mean that . . ." Nolyn held up his sword that was still tarnished with goblin blood. "This blade tends to break others, and we hit pretty hard."

Amicus looked at Nolyn's sword and then down at his own. "Mine aren't general issue, either."

Nolyn moved to the river. He'd waited long enough. Getting down on hands and knees, he pressed his lips to the surface. The water, which came down from the mountains in a thousand little streams, would be uncomfortably tepid by the time it reached the sea, but there it was wonderfully cold. The gurgling froth had a beer-like effervescence, and he drank deeply, sucking the water up until he ran out of air and had to stop. After a long inhale, he bent down and drank some more. After the second draught, he forced himself to pause to avoid getting sick.

A quick look around revealed that he and Amicus were the only two on the little moss-covered bank. "So, what happened?" he asked, wiping his mouth.

"I was going to ask you."

"Me?" Nolyn said, getting to his knees. "When the cliff came down, I cut my way into the darkness and fell behind a log somewhere. Couldn't see a thing."

"Really? I thought your people could see in the dark. You know, like the ghazel."

"*My* people?" Nolyn rinsed his blade in the river. "I've only met one other person in the world like me. And by that, I mean someone who shares human and Fhrey parents. I suppose there's bound to be more by now. The races have lived together over the centuries, but I doubt you've run into any. So, when you say *my people*, who are you referring to?"

Amicus shook his head in disgust. "Forget it."

Nolyn wiped down his blade using the tails of his tunic. Getting to his feet, he dropped the sword into its scabbard.

Whether it was due to the water or Amicus's presence, Nolyn felt significantly better—even safer, which was absurd. Amicus Killian was undoubtedly an amazing warrior, but the two of them stood no chance against the jungle and several hundred warriors from the Ghazel Nation. Still, life was filled with a lot of things that didn't make sense: Nolyn was frightened of spiders that couldn't hurt him but never hesitated when riding a galloping horse into battle, he loved Sephryn but abandoned her, he hated his father yet followed the emperor's every command.

I could have died at twenty and considered my life a happy one. By human standards, I'm practically immortal, but I've done little that brings me joy. My existence is one big, ironic joke.

The river flowed through the canyon, cascading over rocks. The rest was lost to a sea of massive plants, towering trees, looping vines, and a massive—

"Snake!" He pointed to the yellow-and-orange serpent, the thickness of Nolyn's thigh. It dangled from a tree branch, watching them. Another example of Calynia's infatuation with enlarging average everyday things into monsters.

"I've been calling him Rascal," Amicus said.

"You named it?"

"It probably wasn't the best option." Amicus took a second look at the abominable beast, whose head was up, tilted, and looking directly at him. "I should have named him Sloth, or gone for irony and dubbed him Speedy, but hindsight makes everything easy, doesn't it?"

Nolyn peered closely at the First Spear. "How long have you been in the jungle, Amicus?"

He grinned at that. "Not *that* long, sir."

"Good to know." Nolyn walked along the stony bank of the stream but found no sign of anyone, human or goblin.

"Care for breakfast, sir?" Amicus held out a handful of nuts and berries.

Nolyn returned and took the offering. "So, what happened to you last night, First Spear?"

Amicus shrugged. "I heard your order and charged. Ran into a gaggle of goblins, and we had an argument—more than one, actually. I wanted to get by, and they wanted to kill me."

"Who won?"

"Careful, sir, I'm starting to like you. Nothing good can come from that."

"True. My apologies. Go on."

"Well, you were right about it being dark. Couldn't see the swords in my hands, so I just kept on going. Heard shouts and cries. I tried to move toward them but didn't find anything. I shouted out a couple of times, and that was a mistake. I invited visitors, but the ones who arrived were never who I wanted. Sitting quietly made more sense than thrashing about, so that's what I did. At first light, I headed toward water. Been waiting here ever since, just me and ole Rascal. I figured anyone who survived would do the same. Looks like I was right."

"So your plan is to sit here and see who turns up?"

"I don't really make plans. That sort of thing is well above my rank. But I figured I'd wait for a few hours, then start following the river downstream."

Nolyn nodded and popped a sprinkling of berries and nuts into his mouth. "These are good. Are they part of your rations?"

Amicus shook his head. "Found them this morning."

"You know how to forage in these parts? Able to differentiate between safe and poisonous?"

"Nope. That's why I gave them to you first."

Nolyn stopped chewing, his eyes wide.

"Just kidding." Amicus chuckled. "Those are abbra berries and rom nuts. They grow all through this jungle. You can live off them for months."

Nolyn hesitantly swallowed. "Don't you have meals in that pack of yours?"

"Gonna take us a while to get out. No sense depleting our supplies until we need to."

"Strange. I wouldn't have pegged you as an optimist."

Amicus shrugged. "Half the battle is believing you can win."

"Careful, First Spear, I'm starting to like you, too."

"Even knowing who I am?"

Nolyn nodded. "Especially because of that."

Amicus narrowed his eyes.

"I rooted for you against Abryll."

"But you're—" He stopped himself. "Sorry."

"It's the ears, isn't it? Not as pointed as my father's, but not round, either. I wasn't born this way. I guess I grew into them."

"Who is the other one?" Amicus asked.

"Come again?"

"The one with mixed heritage."

"Oh." Nolyn looked at the leather strap around his wrist, and said, "Her name is Sephryn."

"Are you related?"

Nolyn shook his head. "But we grew up together, first in Merredydd, then in Percepliquis after the city got completed enough to live in. We—" Nolyn stopped. Behind them came the sound of something moving through the brush, and he drew his sword.

"What?" Amicus asked.

Before Nolyn could answer, the First Spear's head turned toward the sound, and he drew two of his own blades.

Azuriah Myth and a man Nolyn only knew as the fellow fleeing the justice of the gallows spilled out of the jungle. They both grinned—first at them, then the river. Both of their waterskins were shriveled. Myth's showed creases as if he'd twisted it. The two made feeble attempts to stand straight and offered chest-thumping salutes.

"Go drink," Nolyn told them, and the pair raced each other for the water.

"Seen anyone else?" Amicus asked.

The two nodded but continued to drink. Afterward, Myth lay back on a rock. He gasped for breath and sighed. "Paladeious, Lucius, Ambrus, and Greig." Taking another breath, he added, "All dead. Found them together surrounded by a host of slaughtered gobs."

"How many?" Amicus asked.

Myth nudged the other soldier. "What do you think, Smirch? Fifteen?"

Smirch shook his head, letting the water run off his chin onto his shirt. "Eighteen, at least."

"Eighteen?" Nolyn said. He looked at Amicus. "You killed about twenty last night. That means—"

"I took out forty-two," Amicus said. "You're forgetting about the arguments."

"Okay, so that makes more than sixty. That's a huge bite out of their force."

"Only four of us left, sir," Smirch pointed out. "They got a mouthful, too."

"True. But with a third of their forces lost, they might fall back to replenish their numbers."

"Maybe," Amicus said, but he didn't sound convinced.

Myth and Smirch dunked their heads, then set themselves to the task of refilling their waterskins.

"What made you root for me?" Amicus asked Nolyn.

"Huh?"

"Before. You were saying that during my last arena fight you were on my side. Why?" The First Spear had a hint of skepticism in his tone. "Your father made it clear that Abryll was his choice."

"Yeah, that's actually part of the reason," Nolyn said.

"You don't like your father?"

Nolyn laughed.

"Not real fond of mine, either," Smirch grumbled. "Spent all his money at the Happy Pint, leaving me and my brothers to live off squirrels. The first few aren't so bad, but by the fifth one—let me tell you, bossy—you can really get tired of those big-tailed rats. After ten, you start running short of squirrels."

"Smirch is our own little ray of sunshine, sir," Myth explained. "Always quick with an anecdote to lift the spirits."

"After that fight," Amicus said to Nolyn, "I got on your father's bad side. He ordered my arrest."

Nolyn nodded. "Sounds like him. Doesn't like being outshone; that's for sure. If he could reach it, he'd stab the sun for daring to be brighter, and he sincerely believed that no human would ever defeat an Instarya."

"So you two don't get along?"

"Let me put it this way, I wasn't joking when I said someone sent me here to die."

"Are you suggesting your father would . . ." Amicus paused.

"He's my best guess. We haven't spoken to each other in centuries, literally centuries. The last time was the day my mother died. He told me to pack because I was joining the legion. Two days later, I was sent to fight in the Grenmorian War. I'd never been in a battle before, but ten days after my mother's death, I was going up against giants. At least it gave me something to do with my anger. I survived, and after we won, I was sent to fight in the Goblin Wars."

Nolyn shook his head miserably. "My father probably hoped the giants or the goblins would finish me off. When they failed, he rewarded his son with a post as an assistant to the administrator of a salt mine. That was my reward for taking the Durat stronghold, slaying Lord Rog, and ending *that* Goblin War. I was exiled to that backwater pisshole in southwestern Maranonia for doing my duty. My new charge was to remain out of the public eye until everyone forgot that the emperor had a son, especially one who did so well in the wars."

"Wait, sir, are you saying you fought in the *First* Goblin War? Just how old are you?" Myth asked, sliding his now-fat waterskin over his shoulder.

"I'll be eight hundred and fifty-five in a few months."

"Whoa," Myth uttered. "So you were already four hundred when this war broke out?"

Nolyn nodded his head. "Yep, and I expected to be called up. That would actually make sense because I had so much experience. But no word came. I spent more than five hundred years stranded in that salt mine. Then out of the blue, I was sent here. No one said the orders came from my father, but honestly, who else besides Nyphron cares enough to kill me?"

Amicus looked at Nolyn with new interest. "If you're *that* old, do you remember the Battle of Grandford?"

Nolyn shook his head. "I was born a year after."

"But you knew them?"

"Who?"

"The Heroes of Grandford, the ones in the legends. Did you ever meet Brigham Killian? I'm a direct descendant." Amicus drew his short blade. "This was his weapon, the Sword of Brigham. He was a member of the Teshlor Warriors." Amicus spoke as though he and Nolyn were strangers who'd met in a roadhouse and just discovered they were from the same small town rather than two soldiers in a lethal jungle. "Strange, you don't seem . . ." Amicus hesitated. "Well, you don't act like a person who's been around so long."

"Really? How do they act?"

Smirch laughed. "Walked right into that one."

"It's just that I would expect you to be more . . ." Again, Amicus held back.

"Wise? Intelligent? A master of any weapon? How about mature? People my age certainly ought to be that, right?"

"Sort of, yeah."

Nolyn took a breath. "But you aren't curious as to why I'm not taller, are you?"

Amicus looked puzzled.

"Children grow as they get older, right?"

"Only to a point," Myth said.

"Exactly. When you reach the height you're supposed to be, you're done. A glass can only be filled with the amount of liquid the vessel can hold. You can keep pouring, and some of what went in first might dribble out and be replaced with the new stuff, but the total amount doesn't change. I've met children who are wiser than old men, and I'm sure you have met people older than you who act juvenile."

Myth and Amicus looked at Smirch, who nodded and shrugged.

"Age doesn't endow an idiot with intelligence, and time alone doesn't grant experience, nor does it make you an expert in all things. I suppose if you're the type of person who loves to learn, you could gain a lot of knowledge, but it wouldn't make you a genius. Some things you're just born with. People's personalities are formed remarkably early. Age most often serves to either mellow or harden what's already there. I don't know the first thing about knitting, and I'm a lousy cook, mostly because even after eight hundred and fifty-five years, I've never found those activities appealing, so I avoid them."

He thought a moment. "Sephryn is nearly as old as I am, and she's pretty much the same way. She can't cook, either. But she does have a passion for improving the lives of others. She's a lot like my mother in that way. But Persephone was a chieftain and a keenig, which gave her power. Sephryn's entire life has been under my father's rule. During all that time, there hasn't been a regime change, so the status quo marches on. That still hasn't stopped Sephryn from trying. She never married or had any children because she keeps throwing all her energy against a mountain of stone that will never move. Yes, she's achieved a few small victories, but nothing to significantly change things. And why is that?"

None of the others had an answer.

"Because age hasn't granted her magical abilities. She's not all that different from you or anyone else, just older." He paused. "Well, she does excel at being stubborn. But that's a trait she's always had. Kinda have to be that way, right? Anyone else would have given up by now. I did."

Smirch got up and started heading away from the group. He stopped suddenly and erupted, "Son of the Tetlin Witch!" Pointing wildly, he added, "There's a big-ass snake over here!"

Nolyn and Amicus laughed.

"It's not funny. I was just about to take a piss, and now I have!" He shook his leg.

"His name is Rascal," Nolyn said. "Rascal DeSlothful."

Nolyn guessed it was about an hour later when Riley Glot, Jerel DeMardefeld, and the Poor Calynian appeared. They had found the river farther upstream and were walking down its bank when they stumbled upon the others. Riley was out front, sword in hand, while the wounded Calynian, still with the bloody rag gagging him, was helped along by Jerel. The shiny warrior's expression didn't match his attire until he caught sight of them. Then his eyes brightened, and a joyful smile lit his face.

Seeing Nolyn, Jerel DeMardefeld gasped, rushed forward, and grappled the prymus so forcefully that he nearly took both of them to the ground. "Thank the One, you're alive, Your Highness!" He continued to hug Nolyn so tightly that the man's breastplate threatened to cut Nolyn's lip. Jerel DeMardefeld wasn't a small man, and there was no getting free until he let go. "I feared for your safety, sir."

"He's not kidding," Riley said. "He wanted to look for you last night. I had to take his sword, and if I had any rope, we would have tied him up. Took both of us to keep him from running off." He looked to the Calynian, who nodded in agreement. "I guess we got separated," Riley told Amicus. He had a pitch of shame in his voice, as if he'd committed a crime.

Amicus nodded. "Impossible to see much of anything."

Every squadron had its history: shared memories, past failures, regrets, promises, and debts. From their collective experiences came a secret language. To outsiders, their conversation would sound perfectly ordinary, but Riley's words were coated in a kind of code for those who had bonded throughout the years—an understanding that only those equally cursed by shared memories could read. Having been with the squadron but a few days, Nolyn didn't speak Seventh Sikaria. Still, he knew the secret language when he heard it. Riley was asking for forgiveness, perhaps for something that had nothing to do with the previous night, and with that slight nod, Amicus appeared to have absolved him.

"How long have you been here?" Riley asked, pulling his ax, which was acting as a furca, and his pack off his shoulder. He dropped his burdens to the ground.

"Hard to tell," Amicus replied. "Two hours, maybe."

"That's a lot of time to spend in one spot."

"We were waiting for stragglers like you."

"Don't have to anymore." Jerel pulled a strip of dried meat from a pouch and held it in his teeth while he closed the little bag. He took the meat from his mouth and gestured in a circle at the rest. "This is us. We came across Paladeious, Lucius, Ambrus, and Greig on the way here."

"Smirch and I found them, too," Myth said.

"That still leaves nine unaccounted for," Amicus commented.

Riley shook his head. He glanced at Jerel, that sense of shame filling him again. "When the lights went out, we heard the command to charge. Not everyone heeded the order or maybe they just didn't act fast enough. Yorken, Hamm, and Blanith were crushed."

"I was near the back," Jerel DeMardefeld said. "That order saved my life, sir."

"We were blind," Riley added, that tone of guilt leaking back into his voice. "Just swinging in the dark. Gobs were everywhere, could hear 'em clicking and chattering. Nothing we could do 'cept run, swing, and stab at the nearest sound." The Second Spear let out a mournful sigh. "We went back to the cleft this morning."

"You did what?" Nolyn asked, surprised at the bravery that would have taken.

Riley disavowed his admiration with a smirk. "No great feat, sir. We never got very far to begin with. Yorken, Hamm, and Blanith were mostly buried by the fallen cliff. The others lay scattered but generally within sight of our fire, or what was left of it." He sighed and looked down at his feet. "Sessation and Gammit . . ." He stopped to swallow. "Sir . . ." Riley lifted his eyes to look directly at Nolyn. He held his commander's gaze as if doing so was painful. "Sessation and Gammit didn't have any claw marks. Both men died from sword blows. They were hit from behind." He paused and shook his head. "It was just so damn dark."

Jerel looked at the strip of meat in his hand as if he didn't know why it was there.

"What about the others?" Amicus asked.

"Gobs got the rest," Jerel said. He, too, conversed in the language Nolyn didn't yet speak, and probably never would.

"We should go back and bury them," Riley said. "Now that we're all together, that is. We didn't want to get left behind if others made it out. But now . . ."

"We need to get our asses out of here," Smirch growled, still casting looks at Rascal DeSlothful as if the snake might leap across the twenty feet between them.

Amicus looked at Nolyn. "Sir?"

Nolyn focused on Riley, who looked wounded even though he didn't have a mark on him. "How many ghazel?"

"Sir?"

"How many gobs did you kill? You counted their bodies, too, didn't you?"

"The gobs take their dead," Amicus said.

Nolyn nodded. "They also take the ones they kill, but last night they didn't."

"Fifty-three, sir," Riley answered. "Not counting Amicus's pile."

"Fifty-three?" Nolyn said, stunned.

He stared at the Second Spear, trying to evaluate the man. He'd just admitted to accidentally killing his fellow squadron members, and it was clear he accepted it as his fault. Given that, Nolyn didn't think the soldier would lie.

"All told, this squadron killed a hundred and thirteen ghazel who were accompanied by an oberdaza. Fewer than twenty men did that in the dark, without fortification or much in the way of defenses." He said the fantastical words out loud, thinking they might sound more reasonable coming out of his mouth. They didn't. "Seven of us are still alive—only one wounded. That's . . ."

"That's why they didn't take their dead or ours," Amicus finished. "Too few were left, or maybe none at all."

"True," Nolyn agreed, "But I was going to say—*that's impossible.* A single squadron shouldn't be able to do that."

"With all due respect, sir," Riley said, "the Seventh Sikaria Auxiliary isn't just your average squadron."

"No? What are you?"

"We're special, sir," Jerel DeMardefeld said, but Nolyn already knew to expect nothing less from him. Still, he was surprised when Myth and even Smirch nodded in agreement.

"How so?"

Every one of them raised a finger and pointed at Amicus. "Him, sir."

Amicus looked awkward, then shrugged. "I trained them up a little."

"A little?"

"The Seventh Sik-Aux is the best squadron in the empyre, sir," Riley stated without a hint of arrogance, as if the assessment was common knowledge. "That's why we're always out front—the first to be sent in."

Myth smiled. "We're as effective as a cohort."

"In my day," Nolyn said, "a cohort was five hundred men."

"Still is, sir."

"That's quite the boast." Nolyn turned to Amicus. "Would you agree?"

The soldier nodded. "The legion teaches teamwork above all else. Combat is a group endeavor. If you break up the members, fracture the line, soldiers become nothing but mindless thugs with sharpened sticks. But I teach my men to fight together, and alone, with spear, sword, shield, dagger, or even bare hands. That's what's needed in this jungle. We train over all terrains and in any conditions, even the dark."

Nolyn nodded. He would have argued, but three things stopped him. The first was the spectacle of martial excellence that Amicus had put on the night before. Second, there was no arguing with the reality of six survivors where none should exist. Third, if they wanted to do more than survive one night, they had to get moving. "As much as I hate leaving those men to the jungle . . ." He looked at Riley. "My duty is to the living. Let's get moving."

"Sir," Riley said, "I request permission to bury the dead myself."

Nolyn shook his head. "We can't afford to lose a sword. We might need you to get out."

"I'll be quick, sir, and I'll have no trouble finding you since you're going downriver."

"Those men are dead, and they—"

"Deserve a proper burial. If they don't get it, they won't enter Phyre, and they deserve their rest in paradise."

"He has a point, sir," Jerel said, then to Riley he added, "I'd lend a hand, but, well, you know." He pointed at Nolyn.

Riley nodded. "I'd want to be buried with a stone in my hand, sir. And I'd feel better if Sessation and Gammit found their way safely to the afterlife."

"We should at least collect the gear," Amicus said. "And the ground is easy to dig in."

"Seven of us, thirteen of them," Nolyn said. "There's no time for individual graves. This has to be a one-pit burial, understand?"

"Two," Riley said hopefully. "It'll take less time than carrying Paladeious, Lucius, Ambrus, and Greig back to the others."

Nolyn sighed. "Okay, two, but then we march out of here at double-time. Maybe we killed them all, but perhaps we didn't. I'm not taking the chance that one or two gobs ran off to get friends. Understood?"

Amicus nodded. "Show us the way, Riley."

When the last funeral was finished, the sun was almost at midday. Nolyn didn't dare waste any more time and ordered them to move out.

Everyone who'd lost gear the night before either found their missing items or grabbed new ones from the equipment pile of the fallen. That included Nolyn. Watching the others, he noticed how they each hooked their packs to the heads of axes, mattocks, or brush cutters that acted in place of the traditional furca carrying pole. It made far more sense to employ an existing tool than to use an additional stick to hook the pack to, and Nolyn was reminded that it had been centuries since he'd actively served in the legion. He adapted and did likewise, looping his pack's hang-strap over the head of an ax. Unless he was running, the ax handle on his shoulder balanced the weight of the pack and he didn't even need to hold it.

"Smirch," Amicus called, "you have the boar's head."

"Are you serious?" the man protested, shocked. "I don't know the way out of here."

"Don't need to, just head back the way we came, then walk downstream. Even you can handle that."

"You've never given me the lead before. Why now?"

"You might have noticed we're a bit shorthanded. Do you really want to argue with me?" Amicus smiled at the soldier.

Smirch frowned, hoisted his pack, and started out.

"Did anyone manage to save their own gear last night?" Nolyn asked.

Myth laughed. "Mine is buried under the cliff debris. This was Ambrus's pack."

"I have Yorken's," Riley said. "And Ramahanaparus has Greig's."

"I kept mine," Amicus said.

"Me too." Jerel grinned proudly.

"The two of you are freaks, aren't you?" Myth added.

They moved in a single file down the headwaters, which was treacherous because they were forced to travel over slick rocks and crisscross a forceful current. In some deep places, they walked log bridges covered with algae. Frequently, they had to swing out away from the river then cut back, and on two occasions, they were forced to resort to hand-over-hand techniques as they dealt with waterfalls that dropped twenty feet at a time.

"What about your father?" Nolyn asked Amicus as they trudged together through a patch of thick ferns that grew taller than any of them.

"Huh?"

"We discussed the wit and wisdom of my old man, the Imperial Bastard. Tell me about yours. What's his name?"

"Anthar."

"What does he do?"

"Was a soldier. He died a few years ago."

"Out here?"

Amicus shook his head as he ducked around a massive prickly plant the others referred to as a spiker. "Died in bed of the pox."

"Oh, sorry."

"Don't be. He was seventy." Amicus looked over. "That's old for a human."

"Really? I wouldn't know. Apparently, I'm an idiot."

"Sorry, sir, I wasn't trying to—"

"Forget it."

"I just mean, well, it's especially ancient for a soldier. He taught me to fight. Started training me when I was five."

"It shows. So you were on good terms?"

Amicus smiled wryly. "He asked only two things of me: keep a low profile and never serve in the legion."

"Oops," Nolyn said.

"Exactly. 'Amicus, my boy,' he told me, 'your forefathers' swords have served the empyre since before there was such a thing—since the Battle of Grandford—and what has it gotten us? Centuries of endless marching, poor food, blood, and misery, that's what. Unless you're Instarya, you aren't allowed to succeed, not worthy of respect.' He also told me to avoid profiting too much from my training. Brigham Killian's son Ingram tried that path and regretted it. My dad always said, 'When you're as good as we are at fighting, you become a target.' He was right. I painted a bull's-eye on my back by beating Abryll. Still, I never thought it would be the emperor who would take aim."

"I guess we have something in common, you and I," Nolyn said. "My father hates both of us."

CHAPTER FOUR

The Voice

Sephryn tried to stop the monk from seeing. She did her best to cover his eyes, hold his head. She did everything short of pushing him down the stairs, but he still saw the writing—and of course, he could read. She made him swear to be silent. Demanded it in exchange for allowing him to stay. She couldn't risk him leaving after what he had seen. As it turned out, Seymour didn't need coaxing. After learning her lineage, he was eager to please.

What followed bordered on blind panic. Sephryn ran outside, reached the street, then stopped and examined Ishim's Way. The little neighborhood was shutting down for the evening, but dozens of people were still drawing water, hauling sacks, and chatting on stoops.

Is anyone watching me? She searched for the eyes of a stranger, hoping she would spot someone who might instantly look away or dart down an alley, but the street was the same as always.

Windows! The idea popped into her head, and she made a study of each one. *Someone might be peering out at me, watching to see my reaction.*

She saw no one. Night was coming on; most of the windows were shuttered.

She spotted a pair of city guards: simple leather, short swords, brushed helms. They were having a conversation as they walked past her house on the far side of the fountain.

Tell anyone—he dies.

Her heart raced as she debated what to do. *If I wave them over and no one is watching, how could the culprit know?* She scanned the street again. *What if it isn't a stranger? Maybe it's someone I know. It can't be, and yet—why would anyone kill Mica and take my son?*

None of it made sense. *I don't know enough to do anything yet.* That one thought ran repeatedly through her head as she watched the guards walk past.

Child still alive—will contact you.

With one last look, Sephryn returned inside. She searched the house, although *demolished* was a more accurate description. She tore apart every cupboard and closet. She didn't have a clear idea of what she hoped to find, aside from her son stuffed into some nook or under a bed. She found nothing, not Nurgya or even a clue that might lead her to the identity of who was responsible.

She finally collapsed on the kitchen floor, running a hand through her hair and trying to think. Seymour said nothing, just watched her from across the room. After several hours, he went to the counter, took a cloth and the water bucket, and headed for the stairs.

That got her moving. Together they cleaned the nursery. Seeing her hands shake, the monk offered to do the job alone, but she wouldn't have it. It was her house, and that was Mica's blood—she was certain of it. More important, she desperately needed something to do. Sitting and waiting, she felt certain, would kill her.

Blood was everywhere, but there wasn't as much as Sephryn first imagined. The horror came less from the amount and more from the area it covered. Although she'd never been to war, the death of Kendel wasn't the first she had experienced. She had seen a man crushed by a wagon, a woman trampled by a horse, and two people who fell from scaffolding. She'd even witnessed a number of executions: a man boiled to death and another drawn and quartered. Those occurred back in the dark days before she managed to have such barbaric punishments outlawed. Yet in all her centuries, she'd never seen anything that turned her stomach like the blood in the nursery.

It's as if poor Mica exploded.

As they scrubbed the stains, Sephryn couldn't help thinking of the old woman who had served as Nurgya's nursemaid. Her relationship with Mica hadn't started out that way. Mica was just one of the many destitute people whom Sephryn had taken in. At the peak, there had been sixteen people living with her, all impoverished, which meant a lot of mouths to feed. Even now, she continued to fund a food bank for those unable to find work. Mica was her last invitee and, like Arvis, was a hopeless case. Both were disagreeable, difficult to understand—much less appreciate—and neither was able to take care of themselves. But where Arvis had refused room and board, Mica relented on the condition that she would trade work for a roof over her head. That was how, a little more than a year ago, Mica had become Sephryn's housekeeper. With the birth of Nurgya, that role expanded to include nursemaid. Mica had no immediate family nearby. With the exception of a handful of scattered relatives that she occasionally mentioned as examples of hideous human beings, the old woman had outlived the rest of the DeBrus clan. Sephryn thought she might have a cousin living somewhere in Rhulynia, but even Mica wasn't certain about that. Contacting relatives, at least, wasn't something Sephryn would have to deal with.

She rinsed the red from her rag in the bucket and bit her lip, trying to hold back tears. Mercifully, Sephryn hadn't come across any body parts. Whether Seymour had found and removed them, she didn't know—didn't want to find out.

First Kendel, now Mica, they say deaths come in threes.

By the time they finished the nursery, it was late, and the house was dark and cold. Seymour emptied the buckets of pink water into the sewer grate, the dark of night defending against the prying eyes of her neighbors. Exhausted, her head hurt from examining every possible option. None was useful. Sephryn returned downstairs and sat on the floor like a top that had run out of spin. Seymour lit a fire, found a blanket, led her to a chair, and wrapped her tight.

"It'll be fine. I'm certain," the monk offered in a nearly convincing voice.

Child still alive—will contact you. Dear Mari, she hoped that was true.

Sitting before the fire, she continued to think, tried to focus.

Why was the nut she couldn't pry open. Nothing had been stolen. Nothing damaged.

Blackmail? Everyone knows I'm not rich. Do they think I have the power to enact real change? Was someone angry because—

She remembered Fryln. *Watch yourself, mongrel. That's a thin line to hide behind. Maybe killing half-a-Fhrey would prevent my entrance to Phyre, but there's nothing against inflicting pain.*

She swallowed hard. *He's the one. Has to be. There's no one else.*

Terror gripped her as she imagined him killing Nurgya, but then came a realization. *He can't!* Hope rose. *Nurgya is my son. He has Fhrey blood.* But then hope fled. *He could always pay someone to do it for him.* She shuddered. *But maybe he only wants to frighten me. He wouldn't dare harm Nurgya. Oh, if he does . . .*

Her eyes rose to the long bow that was mounted above the fireplace—her mother Moya's bow.

The night her mother died, Sephryn and her father had sat together in a small dark room for hours. Her father, who always used to entertain his daughter with tales of how he had laughed in the face of his own death, trembled as Moya faced hers. Neither Sephryn nor Tekchin said a word as they sat on either side of Moya's bed, listening to her breathe, a rasping inhaled hiss that gurgled on the way out. For years afterward, anything resembling that noise set Sephryn on edge. But that sound was music compared with the silence when it finally stopped. After waiting so long, after enduring the seemingly unending anguish, Sephryn had imagined that the end would bring relief. She was wrong. What was perhaps even worse was when her father stood up and said, *"It's over. She won't even need a stone. She knows the way."* His tone was what had bothered her. There seemed to be a lack of regret. Her mother's passing—the death of his wife of nearly fifty years—appeared to have had little effect on him. He acted as if she were just sleeping, and he'd see her the next day when she woke up.

That had been the worst night of Sephryn's life—until now.

Sephryn sat in that chair, wrapped in the blanket and praying to a host of gods she'd never needed before. When morning came and the world brightened, she cursed the rising sun. The night had passed without hearing from the kidnapper. There had been no deadline, and yet, she felt the new day was evidence that the slender hope of contact had been nothing more than wishful thinking. She feared facing a reality without her son the same way she'd had to accept her mother's death. Once more, she would do so alone—or nearly so.

"I found some tea," Seymour said, coming toward her with a pair of steaming cups.

Sephryn had moved to the bench at the window so she could watch the street. Lights were on in a few homes. A handful of lonely figures braved the chilly morning air with raised hoods. They carried satchels over their shoulders or pushed carts.

Just another day—for them.

Seymour set one cup down on the table and pressed the other one into her hands. He waited until he was certain she had a grip before letting go. Then he sat beside her and looked out the same window, loudly sipping his tea.

"Do you suspect anyone?" That was the first thing he'd asked since his feeble remarks of support.

"Not certain, but I have an idea. If I don't hear word soon . . ." She forced herself not to look at the bow. She hadn't touched it in years, but she was certain her skill would come back easily. "I'll go after him, track the bastard down myself, if I have to. My mother was known for her temper, famous for it, actually. For good or ill, I have inherited that. No law of Ferrol will stop me."

Seymour nodded. "So, you think it was a Fhrey?"

Sephryn was surprised by his knowledge of Ferrol's Law, but brushed it aside. "If my son dies, no legend will stop me, and that will bring repercussions. I've spent generations trying to build a bridge between humans and Fhrey. Proclaiming that the two could live together in peace. Killing one . . ." She shook her head and sighed. "Murdering the scion of a powerful house could destroy everything I've worked for."

She stood up and moved to the other window. More people were in the square. She reached out and touched the pane of glass with her open palm. "He's out there somewhere. My son still lives. I have to believe that."

"Yes, he does," a voice in her head said. *"And if you don't want me to kill him, you'll do everything I say."*

Sephryn dropped the teacup, and it shattered on the floor. "Did you hear that?"

Seymour looked from the broken pieces then back to her. "Hear what?"

"Shall I continue?"

"That right there!"

"Only you can hear my voice. Would you rather listen to me or blather on with that idiot beside you?"

Her fear must be showing because Seymour looked at her, puzzled. "Are you all right?" the monk asked.

"I don't know," Sephryn replied, terrified. "Something strange is going on." Her heart was thumping, her breath short.

"I thought I made it clear that you shouldn't talk to anyone. So, who is this fellow? You told him, didn't you?"

"No! No, I didn't say anything. I swear!"

"Who are you talking to?" Seymour asked.

Sephryn shushed him with a finger to her lips.

"Don't lie to me. Remember poor Mica? Let me show you what happens when you disobey—"

"I didn't tell him!" she shouted. "He was with me when I found the message. We saw it at the same time."

Seymour stared at her with growing concern. Then he pointed at his own chest and mouthed, *Me?*

She nodded. "Did you hear me? I didn't say anything. He read it himself. We came into the room together—"

"Fine. It's just bad luck then, isn't it?"

"Yes! Yes."

"Well, let's make sure you don't have any more, shall we?"

"It won't happen again. I promise."

The voice seemed so close that it sounded as if the person were right next to her, but it didn't emanate from any specific direction. No matter where she stood or which way she turned, the voice was there. Sephryn didn't recognize it. The speaker certainly didn't sound like Fryln Ronelle or Eril Orphe.

"What did you do with my son? How are you talking to me like this? Who are you?"

"You don't get to ask questions—that's rule one. I tell you what to do, and you obey. If you do, you'll get your son back. Easy as strawberries, right?"

Sephryn had no idea what that last part was supposed to mean, or if it meant anything. Nothing was making sense. Someone had stolen her child, obliterated Mica, and now a disembodied voice was threatening to do the same to Seymour and making nonsensical comments about fruit.

"We're going to make a trade, you and I. I'll give you back sweet little Nurgya in return for the Horn of Gylindora."

And the quagmire of insanity just kept getting deeper. The voice knew her son's name, which was both terrifying and reassuring. That it knew anything about her while she knew nothing of it was paralyzing, but the promise of her son's safe return provided the thinnest of threads to hold onto.

"I don't know what that is."

"It's a musical instrument made from an animal's horn, an ancient thing. Nyphron has it in a safe place in the palace, I suspect. Get it. Then I'll exchange what you want for what I desire. Understand?"

"Not really, no," she said. "How will I find it? What's this all about? Did you kill Mica? Who are you? How are you talking to me?"

"Rule number one. Remember? Or was Mica not a sufficient demonstration? Do you need a reminder? I can still pop your friend. Care for me to paint more of your house in that lovely red color?"

"No!"

"Are you sure? If either of you speaks a word, all three of you die, starting with poor little Nurgya. Can you trust this fellow that much? If not, I can take care of him for you."

Sephryn stared at the monk, who continued to sit on the bench at the window. He held his teacup so tight that his knuckles were turning white. He looked at her, frightened.

"He won't say a word. He doesn't even know anyone in these parts."

"You'd better hope so for your child's sake. Speaking of the kid, you should know I hate children, and I'm not the patient sort. I'll give you some time, but don't take too long."

Sephryn waited, but nothing more was said.

The Imperial Palace stood on the high hill across from the Aguanon, the temple to the Fhrey god Ferrol. As one of the first buildings constructed in the imperial capital in the wake of the Great War, the squat, four-story edifice was more a fortress than a palatial home for the ruler of the world, even more so now after the wall had been added.

Percepliquis was a grand and beautiful city that had no need of fortifications because it had been built at the time of unification. But the palace was another matter. It alone had been successfully invaded.

It had happened about twenty years after Sephryn and her family left the capital and moved to Merredydd, but Nolyn and Bran had been there, and they told her what had happened. Bran had been teaching the art of reading and writing ever since the death of his parents. He used *The Book of Brin* as an educational tool and had students make copies. Then in the year Forty-Five, a dramatic historical play depicting the Battle of Grandford was featured in the city's main amphitheater. Accompanied by flutes, lutes, a full chorus, and a troupe of dancers, the famous battle, known to be the turning point in the Great War, was reenacted.

"It was all wrong," Bran had told her. *"There was no mention of my parents; not a word about my father's ride to Perdif, or Raithe's sacrifice, or Suri's creation of the gilarabrywn. And Persephone was reduced to the doting wife of Nyphron, the hero who forsook his own race to save mankind!"*

In response, Bran sought to set the record straight. He went about the city, standing on boxes in the squares and reading from Brin's original epic account of the Battle of Grandford. He was soon told to stop. The request came from the palace, which, it turned out, had funded and promoted the play. That only made Bran redouble his efforts, recruiting many of his students to go into various squares and make use of their reading skills. Then the emperor himself ordered Bran to stop. Again, Bran refused. He famously and publicly replied, *"This is the exact reason Brin invented writing. She wrote her book to guard against powerful people changing stories of our past to suit their interests."*

The next day, Bran was arrested and locked in the palace.

There was talk of an execution for defying the emperor, but few believed that would happen because Bran was a popular figure. Plymerath, one of the legendary Instarya heroes of old, was said to have been among those who had spoken on Bran's behalf. Although Bran wasn't killed, neither was he freed, and he spent two months in prison. He might well have been in there the rest of his life if not for Nolyn.

The emperor's son had returned from the Grenmorian War to find his childhood friend locked up by his father. Nolyn had tried to speak to Nyphron and was stunned when he was unable to get an audience. The First Minister had declared that Bran was stirring up trouble and would remain isolated until he accepted proper imperial history. Bran said he would die first. Fearing that was an actual possibility, Nolyn went to the one person he knew could help—the old mystic, Suri. She had been like an aunt to all of them and still lived in the forest of her birth. Ancient by human standards, she hadn't left the Mystic Wood in decades, but for Bran, she made an exception.

As Nolyn explained it, the old woman—who wore a ruddy cape and leaned on an ancient staff—entered the palace without fanfare or resistance. She walked out with Bran, who laughed uncontrollably. Bran said it had been the expression on Nyphron's face that had elicited his reaction. *"The ruler of the world was as powerless as a child when facing a little old woman."*

The next day construction began on a wall that surrounded the palace. Nothing fancy. Only six feet in height, the wall didn't appear worth the effort, but it did have one interesting feature: a continuous band of symbols that ringed the top. The symbols appeared to be merely decorative, and why the wall had been built at all remained a mystery to everyone. To Sephryn, the markings were vaguely familiar, but she didn't know why.

In addition to the wall, the emperor instituted a new tradition of stationing a guard at the gate, presumably to stop feeble old women from walking in and freeing prisoners. Five men took turns at the post. That day, it was Andrule.

"Good morning, Andrule." Sephryn waved as she approached, hoping he couldn't see the terror behind her eyes.

What if he doesn't let me in?

That was a ridiculous thought. The Imperial Council had its offices in the south wing of the palace. She passed through the same gate nearly every day and had done so since before Andrule was born. And yet . . . this was the first time she ever *had* to, the only time walking to work had felt criminal, and she was certain the guilt showed on her face.

"Morning, Sephryn." He smiled at her. "Is there a meeting today?"

There wasn't. Truth was, Sephryn had absolutely no reason to be there. Luckily that didn't matter. Sephryn Myr Tekchin was a well-known workhorse. No one ever saw her dancing at a festival or drunk in a Mirtrelyn hall. She didn't lounge in the bathhouses or take extended holidays to the remote corners of the empyre. In a little over eight hundred years, Sephryn—the daughter of two long-forgotten heroes—hadn't been anywhere except Percepliquis, Merredydd, and the Mystic Wood. And she hadn't been to Suri's home since childhood. After having fought for so long to secure a right to the council chambers, she spent nearly all her time working in the eight offices and one meeting hall. That was partially because she felt an obligation to those who had helped make the advisory body a reality. But if she were honest, she was also proud of the Imperial Council, the greatest and most lasting achievement of her life. Wrapping herself in that accomplishment helped blunt the stings of not yet having managed to make the world a paradise for all. Change on that scale was a long journey made by small but determined steps.

Sephryn shook her head at the guard. "I left my scarf inside. At least I think I did. Can't find it, so I hope it's here." That was a lie, and while not an unlawful thing, she saw it as her first criminal act on behalf of the Voice. She didn't need an excuse to enter the palace, but Sephryn wasn't planning on following her normal routine, and she wanted to get ahead of any questions. If someone found her wandering, she hoped to explain herself by stating she'd lost her scarf and was searching. Her ruse was far from an ironclad defense, but no one in the palace had any reason to doubt her, and she guessed even a flimsy excuse would be more than enough.

"Don't want to do that," Andrule said, and for an instant, she feared he knew—knew everything. As her heart began to thunder, he added, "Don't want to be without a good scarf. Still cold. I swear this year's Founder's Day Festival will need to be held indoors."

She nodded and smiled, more from relief than anything, not daring to say another word as Andrule waved her through.

The wall that Suri had been responsible for created an enclosed little courtyard, most of it paved with flat stones. There were purposeful gaps, decorative circles where trees grew. Sephryn remembered when they were saplings. Now budding with new leaves, the trees were mammoth, and their root systems upended the once carefully placed stones. Having no clue where to begin her search, she walked straight to the front door. She didn't even know what she had come to steal. *A musical instrument?* That just sounded too bizarre. Her son had been taken and an old woman murdered for a horn? So much about the request was beyond comprehension. She was hearing voices in her head—*not voices,* she corrected, *just the one. Does that make it better?*

If she hadn't seen her son's nursery painted in Mica's blood, and if Seymour hadn't been there to witness the scene, Sephryn would have convinced herself she'd surpassed Arvis and won the award for Most Detached from Reality.

But we both saw the message. And while the monk hadn't heard the Voice, that aspect didn't seem so strange when compared to the whole. In many ways, the Voice had provided a degree of structure to the incomprehensible. She had no idea what was going on, who the Voice belonged to, or how she was hearing it. But the words, awful as they were, lit a path toward purpose and provided direction. Sephryn's entire life had been dedicated to goals, not an unusual pursuit for a workhorse. She had a problem to solve, and as frightened as she felt, she would persevere.

The interior of the palace lacked the subtle beauty employed in later buildings. The entrance hall was four stories tall, with narrow windows lining a high gallery. Painted on the upper walls and parts of the ceiling were astounding scenes of battles from the Great War. Warriors rode on horseback with streamers flying from long poles, vast valleys were filled with thousands of soldiers, and fortress gates were defended by archers. In one scene, three figures stood on a hilltop. One fought against what looked to be a dragon.

The scene was famous. The three individuals were said to be Cenzlyor, Techylor, and Nyphron, and the painting depicted the moment when the emperor slew one of the conjured beasts in the last epic battle of the war. Little of what was depicted was accurate. Nyphron had actually fought and slain a great beast on a hill, but it wasn't a dragon or even an enemy. The creature had been an ally. And Cenzlyor and Techylor were just artistic metaphors, not actual people. Cenzlyor, which meant swift of mind, was the symbolic stand-in for Arion and Suri, the women who had aided the cause with their magic. And the male figure known as Techylor represented the thousands of human warriors—those with swift hands—who had fought and died. That's how Empress Persephone had explained the painting, although the words engraved in a band encircling the room could easily give the impression that Techylor and Cenzlyor were actual people. The empress had insisted on the engraved writing, even though she had never learned to read. She recognized its importance, and she would have been outraged that the emperor had outlawed the practice after the incident with Bran and Suri.

Off to the right was the North Wing, home to the imperial bureaucracy comprising the office of taxation and other domestic concerns, and also the headquarters for military matters. On the left lay the South Wing, which housed the servants' quarters, kitchen, storage rooms, and the offices for the Imperial Council. Low ceilings held up by heavy stone pillars and a lack of windows made that wing feel like a tomb. Because this was where Sephryn had had her first encounter with death, that notion was amplified. She had been twelve when Empress Persephone—the woman she'd been named after—died. She'd passed away in the room directly above the chamber where the Imperial Council now held its meetings.

Sephryn quickly crossed the black-and-white checkered floor to the majestic stair that gave access to the gallery above. For the first time, she climbed. At the top was a series of doors, which made up the Imperial Residence, Nyphron's private quarters. It, too, was divided left and right. The right was the emperor's personal living space, while the left had been reserved for Empress Persephone. Sephryn had always thought it odd that the two rulers not only had individual bedrooms but entirely separate apartments.

"Nyphron has it in a safe place," the Voice had said, *"in the palace, I suspect."*

Sephryn assumed that anything the emperor considered valuable would be in his personal quarters. She also guessed her scarf excuse might not hold up if she were discovered in that part of the palace. Her plan—if push came to shove—was to claim that she believed a servant might have taken the scarf upstairs after thinking it was Nyphron's. That was weak, and she doubted anyone would believe an item of hers could be mistaken for something owned by the emperor—but it had the benefit of being impossible to disprove. The excuse was also all she had. Why else would she be wandering the private residence? At least if she were caught, the most likely outcome would be a request for her to leave. Anyone else would—

That's why the Voice chose me! The thought surfaced late, making her feel stupid. *Relax. It's difficult to think straight after all of this: Mica's blood dripping off the walls, not knowing if Nurgya is alive or dead, being forced to commit a crime against the emperor. Oh, Mari, this isn't going to end well.*

Still, the puzzle piece fit, and that helped. The more things made sense, the better she felt. The biggest mystery was the source of the Voice. Sephryn didn't have a clue on that score. If she ruled out the idea that she had lost her mind—which actually could be the most likely possibility—what was left?

Is it a god? Possibly. Who else has that kind of power? And if so, which one? It didn't sound benevolent. Maybe it's Ferrol. No, that doesn't fit. The Voice was definitely male, and her mother and father had always insisted that Ferrol was a woman—and they ought to know since they claimed to have met her.

Sephryn came to the split and stopped. A door stood on either side of the hallway. She'd reached the point of decision.

I have to start looking somewhere—

Just then, the door on the right opened. Behind it, and looking squarely at her, was Illim.

ℒ

Sephryn couldn't speak. She just stood there and stared.

Illim was the Imperial Steward. Older than the emperor, he had held a similar position long ago when Alon Rhist had been the foremost stronghold on the imperial side of the Nidwalden River. Although thousands of years old, Illim didn't appear a day over forty-five. He was barefoot and wore a comfortable, loose-fitting tunic. His attire seemed strangely casual until she realized that, as the emperor's personal aide, he likely lived there.

Illim began snapping his fingers over and over, an irritated expression pulling at his mouth. Then he stopped and pointed at her. "Sephryn, right?" He followed his conclusion with a grin of triumph.

She nodded.

"Knew it." He continued to smile. "And your mother was . . . Moya."

Again, she nodded.

"I liked her, but I suppose she's dead now?"

"For eight hundred years, yes."

"That long?" He shook his head sadly, then studied her carefully. "What about Tekchin? Is your father still alive?"

"Yes, he still lives in the same house in Merredydd."

"I remember him well—wonderful days. Good old Tekchin. Is he with you?" Illim looked down the corridor.

"No, sir."

Illim waved a hand dismissively. "Don't call me *sir.* I'm just a glorified servant, always have been."

"You're a bit more than that."

"Perhaps," he said and sighed. "It's a shame your father isn't here. I'm sure the emperor would be delighted to see him. They are the only Galantians left, you know." He scratched his head, and she noticed his blond hair was starting to turn white.

"My father—"

"Hold on." He waved for her to follow. "No point standing in this drafty hallway. I was just checking to see if the linens had arrived. Let's go to my chambers, but please ignore the mess."

He led the way through a suite of rooms, moving quickly. She followed, feeling both fortunate at the invitation as well as concerned. Although he didn't look like it at that moment, the Fhrey before her was likely the second most powerful being in the world. Imperial Steward was a simple title, but Illim was also the emperor's best friend and confidant.

The room he led her to wasn't what she had expected. Sephryn had anticipated an impeccably neat and austere chamber because of Illim's fastidious nature, but she found a mess. The furniture and adornments were lavish, but clothes were scattered everywhere, and a plate of leftover lamb rested on a gold-inlaid chair. The steward invited her to sit, even though all the furniture was covered in dirty clothes.

"Thank you," she replied but remained standing just the same.

"You were saying?" he prompted.

"I was?"

"Something about Tekchin?"

"Oh—ah, I was about to mention how much I enjoy his stories about your adventures."

"Not mine," Illim said. "I was never a Galantian, not part of that elite band of warriors, but I did know them all, even Nyphron's father. In truth"—he leaned in—"Zephyron was twice the leader Nyphron is."

"That sounds like . . . ah . . . a dangerous opinion."

Illim laughed. "Not at all. I tell Nyphron that all the time, usually when I'm mad at him."

The steward collapsed on a mound of clothes piled on a couch and threw his feet up. "Here's a tale your father probably doesn't know about. One spring, when Nyphron and I were stone-faced drunk on apple wine, his father caught us preparing to brave the Grandford rapids in a raft—at night, no less!" He smiled at the memory. "Zephyron didn't stop us. We both nearly drowned that night. I broke my leg and shattered this little bone right here." He pointed to his collar. "Nyphron banged his head and lost all sight out of one eye for a week." He followed the statement with a laugh. "Dear Ferrol, I miss those days. I really do. Life was . . . well, it was life, wasn't it?"

He looked at her as if expecting an answer, but she had no idea what to say.

"When I think of how much he wanted this"—he gestured at the chandeliers, cut-crystal decanters, and a floor layered in exquisite rugs—"I wonder why."

Illim wagged a finger at her. "You've been seeing Nolyn, isn't that right?"

The question surprised her, and she took a moment to answer, "Ah, yes, sir." Then she quickly added, "But not recently, it's been more than a year. He's currently in southwestern Maranonia."

"Still in his first millennium, right? Ah, those were the days." He shook his head as if waking from a pleasant dream. "Nolyn will look back at his time in the legion fondly. Just like your father and Nyphron cherish their years as Galantians. Trust me. I've seen it all. When the fighting ends, blades grow rusty."

He kicked his feet off the couch, righting himself, and gathered a pile of tunics, palliums, and braccae. "How have you been? Everything all right?"

She almost told him, nearly blurted everything out right then and there.

"If either of you speaks a word, all three of you die, starting with poor little Nurgya," the Voice had said, and she assumed he would be watching her—now more closely than ever, listening to every sound she made.

"I'm fine," she said.

"You're not," he challenged and stared knowingly. "I know why you're here."

She held her breath.

"You've been trying to gain an audience with the emperor for years. Now, I know how frustrating that can be. Trust me, I've had to stand in the way of legion generals and provincial governors, including Sikar."

Illim smirked. "Oh, dear Ferrol, he can be a handful. When he served in the Rhist, none of us liked him. But can you imagine telling the governor of Merredydd that the emperor isn't available? Especially after he's traveled for days? *Pitching a fit* doesn't describe it. So you see, I can't intervene on your behalf. Protocols really must be followed. I suggest you submit a request to the minister's office. I'll try to put in a good word for you, and if it can be arranged, it will be. But you must be patient."

He got up.

She couldn't leave, not yet. As scared as she was, she had an opportunity that she couldn't squander. "There is one thing," she began slowly. "It's regarding the Founder's Day Festival, which will be here before we know it."

"Yes?"

"I thought . . . that is, I was wondering if . . . well, you see, the Imperial Council is planning something special. A . . ." She was improvising, making everything up as she went, and that wasn't a talent of hers. "A display, a historical one to commemorate the events leading to the founding of the empyre. We thought—that is, the Imperial Council determined—it would be far more impressive if we had a few things to bring the past to life."

"Such as?"

"Well, like antiques and general memorabilia. Things like the flag that flew over Alon Rhist during the Battle of Grandford, for example. The emperor's chariot from the war, perhaps. Maybe even the Horn of Gylindora." She hoped she remembered the pronunciation correctly.

"The Horn of . . ." He was shaking his head. "How do you know about that?"

She smiled, trying to look innocent. "My parents."

"Oh, right." He nodded. "Well, they should have explained that the horn isn't a toy. It's a holy relic and not to be gawked at in public." He chuckled at the thought. "It stays locked up." His eyes shifted to what Sephryn had previously thought was a decoration in the wall, but she now wondered if it was a small door—one without a handle and made of stone.

But why would it be in Illim's room?

"Oh, all right," she told him while staring at a crumpled tunic, trying to puzzle out the mystery.

"I know what you are thinking," he said.

"You do?"

"I've always been a stickler about keeping the palace neat and orderly, so why is my place such a disaster?"

"I didn't mean to insinuate or insult. I suppose it's like the old saying about the cobbler's children having no shoes."

"No, that's not it at all. In this case, my children prefer to go barefoot."

"Sorry. I'm not following."

"Nyphron. He's the problem. The truth is I live with a slob. I simply can't keep up with the emperor's commitment to chaos. This is all his mess."

"So you and Nyphron are . . . you share . . ."

Illim shrugged. "We both sleep here, if that's what you mean. Sharing is a whole other matter. One that Nyphron isn't good at. But that's my problem, not yours."

That explains it; the horn is here! Locked up in some sort of vault.

"Oh, I see, but I really would like to present my request about displaying the horn directly to the emperor. Perhaps I could wait here for just a little while?"

He smiled but shook his head. "Protocols, remember? But I'm certain we can provide the other things you requested. Please say hello to your father for me the next time you see him." He laughed again.

"Ah . . . yes. I will. Thank you," she said and then retreated to the hallway. She moved quickly and didn't slow down until she reached the empty courtyard.

"It's sealed in stone!" she whispered aloud. "The horn is locked inside the emperor's private quarters." She hissed the last part, trying to keep her voice down but wanting to scream. "Are you hearing me?" She paused, listening. She wanted to have it out with the Voice there rather than on a public street. "I can't get it. There's no way I can do this!"

She waited.

Nothing.

"Say something, dammit!"

Silence.

Sephryn ran for the gate. She had to get out, wanted to get free of the palace before the tears came. They were there, lurking beneath the weight of fear, stress, and exhaustion.

"Did you get it?"

Sephryn looked sheepishly at Andrule. "No. It must be somewhere else."

"Oh—that's too bad," the guard replied, appearing puzzled.

"Not the scarf, you idiot. The horn! Do you have it?"

Sephryn realized her mistake, and with an embarrassed smile, she quickly stepped back onto the Grand Mar and headed for home.

Ducking into an alley, she said, "It's locked inside a stone wall. I can't get at it. You'll need to find someone else. But if you give me back my son, I can tell them where to find it."

"That's not how this works. The deal was the horn for the child. If you can't hold up your end, then I won't, either. And if the child no longer has any value, I guess I'll just have to kill him. Is that what you want?"

"No!"

"Then what do you propose?"

Sephryn stared at a puddle, seeing her reflection. What she saw was the face of desperation, and for the first time in her life, she thought she looked old.

"I'll figure something out, but it will take a little while."

"That's better, but don't take too long. I don't think little Nurgya likes it here, and you wouldn't want to scar him for life, would you? So do hurry, for his sake."

CHAPTER FIVE

One of Them

Nolyn walked directly behind Jerel. Being taller and broader, DeMardefeld was forced into contortions to duck thick stalks of palmy vegetation that began purple at their bases and shifted to yellow-green as the leaves fanned out. As the larger man dipped and twisted, shafts of sun pierced the roof of the jungle and scintillated off his armor, which inexplicably managed to retain its luster.

"This morning, I had my doubts about finding you alive, sir. I shouldn't have doubted the One," Jerel said as he ducked under a large jungo leaf.

\"Oh, don't ask about *that*, sir." Myth let out a moan. He was somewhere behind them, close enough that Nolyn could hear his heavy breathing. Azuriah Myth was one of those people who not only spoke loudly but even breathed with excessive volume.

"Why? Is it a secret?"

"What we wouldn't give for that to be so," Smirch muttered. He, too, was somewhere behind Nolyn.

Amicus had set the order, with Riley having the boar's head, a position Nolyn guessed the First Spear often took because of his experience; then came Jerel, as the boar's tusks. Amicus put himself at the boar's tail. Nolyn suspected the little fortress of men was designed, fore and aft, to keep him insulated from harm. The prymus was considered the brain, the most valued component in the body, and so the men acted in his defense. Nolyn had never understood the reasoning, since a body without a heart or lungs would die just as certainly.

They walked in a ragged single file line as they descended from the start of the ravine to where the ground was less steep. There, the flora was larger and more abundant, and the once-thrashing turmoil of wild cascades calmed to a legitimate river. Because the water was too deep to walk in, the men were forced to hack their way along the bank.

"The One is the reason I'm here, sir," Jerel declared in the dauntless tone with which he responded to everything.

"He's your regiment officer?" Nolyn joked.

That drew a number of chuckles, more than expected, but then legion officers weren't known to be well thought of.

"No, sir!" Jerel responded, clearly not getting the jest. "The One is God."

"Yes, I gathered that much, but which one?"

Nolyn considered himself something of an expert on the gods, mostly because of his mother and her friends. While he had been entirely ignored by his father, Nolyn had found plenty of attention from his mother and those closest to her, whom she had called his aunts. Being from the same clan, they *were* all related but none of them were Persephone's sisters. Women of the village commonly served as caregivers to young children, but these ladies were anything but *common*. If stories were to be believed — and some just couldn't be — they had fought man-eating bears, huge magical monsters, and even passed through the underworld to save their entire race. As a child, he had loved the stories, especially the ones about the evil dwarf Gronbach. But as he grew older, he realized most of these tales were too tall to be true.

One of his *aunts* was a woman named Brin. She had died when Nolyn was still young, and he had only vague memories of her. According to his mother, Brin had invented writing and created an incredible book that chronicled not only the history of their people but also details about the gods, which she learned from reading ancient stone tablets in the dwarven city of Neith. Nolyn, Bran, and Sephryn were all tutored from *The Book of Brin*. According to it, there were five primary gods: Ferrol, the god of the Fhrey; Drome, the god of the dwarfs; Mari, the goddess of mankind; Muriel, who was nature itself; and Erebus, the father of them all. These were the ones Nolyn was the most familiar with, but he knew there were many others, such as Eton, the god of the sky; Arkum, god of the sun; and Fribble-Bibble, a favorite river spirit of Suri the mystic. Then there were the Mynogan—gods of battle, honor, and death—and Eraphus, the god of the sea. All of these were mentioned in *The Book of Brin*. There were also a slew of other gods or demigods that Nolyn discovered after leaving home. The Grenmorians worshiped the Typhons, and Uberlin was the god of the ghazel. But in all his travels and the combined teachings of his aunts, Nolyn had never heard of any god being referred to as *the One*.

"The only One, sir," Jerel insisted. "The true God. All others are merely legends. Perhaps they were great people once, but they suffered the same fate—they died. Only the One is immortal. Only the One *is* God."

"And how do you know all this?"

"He told me."

"He speaks to you?"

"Just like you are now, sir. He said I must leave the comfort of my happy home in lush Maranonia and join the ranks of the legion."

"Would take more than a request to get *me* to leave all that and come here," Smirch grumbled. "No doubt about it—I can tell you that, bossy."

"Jerel's father is a wealthy landowner," Myth explained in his deep, throaty voice, which reminded Nolyn of how a seasoned hound might sound if it spoke with a Calynian accent. "Has a sprawling villa outside

Mehan, an army of servants, and herds of sheep and cattle. Jerel used to spend his days drinking wine with women in lush green glens. He gave all that up to come to this disease-infested muck hole."

Smirch was shaking his head in disbelief. "Volunteered for the auxiliary, too. Bright as a blindfold, that one. If I was him, I'd be back home, drunk off my ass, having my nails done on the veranda by some beauty in a short, sheer palla. But no—he's here, and happy for it, too. That's the rub, right there. The whole thing goes beyond simply stupid and wanders off the Cliffs of Insanity."

"When God tells you to do something, it's the fool who turns a deaf ear," Jerel replied.

"If that's true, foolishness is highly underrated."

"So what does this one true god look like?" Nolyn asked. "Is he a giant? Half man, half animal? A floating light? What?"

"To be honest, sir, he looked like a tailor."

"A tailor?"

"That's what I took him for, sir. He said he'd come to *size me up*, and I assumed my father had sent him to take measurements for a new set of clothes. I was quite wrong. He'd come to evaluate me, sir—not the dimensions of my body, but the magnitude of my character. He asked me a series of seemingly innocuous questions, and then he told me I must join the legion and seek out active duty in the Seventh Sikaria Auxiliary, which is always sent to the most hazardous areas."

"And you just accepted this advice?"

"It wasn't what I would call advice, sir. It'd be more accurate to describe it like he was telling me what already happened, even though it hadn't yet, and no, sir, I regret to say that I didn't believe a word he said—at first."

"What changed your mind?"

"I would have to say it was the two-headed sheep."

"Did you say, two-headed sh—"

"As wonderful as this story is," Amicus cut in, "it's getting late. We need to make some decisions. Should we set up some sort of defense on the river? Or leave it and seek shelter elsewhere?"

"How far are we from Urlineus?"

"We won't get there tonight, if that's what you're thinking."

Nolyn looked out into the dense jungle surrounding them. They'd left the narrow end of the ravine, and the cliff walls had retreated too far to be visible. "Odds of us finding shelter out there are slim, while the chance of getting lost, I suspect, are high, and the cost in effort and time isn't worth it. We might as well set up here. At least we have the river on one side."

Nolyn looked at Amicus for approval or doubt. They were in the First Spear's neighborhood. Although Nolyn was nearly eight hundred and fifty-five, the one consistent thing all those years had taught him was that every individual had a lesson to impart.

Amicus, however, wasn't in a teaching mood. He showed no sign of disagreement or approval and quickly said, "Then I suggest we get started on a fire."

Nolyn knew that the ghazel, angered by their failure in the ravine, would retaliate by sending an even larger force, and unlike before, his troop wouldn't have the protection of cliff walls. However, a fire and a river were better than nothing. After witnessing the incredible events of the night before, Nolyn wasn't so quick to forecast defeat. He clung to the glimmer of hope that they might yet survive their ordeal.

Then it began to rain.

They heard the first telltale pitter-patter not long after dragging over some logs. A few minutes later, it grew to a roar that required shouting to be heard over. And while night hadn't quite fallen, the increased darkness declared it was no longer quite day, either. Rivulets formed at their feet. Heavy droplets blasted through the canopy, soaking the ground. There would be no fire.

No one said anything. They just stopped gathering wood and came together on the riverbank where they had cleared away most of the leafy plants. The little troop of survivors took seats on the few logs they had already dragged over. Smirch and Myth ate from rations. Amicus and Jerel looked to their weapons and armor.

"So what are your plans once you become emperor, sir?" Riley asked. He, too, had pulled a strip of cured meat from his pack.

"Not going to happen," Nolyn replied.

Riley sent him a work-with-me-here look and gestured at the others.

"I didn't mean to imply we aren't going to survive. It's just that my father will most certainly outlive me."

"He could die from falling down the stairs," Riley said. "You don't know."

"My father is a full-blooded Fhrey, which means that's about as likely to happen as a cat tripping."

"But if it did, what would you do?"

Nolyn took a deep breath and drew his cloak tighter. The garment was getting soaked, but it still provided protection. Nolyn hated the feeling of water running down the back of his neck. It reminded him too much of spiders on his skin. "Well, a long time ago, Sephryn and I had a friend named Bran. Sephryn is like me, the child of a human mother and Fhrey father, but Bran was different. Both his parents were human. As we got older, we saw how poorly he was treated, and that bothered us. When Sephryn's family moved back to Merredydd—do you know anything about that place?"

"Mostly Instarya living there, right?" Amicus ventured.

Nolyn nodded. "Used to be a Fhrey fortress even before the Great War. We all lived there for a while when Percepliquis was being built. After the city was finished, most of the humans moved to the capital. Then the remaining Fhrey built the fortress into a proper city, and they weren't happy living elbow-to-elbow with the humans who had stayed behind. An Instarya named Sikar is the governor now. Incidentally, that's the same guy our legion is named after. Anyway, when Sephryn went back, she discovered firsthand what it's like to be singled out because of her birth. The citizens of Merredydd could only see her human half, and they treated her like dirt."

Nolyn popped the few remaining nuts he'd gotten from Amicus into his mouth, chewed, and then went on, "When she later returned to

Percepliquis—a city where humans are treated as outcasts even though they outnumber the Fhrey—Sephryn stopped being just bothered; she became outraged. Ever since then, she's been working to make significant changes but hasn't gotten too far. She has a lot of crazy plans, and some that are actually pretty good. One night we came up with the idea of a Citizen's Charter, a list of laws that would apply to every imperial citizen regardless of their race—rules that would be consistent, with punishment and reward that would be applied fairly to all." Nolyn laughed self-consciously. "You have to understand that a lot of wine was involved." He wiped the rain from his face, where a droplet was tickling his nose.

Jerel nudged Amicus and pointed to Nolyn. "See? I told you."

Amicus frowned. "Doesn't prove anything."

"What doesn't?" Nolyn asked. "What are you two talking about?"

"The One prophesied that if I joined the legion, I would help change the world for the better by protecting Nolyn Nyphronian, the next emperor."

"He said that, did he?" Nolyn chuckled. "This god of tailors actually used my name?"

"He just looks like one, but yes, he did. Furthermore, he declared you would rule with the compassion and wisdom of your mother. Your idea for a Citizen Charter proves the truth of his words."

"Your god is wrong. There was only one Persephone, and Nyphron isn't going anywhere for another thousand years, and I'll be dead long before then."

"We didn't believe Jerel, either," Riley admitted. "But then you showed up."

"And yet, you still didn't change your mind," Jerel retorted.

"It's difficult to accept anything you say, DeMardefeld," Smirch said. "You're just so damn shiny. Inside and out, I suspect. That's just not natural."

Myth was nodding. "Jerel told us the crown prince of the empyre would breeze into the Seventh Sik-Aux. What were the odds?"

Before Nolyn could answer, he noticed faint movement in the ferns. The night was a noisy crash of rain, but that brush against plants resonated as a counter-note, the audible equivalent of brushing fur the wrong way.

Amicus noticed the turn of his head, the widening of his eyes. "What?"

"Movement."

Amicus smiled. "Showtime."

The soldiers scrambled to their feet. Blades were drawn and shields raised.

"Protect His Highness," Amicus said. "And, sir, if you see a chance to save yourself—you take it. That's an order."

"I'm your superior officer and the emperor's son. You don't give me orders."

"I do today, sir. And I don't want you coming back here to bury us, either. If a god sent Jerel to protect you, maybe he knows something we don't."

Ghazel crashed through the brush. Intermittent, filtered moonlight reflected off the surface of the river and provided adequate illumination for Nolyn to see. Dark, twisted, and hunched bodies charged in. Amicus and Jerel stood in front of Nolyn and met the advance with Riley Glot and Azuriah Myth flanking. Once more, Amicus Killian performed his magic, hewing goblins in his perfect dance with a mesmerizing rhythm. Now, however, Nolyn had the chance to witness the others. Jerel, Riley, and Myth mimicked the First Spear, not as perfectly, not as elegantly, but they, too, killed goblins with remarkable skill—the same techniques. They weren't equal, but the relationship was obvious. Nolyn was listening to one melody played on four different instruments, and the concert was a bloody one.

Ghazel came at them like rampaging bulls only to slam into a wall and collapse in a pile. More attacked from behind. Smirch and the Poor Calynian were there, but not nearly as proficient as the others. Nolyn lent his blade to theirs, and in comparison, he felt like a new recruit.

Blood and rain mixed; thunder and metal crashed. Then, as suddenly as it began, the attack stopped.

"That's the first wave," Riley said, puffing clouds in the supersaturated air.

"No arrows this time," the Poor Calynian said.

"Didn't help last night," Riley replied. "Guess they're learning."

"Not sure why they don't just start with the oberdaza then." Myth shook the wet off his head and beard.

"Don't give them ideas."

In the depths of the jungle, within the dark of the unknown, they heard the wailing of a long, single note.

"Oh, by the short hairs of the emperor!" Smirch cursed. "What is that?"

"That's a *legion* horn, you idiot!" Riley shouted.

They all looked at him as the truth of his words sank in. In that span of time, the horn cut out and sounded again.

"That's definitely a legion horn," Amicus said, shocked. "How is that possible?"

They watched the brush around them. Amid the crash of rain, they heard the clash of combat. Somewhere in the trees, hidden by the big leaves and the inky black that filled in the cracks, a war erupted. The sound, like the rain, ebbed and flowed. It rose to a climax, tapered off, then silence. Still, they waited with swords in hand as the rain cleaned the blood from their weapons.

Something moved toward them: something loud, something big. It thumped through the trees, snapping branches as it approached. Nolyn could hear heavy breathing, too loud to be human, ghazel, or even Azuriah Myth. A jangling accompanied it as if the creature was adorned in ring mail. They prepared themselves for whatever hideous beast was about to emerge. Then it came, taller than any man. The moonlight revealed—a horse.

Acer! Nolyn recognized his mount, and upon the animal's back sat—

"Everett!" they all shouted.

The young scout grinned and dismounted. He held out the reins to Nolyn. "Your horse, sir."

"Everett, how—" Amicus paused as out of the dark came several legionnaires. These were regular infantry wearing heavy armor. "How did you get to Urlineus and back so fast?"

"I didn't," Everett replied. "I ran into the Fifth Regiment coming down from Craken's Firth. I told them the Seventh Sik-Aux was in trouble, and they didn't hesitate. Their commander split off a detachment and sent them with me." The scout couldn't stop grinning.

Neither could anyone else.

Then a rugged old soldier with a First Spear brush on his helmet stepped out of the murk, and Amicus began laughing. "Well, look at that—Brac Bareith. I thought you retired to a rocking chair."

"Amicus Killian—you just don't die, do you?"

"You sound disappointed."

"Not at all. Saving you and the famous Seventh Auxiliary will be something I'll boast about for years to come."

"Saving me?"

Bareith grinned while wiping rain away with one hand and reaching for his water pouch with the other. "We just pulled your ass out of the jaws of an angry hive of ghazel."

Amicus chuckled. "Oh, I see. You thought we needed your help."

Brac narrowed his eyes, rose up on his toes, and took a head count using a finger. "There are only *seven* of you and more than a hundred ghazel. If we hadn't caught them by surprise and from behind, they might have put a serious dent in *our* detachment."

Amicus nodded. "Of that, I'm certain. But we were fine."

Brac appeared dumbfounded. "Bull's wool!"

Amicus looked at Riley. "Do *you* think we needed any support?"

"With what? These cute little buggers?" He put a foot on the body of one.

Amicus looked to the others. "Does *anyone* think we needed assistance?"

Myth and the Poor Calynian shook their heads. Smirch was the only holdout. "Well . . ." he said, "I wouldn't mind a little help. I got an itch I can't quite reach. It's on me bum. Here, I'll lift my skirt for you, bossy."

Brac frowned. "You're all full of bosh." Then he spotted Nolyn. His eyes registered the uniform, and he snapped to attention, offering a smart salute. "Sorry, prymus. I didn't notice you there, sir."

"Relax, First Spear," Nolyn replied.

"Thank you, sir." He eased his stance, then a smile came to his lips. "Surely you have a grip on reality. You're required to make an accurate report to Legate Lynch. You'll set the record straight about how we saved you, right?"

"Saved? From what, First Spear?" Nolyn asked.

Brac Bareith's eyes widened. "Oh, by the beating heart of Elan!" He glanced at his fellows as they came out of the jungle, forming up to either side. "The emperor's son . . . he's one of *them* now."

Amicus looked at Nolyn, smiled, and nodded. "Yes, I suppose he is."

CHAPTER SIX

Divine Providence

Mawyndulë slapped his neck and killed another of the monstrous insects that sought to bleed him dry. He pulled his hand away, rubbing the tiny bug between his fingers, taking pleasure in crushing its dead body, smearing it across his skin. Hideous flies, ridiculous heat, and the ever-present wetness plagued him. It rained every day. Even when it didn't, the air felt poised to spit. That's how it felt, like he was trapped in the mouth of some vile beast, inhaling secondhand its hot, moist breath. In a bout of delirious, wishful thinking, the empyre had nicknamed their newest city Urlineus—the Gem of the Jungle. Mawyndulë could agree only if the said gem was presently jammed up a boar's ass.

Wretched Ferrol! How I hate this place, he screamed in his head as he dodged a mud-spraying chariot and nearly fell into a lake-sized puddle. After all these years, Mawyndulë still enjoyed speaking the name of the Fhrey god in vain. As a youth, he'd recoiled if anyone dared to do so. Now, he did it as a personal right. Ferrol was no longer his god. If ever there was a godless creature, Mawyndulë was it.

Making his way around the noisy city construction, Mawyndulë stopped, dumbfounded. Eight men dressed in auxiliary legion uniforms entered the city from the east. Capes torn, helms dented, mud and blood on their unshaven faces, they looked like they'd been dragged by horses. Scores of other legionnaires with different insignia flanked them. They, too, were fresh out of the bush, but not nearly so battered, and all of them—especially the eight—smiled and laughed as they marched.

No, not eight men, Mawyndulë corrected himself, *seven humans and a crossbreed. The prince is still alive!*

He peered up at the milk-white haze that he assumed was the sun. *Barely midday, and already I have to deal with my second major setback. One mishap was bad luck but two in a single morning?*

Trilos said it would work. But I guess he was wrong. Should have known better. If I say it's going to rain tomorrow and it does, am I a seer or just lucky? Okay, it rains every day here, so that's a bad example. But the point is that just because Trilos makes a prediction doesn't mean it'll come to pass, or that he's telling the truth. I can't trust him. After all, Trilos is a demon.

Mawyndulë was standing in the middle of the street as he mused, and the sight of the apparently unscathed prince made him more than a bit cross. So when another chariot charged his way, he was in no mood to dodge it. Instead, he clapped his hands, and the forelegs of the horses pulling it immediately buckled. With a whinny, they went down. The yoke and crossbar did as well, propelling the vehicle up and over, tossing its occupants.

Mawyndulë completed crossing the street amid the sounds of screams and shouts. He didn't look back and grumbled to himself, "I shouldn't have done that."

It wasn't that he cared about the riders or the horses, but his plan required invisibility. Everything hinged on acting in the shadows. He consoled himself with the knowledge that none of the Rhunes around him would take note of the cause and effect. With one notable exception, their kind was too primitive to wield the Art, and as such, they wouldn't recognize magic when they saw it.

His foul mood descended further.

Two setbacks in one day? It's a wonder I didn't blow up a building. First, that useless idiot Sephryn couldn't get the horn, and now the prince—whose liver was supposed to be the leftovers on a ghazel's plate—just strolled into Urlineus.

Mawyndulë moved up the street, away from the turmoil he'd caused, then stopped to think.

What do I do now?

Mawyndulë had diligently worked for centuries to make his dream come true. Some of that time he'd spent in a hideous castle on the Green Sea, some in Percepliquis, and the rest in the southern province of Maranonia. But recently, most of his time had been consumed in the jungles of Calynia, prepping for the first act of his *Big Show*. Finally, he had unleashed his grand scheme—but its wheels fell off the instant he gave it a shove.

"You'll succeed," Trilos had once predicted through the thin lips of a young woman who had apparently died from starvation. *"You'll have your revenge, at least."*

In some ways, Mawyndulë missed his old mentor, but at the same time, he didn't. Over the eight centuries they had been together, Mawyndulë suspected he had learned more about the Art from Trilos than in the entire history of the world. Learning to fabricate strawberries from thin air was just the first of many wonders he'd picked up, and broadening his magical abilities was one of the two reasons Mawyndulë had stayed with the demon for so long.

He has to be a demon. What else can he be?

Mawyndulë still had nightmares from the time Trilos came back wearing the body of a mutilated child. He explained it had been an emergency relocation. Soon after, the demon took up residence in the recently vacated body of a beautiful female Fhrey. Mawyndulë felt, in part, that Trilos was trying to make up for the previous choice. In a way, that body was worse. Mawyndulë found he was attracted to Trilos—or rather the dead body he inhabited. The whole thing was confusing and more than a little troubling.

Now that Mawyndulë was finally free of his mentor, he felt a bit lonely, a tad nervous, and even a dash frightened. He had bided his time and let centuries pass to ensure that any Rhunes who had known about his part in the Great War had turned to dust. He suspected even most of the Fhrey had forgotten him. Mawyndulë had been the crown prince of the Fhrey, but he hadn't been well entrenched in the hearts of those he was supposed to rule. Having killed his own father, he was an outcast, forgotten, and likely presumed dead. After more than eight hundred years, no one would be on the lookout, no one on guard.

The soldiers, freshly back to civilization, stopped for food. The men would be at the canteen for a while. Then they would likely take time to wash, change clothes, and then get drunk.

I still have some time.

He looked up the hill at the only decent building in the province. The city of Percepliquis, having been proclaimed as sheer perfection, served as the model for all imperial cities. So just as the palace formed the heart of the capital, Urlineus's center would one day be the governor's residence—when the city finally obtained one. For now, it was the office of the legate, the commander of the Seventh Legion who was tasked with building the city and taming the frontier.

Maybe staying invisible isn't the right approach after all.

Another fly bit, just behind his ear.

He slapped at it and missed.

As Mawyndulë entered the command quarters, a man behind a desk was tying scrolls into neat tubes and placing them in cubbyholes built into the wall. That was the sort of activity Mawyndulë imagined worker bees did deep within a honeycomb. It had to take about the same amount of mental acuity.

"May I help you?" The staff officer and general secretary, known as the palatus, hadn't so much asked a simple question as insinuated Mawyndulë had no business being there.

The creature was the glorified servant to the legate, the sort to fetch things and make appointments. A miserable, spindly little man with pale skin, small eyes, and a hatchet nose.

If the little palatus were dead, it would be just the sort of body Trilos would use to needle Mawyndulë. *"How do you like this one, Mawyndulë? Look, it's got all its teeth. See! And don't you love the whine of its voice? It sounds like a late-summer cicada. Want me to sing a song? How about* The Wicked Brothers, *eh? You like that one, don't you?"*

Trilos had to be a demon. What else lived longer than a Fhrey, inhabited dead bodies, and knew more about the Art than all the Miralyith combined?

The palatus at the desk leaned forward in his seat. "I *said*, may *I—*"

Mawyndulë didn't answer the clerk, just as he wouldn't engage a barking dog on the front porch of a tenement where the rent was overdue. With long strides, he crossed the room, made his way down the hall, and with a casual flick of his hand, the door to the legate's office burst open. It banged hard against the inner wall.

"Demetrius! What is—" Legate Lynch, the legion commander and acting governor of the Imperial Province of Calynia, stopped the moment he saw Mawyndulë. The two had but a brief history, but Mawyndulë had obviously made an impression.

"I'm sorry, sir!" Demetrius shouted. The little man came running.

Mawyndulë slammed the door shut the same way he'd opened it, hoping to time it to hit the staff officer. He missed but still enjoyed the satisfying *thud* when Demetrius, who was unable to stop in time, banged into the door.

"He's still alive," Mawyndulë declared to the legate. Then, after seeing Lynch's sight track to the door, Mawyndulë frowned. "Not the palatus, the prince."

As if in confirmation, the door latch rattled as Demetrius struggled unsuccessfully to open it.

"You again," Lynch said, demonstrating far less respect than Mawyndulë felt he deserved. Although, if they were going by that scale, nothing short of Lynch groveling at his feet would do.

"Yes. Did you think I wouldn't wait to see if the job was done?" Mawyndulë snapped. "I gave—I mean, the emperor gave—strict orders to arrange for his son's death. Nyphron didn't want Nolyn returning from that assignment, and yet, he's back. Did you happen to forget?"

"I appointed Prince Nolyn as the prymus of a tiny scouting party," Lynch replied, "and ordered him into a dead-end gorge deep in goblin territory. The chances of his survival were nonexistent."

Lynch was the worst sort of Rhune—or human, as they were called these days—old, sagging, white-haired, and worn out. His skin had the pitted texture of a rotting gourd. Mawyndulë guessed his mind suffered in much the same way.

If his head is rancid on the outside, how good can it be inside?

"And yet, he lives."

"Exactly. So how do you explain that?" The legate pushed back his chair and folded his arms with an overdeveloped sense of confidence.

Mawyndulë was baffled about why the buffoon was posing the exact same question that Mawyndulë was demanding an answer to. "Obviously, you're terrible at your job."

"I didn't rise to the rank of legate by being incompetent."

"Oh? Then what's your explanation?"

"Providence," the legion commander declared, saying the word as if it held magical attributes. "That order was wrong. The emperor shouldn't murder his own child—especially without cause and in such a cowardly manner. Although the emperor may want his son dead, the gods clearly don't. There is no other possible explanation."

Mawyndulë stared at the fool for a moment, considering his absurdity. "And you fear the gods more than the emperor?"

"As any sane man would."

"Huh." Mawyndulë nodded, making a mental note that in the minds of humans, gods trumped emperors.

Mawyndulë's improvisational plan was merely to threaten Lynch further. As Nolyn's commanding officer, the legate could once more arrange for the prince's demise. Now, however, a completely new idea took shape—a wonderfully poetic payback that was just too glorious to resist.

If providence is in play here, then never before have I been dealt such a wonderful hand.

"Okay, fine, but what if I told you that I'm not an imperial envoy sent by the emperor? And that the soldiers who were with me last time were paid to act as escorts and give false credentials on my behalf, and that I stole this uniform and forged the imperial seal on the document I presented? What if I said I had been making plans for decades, which is why I knew the protocols, all the right names, and the correct terminology."

"I wouldn't be surprised." Lynch got to his feet, and a smile rose on the man's lips.

Because he's bigger and I'm unarmed he has no fear. And being commander of over five thousand men, he wrongly believes he's in control.

Mawyndulë nodded. "But what if I revealed that I am a god? You seem to believe they can overrule emperors."

Lynch laughed. "You've got some big ones. I'll give you that."

"Ah, I see, you don't believe me. You need proof." Mawyndulë called out, "Demetrius!" As he did, the latch finally worked, and the door swung wide.

The staff officer stood on the far side, staring suspiciously at the door.

Mawyndulë made a curling motion with his forefinger and coaxed Demetrius into the office.

The legate took another step forward and stood even straighter, arching his back and puffing out his chest. He wasn't wearing a uniform. Instead, he was dressed in a robe similar to the imperial version of the ancient Fhrey asica, a fashion choice that Mawyndulë didn't approve of. Lynch, it appeared, was growing a bit too used to his role as governor.

Lynch commanded, "Demetrius, this fool has just confessed to treason. Fetch the guards."

The palatus made a crisp nod and pivoted toward the exit. He took one step before the door slammed shut again.

"How is it doing that?" Demetrius asked, mostly to himself. He looked around. "A draft?"

"No," Lynch said. "This impostor has rigged up some kind of trick. He's trying to impress, make us believe he's a god." He shook his head in disgust. "Out here, it takes more than slamming doors."

"Fine. You need a demonstration." Addressing the clerk, he said, "Demetrius, walk around in a circle for me, will you?"

"What?" Turning back toward the other two, the palatus had a confused expression.

"My error," Mawyndulë said. "I didn't mean to form that as a request. Do it. Now!"

The palatus began circling the office. He, too, was dressed in the pallium style of robes, but his attire was not nearly as well tailored as the legate's and lacked the fine gold edging. He strolled with arms swinging at his sides.

Hmm, he has a short gait and a simple heel-toe step.

"Demetrius, I gave you an order," Lynch snapped.

"I'm sorry, sir. I—I don't know what's going on. I can't stop myself."

Mawyndulë held up a hand, and the palatus halted. "Look left," he said, and Demetrius turned his head, presenting his profile. Mawyndulë studied it for a moment. "Now right."

Frustrated, and more than a little angry, Lynch crossed the room and tried the door handle himself but found it just as inoperable.

"You have an extremely stiff posture and sort of a waddle when you walk," Mawyndulë told the palatus. "Okay, now I need to hear you speak and not just a few words. I'll require you to—oh, I know, why don't you recite that awful poem that's so popular among the soldiers. The one about the Wicked Brothers. Surely you know it. Everyone seems to these days."

Squirming, Demetrius took a deep breath and began,

> *"Dill and Will Wicked and Nasty Bill Fricked*
> *were pirates who sailed on the sea.*
> *They decided to steal their very next meal*
> *from the people who ruled McFee.*
> *The job didn't go as they hoped.*
> *Poor Bill drowned in the moat.*
> *And the Wicked boys' luck got stuck in the muck,*
> *leaving both far away from their boat."*

"Demetrius, what are you doing?" Lynch admonished. "Stop that and get over here and help me with this stupid door!"

Demetrius continued,

> *"The two were caught and hopelessly brought*
> *to trial, which made quite a scene.*
> *Locked in a cell not much more than a well,*
> *the judge both vicious and mean.*
> *He laughed at the two, said this day you will rue;*
> *you shall never again be free.*
> *You'll stay here forever chained helpless together,*
> *I'm throwing away the key."*

Mawyndulë walked around Demetrius, studying him, listening to how the words were pronounced, his accent, the lilt of his voice, and placement of the inflections. Mawyndulë didn't think he had to get the mimicry perfect, but he wanted at least a good understanding of the palatus's basic speaking style. The man's mannerisms were easy when compared with his speech patterns.

Demetrius went on,

> *"You'll never be fed, released when you're dead,*
> *proclaimed His Excellency.*
> *You'll get sick and have at least one tick,*
> *the punishment for stealing from McFee.*
> *Dill and Will Wicked thought maybe Bill Fricked*
> *was more fortunate than they.*
> *For drowning was better than living forever*
> *chained on a pile of hay."*

"For every god's sake, shut up!" Lynch shouted.

"Yes, that's enough." Mawyndulë raised a finger, and Demetrius took another breath, but said no more. Turning to Lynch, Mawyndulë added, "Now for that proof. Watch closely or you might miss it."

Mawyndulë snapped his fingers, and the palatus exploded.

CHAPTER SEVEN
The Thief and the Poker

"It's just like Gronbach, isn't it?" Seymour said, sitting before the hearth in Sephryn's home. He wasn't looking at her anymore; instead, the monk stared into the fire he had built, using the iron poker with an odd sort of precision to adjust the logs. He sat on the little maple-wood stool, the one Sephryn had bought for Nurgya that stood just a foot off the ground. Still an infant, her son had yet to use it. The thought that he never would knocked on the door to her mind, demanding admission—a door she braced against with all her might. She couldn't let it in. If she did, Sephryn knew anguish would consume her. She had to keep her head clear, had to think, but that was so difficult with the constant *knock, knock, knock* drumming inside her consciousness. In her mind, she saw flashes of Nurgya: his pudgy face laughing, his mouth gurgling, his hands reaching, fingers clenching only to open and close again. So small, so helpless, and now gone.

What's happening to him? Is he locked in a box somewhere, crying for me?

Sephryn felt as defenseless as her son. She couldn't cry—there was no time for that. She had to think, had to do the impossible. The tears would come later. They would follow the last roll of the dice, when she either got him back or lost him forever.

"I mean, the way he's preying on you, forcing you to do his bidding. It's classic Gronbach."

Sephryn had told Seymour about her trip to the palace because he was the only one she *could* tell. Exempt from the Voice's edict of secrecy, the monk became her sole confidant. Their chance meeting and mutual discovery of the bloody message had placed Seymour in danger, and yet, Sephryn was so grateful for his company that she wondered if his arrival was truly an accident. Perhaps it had been the gods who put her feet on such a horrific tightrope, but they'd also provided a balancing pole. If so, they likely did it more for entertainment than empathy. They wanted a dramatic show with many acts. For that, Sephryn's sanity had to last, and to last, she needed help.

The monk looked at her, and his eyes widened. "Maybe that voice in your head *is* Gronbach!" His shoulders bunched as if with cold, and he shivered.

"It's not him," she said with more contempt than she'd intended. Seymour was only trying to help, but his idea was preposterous, and she couldn't entertain ridiculous notions with her son's life in jeopardy.

The fable of Gronbach was a child's tale. The story told of a deceitful dwarf who made a deal with a group of women, whom he'd promised to reward if they rid his town of a monster. Against impossible odds, they accomplished the amazing feat, but the dwarf refused to honor his word because he was greedy and dishonest.

The story was blatantly partisan and insulting to dwarfs, and she couldn't tell if it was the result of a long-standing prejudice or the cause of it.

Sephryn had both read the story and heard it directly from her mother, who claimed to have been present at the famous betrayal. But her mother insisted on a great many things that were too far to fetch. Moya's version, unlike the one in *The Book of Brin*, wasn't a children's story, since it was laced with old-world profanity—curses in a wide variety of languages including a vast assortment of Fhrey obscenities. Moya had also added a few new scenes regarding conversations that Brin hadn't heard. Sephryn had concluded long ago that the story was utter crap. That she had ever believed it—or any of her mother's crazy tales—embarrassed her. But children were apt to accept the word of their parents because they trusted them.

"Who it is doesn't matter. What's important is how do I get the horn."

"So what are you going to do?" Seymour asked.

"I'll have to find help. I can't do this alone." Seeing the hurt look, she added, "*We* can't do this by ourselves. We need someone who can open the vault, and it would be helpful if we knew more about the horn. I can't afford to make a mistake and grab the wrong item."

"Being as old as you are, I'm surprised you aren't already familiar with it."

She rolled her eyes. "Just because I've lived a long time doesn't make me an expert on everything."

Seymour's hurt expression deepened.

"I'm sorry. I didn't mean to snap. It's just that people always bring that up. It's become a personal tic. Although . . ." She thought a moment. "When I mentioned the horn to Illim, he knew exactly what I was talking about and seemed surprised I had heard of it. He even questioned how I found out."

"What did you say?"

"That my parents told me—a total shot in the dark, but he accepted that explanation. That probably means my father knows about it."

"You can't tell anyone. The kidnapper will kill your son if you do."

Sephryn nodded. "Trust me. I'm well aware of that. I'd love to go to my father. He and Nyphron were close once. He could likely get this horn, no problem." She shook her head. "If only he weren't so far away, I might . . . no, it's too dangerous. Losing Nurgya would kill me; losing them both is unthinkable. I considered talking to the First Minister or even Havilinda. She's the council's secretary, loves to gossip, and knows practically everything. But you're right. I can't *tell* anyone anything. But I can *involve* others. I just can't tell the *truth*. I'll have to make something up."

"Like what?"

"I have no idea, but what I do know is I need a thief."

"Sorry. Can't help you there."

"True, but I know someone who might."

"Who?"

"Arvis Dyer. She knows everyone on the shadowy side of the street. Maybe she can help me find someone who knows how to break into a stone vault. If she can't, I have no naffing idea what to try."

"Naffing?"

"It's one of my mother's profanities." Sephryn wasn't sure what it meant, but she was clear on how to use it.

"What can I do?" he asked in a gentle voice.

"You? Nothing."

Again, the puppy face. "You don't want my help?"

"No, that's not it. I just don't want to put you in more danger than you already are. Besides, you shouldn't be volunteering. I'm plotting a crime against the leader of the known world because of a wayward voice in my head. You'd be insane if you don't run from here and turn me in to the first city guard you can find."

Seymour looked toward the stairs, and Sephryn could guess what he was thinking. Even after scrubbing, a few bloodstains had remained.

"I don't think reporting you would be healthy. And as I can't unlearn what I know, leaving you might be dangerous. I don't hear the Voice, but we are in this together. If I'm seen as a help, perhaps I can avoid . . ." Again, he looked at the steps.

She looked, too. "You might be right."

"So, once again, what can I do?"

"Well . . ." She thought a bit. "There is something you would be perfect for."

Seymour's expression brightened.

"Can you write as well as read?"

"It's a requirement of my order. Bran demanded that all monks spend a portion of our day creating copies of *The Book of Brin*."

"Okay, so maybe you could find a description of the horn or maybe even an illustration. You could make a copy and bring it back here. That would help me identify it, assuming I can get the vault opened." She paused, waiting for approval or condemnation from the Voice. Then she looked at the ceiling as if the owner of the Voice lived on the second floor and asked, "Is that okay?"

No answer. The Voice either didn't care or wasn't listening at that moment, and she guessed the latter to be the case. It seemed unlikely that even a god would spend all his time listening to every random conversation she had.

"It's called the Horn of Gylindora. If my mother knew about it, that would suggest it has something to do with the Great War or the times shortly after. She lived to age seventy-four, so it had to exist before the Imperial year of Forty-Four. If you could search through the parchments at the records office and write down anything you find about the horn, that would help."

"Where is that?"

"At the palace. There's a little building just inside the gate to the left of the entrance. I can show you tomorrow. There are a lot of parchments down there, many of which are related to the founding of the city."

"Is it open to the public?"

"No, but I can get you in. I'll just have to tell them you're working for me. So, congratulations, you're my new scribe."

Sephryn looked for Arvis Dyer in West Market Square. Being the premier location to buy and sell food in the world's greatest city, the cobblestone plaza offered visitors the greatest variety of comestibles ever known, pulled from the far reaches of the empyre: ostrich steak, sea urchins, starlings, woodcocks, scorpions, fish eggs, peacocks, dolphins, herons, nightingale tongues, parrot heads, camel heels, and ground elephant trunks. A circular arcade of white pillars provided shelter to hundreds of merchants, and since almost everyone visited the market at least once a day, it was the pulsating heart of the city. Six streets converged on the aromatic gallery, and its center was always crowded with basket-carrying customers and delivery carts. Sephryn spotted Arvis, as she usually did, on the northeast side.

"Give it back!" A balding baker was yelling at Arvis, who cowered, retreating with a loaf of bread. She held the small round to her chest, clutching it like a baby.

"It's mine!" Arvis shouted back with a fury so intense that spittle flew from her lips.

"What's going on?" Sephryn stepped between them, which took a bit of courage given that the baker was menacingly holding a rolling pin.

The baker's wife had a worried look on her face as she stood behind the table of baked goods with one arm on her young daughter's shoulder.

With Sephryn's arrival, the baker's demeanor changed. His shoulders dropped, his face lengthened, and he took a long breath of—well, not relief. He didn't look happy to see her. He appeared . . . *what?* Sephryn wasn't certain.

"What's going on?" she asked again.

"She stole that."

"It's mine," Arvis snapped. "I paid for it."

That caught Sephryn's attention. "Arvis? How did you get the money?"

The woman opened her mouth and wiped the underside of her tongue over her lower lip, her eyes shifting left and right in countermeasure.

"Arvis?" Sephryn took a step nearer. "Where'd the money come from?"

"I . . . I don't . . ."

"She never gave us any money," Rodney declared. "She walked up and grabbed it. Took it right off my table." He gestured to a handful of onlookers who had paused to watch the shouting. "They all saw her do it. Didn't you?"

Sephryn saw most of them nod.

"Grabbed it without so much as a good morning and just walked off with it," said a woman who stood a little too straight while holding a big basket in front of her. "Bold as could be. Didn't hide it. Didn't care that people saw."

Sephryn turned back to Arvis. "Is that true?"

Arvis was still letting her eyes and tongue glide back and forth. "I—I did take it, but . . . but it was promised to me. They said I could have it."

"We said no such thing." The baker emphasized his exasperation by throwing his hands up. "That woman isn't right in the head. Everyone knows she's got a crack in that pot of hers."

"Arvis," Sephryn said softly, gently, "why would they give you a loaf of bread?"

"I don't . . . I don't remember." Arvis frequently had difficulty recalling things. "But I know it's mine. I'm sure they promised me. You believe me, don't you?"

Sephryn sighed. She honestly didn't believe Arvis. The baker was right. Everyone knew Arvis Dyer's pot was cracked. The woman was disturbed in a number of ways. She lived on the street, never washed, shouted at and sometimes spat on people. Everyone except Sephryn avoided her when they could. And because Sephryn treated her like a human being, talked to her like a person, Arvis awarded Sephryn the title of Best Friend—a dubious honor since she was most certainly Arvis's *only* friend.

The relationship did nothing for Sephryn's reputation. In fact, it hampered her efforts to enact changes. Sephryn's political enemies used Arvis and a few other undesirables as proof that Sephryn was unfit for leadership based on those she associated with. Fellow members of the board pressed her to publicly denounce these social anchors, but Sephryn could no more shun the disregarded than she could kick a stray dog that came begging. They suffered so much and asked for so little. People like

Arvis Dyer just wanted to be acknowledged, to be seen and heard, to be a part of the world without having to dodge rocks and sticks.

"I'll pay for it." Sephryn reached down for her purse, which was a habitual part of her attire, but she'd been too preoccupied to tie it on. "Damn."

She saw the look in Arvis's eyes that revealed little hope of prying the bread away. In Sephryn's head, she saw the two of them wrestling for it in the street and cringed.

"Allow me," said a thin man in a simple off-white tunic and a tattered hood. He had been one of those in the thickening crowd, and he didn't look the type to have money to spare. Yet without needing to ask the amount, he produced the proper number of coins and held them out.

"She'll just steal another tomorrow," the baker said.

"Everyone must deal with the future when it comes," the man replied, holding out the coins, but his sight was focused on the baker's wife and daughter. "And what joy can be purchased with but the price of a loaf of bread."

The baker didn't appear to like the way the man looked at his family. He sneered, snatched the coins, then turned back to his wife, who now clutched her child in much the same way that Arvis held onto the bread.

"Thank you," Sephryn told the man, whom she had never seen before. He was neither old nor young. His simple tunic and cloak revealed no clue as to who he might be. Although Sephryn's impression of him may have been the result of his unlikely generosity, she felt he had a compassionate face. "That was extremely kind."

"I only wish I could do more," he said. Then looking at Arvis as the woman and her bread began walking away, he added, "But I fear that would take a miracle."

"Please excuse me," Sephryn told the man as Arvis disappeared into the crowd.

She raced after Arvis. Catching her by the arm, Sephryn dragged the woman into a nearby alley. Arvis's jaw was clenched, her eyes hard. She was braced and ready for a verbal beating.

"Arvis," Sephryn began. "I need your help."

The woman stared back, looking like a terrified turtle. Her shoulders were up, her head down, her eyes squinting despite the shadows.

"Did you hear me? I need your help."

Slowly, the words seemed to seep in. "I don't understand. The bread—I . . ."

"I don't care about that, okay? I'm desperate."

Arvis began nodding. "You need *my* help?"

"Yes." Talking to Arvis was like yelling through a closed door.

"Okay." Arvis blinked and emerged from her turtle's shell.

"Will you do something for me?"

"I'll do anything."

Except give up a stolen loaf of bread, apparently.

"I'm serious, Arvis. This could be dangerous."

The woman laughed so hard she nearly dropped her beloved bread. "Do you think I care about *danger?*" Arvis said, wiping tears from her eyes. "Every morning that I crawl out from under the butcher's stairs is *dangerous.*" She paused, thought, then shook her head. "Actually, I was bitten by something last night, too. My whole life is filled with peril." Arvis looked down at the bread. "And I was speaking the truth." She held the loaf out to Sephryn. "I'd do anything for you."

"I don't want the bread, Arvis."

"You don't? Then neither do I. I don't deserve it. I can't take care of it."

How much care does a loaf of bread require?

Sephryn pushed the loaf back into the woman's arms. "Arvis, pay attention. Focus. Do you know any thieves?"

"Sure, lots."

"I'm not talking about common cutpurses or highwaymen. I need a . . ." Sephryn didn't know exactly what she was looking for. "A very *good* thief. One who can open a really difficult locked box."

"You want Errol."

"I do?"

Arvis nodded. "He's the best."

"Okay. Where do I find him?"

Arvis's scraggily brows rose in objection. *"You* don't. I'll tell him you want a meeting."

Sephryn shook her head. Centuries had taught her not to rely on anyone for something she could do herself. Most people were frustratingly incapable, giving up at the first sign of difficulty.

Surrender was a concept Sephryn didn't understand. Literal centuries of fighting to defeat an unfair system, chip by meager chip, proved that. *"There's always a better way,"* Bran used to say, a favorite declaration of his mother, but given Sephryn's struggles against an unmovable and often indifferent ruler, she had changed it to *"There's always* another *way."* When finding an obstacle, she went around it if possible and right over the top if necessary.

That was how she'd created the Imperial Council. When petitions were repeatedly ignored, she led protests. When three protesters were killed by imperial soldiers, she organized a citywide shutdown. For a week, there were no carts on the streets, no food in the markets, no workers on the docks, and perhaps most distressing of all to the emperor, no servants — even in the palace. That had been a tense standoff. People were terrified of starvation or imperial retribution. Sephryn couldn't recall sleeping that week. She had to be everywhere, reassuring everyone that her plan would work. And only she could do that. The more crucial the outcome and the less time allowed, the more Sephryn felt compelled to take matters into her own hands. That counted triple with someone like Arvis. "I have to go. This is too important."

Arvis shook her head. "Doesn't work that way."

"Fine. We'll go together."

"No," Arvis said. "You can't."

"Of course I can. Is this place secret? I don't care. Blindfold me, spin me around, knock me out and drag me."

"No," Arvis insisted.

Time was wasting, and Sephryn didn't know how much sand was in her hourglass. She feared the Voice in her head, saying, *Sorry. You took too long. Your boy is dead. So is the monk. All because you couldn't—*

"You don't understand what's at stake." Sephryn lowered her voice to a no-nonsense level. "I'm not leaving this to you, Arvis. I can't. You—for the empyre's sake! You forget things all the time! You can't even remember why you thought you were promised that bread!"

Arvis shrank, the turtle's shell rising again. Sunlight bouncing into the alley glinted in her eyes, exposing a well of tears. Still, she didn't give in. Arvis sucked in a short breath. "No," she repeated softly.

"Why not?"

"It isn't a nice place."

"I don't care if—"

"I won't let you go there. It's not for people like you." Arvis wiped an eye clear. "They can't burn ash or topple a fallen tree. Don't you see? I can't be hurt any more than I am. But you can. You're still whole, still breakable. And you're a good person, pure and decent. I don't care what you say. I won't let them hurt you." She wiped the other eye. "I'll find Errol. Tell him you want to hire him." Arvis began to move away, slipping deeper into the alley.

"Let him know I'll pay any price!" Sephryn shouted to Arvis as she began to run.

"Okay. I'll say that you'll sleep with him."

"What? No. Wait, Arvis?"

But the woman had turned a corner and was gone.

By the time Seymour returned home, darkness had fallen, and Sephryn had snapped a sandal strap from pacing the floor. She hadn't bothered to light a lamp or start the fire, and the room was dark and growing chilly. She'd lived in that house in the little square for centuries, but for the first time, she noticed how dark it could get—dark and frightening.

*Yesterday, long before this same time, someone or perhaps some*thing *had entered this place, murdered Mica, and painted on the wall with her blood.*

Sephryn had never lived alone. For ages, she'd been with her parents. After moving to Percepliquis, she had been a renter, then a landlord, then a shelter for an army of the needy, but always there was at least one other person.

An empty house is a lonely place, an oversized coffin with furniture and windows.

She was relieved when Seymour entered, giving her more to look at than the dark, more to hear than her heartbeat, and more to meditate on than her own horrific thoughts that returned to her son no matter what she tried to focus on.

Seymour crept in, peering around the edge of the door. Without a lamp burning, he must have expected to find another gory scene, one that starred her, or at least her foot, or a hand, or a severed head, but the bloody message would be for him:

YOUR TURN, SEYMOUR. DON'T FAIL ME LIKE SEPHRYN DID. REMEMBER, DON'T TELL ANYONE!

"Find anything?" she asked even before he cleared the door.

The monk jumped. "Oh! Ah, no." He drew back his hood and caught his breath. "Sorry. I didn't. To be honest, there's a lot down there. Boxes and boxes stuffed full of scrolls, maybe hundreds, maybe thousands of containers. It will take me weeks, perhaps months. And that's if there is some sort of order, which from what I've seen so far is doubtful. Quite frankly, it's a mess. The parchments are dry and cracking. Some are too far gone to read. Others I think have turned to dust. Those were the ones near this gutter in the back where water seeped in through the foundation. And there isn't any light. They don't allow lanterns or candles for obvious reasons."

"No light?" She looked at the black glass of the window. "It's been dark for hours. What were you doing all this time?"

Seymour hung his head. "I got lost on the way back. I missed the little street with the mask shop."

"Ebonydale."

"Right, that one. I ended up wandering past the palace again. That's when I knew I was *way* off course. I doubled back three times, but in the dark, everything looks so different. This city is a maze." He looked at the hearth, then at the pile of wood beside it. "Why no fire? Getting cold, don't you think?" He rubbed his arms briskly.

Sephryn shrugged.

"May I?" He pointed at the hearth.

"I couldn't care less."

Kneeling down, Seymour began brushing the ash out and loading new logs. "How about you? Find any help?"

"I don't know." She watched him methodically prepare the fire. Something about the orderly manner of the operation made her feel better.

The whole world isn't lost in chaos, just my little corner of it.

"I talked to Arvis. She said she would ask a thief named Errol to contact me. Said he was the best — as if Arvis Dyer, professional beggar and all-around lunatic, could tell the difference."

"You didn't have her take you to this person?"

She glared at the monk.

"Just asking." He quickly returned to the task of fire building.

"She refused!" Sephryn exploded. Throwing up both hands, she began pacing. "I spoke to her around noon — right after I dropped you off at the records office. What is it now?" She slapped the window frame. "Midnight?"

"It's not *that* late. I don't think."

"It's been hours! Hours!"

Seymour cringed at her raised voice.

"And I don't know if she's even talked to anyone. I've been sitting here waiting—and for what? I have no idea!"

Seymour spotted her broken sandal. "You haven't actually been *sitting*, I suspect."

She looked at the broken strap, just now noticing it for the first time. "By the Unholy Twins!"

"Unholy Twins?"

She waved a hand at him. "It's something my mother used to say. And that's another thing." She stomped her heel on the floor, making the row of ceramic spice bowls on the meal table chirp. "On top of it all, I'm becoming my mother!"

Seymour looked up at the bow above the mantel. "Moya was a legendary hero. There are worse things to—"

"My mother was a bitch!" Sephryn also looked at the bow as if Moya herself sat there grinning. "She treated everyone like crap. My father is the nicest person you will ever meet. He's Fhrey—a full-blooded Instarya warrior."

"Yes, I know all about Tekchin of the Galantians. He's featured in *The Book of Brin*."

"Right, well, he doesn't age much. At least he doesn't look like it. I'm almost eight hundred and fifty, and I look like his older sister. He's over seventeen hundred. He'll probably live another thousand years. My mother . . ." She paused and shook her head. "Moya was in her seventies when she died. She had been beautiful in her day, but like everyone, she got old. Near the end she was wrinkled like a shriveled prune, and her white hair was so thin that you could see her scalp. Still, my father . . . I mean, you're right. He's a hero. Everyone knows it, and he looks the part, too. His bronze armor still fits. The guy is as dashing as the day he met her." She shook her head. "Not once did he consider leaving, even though she treated him so horribly. Screamed, threw things, but he never once . . ." She paused. "I think she resented that he was still young, still handsome, while she had lost all her beauty. Or maybe . . . oh, I don't know. They were never formally married, not like people do now. One day she told him to leave. She was drunk, of course, but the tone was so cruel. My father shrugged it off. So she asked him flat out why he was still with her."

Seymour had paused in his construction to look up. "What did he say?"

"That she was still beautiful *to him*. He reminded her that he had died for her once and would do so again. That's the sort of person he is. Later he made excuses for her. Tried to convince me that she didn't mean the terrible things she said and did. He explained that my mother hated herself, not him, and despised being a burden. Moya was a great hero of a forgotten age, and by then she was too weak to draw Audrey. After a while, she became too feeble to get out of bed. Maybe anyone would be bitter, but I hate how she treated him near the end. You know, it has been hundreds of years now, but my father is still alone. He keeps busy teaching young Instarya how to sword fight. I told him he should find someone new, that being alone wasn't healthy. But he won't even consider replacing Moya. He told me, 'There isn't anyone else, and there never will be.' Then he laughed and said, 'After I die, I don't want to explain myself to a woman who can shoot a bow the way your mother could.' He was so good to her, and she was a horror to him. So maybe you can see why I'd rather not become her. Everyone has to pay, but heroes—I think, they have a higher price than everyone else. And maybe they never erase their debts."

Seymour used oil from the little bottle, a wad of tinder, and the flint-and-steel scratcher to ignite the stack. As the wood caught, the room filled with light, the shadows chased away.

"Such a sad story," said a figure who stepped out from behind the drapery.

Sephryn staggered backward until she hit the far wall, clanging a set of three copper ladles that dangled from hooks. Seymour jumped up, retreating to stand beside her. The two focused wide-eyed on the figure wrapped in a long cloak who moved forward and settled onto the bench near the window. A large hood hid most of the face, so it was hard to tell if he, she, or it was human.

This is who killed Mica and took Nurgya. Time's up!

Sephryn glanced at the bow. It had been years since she'd used it. The idea was rendered pointless because the arrows were sealed in a box upstairs. She looked back at the figure on the bench. "Who are you?" she summoned the courage to ask.

The hood lifted no more than an inch. "Name's Errol Irwin. I was told that you wanted to speak to me about a job."

"You're . . . you're Errol?" She was so convinced it was the kidnapper, the monstrous killer who had invaded her home and her head, that she refused to accept any other idea. "Arvis's Errol? How—how did you get in here?"

She still couldn't see his face well, but she heard him laugh. "None of your doors or windows are locked. I didn't check them all, but I'm confident of that statement. Mostly because you don't *have* locks. Not even one on the front door. That's more than lazy. It's negligent, especially given that you have an infant—or did. Your two-month-old boy was kidnapped, and I think that's enough evidence of your irresponsibility and lax parenting."

Sephryn's mouth dropped open in shock. "How do you know that?"

"Well, you're not exactly unknown around these parts. And it's no secret you have a child. But the nursery upstairs is empty, and you have the look of a terrified mother."

"How long have you been here?"

"That ought to be obvious. You're Sephryn Myr Tekchin, the Director of the Imperial Council—half Fhrey and on alert, which means if I had entered while you were here, you'd have seen or heard me. I'm quiet, but perhaps not so silent as to escape Fhrey ears. But I doubt even a full-blooded Fhrey could hear just my breathing or heartbeat. Yet to answer your question, let me say, I've been here long enough. And as entertaining as the two of you have been, life's too short to waste, so I'll be going." The thief stood up.

"What?" Sephryn blurted out. "No! I've been waiting for you."

"Yes, I know. You want to hire me to help get your son back, but that's not going to happen."

"Why?"

"I don't do charity. I'm a highly compensated professional, and you can't pay me."

"How do you know?"

"I've been through your house. There's nothing here of value, which is actually to your benefit because if I'd found anything worth stealing, I'd have already done so and disappeared. I only lingered this long to satisfy my curiosity as to why a woman like you would seek out a thief such as me. As it turns out, your story is sad, pathetic, and dreary. I'm guessing the father made off with the boy or perhaps tax collectors? They likely have him imprisoned somewhere—Arvis said you needed me to open a locked box. She implied sex as a payment. It's not that I have no interest, but I suspect that wasn't a serious offer. So . . ." He spread his hands. "Since there is nothing here for me—"

"It's not his father, and it's not tax collectors," Sephryn said.

"Fine. I was wrong on that part. I'm not perfect, never claimed to be, and I knew I was reaching, but I wasn't wrong about the rest. I don't work for free, and you have nothing to offer."

"How can you say that? You know who I am, and—"

"Yes, yes, I know all about you. You loved your father, hated your mother, apparently adopted a pet monk the moment you lost your son, just like the way families get new puppies when their old dog dies." He pointed at the monk. "Your name is Seymour. One of those Monks of Maribor, a member of that lunatic sect, right? You're the fellows who live in caves together. Here is what I don't get. How does isolating yourself in the wilderness help you understand the world? Sort of like moving to the desert to become an expert swimmer." He stepped toward the door. "Now, I'm certain there's someone somewhere who has far too much wealth and needs my assistance. So, if you don't mind, I'll be—"

Sephryn moved quickly to block him. "Wait! I can get money."

Once more, the thief paused and frowned, then shook his head. "Look, I get it. Your child was taken. You're insane with worry, but think of it this way, kids die all the time. If it isn't pox, it's a breaking tree branch or an icy pond. Odds of your son reaching maturity were poor at best."

She opened her mouth to protest.

"Epp-epp-epph," he muttered, holding up a hand to stop her. "If you don't believe me, look at how many locks you have protecting your son from abduction. And of course, he's gone, isn't he? So let's not argue a point already proven. Now, if you'd get out of my way . . ."

"I can't. I need you to—"

"What did I say about talking to others?" The Voice joined them.

"I'm sorry, but I need help," Sephryn said, looking up at the ceiling out of habit.

"That much is quite clear," Errol said. "But that's not my problem. Now if you would just get out of my way."

Sephryn continued to block him. "This is Errol. He's a master thief. I'll need him to get the vault opened. I told you I can't do this myself."

Errol looked at Seymour. "Who's she talking to?"

"I don't think I'm allowed to say," the monk replied.

"Okay, I'm gone. Have a nice hallucination." He dodged right, then spun left and stepped past, reaching the exit. "Sorry for your loss. I'm referring to my services, of course. I am the best." He pulled open the door, but before he could step out into the night, it slammed shut.

The thief stared at it, then glanced back at the two of them. "What's that about?"

Neither Sephryn nor Seymour spoke.

Errol eyed both of them carefully. He grabbed the handle and pulled. The door didn't budge. He bent over and studied the latch. Then he straightened up and tried the door again. "Okay, so I can see why you don't need locks. Your house is so shoddily built that the door jams after closing."

Just then, the spice pots on the table exploded one after another, bursting from left to right in perfect precision. Ceramic shards ricocheted off the walls and salt, ginger, cloves, nutmeg, basil, rosemary, and sage rained across the table and floor.

No one moved. No one spoke. All three looked left then right, eyes shifting, waiting.

"You have a ghost problem, too?" Errol said slowly.

All three ladles tore themselves from the wall. They flew at the thief, and in mid-flight, they changed into sharpened blades. Their points struck the door, stabbing the wood to either side of Errol's head.

He stood frozen, not daring to so much as blink as he stared at Sephryn.

"All right. You can involve him," the Voice said. *"And if he wants a reward, ask him how much his life is worth."*

Sephryn recounted the events that had transpired since the previous day. She was as thorough and accurate as possible while keeping in mind that the Voice was listening, and any mistake might cause their deaths. Well, perhaps not hers, but she imagined the Voice found Seymour and Errol expendable. The story took several minutes, and in that time, Errol Irwin didn't move a finger. She couldn't even be sure he was breathing.

"I'm sorry," she said after concluding her tale. "I didn't mean to put you in jeopardy. I just needed someone to help me open the vault. I would have found some way to pay you."

The thief looked around, warily. "And you don't know anything about this Voice?"

She shook her head, warning him with her eyes. Looks were poor tools for communicating complicated messages, but from what little she knew about his profession, she guessed he was fluent in subtle body language.

The thief looked at the transformed ladles still stuck in the door. "Has he ever talked to *you,* Seymour?"

The monk shook his head.

"So you'll help us?" Sephryn asked.

Errol's brows raised with surprise. "Is there a choice? I mean, beyond the obvious." He looked toward the broken pottery and the piles of spice residue on the table and grimaced.

Again, Sephryn shook her head. "He told me to say, 'If he wants a reward, ask him what his life is worth.'"

"Oh, well that's just—" Errol paused, his eyes narrowing. "*He* told you? The Voice is male?"

"In my head, it sounds like a man."

"Is there an accent? A dialect perhaps?"

The poker near the hearth fell over with more force than a mere toppling would grant. Errol stared at the iron rod as if it were a deadly snake.

Apparently, the thief wasn't as fluent in warning glares as Sephryn had hoped. Either that or Errol's curiosity had simply gotten the better of him. In any case, she thought for the good of everyone it was best to be blunt. "I don't think he likes those questions."

"Clearly," Errol said, not taking an eye off the fire iron.

"So? What do we do next?"

Errol looked at the door that was still closed.

Don't, she thought. The sharp end of the poker slowly rotated until it was pointing in the thief's direction. So far, the Voice hadn't given her the impression of being patient.

Errol sighed. "Okay, listen. What you're describing is a dwarf-made *safe*—a carefully built box to keep valuable items, well . . . *safe.* Therefore, it is most certainly gemlocked."

"What does that mean?"

"That it can only be opened with a specific key, a gem. These dwarven locks are famous for their impregnability. If you don't have the gem, you can't get past them. Simple as that. And since you appear oblivious to the very existence of gemlocks, I'm guessing you have no idea where the gem is or what kind it might be."

"The emperor isn't really the jewelry-wearing type. He does have a few rings, but none of them have any gems. But there is a gold chain around his neck that holds a pendant that has a red crystal."

"I've seen the emperor many times at festivals and proclamations, and I don't recall seeing that bit of jewelry," Errol said. "And I tend to notice such things."

Sephryn tapped a finger to her lips. "Now that I think about it, only saw it on a few occasions when visiting the empress. These weren't formal occasions, and Nyphron was just dropping by to ask Persephone a question. I only remember because when he saw there were others in the room, he tucked it inside his tunic. At the time, I took offense, thinking he was making a judgment on my character. So maybe the necklace is something too important to leave lying around but too secret to show off."

Errol considered her words. "Well, if I had to guess, and at this point it really isn't just idle speculation, I would say the necklace is the key to the safe in his private quarters. All you have to do is get it, tap it against the safe's door, and it will open." The thief dusted his hands ceremonially, then focused on the poker. "There you go. You're all set. Glad to be of service. Don't bother sending a bill. I was happy to help. Now would you mind releasing the door?"

"I can't take the necklace off the emperor," Sephryn said quickly, to both him and the poker. "The last time we met face-to-face was at the empress's funeral. That was over eight hundred years ago, when I was sixteen. Even if I could get close to him, what am I supposed to do, reach up and rip it off? Ask to see it and run away?"

"Look, I told you what needs to be done," Errol said. "The rest is up to you."

The poker rattled on the wooden floor, making all of them flinch.

"I think the poker disagrees," Seymour said, inching away from both it and the thief.

"You have to help us," Sephryn demanded. "My son —"

"Yes, yes, of course. Wouldn't want anything happening to little Nuggy," Errol said, without taking his eyes off the poker.

"Nurgya."

"Whatever."

"She's right," Seymour said. "Nyphron isn't an idiot. History makes it abundantly clear the emperor is extremely clever. He's an accomplished swordsman and the leader of the Galantians who are known to be the greatest warriors the world has ever seen. According to the writings of Bran, Nyphron won the Great War by defeating the Fhrey prince, who was a powerful sorcerer. This isn't a person who could be hoodwinked or fall victim to a slash-and-grab."

"Right," Errol said. "So that leaves you —"

The poker slid and inched forward.

"I mean, that leaves *us* needing another solution."

"*Is* there such a thing?" Sephryn asked.

"You could kill him." He pointed at the bow. "Are you any good with that?" The thief smiled sardonically.

"I don't think assassinating the emperor is a smart plan," Sephryn said. "Think of something else."

Errol pursed his lips and rubbed his hands together. "I honestly don't know anything else that has a chance of success."

The poker rumbled, but Errol put out a wait-a-minute finger. "However, while I know *about* safes and gemlocks, I'm not an authority on the subject. Turns out, I know a guy."

"And is this *guy* an expert?"

"He is."

"Wonderful!" Sephryn said. "When can we see him? Can we go now?"

"No. He keeps business hours. It'll have to wait until tomorrow. I'll take you in the morning." Errol grabbed the door latch and tugged. The door held firm.

"I think the poker wants you to spend the night," Seymour said. "Must be your affable personality."

Sephryn offered the thief a sympathetic smile. "Sorry."

"I don't feel that quite covers it," Errol told her.

"Looks like we're in this together," Seymour said.

"That doesn't sound at all ominous."

They all jumped when the poker leapt back into place beside the hearth.

"I was being ironic!" Errol shouted at the fire iron. "Gallows-style wit, if you will. Don't be so touchy."

Seymour looked at the black metal rod tilted slightly against the stone. The bottom end was still coated in ash. "I don't think the poker has a sense of humor."

CHAPTER EIGHT

Escape from Urlineus

The city of Urlineus was a work in progress. Little more than a stone fortress haphazardly built into the jagged cliffs at the headwaters of the Estee River, it suffered from a profusion of domes. Stone towers and grand rotundas were roofed with copper caps. These fanciful cupolas had quickly surrendered to the steamy miasma of the jungle, forming bluish-green patinas that no amount of cleaning could reverse. Although men and goblins fought within its depths, the wild and untamed region held dominion over all of them. Carving civilization out of the harsh environment of the Erbon Forest was chore enough; insisting that the newly founded city adhere to the universal building style of the empyre was pointless arrogance.

Isn't hubris always pointless? Is wondering about the value of arrogance useful?

There were times, far too often lately, that Nolyn felt long life was equally *pointless*. An indicator of that realization was when he began pondering the value of such things as arrogance and worth. Only someone who had lived far beyond his usefulness could waste time evaluating such things. Purebred humans never bothered with such trifles. They were racing the sun, hurrying to reproduce before their brief dash was over. Only people like Bran and Sephryn sacrificed home and family to reach for greater things because they must choose between one or the other; no time was granted for the luxury of both. Nolyn was born with the nature of men and the longevity of the Fhrey.

A horrible cocktail, he mused, *all mixer, no alcohol.*

Returning to the city in the protective bosom of the Fifth Regiment, the members of the Seventh Sikaria Auxiliary had only stopped long enough to eat. While the remaining survivors of the squad were given leave to clean up, Nolyn and Amicus were eager to report.

The clerk outside the governor's office watched as Nolyn and Amicus entered. That was Legate Lynch's palatus, his chief secretary and quartermaster whom Nolyn had met only once. As usual, the man's name escaped Nolyn. The palatus made no effort to stop them, didn't say a word, nor did they ask for permission before entering the office of the legate.

Recalling the fuss the palatus had made on his previous visit, Nolyn had expected a protest, but the little man stood silently by as they walked past him. Filthy and covered in blood, they marched directly into the legate's office. Mud splattered their calves. Stiff and oily, their hair lurched at odd angles, pressed into position by sweat and hours beneath helmets. The two appeared both a mess and impressive, as only soldiers fresh from the bush could. Lean, dirty, alert, and raw, they had the look of animals—wild and dangerous.

In stark contrast, Lynch sat at a broad desk, white-haired and plump. The aging legate had the dull, sedentary sag of a man who smiled only at hangings. Nor did he dress like a soldier, having given up his leather and bronze in favor of more comfortable robes. His frown only deepened as he beheld them.

"You've returned," the legate said, his voice betraying a bit of nervous concern. "Could have cleaned up a bit before presenting yourself, don't you think? What is your report?"

"Utter failure to complete all objectives, sir," Nolyn replied. "In addition, I lost the majority of the Seventh Sikaria Auxiliary. Only eight left, including myself."

Lynch straightened and glanced at Amicus. "The Seventh Sik-Aux?" Then the legate nodded in understanding. "The First Prymus knew you were the imperial prince, so he assigned you to our best squad. Of course, that makes sense."

Nolyn looked at Amicus and smiled. "The missing piece."

"What are you talking about?" Lynch asked.

"We've been speculating about the culpability in the chain of command regarding our orders."

"What are you getting at?"

"Just that it was unreasonable to expect success, when you failed to tell me that the major objective was my death. Had I known, I could have tried harder. But with so many mixed signals, you made my job quite difficult. Instructing the First Prymus to assign me to a sub-standard troop would have looked too suspicious, I suppose." Nolyn glanced at Amicus. "I mean, that's clearly treason—and who would expect such an action from a legate, right?"

Lynch looked toward the doorway where the palatus stood, watching the conversation unfold. Then he slammed his hand on the top of his desk, which was covered in dispatches and rough-drawn charts. "Are you accusing me—"

"Of course not." Nolyn chuckled. "Implicating you in my attempted murder is"—he smiled to himself—"*pointless.* I'm here to find out who else is involved. Apparently, the First Prymus is innocent. Good to know because I like him. If you're cooperative, we'll let you take your own life. I assure you it will be less painful than anything I have planned."

"How dare you! I'm the legate of Urlineus! Acting governor of this city. You will be—"

With the concert of muscle and steel that only Amicus Killian possessed, the First Spear of the Seventh Sikaria Auxiliary drew his short sword and severed the hand of Legate Lynch just above the wrist.

It came off cleanly, and Amicus's blade never touched the surface of the desk. Nolyn imagined Amicus could kill a mosquito on his arm without touching his skin.

The legate stared in shock at his bleeding limb. He pushed back on his chair, as if thinking he could flee from the horror. The man tripped and ended up falling over backward. That's when he began screaming.

"Shrieks like a coofa bird," Nolyn observed while untying a strip of leather that hung from his belt.

"Oh, yeah." Amicus nodded as he put his sword away. "I hate those things."

"Grab his arm," Nolyn ordered as he deftly applied the tourniquet around the stump. The hand remained on the desk, a pale, fingered island in a pool of blood. "Don't want you passing out, sir. We need information."

Lynch's face was white, his eyes wide, jaw clenched in pain, lips trembling.

"Tell me who ordered my death, or we'll have that other hand—your feet, too, if you're really stubborn. Was it my father? It's okay; you can tell me. It won't hurt my feelings. We haven't exchanged Wintertide gifts in centuries."

Once Amicus let go of him, Lynch rolled side-to-side on the floor, growling in pain and anger. He clutched his bloody stump, which made dark red streaks across his bright-white robes. "You're dead, Nolyn!"

"I don't think so. I'm certain my ghost would look better than this."

"You won't get away. He can end your life at any time. He can kill *anyone* whenever he likes."

"How nice, and who is *he?*"

"You think this was some kind of political maneuver? You're a fool. You're dealing with real power. He can destroy you with a snap of his fingers. Burst you like a bladder of blood. And then"—he looked at the walls—"make it all go away as if it had never happened."

Nolyn looked at Amicus, who also appeared puzzled. "Burst you like a bladder of blood? Is that a local colloquialism I'm not familiar with?"

"Never heard it before," the First Spear replied.

Nolyn shrugged. "So, who are you talking about? Give me a name."

The rapidly receding sound of sandals slapping the marble floor alerted them that the palatus—who until then had remained a fixture at the door—was running.

"Dammit!" Amicus cursed.

Weak from blood loss and slipping into shock, the legate wasn't going anywhere. The real threat was the palatus and what he might do if he got clear of the residence and found a squadron of imperial soldiers. They raced after him. By the time the two were halfway down the corridor, their prey had slipped out the front door, banging it shut behind him.

"Great," Amicus said. They both halted short of the door. On the far side was the churning city filled with soldiers. Chasing the palatus through the streets would not only be pointless but stupid.

"What's the punishment for dismembering a legate and acting governor of an imperial province?" Nolyn asked.

"For you, prison. For me, execution."

"Let's grab Lynch. We'll take him with us. I can—"

A *thud* followed by a *splat* emanated from the direction of the office, as if someone had thrown a melon against a wall.

"What was *that*?" Amicus asked, concerned. What they'd heard hadn't been a pleasant sound.

Nolyn suspected Lynch might have tried standing, then passed out and collapsed. The legate seemed the sort to be both determined and stupid in that unrelenting worry-about-it-later sort of way. That would account for the *thud*, but not for the disgusting *splat* and . . . there was another sound: a horrible ripping *pop!* That noise contributed to Nolyn's feeling that their situation had gone from bad to worse.

Together they hurried back toward the governor's office, but both men slowed before entering, hesitating before looking. Still fresh in their ears, that sound had conjured ugly thoughts, yet not one of them came close to what they found. Imagination, at least in this case, fell short of the creativity of reality—but the world always had a way to amplify gruesome.

Lynch was dead. No need to check the corpse—couldn't even if they wanted to—there wasn't one, not in a usual sense. The legate's body had been blown apart. Lynch's legs were on different sides of the room, and his head had rolled under the desk, eyes open, face still frowning. Blood drizzled down the walls, beaded on the polished floor, and dripped from the twelve-foot-high ceiling. Centered at the toppled chair, a spray of blood radiated in all directions.

"Burst you like a bladder of blood."

Nolyn and Amicus looked at each other with open mouths.

"What in Phyre just happened?" Nolyn asked.

"I have no idea." The First Spear stared at the gore in stunned wonder. "I don't like it, though."

"I'm inclined to agree with you."

The two backed away from the sight.

The palatus was likely reporting their attack on the legate to the first soldier he found. The jungle with its ghazel horde and poisonous snakes felt friendly by comparison. Without another word, the two bolted for the exit. Stepping back outside onto the sun-bleached steps of the gubernatorial residence, Nolyn expected to be met by a contingent of soldiers, and he was. But these men weren't the angry personal guard of the legate.

"Hope you don't mind, sir," Riley Glot said, holding the palatus by the arm. "He seemed in too much of a hurry to let him run off."

What remained of the Seventh Sikaria Auxiliary stood at the bottom of the steps on the muddy street. He had expected them to be in the baths; instead, they remained as filthy as Amicus and himself.

The construction of the fledgling city created a chaotic mess, and few residents took notice of the battered soldiers trapping the palatus among them. No hand covered his mouth, and no dagger was at his throat. The staff officer could have screamed or called for help to save himself, but he remained resigned to his situation. Riley may have threatened him, and after what he'd witnessed in the governor's office, the palatus would certainly take any intimidation seriously.

Chariots filled with men, and wagons full of logs and stones, rolled by while in the distance a loud voice called drills and a chorus of men responded in rhythm and rote.

"Did your meeting go well, sir?" Jerel asked in a voice far too bright and cheery.

"It did not."

No one said anything more, but the silence heightened by an exchange of concerned looks spoke for itself. Riley's expression darkened. "Then am I to assume we are in need of quick transportation?"

"No," Nolyn said. "I mean, I certainly could use a chariot. Amicus, too, I suspect. But the rest of you . . ." He focused on the palatus. "They didn't do anything. Weren't even there. You saw that."

The slender, elderly man showed no form of recognizable response as he continued to be restrained by Glot.

"Didn't *do anything,* sir?" Jerel asked suspiciously.

"Myth, Smirch, chariots. Now!" Riley barked.

The two men stepped out into the street, waving arms and blocking traffic. They found three big ratha chariots, each pulled by a set of four horses, and forced them to the side of the avenue.

"Sorry, boys." Myth took hold of the horses' tack. "Gonna need these carts of yours."

The drivers opened their mouths to protest, but Myth was quick to point toward the stairs. "Emperor's son needs them." Smirch advanced on the second team of horses. "If you want to argue, Nolyn Nyphronian is right over there."

Mouths snapped shut. One of the soldiers in the lead chariot extended a salute. Then all the occupants climbed out so quickly that they left their spears behind.

"Your Highness." Amicus waved him forward.

"What about Demetrius?" Riley asked.

Sweet Deity! Demetrius, that's the palatus's name! "Bring him for now."

"Where we going, sir?" Smirch asked as he took control of the third chariot.

"The river."

ल्

Luckily, a line of chariots driving through the streets of a military camp that was quickly becoming a city wasn't unusual. Some of the roadways were narrow enough to cause pedestrians to jump out of the way, but no one seemed to think that racing soldiers playing fast and loose with horses was odd. Bringing Demetrius bought time, but Nolyn had no idea how much. Working from a long-held theory that the gods had cursed him, he feared someone had already found what was left of Lynch. Under the rules of that same said theory, others would have noticed them leave the governor's residence, confiscate the chariots, and head for the river. That meant they were only a few minutes ahead of pursuit. His one thread of hope came in the form of a missing sound. The city itself was loud with voices and noise, and the racket of the metal-rimmed chariot wheels on the stone road was deafening, but Nolyn didn't hear a horn or a bell. If someone had found the dead legate—who wasn't just murdered but brutally slaughtered—an alarm would be sounding across the city. Its absence was encouraging.

Amicus was as brilliant a charioteer as he was a sword master, and the white-knuckled trip quickly brought them to the port along the river, wheels skidding across the quay until they bumped to a stop against the dock's cleats. There, half a dozen bireme warships were tied to the pier. Nolyn had come to Urlineus by sea and knew the single-mast galleys could take him to Percepliquis, or at least away—he hadn't yet decided where he would ultimately go, just knew he was leaving.

They climbed off their chariots and looked down the length of the pier at the moored ships with double rows of oar ports and dragon faces painted on their bows.

"As of now, none of you are under my authority," Nolyn said. "I'm not a prymus anymore. I attacked the legate. I'm a fugitive, a criminal of the empyre. As such, I have no authority to command any of you to serve—"

"You cut the man's hand off!" Demetrius finally found his tongue. His face was red, and he struggled against Riley, who held him fast.

"No, *I* did that," Amicus corrected.

"Doesn't matter," Nolyn said. "Lynch is dead."

"Dead? You killed him?" Riley asked.

"No, oddly, we didn't," Nolyn answered. Then looking at the palatus, he added, "I don't expect you to believe me, but I never wanted to *kill* your boss. In fact, he was my evidence. His death is a problem I didn't want to have. Nevertheless, I'll be blamed for his murder." He once more addressed his men, "Anyone helping me will be branded a traitor. If caught, you will be executed. Given this, I strongly suggest we part ways here."

"I'm the one who cut the man's hand off," Amicus said. "I can't claim innocence."

Nolyn nodded. "Fine. It will be the two of us then."

"Three, sir," Jerel said.

"Oh, of course," Nolyn conceded.

"I'm staying with you, too, sir," Everett said. "The others mentioned how you tried to save me. Likely did, too. I owe you at least one life."

Nolyn smiled. "That's nice of you, Everett, but—"

"We're all coming, sir," Myth declared.

Nolyn saw the same expression of amused agreement on the other faces.

"You don't get it, do you, sir?" the Poor Calynian said. "You're one of us now."

"For pity's sake, what *is* your full name?"

The man smiled and winced from the pain in his mouth. "Ramahanaparus Mirk, sir."

"Mirk? Why didn't you mention that before? Even I can remember that."

Riley said, "Mirk is right, sir. You're now one of the Seventh Sik-Aux."

"But I'm not. That's what I'm trying to tell you. I've betrayed the chain of command. I'm no longer fit to wear this uniform."

Jerel said, "I joined the legion to serve you, not the empyre, and certainly not the emperor."

"Everyone here knows I'm a wanted murderer," Weldon Smirch said. "That's why I joined the legion. Killing the legate, well, that only raises your status in my book."

"The Seventh Sik-Aux has always been more than just a squadron," Riley said. "When you became one of us, you joined our family. We don't abandon our own. Lynch tried to kill us all. You dealt justice. If it comes down to it, I'd be proud to be executed alongside you, sir."

"With so few of us left," Myth said, "the commanders will split us up. I can't bear that. I think it's time we stepped into the status of legend."

"So you're all determined to desert with me?" Nolyn shook his head in disappointment. "Stupid, but touching."

"What about him?" Riley shook Demetrius.

"Need to kill the little weasel," Smirch said. "He knows where we went, how many of us there are . . ."

"You're probably right," Nolyn said. "But I'm not in the habit of killing innocent people."

"Perhaps it's a tradition you should consider adopting," Smirch replied. "Now that you're embarking on a life of crime and all."

"I have no intention of being a criminal on the run. Maybe I should go to the palace and confront my father. Have it out with him once and for all. How dumb would that be?"

"And the palatus?" Riley asked.

"Demetrius," Nolyn said, "I won't kill you, but I can't afford to leave you, either. So you're coming along. Be a good boy. Be quiet and don't cause a fuss. If you behave, we'll let you go as soon as it's safe."

Nolyn turned and scanned the ships. "That one." He pointed to a ship with emerald eyes painted on its prow. "Do you think if we ask nicely, they would be willing to give the emperor's son a ride?"

‿‿

As with all military vessels, there was precious little space on the imperial bireme *Stryker*. To accommodate the hundred men aboard, the ship had five decks; although one was given over to ballast and another was too small for anything other than supplies. That left the two levels where the oarsmen rowed, and the top deck that was exposed to wind, rain, and sun. A four-story castle built directly behind the single mast provided shelter for the soldiers. The sailors—those who operated the big sail and the smaller one that they sometimes extended out before the bow—had no place but the rigging.

Nolyn had chosen the ship from those berthed at the Urlineus dock for no other reason than the color of the eyes painted on the prow. All humans had brown eyes; the Fhrey were blessed, without exception, with blue; Belgriclungreians shared amber as their standard eye color; ghazel eyes, Nolyn had come to notice, were always yellow. The only one in the world he knew besides himself who had green eyes was Sephryn. And the *Stryker* had emerald-colored eyes: large, acute, and feminine, peering just above the waterline. His choice was only a shade short of arbitrary: a wholly emotional decision. The eyes were likely modeled on those of a mermaid, which were rumored to rival the green of the most precious of gems. But in a vacuum of information, emotion was all he had. He'd made many decisions based on a feeling. Women referred to it as intuition. Men called it gut instinct. His father believed such things to be foolishness, but his mother had referred to it as the Voice of Elan. Suri once told him his feelings were the sounds his soul heard when listening to the world singing the music of truth. Nolyn didn't know which to believe, but he missed Sephryn, and those eyes reminded him of her.

They'd had no difficulty boarding the ship. Their uniforms were more than adequate for admission. Soldiers were welcome on ships as added protection, and Nolyn's word as an officer was accepted without question. Insisting that they set sail immediately was a trickier proposition.

For that, Nolyn was forced to reveal his name, which meant that any pursuers would have little problem guessing where the Seventh Sik-Aux had gone after Lynch's death.

Although the legate had been given authority over Nolyn by virtue of rank, everyone else had a more reverent reaction when meeting the prince. When the ship's commander learned his new cargo was the heir to the empyre, he handed over control of his vessel. *The Prince*, as Nolyn was thereafter referred to by the crew, refused the offer of wine and cheese—premium stores that had just been brought on board. That had received a frown from Smirch but goodwill from the crew. Two decks of oars reached out, and the imperial warship *Stryker* entered the Estee River and headed south toward the sea with the remnants of the Seventh Sikaria Auxiliary aboard.

"Sure beats walking," Myth said as the eight of them lined the sides of the ship, watching the thick green of the riverbank pass by.

"Where is the palatus?" Nolyn asked.

"Over there," Riley replied, pointing to the little man sitting on the deck with his back to the gunwale, his thin robe wrapped tightly about him. "He seems content to stay put. I think he's a tad frightened of the water. Don't think the sod can swim."

"How long will we be aboard?" Ramahanaparus Mirk asked Nolyn.

"That depends," Nolyn replied. "Getting out of Urlineus was my first priority. Now that we're on our way, I have to think things through."

"I thought you'd already decided." Amicus, having finished with the jungle, turned his back and rested both elbows on the rail. "You said you were heading back to face your father."

"I also said that was a dumb idea. And since he wants you dead, too, leading you there would be rude, don't you think?"

"What is it between you and your old man, anyway?"

Nolyn threw up his hands. "If only I knew. We've never gotten along. I suppose a big part of it is because I'm half human."

"But he married your mother," Jerel said.

Nolyn looked over the edge at the dark, swirling water as it rolled past the hull in undulations that couldn't be felt. "Persephone was the keenig. She ruled over all the human clans. My father needed her armies. But after the war, the balance of power shifted, even more so after she died." He sighed and turned to peer out over the curved head of the prow. "I dunno. The ship's captain seems accommodating enough. Maybe we should ask him to drop us off in Caric. We could live like giants there." He forced a laugh. The others provided empathetic chuckles.

"I'd like to go to Percepliquis, sir," Mirk said. The lad no longer had his face wrapped, but the red scabs on either cheek still stood out. "I've always wanted to see the great city."

"Been years since I left," Amicus said.

"I only passed through as I ran from Rodencia." Smirch wiped his nose with his forearm. "Don't get to see much when you're running for your life."

"It's a wondrous place," Jerel said. "I used to go there twice a year with my father for stock auctions. The thing I remember most is the food. There are so many different kinds. I first tasted tiger in Percepliquis."

"How was it?" Everett asked. The boy had the eager face of innocence, and Nolyn guessed he hadn't been long in the jungle or the legion; both had a way of leaching curiosity. He was still more child than man, and yet, Nolyn recalled how Bran had been gray-haired and managed to retain that same uncorrupted spirit. Perhaps not all miles were the same.

Jerel thought a moment. "Tiger meat is . . . well, like the animal, I suppose—pretty to look at but tough. I chewed that piece of meat until my jaw ached. I spat it out when no one was looking because I was afraid it would choke me if I swallowed."

"I like the fountains," Amicus said, his eyes looking above the tree line as if he could see them. "Fresh water bubbling up throughout the city. And the baths! Oh, dear deity, they are joyous."

"Yes!" Nolyn smiled at the memory. "They're incredible. There's nothing better than settling into steaming-hot water for drawing out the pain of sore muscles and rinsing away filth."

"Add a woman and a bottle of wine, and I'm there," Myth said.

"What about you, Riley?" Amicus asked. "What do you remember?" The man shook his head. "Never been. I'm a Rhulynia boy. Haven't even crossed the Bern River. Grew up in a little village northeast of Vernes, an old mining town. My father, all his brothers, and their grandfathers before them worked the foothills, digging iron and coal. A stooped back and a hacking cough didn't seem like a good enough reward for a life of hard work. So being the genius I am, I joined the legion. Twenty years later, this is what I have to show for my life." He clapped his dented armor. "The idea of coming home to a wife and family seems oddly grand now. But I'll go see this amazing city if that's where His Highness leads."

Nolyn said, "I have no idea where we should go, and this might sound strange, but when I was young—some eight hundred and forty years ago—there was a woman named Suri. She was a"—Nolyn didn't know exactly how to say it and settled for—"a mystic. She understood the language of the world. It talked to her and she could answer back. Suri could do amazing things, stuff you wouldn't believe. She told me that the feelings we sometimes have is Elan telling us what we need to know."

"You mean like how you get a cold shiver when someone is aiming an arrow at your back?" Myth asked.

"Well, yeah, I guess so, but it can be more complicated than that. It's a way of knowing things with your heart that you couldn't possibly work out with your head. Sometimes you get it wrong, just like you make any other mistake, but that doesn't make it false. Suri taught me to trust that voice even when it's painful to hear."

"This voice?" Amicus asked. "Is it what's telling you to go to Percepliquis?"

Nolyn shook his head. "Honestly, that voice has been silent for centuries, but common sense says that going home is crazy."

"It's not, sir," Jerel said. "It's what you're meant to do. It's the will of the One."

"Well, then let's hope this *One* knows what he's doing."

CHAPTER NINE

Inside the Gem Fortress

At first light, Sephryn's door finally released, and the three left her home. Seymour returned to the records hall, while she followed Errol to the upper east side, where the most successful businesses took advantage of the river to import and export goods by barge. They stopped in front of West Echo Precious Gems and Jewelry Creations, a formidable building of meticulously cut and set rose granite blocks that dominated the trade center like a swan in a flock of ducks.

"You've got to be kidding," Sephryn said, looking up at the massive building that everyone referred to as the Gem Fortress. It didn't look like a shop at all. The five-story structure that extended along one whole side of the trade square towered over them. "Augustine Brinkle the jeweler? *That's* the guy you know?"

Errol Irwin nodded. The thief had said precious little that morning while he sped through the streets so quickly that she considered he might be trying to lose her. The sky was dark with clouds, the air damp with the promise of a forthcoming outburst. To Sephryn, the dirty overhead puffs looked as heavy as snow clouds, but although the air was chilly, it wasn't that cold. They had seen the last of winter; what was approaching was a spring storm.

"You've heard of him, too?" Errol asked.

"*Everyone* has! Not only is he the city's most prominent businessperson, he's also the Belgriclungreian ambassador," Sephryn replied.

"I'm impressed you can say that word. Rumor has it that a man once sprained his tongue while trying. Most just use *dwarf* for obvious reasons."

Sephryn looked back at the storefront and its set of bronze doors decorated with relief panels of dwarven craftsmen laboring at various workstations.

"Incredible," she said and reached for the door.

"Wait." Errol stopped her. "Not yet."

"What? Why? You were in such a hurry to get here that I thought you had other pressing appointments to get to."

Errol pressed his palms together and used them as a pointing paddle. "Two reasons." He aimed his hands at the Gem Fortress's doors. "First, they won't let us in. Second, Brinkle isn't here yet." He pointed his fingertips up the street. "Augustine will arrive precisely two minutes from now."

"What makes you think that? How can you even tell time so accurately?" She looked over at the massive sundial in the center of the plaza. The heavy cloud cover made it impossible to see even the faintest shadow. "I have excellent eyesight, and I can't see —"

The thief rolled his eyes. "Oh please, the number of things you don't observe would take too long to list. We only have one minute, forty-two seconds left."

"But I still don't understand how you know any of this."

He wiped a hand over his face to further emphasize his exasperation. "Didn't you notice the bakers placing their rolls out on Griffin Street? The first two nearly empty trays were steaming; the third and fourth were not. The bakers *always* set out their first doughy treats before dawn to catch the zombie parade of the city's poor as they march to the rock quarry. They put their second batch out exactly one hour later so it will be releasing an irresistible aroma just as the merchants pass by. Likewise, jugs of milk were on the stoops of the homes in Brighton Heights, which means they had been delivered, but not yet brought in. And although the dairy and bakery carts were set up along Bristol Street, the ice wagons haven't yet arrived. Need I go on?"

"All that means is that it's morning. No one is so exacting in their daily routine."

"Mister Brinkle is. I've done quite a study on him and his establishment. I'm intimately familiar with the fellow's habits. And he is a stickler, let me tell you."

"Hold on." Sephryn narrowed her eyes. "You've been *watching* him? You don't *actually* know Ambassador Brinkle, do you?"

Errol shrugged. "I know *of* him."

"So does everyone! Why did you say you *knew* him?"

"I said I *knew a guy.*"

"But you don't. You lied."

"I didn't. The fact that I know Augustine Brinkle exists is the truth. You chose to assume my statement meant more than it did. That's on you. Besides"—he shrugged—"I didn't like the way the poker was looking at me. Death by fireplace implement wasn't what I wanted for my future. It seemed wiser to suggest I had a valuable part to play in your little melodrama than to admit I couldn't help."

"Melodrama? You act awfully superior for a common street thief."

Errol's eyes widened. "I can assure you I am *anything* but common. You tasked Arvis Dyer to find the best abactor, and surprisingly, that crazy bat actually succeeded."

"The best what?"

Errol frowned. "Technically, it's someone who steals livestock, which I don't deal in, not as a general rule at least. But I do prefer the term over *robber, burglar, bandit,* or *crook*—all of which are tainted by poor practitioners of the craft—and *criminal mastermind* is too pretentious even for me."

She couldn't make sense of Errol Irwin. He seemed clever, but appearing smart and being intelligent were often two different things, and Sephryn had no idea which she was dealing with. Standing in the brisk morning air in front of the Gem Fortress, she began to think Errol was neither a criminal mastermind nor even a thief but merely a flashy swindler. He had impressed her with his keen observations and quick mind, but the result of his mental acuity had left her standing out in the cold, awaiting a storm.

"Ah, right on time," Errol said, nodding ever so slightly up the street to where a litter was carried by four men. "The dwarf is wonderfully punctual. The sun likely looks to him for the signal to rise. They're all that way, you know."

"I have no idea what you are referring to."

"The little folk—dwarfs. They are all obsessed with precision. Helps with their crafts. Even the smallest of mistakes can turn a diamond to dust or collapse a bridge."

Sephryn's estimation of the man's intelligence dropped another rung. "Seriously? You paint with that broad a brush, do you? How would you feel if Augustine said all humans were exactly like you?"

"He would never say such a thing. He would know I'm unique. And lumping me in with the rest of humanity is like comparing a hawk to a housefly."

"What I'm getting at is that you're speaking about opinion, not fact. And while you might feel strongly that your hypothesis is true, it might not be. You don't know."

"But I do."

"How?"

"I've already explained." Errol sighed. "And I must say, it's quite frustrating speaking to a person who doesn't pay attention. Augustine Brinkle wouldn't say other people were like me, because dwarfs are *precise*."

A dozen different outraged responses welled up in her, but Sephryn had no time to reply as a litter arrived and stopped at the Gem Fortress's big entrance.

The carrier, which looked like a little lacquered and richly ornamented house complete with a peaked roof, windows, and curtains, was set down on its support legs. A man—not one of the four sweaty ones who carried the litter, but another fellow entirely, one dressed in clean robes who had jogged along behind the litter—stepped up and opened the door to the travel seat. He also extended a hand to help Augustine Brinkle step out.

There were no Belgriclungreians in Merredydd, and precious few in Percepliquis. Because Sephryn had been to only a few other places, she hadn't seen many dwarfs. Ambassador Brinkle performed his trade negotiations with the First Minister in the right-hand wing of the palace, which was far away from the Imperial Council. Sephryn vaguely recalled meeting King Rain of the Kingdom of Belgric when she was a child, but that memory was now just a set of faded impressions. What she recalled the most was that her mother and father held King Rain in high regard, which was odd given her mother's general dislike of dwarfs—especially the one named Gronbach, whose name Moya often used as a curse.

Seeing Brinkle, Sephryn's first thought was that the gem mogul was bizarrely small. The few Belgriclungreians she had met were a solid four feet or so in height. Brinkle wasn't anywhere near that. He gave the two of them only a brief glance as he hopped down the half-foot step to the street, managing the descent without spilling a drop from his porcelain teacup.

"Good morning, Augustine," Errol said brightly.

"I know you, don't I?" That response produced a self-satisfied smile on Errol's face until he realized Augustine was speaking to Sephryn. The dwarf thought a moment, tapping a ridiculously delightful miniature finger against his cheek. "Oh, yes! You're Sephryn, the mixed-blood daughter of Moya and Tekchin, isn't that right?"

"Yes," she said. The word *mixed-blood* was a tad off-putting. She'd heard it before and never cared for the adjective; it had the tone of a slur. She fleetingly wondered how he'd like to be categorized as *midget,* but realized he'd meant no malice. Words came and went, and with time many changed their definitions. The intent behind the words was what mattered. Sephryn also knew that if everyone took offense at everything, society was doomed. For good or ill, she had put herself in the business of making certain that didn't happen.

"Tell me," Brinkle said, "was your mother really as good with a bow as they say?"

Sephryn was surprised. Few people remembered Moya, and Sephryn wouldn't have expected a foreign ambassador to be familiar with the legend. "The way she told me . . ." She paused while recalling an oft-repeated comment of her mother's. "*They* don't know the half of it."

That made the dwarf grin. Behind him, the litter was carried away. The door wrangler had also moved off and was holding open the entrance to the Gem Fortress, but Augustine appeared in no hurry. "You're still the Director of the Imperial Council—isn't that right? Been there awhile?"

She rocked her head from side to side, evaluating the term *awhile.* "Given that I founded it four hundred years ago, and have been the director since day one, I'd say I'm past the initiate stage."

The diminutive dwarf laughed, and just as high-pitched as one would expect. "I like you, Sephryn. How is it we haven't met before now?"

"Because the emperor doesn't give the Imperial Council the respect he should, and I don't wear jewelry." She held up her hands as evidence.

Augustine nodded, then glanced at the sky. "Looks like rain. Are you busy, or can you come up? I'm due for a refill." He looked mournfully at his cup.

"I would love to."

"Wonderful," Augustine replied.

Her eyes shifted sadly toward Errol. "But what about my manservant?"

"He can come, too, if you'd like."

Errol opened his mouth, but Sephryn shook her head, silencing him with a look.

❧

The interior of the Gem Fortress was nothing like the exterior of the brooding stronghold. Within was a world of delicate stairs and branching corridors lit from hidden skylights that reflected off polished mirrors of white marble. The lower floor was a warehouse and loading dock, while the middle floors were filled with workshops and diminutive ovens designed to melt small bits of metal and glass. Craftsmen on the upper stories cut gems and created works of art that had been designed by those on the top floor.

The instant they entered, Errol's gaze darted about as if he were a starving dog in a slaughterhouse, studying, calculating. She knew what he was thinking—well, not *precisely*. She didn't believe anyone could fathom that particular abyss. But it didn't take an Errol Irwin to know he was plotting a heist, looking for weaknesses, marking the best targets.

Augustine maintained a luxurious, albeit miniature, office on the top floor. They reached it by way of a vertical moving room that Brinkle referred to as the elevator, literally "one who rises up." Almost everything in the space was Brinkle-sized. Chairs, a desk, and even the cups and fireplace were half scale. The ceiling, however, was high, so Sephryn and Errol didn't need to crouch.

There were two normal-sized chairs. Whether these were always there or brought in for them, Sephryn didn't know. They took seats beside the morning-stoked fire as a teapot arrived, carried in by a servant who poured out three cups.

"I'm surprised you know about my mother," Sephryn said. "You don't look terribly old."

"Don't let my size fool you." He frowned. "I'm not a child."

"I didn't mean anything by that," Sephryn was swift to say, frustrated by how quickly some people took offense. "It's just that my mother died nearly a thousand years ago, and I didn't think Belgriclungreians lived so long."

The smile returned. "Dwarfs live longer than humans, but not nearly so long as Fhrey. I'm fifty-eight and look good for my age. I know about your mother from the stories." Augustine moved to the open hearth, briskly rubbing his hands against the morning chill.

"You've read *The Book of Brin?*" Sephryn asked.

"Book of what? Never heard of it."

"Then how—" she started.

He chuckled as if he were in on a joke. "King Rain, the founder of the Belgriclungreian Second Kingdom, was one of the heroes that entered the underworld along with your mother and father. The tales of that adventure have long been passed down by my people, along with many of the exploits relating to members of that valiant troupe."

"Oh . . . *those* stories." She almost said *myths* but caught herself. Brinkle's tone suggested he didn't see the tales the same way. She had realized long ago that her parents, like most adults, enjoyed delighting their impressionable children by presenting a world that was more fantastical than the real one.

"It's just so exciting to think that you knew—actually spoke to—members of that famous fellowship. And your father? Is he still alive?"

"Yes, he's just a few years younger than Emperor Nyphron in fact."

"And you were born before Percepliquis was built, isn't that right? You met Persephone and . . . did you know . . . did you meet . . . Suri?"

"Oh, yes." She smiled at the name. "The old woman was like a great-aunt. My mother used to take us for visits."

"Us?" Augustine asked, his eyes wide and attentive.

This is so much more than a myth to him.

"Yes. Nolyn, Roan and Gifford's son, Bran, and me. Every summer we'd go to the Mystic Wood, a magical place, and it would have been even without Suri, but with her . . ."

Fleeting, untethered memories blurred by time flooded her mind. Sephryn recalled a white wolf whom Suri conversed with. *But she was only pretending . . . right?* Sephryn remembered the softness and smell of the wolf's fur when hugging it. *Why would adults let me get so close to a vicious animal?* And there was that tree, the one that supposedly housed an evil creature. *Surely, that had to have been a fable . . . wasn't it?* And whenever Suri visited the still pond by the old willow, the fireflies had blinked in unison. *That had to be a distorted recollection because magic*—real *magic*—*doesn't truly exist. Or does it?*

Everything had seemed so real back then, but eight hundred years later, separating childish fantasy from adult reality was difficult. Regardless, some things she was certain about. She knew that those summers were the best times of her life, filled with friendship, laughter, music, and dance—for Suri loved to twirl. "Such a wonderful place to grow up, but . . ."

"Yes? Go on."

"Well, it made everything that came after a bit disappointing."

Brinkle laughed again, his chuckling inviting and infectious. "I can just imagine. Or rather, I wish I could. I grew up in brutal stone halls—and it wasn't just the walls and floors that were cold. The only warmth I received was listening to those grand tales of long-ago." He shook his head in awe. "Those people, those heroes—so brave, so fearless—they truly cared for one another, and risked more than their lives to save the world. You don't see that sort of selflessness anymore. These days everyone is out for themselves. If something doesn't benefit them, they don't bother to lift a finger. I grew up wanting to be Rain—not King Rain, but Rain the Digger—the member of that team who adventured above and below. My brother always got to be him when we pretended. I had to be Frost or Flood. No one wanted to be them. They were just builders and never went into the underworld, didn't meet Drome." Augustine looked at her with a whimsical flash of his eyes. "Your mother insulted him, didn't she?"

"No. She was rude to his servant, if you can believe what she said."

He gave her a sidelong stare. "You don't?"

"Well, it is a bit inconceivable, isn't it? The idea that my parents died, visited old friends and family, and came back? And does it make any sense that they are the only ones to accomplish such things? I mean, in centuries of searching, no one else has found the witch's hut, or spoken with gods, or claimed to stride the halls of Drome's castle or Ferrol's white tower." She shrugged. "Just seems made up. None of it is in *The Book of Brin*, and if you met my mother, you'd know she wasn't always a close friend to the truth."

"I see. Well, perhaps you can take comfort in the knowledge that King Rain confirmed the stories, passing them along to us, and we've handed them down word for word."

"But how do you know they weren't distorted in the retellings?"

"Precision," Errol said.

Sephryn dropped her face into her hand. "Please don't."

Errol crossed his legs and folded his arms. "I'm just saying that dwarfs are an extremely punctilious people, that's all."

"How about you?" Augustine's attention could not be drawn away from Sephryn.

"How about me, what?"

"Can *you* do it? Can you shoot like your mother?"

"Oh." Sephryn sighed. She shook her head. "No one could shoot like Moya."

"But she taught you, yes?"

"She taught me a great many things. Mostly things I wish she hadn't. Did you know that she could curse fluently in five different languages? I mean, really, what use is it to know how to profane the dead in Fir Ran Ghazel? How often does that come in handy?"

Augustine gave her a tell-me-more smile as if he hadn't heard a word she'd said. "I bet you can. I'm sure you're incredible. They say Moya was the best ever because she invented archery and used a magic bow carved from the famous oracle tree of the Mystic Wood, but the Fhrey have a dexterity that humans and Belgriclungreians lack. We've all seen it. That's why it was so incredible when Amicus Killian defeated Abryll Orphe in the arena. Of course, brute force is needed in hand-to-hand combat, but in archery . . . the daughter of Moya the Magnificent, who is also endowed with the Fhrey blood of an Instarya father, would be amazing."

Sephryn sighed again. "I suspect you'd be sadly disappointed. And just so you know, a good amount of brute force is required. Drawing Audrey is no easy feat."

"So you *have* used that bow?"

Sephryn nodded. "Since I was a child. Mother insisted. They aren't my happiest memories."

Time to change the subject, Sephryn thought. "Ambassador Brinkle, we weren't lingering outside by accident," she began. "We actually did wish to speak to you."

"Oh?" The dwarf's eyes lit up with the firelight that he now faced, as his backside was adequately toasted.

"We had a couple of questions, I believe?" She looked at Errol.

He nodded. "I assume you know about gemlocks?"

Alerted by overhead patter, they realized it had begun to rain.

Augustine's cup stopped halfway to his lips. He stared at Errol, as if just realizing the thief had been sitting with them. "This isn't your manservant, is it?"

Sephryn shook her head. "This is Errol Irwin, who considers himself a criminal mastermind, but wouldn't call himself that because he finds it too pretentious."

Errol's eyes widened, as did Brinkle's. Each was shocked by opposite ends of the same idea. Both attempted to speak, but Sephryn pressed on over both. "I'm telling you this, which I'm certain is infuriating Mister Irwin, who has invested a great deal of time planning to burgle your business, in order that you understand I'm being completely honest."

"And *why* are you doing that?" Brinkle cast repeated glances at Errol.

"Yes," Errol said with angry eyes. "Why?"

"Because I desperately need your help and your trust, but I can't say why."

"How come?" Augustine's face was developing an angry expression.

Sephryn realized how idiotic, how deceitful, all of it must sound, but she pushed on anyway. "If I told you the full details, your life and the lives of others would be in jeopardy, and truthfully, sir, you seem like a nice person—I wouldn't want that."

"She's not kidding about the jeopardy," Errol said hotly. "I only wish she'd extended me the same courtesy."

The ambassador squinted at them. "At this point, I think it unwise to believe anything you say," Brinkle said while looking at the thief. "I can't believe I let you in here. I suppose I was simply so . . ." He gestured at Sephryn with an open palm. "I had no idea you—you of all people—would associate with his sort." He looked again at Errol as if the thief were a hissing adder.

Errol frowned. "I assume that by *his sort,* you mean an elite malefactor and premier intellectual."

Augustine continued to stare at the thief.

"Ambassador Brinkle," Sephryn said, "I must implore you to ignore him, for now. And no, I don't normally associate with Mister Irwin. I only met him last night, and I'm forced to work with both of you because of extreme circumstances that have left me desperate. I have employed this man to aid me in obtaining a vital but difficult-to-acquire item."

"You've hired him to steal for you?"

"Yes. And he has told me that your expertise is needed."

"Because what you are after is protected by a gemlock."

"That is correct."

"And you won't tell me what this item is or why you need it?"

"I could tell you, but I'm absolutely certain that once you either refused to help or told me what I need to know you would die a most horrible death."

Again, Brinkle narrowed his eyes.

Sephryn looked up at the ceiling. "If you're listening, I'm not going to tell him anything specific, but I do need to say a little—okay?"

Both Sephryn and Errol looked around the room for anything that might fly. Nothing did. Sephryn took that as a yes and prayed she was right. "As you might guess, we are likely being overheard. By whom or what, I have no idea, except that the individual is extremely powerful and capable of killing any of us where we stand. Therefore, I need to be careful about what I say."

"This is most unusual," Augustine said, then took a sip of tea, using both hands to lift the cup. "If you were anyone else, I would have thrown you out already. But I do find it hard to believe that the founder and Director of the Imperial Council is planning a greedy heist. And I find it utterly impossible to believe that the daughter of Moya and Tekchin would be so vile."

"And yet," Sephryn began and sighed, "I quite expect you *will* be throwing us out. But before that happens, allow me to add that what I'm asking is a matter of imperial security and your help is needed to safeguard the future of the empyre."

"Are you serious? Do you really expect me to believe that you are acting—that you are stealing—for the good of the empyre?"

"I swear on the soul of my late mother Moya and the name of my still-living father that I speak the truth," Sephryn said, looking hard and unblinkingly into Augustine's eyes. It wasn't a lie; it only felt like one because she alone knew the truth. Sephryn hadn't told anyone—not even Nolyn—that he had a son. Nurgya was heir to the imperial throne. Nolyn had been sent to war in the past and could be in the future, and Nyphron was likely entering his last millennium. Given that, her missing son might be all that stood between a peaceful transition of power and imperial implosion.

The moment she swore by her famous mother, Sephryn saw what she had hoped for in the eyes of the dwarf—not belief but doubt. The ambassador wasn't certain what to think. His disbelief left the door to his mind open a crack, just enough to slip a pry bar in. "My mother told me that before the Battle of Grandford, she, Persephone, and many of those you know as the Heroes of Legend went to seek help from Gronbach of the Belgriclungreians."

Brinkle's face darkened. "I know that story, too. It has been the cause of great . . . problems between our peoples."

Sephryn nodded. "According to my mother, that dwarf's betrayal brought about the destruction of the ancient city of Neith, the original home of your people."

"Yes. Sadly, King Rain's recounting of that terrible day confirms that as well."

"Then tell me, ambassador, who do you want to be like today? Rain or Gronbach?"

"That's unfair." He responded as if she'd threatened him with a caning.

"I'm as desperate as Persephone when she arrived on the shores of Neith. This is a matter of life and death—no exaggeration. I need help just as certainly as my mother did."

The jewelry merchant and representative of the Belgriclungreians clutched his arms behind his back as he walked in a circular track around the room. He orbited the long table with its silver serving set and elaborate candelabrums, then paused to tug on his beard. "What is it you want to know *exactly*?"

"*Exactly*. See? What did I tell you?" Errol smiled. "Precision."

Sephryn shook her head in embarrassment. "We need to know how to open a gemlock. Isn't that right, Errol?"

He nodded. "It's a permanent safe. Can't be moved, and there's no chance of obtaining the gemkey. We need another way in."

Their host rubbed his hairy chin. "Has the original key been lost?"

"No, the owner has it and isn't going to lend it out. Is it possible to make a duplicate?"

"Perhaps. If I had the original, but you're telling me that's not a possibility."

"That's correct."

Someone knocked on the door, which was absurdly tall for an office of half-scale tables and chairs. The giant bronze door inched open hesitantly and a little man popped his head in. "Your morning staff meeting is awaiting you, sir."

"Tell them to hold it without me," Augustine replied.

"But, sir, Hammerman is unveiling the Sapphire Sprite today. I ordered fruit pies for the occasion."

Brinkle frowned. "I can't help it, Lindy. Tell them to go on."

"I'll save you a piece of blueberry, sir."

"Fruit pie this time of year?" Errol asked.

"They pack them in ice."

"Ah. And the Sapphire Sprite?"

Augustine frowned. "Don't try to play me like a fool. I'm trying my best not to think you're a common *hiben*."

Errol didn't know what to make of that, but as the daughter of a legendary expert in international profanity, Sephryn did and struggled not to smile.

"How does a gemlock work?" Sephryn asked.

Augustine turned his attention to her. "A gemlock is a highly precise mechanism that works on the principle of complex resonance, vibrations created by gems." He trotted to his short desk, where he picked up a gorgeous mahogany box and dumped it over, spilling out a pile of rough-cut gems. He picked up what looked to be a ruby the size of a human's thumb and held it up.

"Crystals are sensitive to energy that surrounds all things. This leads to oscillations and causes them to emit specific vibratory frequencies. The structure of a crystal, the lattice that makes it so balanced and ordered, releases a consistent vibration. In other words, a jewel hears the Voice of Elan and sings back to her, and each crystal has its own unique song. You can alter the tone by cutting the gem. The idea behind a gemlock is that you create a container whose locking mechanism will only react to a specific gem's voice. Some common gemlocks are designed to react with any jewel of the same family, regardless of size or cut." Augustine held up a little stone box and tapped the ruby to it. The top popped up. He then closed the lid and fished around on his desk for another ruby. Finding one, he tapped it and the box opened again. "This is a Courier Gemlock. It got its name because it was designed to transfer messages among two or more people, all of whom needed to be able to open it. Anyone with a ruby can do so. In this case, I suppose you could say that the voice of the gem isn't as important as the song it sings, and like birds of a feather, all rubies sing the same tune."

"Can we do that?" Sephryn asked. "We could use another ruby. I'm pretty sure that's the gem we need."

"I doubt we are dealing with a Courier Gemlock," Errol said. "I imagine this vault has an extremely sophisticated device."

"In that case, you are speaking of a mechanism that's so finely crafted, it listens not only for the song but also for the specific voice of the gem. To open it, you'll need either the gem made for that particular lock or an exact duplicate. And, of course, to make a copy would require obtaining the original."

"That's impossible." Sephryn looked at Errol.

"There is another way," Augustine said. "It's possible to confuse the lock."

"How?" Errol asked, his eyes studying the diminutive ambassador with keen interest.

"You can use a nullifying stone. If you know the gem family used to open the lock, then you could employ the opposite crystal."

"Opposite?"

"Gem vibrations work a bit like pigments. There are three primary colors: red, blue, yellow. If I were to mix yellow and red together, they make orange. Green is created from yellow and blue, and purple comes from mixing red and blue, but if I put all of them together, I get black. This is *complete* color, or the utter lack thereof. However, if I mixed, let's say, orange and blue, I would get gray, which is also a lack of color because orange and blue are complementary—not to be confused with complimentary, as in speaking well of, but rather the idea of completing something. Orange and blue cause the color intensity, or chroma, to be reduced."

"What does this have to do with gemlocks?" Sephryn asked.

Augustine held up his finger. "Well, the same principle applies. Gem frequencies work much like colors. Just as using complementary colors nullifies the chroma, using the complementary frequency nullifies the vibration—or rather, it creates a complete vibration."

Sephryn looked at Errol. "You're the self-proclaimed genius. Do you understand any of that?"

"Not really."

Augustine sighed. "By placing a crystal inside the box and then applying its complement on the outside—the two will complete each other and the lock will disengage."

"Inside?" Sephryn asked. "But if we could open the box to put something in, we wouldn't need any kind of key."

"Yes. That's why it's generally not an approach that can be used to any great effect."

Errol cut in, "You have to persuade the . . . *owner* to help. Make them put it inside."

"And how do we do that?" Sephryn asked.

"Well," Augustine said, "people put valuable things in gemlock boxes. You could give the emperor an expensive gift. A wonderful bit of jewelry."

Sephryn stiffened. "We never said anything about the emperor."

Augustine smiled such that his eyes seemed to sparkle in the firelight. "A high-end, single-voice gemlock safe that is opened with a ruby key? I doubt there are two such devices in the city—perhaps even the world. That particular box was a gift from King Rain to commemorate the dedication of the city on what you now celebrate each year as Founder's Day. My great-great-great-grandfather, or so, created that masterpiece." He glanced at Errol. "And you're right. It is quite sophisticated."

Sephryn and Errol both looked at the bronze exit door, neither of them happy to see it was closed.

How long has he known? Was "Sapphire Sprite" a special code? Did "I ordered fruit pies for the occasion" really mean "I summoned the city guard"?

Sephryn felt her heart sink.

"The thing is," Augustine said, "Nyphron never thanked Rain, never even acknowledged the gift. That grand gesture has long been seen as a snub to the Belgriclungreian Kingdom. It was further tainted by being delivered on the day Persephone died, and it was well known that Rain intended the present for her, not Nyphron. As the Belgriclungreian Ambassador, I'm not at all pleased with the treatment of some of my people who live and conduct business in the empyre, but because Belgreig doesn't have the power of seven legions backing it, I can rarely do much. On the other hand, should I have the support of the Director of the Imperial Council, perhaps I could achieve more."

Sephryn frowned, hating herself for what she was about to say. "As much as I wish it weren't true, I have to tell you that the Imperial Council doesn't have a great deal of influence with the emperor."

"I know that," Augustine said. "But some is better than none. I suspect you agree, or you wouldn't still be trying after so many centuries. Look, if anyone asks me about this, I'll say, 'Sephryn who?' But you have no idea how long I've waited to be Rain. You'll need an emerald and a ruby of exquisite quality to reach the level of frequency required. One of them will need to be placed in an amazing setting, something the emperor will value but not wear." Augustine picked up a green stone the size of his palm. "Give me a week."

"A week?" Sephryn began to panic. "I don't know if I have that long."

Augustine's face showed more concern than she expected. "You're in trouble, aren't you?"

She nodded.

"But you can't tell me what sort?"

She shook her head.

"I've always hated Gronbach and wished I had been there. It may be arrogance, but I always believed I would have saved Neith, playing the hero who stood up for what was right." He looked down at himself and laughed. "Can you imagine that? Me, a hero?"

Sephryn smiled.

"Funny how life has a way of presenting opportunities, never what or when you expect, but the marrow is the same. At its core, the question being asked and the courage to answer correctly remain identical. I wasn't in Neith when Persephone needed help. I couldn't stand up to Gronbach, or willingly enter the underworld, but maybe I can do something now. Gronbach's greed and deceit have cursed my people. Maybe my actions will be a first step toward removing his stain—perhaps this is a path to positive change. I'll work as fast as I can."

The possibility of saving Nurgya was too much to contain. Sephryn couldn't help herself. She reached out and hugged the gem merchant.

CHAPTER TEN

Death Pays a Visit

The midnight bell was ringing.

Arvis Dyer knew the sound better than most. Nearly everyone in the city—those unhappy enough to still be awake at that dismal hour—heard it through the walls of a building. Such a muffled conversation lacked intimacy. Arvis heard the clarity of that toll whispering directly into her ear like a late-night lover as she huddled beneath the steps of Chuck's Butcher Shop. Charles Jenkins, slaughterer of all things meat, lived above his bloody little business on the northeast side of Market Square. Arvis lived below it, although if asked, *lived* isn't how she'd have put it.

Living suggested a certain degree of balance between happiness and misery, success and failure, warm and cold, friends and enemies, want and satisfaction. Most observers might describe her situation as mere existence. Arvis believed such an assessment would be strangely optimistic, but then observers only got to see her circumstance from the outside. They glimpsed a woman who was past youth, but short of old, who lived beneath a rickety set of wooden steps. Wild hair and a mishmash of filthy clothes harvested from trash piles pointed to her being either a troll or a witch. Her accusers failed to grasp the fact that she charged no toll for crossing her steps, and if she could perform magic, she certainly wouldn't be living where she did. Yet the true depth of her misfortune wasn't on display, not visible to the naked eye. Arvis's torment wasn't that she had no home, bed, decent clothes, money, or food, but that she had no mind—or rather very little of one. Arvis still had some wits left, but she suspected even that meager store of sensibilities was dwindling.

It's all because of the bread.

She considered the thought as she hugged her knees beneath the steps. On her right side was the broken ceramic urn. The top was gone, as if someone had cleaved it at an angle, but the bottom was still intact enough to reveal the dancing deer painted in a ring around its base. Arvis kept her most prized possessions in that container: a string of wooden beads whose cord was now too short to wear after numerous breaks, a partially crushed tin cup with a missing handle, a stiff bloodstained drop cloth from the butchery that she used as a blanket, a well-worn sack with one busted shoulder strap, and a weevil she'd named Bray.

The bakery across the street was closed, as were all respectable businesses and homes at that hour. Only drunks, thieves, trolls, and witches breathed the late-night air and heard the naked tolling of the midnight bell.

They owe me bread.

She was certain of that truth, but why she was so sure, she hadn't a clue, and Bray was of no help whatsoever. The little beetle rarely even moved.

"Bread. Bread. Bread. The secret is in my head, head, head," she whispered to herself.

There was most assuredly a secret, a memory she'd lost, one of the many mental crumbs that had broken away. "Leaving me a few short of a loaf." She giggled to herself as she huddled beneath the steps, struggling to keep her one bare foot under the bloody tarp. The night was growing cold.

Nothing worse than cold feet—or foot.

She struggled to remember what she had been thinking about and lifted a hand to the side of her head that had the scar. She felt it, long and thick, running up her scalp under her hair like an awful seam.

That's where my mind went. Leaked out through there and dribbled away. Still dribbling, and the secret went with it.

She could no more remember where she got the scar than she could recall the Secret of the Bread. These were the two grand mysteries of her life—the two pillars she was certain supported the rest of her euphemistically styled existence. Arvis also believed the two were linked: the bread and the scar, the lost memory and the secret. All of it devastatingly important, but also horrible. Why else had her mind ejected them? And why should that part of her life be any different from the rest?

"What do you think, Bray?" she asked the beetle, who remained quiet. She nudged the urn. The weevil slid an inch across the smooth bottom. Not a sound.

There was a chance Bray was dead. There was also the possibility that he simply didn't like rye crumbs. All weevils preferred wheat.

Footsteps.

Arvis heard them growing louder, coming out of the echoes of the bell. Footsteps at night wasn't a sound she liked. The slow, lonely, rhythmic clap of leather on stone chilled her more than the cold.

No businesses open. No business being here.

Arvis knew the habits of the people living nearby. No one wandered the square on a raw spring night. Chuck and his wife worked hard all day, murdering animals, and they enjoyed the sound sleep of the virtuous. Rodney the Crooked Baker and his wife Gerty the Turdy, the one with the cold accusing stare, locked themselves in after dark with their daughter, as if afraid Death would come knocking.

Is that who's coming?

Arvis found the thought strangely comforting. Death, she imagined, would be a gentleman compared with others she'd met after the tolling of the late bell.

He's coming back to finish the job another started.

Arvis didn't move, merely hugged her legs tighter. The still-functioning residue of her remaining brain was trying to make her smaller. Smaller was better. Smaller was harder to find, more difficult to see. She bowed her head to her knees, and closed her eyes tight, trying to disappear.

The sound came closer. No hesitation, pause, or meandering. The steps were deliberate.

Someone is visiting Chuck—the-butcher—Jenkins.

The reasoning was perfectly sensible, abundantly logical, and quite unlike her normal starburst of thoughts. Arvis also knew she was wrong. She desperately wanted the owner of those noisy feet to climb the stairs above her and rap on the butcher's door. That was the primary reason she knew it wouldn't happen. Evil had a habit of finding her.

The footsteps didn't go up the wooden stairs. They came around the side and stopped, sliding to a noisy halt just inches from her.

"Arvis?" An unfamiliar voice spoke.

She kept her eyes closed. *If I can't see Death, Death can't see me.*

"Arvis, come with me."

She shook her head.

"Please."

Arvis had heard the word before, but never had it been spoken to her, and certainly not in that way, with such a tone of sincerity, with such politeness.

She inched out and looked up. A figure stood before her, draped in a long cloak that started with a billowy hood and ended where excess material gathered on the cobblestones. In the darkness, she saw no face.

Death. It has to be Death. He is a gentleman.

Death held out a hand to her. All she saw were the tips of fingers that extended beyond the length of loose sleeves.

Not claws, at least.

Feeling she had little choice, as no one does when Death comes calling, she took the hand, and Death pulled her up. Still holding on gently, Death walked with her across the square as if they were a young couple on their first date. She glanced back, concerned about Bray. He hadn't been looking good. Bray might be a *she;* Arvis wasn't at all certain what Bray was.

Death led Arvis down Carvo Street, the smallest of the six roads that spoked out from the square, the area known as the garment district. Most of the homes were owned by tailors or fabric merchants. Nice places, but not *too* nice. Some at the end of the street were so old and neglected as to be called run-down.

Arvis saw no reason to speak to Death. What was there to say?

No, wait, you made a mistake? I'm Arvis Dyer. You want another Arvis.

And small talk would be even more absurd.

How are you doing? Looking forward to Founder's Day? Nice robe. I bet that really scares the pifflepuff out of most people.

Arvis resolved herself to a quiet march to her demise. No whimpering, no begging; she would face her end bravely. She wasn't leaving much behind anyway, just Bray, and now she was certain he had already left her. Almost everyone she knew had.

As they turned into the little alley south of the charred remains of the milliner's shop that had burned down two years before, Arvis became curious where Death was taking her. With anyone else, she'd be terrified. They were now entering a decidedly unsavory part of town. Given that she had already accepted she was traveling to her final resting place, she wasn't terribly worried, merely curious about where the ultimate act would take place. And of course, there was the one remaining concern . . .

"Will it hurt? I mean, sure, I know it'll hurt, but will it hurt a lot? Will it take a long time?"

Death turned, and she saw the tip of a nose poking out of the hood. Death, it seemed, had a face after all. "I'm not going to kill you, Arvis."

"Really?" She was both shocked and oddly let down. The degree of disappointment was surprising. Only then did she realize that while she was frightened, she was also clearly looking forward to it. "But—"

"I need your help."

Death needs my help?

A sudden panic welled up. "You don't want me to . . . I can't *kill* anyone. Please don't make me kill—"

"No, it's nothing like that."

"Then what?"

"It's about the bread, Arvis."

The fact that Death knew she lived under the steps of the butcher shop and knew her name hadn't affected her nearly so much as his knowing about the bread. She stopped and stared at the shadow beneath the hood. They were in a lonely alley formed from the backs of mud-brick hovels. The only light came from moonlight that glanced across one side of the narrow passage, spilling like pale paint on dirty clay blocks and poorly set mortar.

"The bread?" she asked, both terrified and hopeful.

The bread had confused her for so long. Just thinking of it produced a mixture of feelings and ideas that were so deeply tangled that the idea of unraveling the snarled web of mystery had been hopeless—until now.

Death raised a pale finger. "Can you hear it?"

"What?" she asked.

"Listen carefully."

Arvis pulled back her hair and paused, taking inventory of the nightly noises: somewhere something creaked faintly, a dog barked, wind whispered as it raced through the alley, a shutter clapped, and far away she heard the peeps of spring frogs. She heard nothing that—

A cry.

Desperately faint, high-pitched, and weak, Arvis heard the unmistakable wail of a child—an infant. The sound almost killed her. The cry stabbed into her heart with a multitude of claws ripping it open and laying it bare. She gasped.

"Over there." Death pointed deeper into the alley. "Be courageous, Arvis. It's time to face your fear."

Shaking, Arvis stepped ahead of Death and moved deeper into the alley. With each step, the sound of the cries, while still muffled, grew louder. She searched frantically for the source but saw nothing but bricks and cobblestone, old leaves swept into mounds, broken clay shards, rags, and horse manure that had been heaped against the wall so that she had to step carefully around it.

Is something in the piles?

She moved past the rubbish, and the wailing compelled her deeper still.

Her ears and nose were cold, her bare foot threatened to go numb, but Arvis felt hot, sweaty, and horrified. Then she passed it. The sound was behind her. She turned. The cries came from below her feet.

Kneeling down, Arvis swept away a crate, a sack of rotted vegetables, and the cluster of brittle leaves that had gathered. The moment she did, the instant she exposed the sewer grate, the wails grew louder.

"It's coming from down there. What am I supposed to do?" Arvis looked up but was alone in the alley. Death had abandoned her.

∾

She wasn't entirely certain Death had left. Just because she couldn't see life's little reaper didn't mean he wasn't still there. If he was, however, he wasn't talking. Arvis concluded he was watching, but from that point forth, she would be on her own.

The cries continued to ring, to beckon from the far side of the grate. The sewer cover was a two-foot square of limestone with four petal-shaped holes cut through it, creating a simple flower pattern. Nothing but its weight held it in place. She placed her hands on the rough surface of the cold stone.

Is a baby down there? How can that be?

"Do you want me to climb in?" she asked, but Death was still nowhere to be seen.

Arvis shuddered at the idea of squeezing through the tight hole and dropping into darkness. She would be forced to fall into that unknown world of who knew what. Everyone knew the sewers were the very bottom, the realm of vileness so wretched that only the most desperate entered.

How could a baby be down in a sewer?

Even as she recoiled in disgust at the idea, her fingers slipped into the petal-shaped holes. The stone was heavy, a good fifty pounds at least.

I'll never get this off.

The wailing from the sewer had a different opinion, and Arvis found enough strength to lift and drag, grinding the stone aside. Thrusting her head in, she saw nothing; still, the sound of the cries was magnified as they echoed eerily, hauntingly in that netherworld of sunless gloom.

Is this an actual child I'm searching for or something else?

Having mostly leaked out of that cracked skull of hers, Arvis's mind was of little use. In its truancy, her heart had taken over, and answered her with a confident, yet confusing *Yes!*

Wait! her mind shouted as her heart put forth the bare foot toward the inky brink. *Light! Can't see in the dark, you idiot.*

Arvis's heart reluctantly granted that concession. Running out of the alley, she frantically searched for a lamp. Now that her heart had assumed control, panic gripped her. A frenzy of fear took hold and cried with the voice of a terrified child that doom was seconds away.

Arvis found a half-burnt torch discarded beside the front door of a home. Maybe it wasn't thrown away. Perhaps it was left there for use in lighting the door lamp, and by taking it, she was stealing. But speculation was an instrument of the mind, and the heart would hear none of it. She snatched the torch up, caught the end on fire using the lamp by the door, and off she ran—a wild woman armed with flame and fury. Back into the alley she charged, torch spitting sparks as she skidded to a stop at the ominous square of black cut into the ground.

Arvis's mind objected, but her heart was deaf to protests, and into the hole she went. Feet-first she fell with no thought, no precaution, no plan. In her chest, a drumbeat pounded, a rapid call to action that dismissed everything else as cowardice. She hit the bottom by slapping into sludge and ankle-deep water with a splash. She chose to believe it was water, and maybe some of it was, but it didn't smell that way. The moment she landed, she gagged at the thick stench that made breathing a conscious decision.

She stood in a narrow corridor that ran parallel to the alley above. The walls were formed of thick blocks of mortar-free stone. She couldn't see the end of the passage in either direction, but then her lone torch was ill suited to the task. Without it, she would have been at a loss, and her heart grudgingly acknowledged that her mind wasn't a total idiot.

The ongoing cries, a series of now staccato eruptions and gasps, led Arvis in a direction—which direction she failed to register. Reaching a four-way intersection, again she charged ahead, led by her wailing north star. Overcoming the stench, the slime-covered walls, and the muck squishing beneath her feet, she drove on.

The rats she noticed. More than a couple, more than a few, the chilly spring night had driven the rodent nation underground. The corridors were filled with a constant flow of scurrying piebald bodies and naked tails. They moved with nearly as much purpose as she, climbing over the bodies of those before them who dared to pause. At times, Arvis struggled to find free real estate to land her feet on, and she often crushed several of the creatures, and not always with the sandaled foot.

Another turn, another corridor and then . . .

She waited.

Silence.

Arvis stood in the water, listening, but the crying had stopped.

I'm too late. The bread, the bread is . . .

Arvis began to sob, as much for the loss of the child as for her own mind.

CHAPTER ELEVEN

The Orinfar

By the third day, Nolyn was feeling better. He'd always suffered chronic seasickness, and the current trip had been no different—ironic though, given that the imperial warship *Stryker* had been bobbing cork-fashion down the Estee River and didn't actually reach the sea until then. All oar and rudder work, there was no need for sails while riding the current. The billowing of the canvas was what tipped him off that things had changed. Nolyn had been crouched in his usual ball of misery near the bow when he heard the canvas being let out. Lifting his head, he noticed the great gold dragon on the blue field, the symbol of the imperial House of Nyphronian, his own standard, blooming out like the chest of a proud father. Feeling sun on his skin, Nolyn breathed deeply. Air—cool, fresh, and salty—tousled his hair and blew across sweat-stained cheeks.

I don't need to vomit.

The thought came as a surprise. For three days, he'd been either retching, on the verge of doing so, or in that pre-heave stage that promised those miseries to come. For the first time, he felt none of that. In exchange, he now suffered a painful emptiness in his stomach, a dash of dizziness, and a general weakness, all of which were welcomed, since they heralded the end of his anguish.

Seasickness had always progressed the same way. He knew the signs of each stage and was finally done with the middle one where he cocooned himself, obsessed with his own agony. That was the worst part, the *blackout* period similar to a fever when he knew nothing and cared less. The last stage, which he labeled *post-storm*, would come soon, but the worst was over; all that remained was the grim task of assessing the damage. He hadn't managed to keep anything in his stomach for three days, which left him weak. Despite his lack of food, he wasn't overly hungry, and he worried that eating would send him back to the blackout stage.

Water. He needed that more than anything. The thought ignited a desperate want, and he was about to take the chance of standing up when he spotted Amicus Killian crossing the deck with a cup in his hands.

"What's that?" he asked hopefully.

"Beer."

"Isn't there any water?"

"None that you'd want to drink," Amicus said, handing the cup over and sitting beside Nolyn. "The *Stryker* had only docked for a few hours before we insisted they leave. Like any sensible commander, the captain ordered the restocking of his beer barrels first. The water has a nice green scum. But if you prefer . . ."

Nolyn waved his hand to make Amicus stop, then pressed the metal cup to his lips. He wanted to guzzle it all, but he had learned from experience that doing so would be bad. So he forced himself to endure the torture of sipping. As expected, it was sailor's ale, the typical watered-down cousin to real beer. No sane captain would stock the genuine article on a vessel full of armed men.

"You've done this before," Amicus observed.

"What? Been sick?"

The soldier nodded. "I partially filled that cup on purpose, so you couldn't gulp down too much."

Nolyn revealed a pathetic smile. "Not my first voyage. Ever since my father established the Imperial Navy, he's enjoyed torturing me with it. That's . . ." He paused to think, but his mind was still too befuddled to be exact. "Well, several hundred years of misery, at least. You don't suffer from Eraphus's Wrath?"

"If you mean seasickness, no. What did you call it?"

"Eraphus's Wrath," Nolyn said. "Eraphus was the ancient god of the sea, from pre-imperial times."

With an amazed expression, Amicus shook his head. "I keep forgetting how old you are. Must be strange. The world must have been very different when you were young."

"True, but the changes happen so slowly that it's not as odd as you might expect. But yeah, I've seen a lot. When I was young, there weren't really any human cities, just clusters of small pockets where homes were built on hilltops surrounded by wood-and-earth walls. People huddled in fear of the night, gods, and spirits. After the Great War, we became *civilized*. My mother made that possible. She was amazing—so courageous, so wise. I wish I were more like her. Although at times, I suspect she longed for simpler days."

"Why do you say that?"

"Just the way she used to talk about living in Dhal Rhen. Everyone knew everyone else. The clan was one big family. They took care of one another. Now . . . well, people starve in the streets of Percepliquis because they don't have money to pay for bread."

"Your mother knew Roan of Rhen, yes?"

Nolyn nodded. "Of course."

"An amazing person. I suppose people were smarter back then, or maybe there were more things to invent. I've heard it said that there's nothing left to discover now. Still, it seems incredible that one man managed to single-handedly create hundreds of inventions in just a single summer before the Battle of Grandford: the wheel, metallurgy, the bow and arrow, and all sorts of other things we now take for granted."

Nolyn smiled. "Your information is a little faulty."

Amicus looked surprised.

"First of all, Roan was a woman."

That was met with a facial crush of confusion.

"The rest is gross exaggeration. I mean, she *was* an undisputed genius, perhaps the greatest mind the world has ever known, but in retrospect, people are fond of simplifying to suit their narrative. Even my mother often referred to the *thousands* of discoveries Roan had made without realizing people would take her literally. In truth, during that summer before the Battle of Grandford, Roan only invented two significant things: the pocket and the bow and arrow. And the pocket did little to win the war."

Amicus looked unconvinced. "What about the wheel? She created it, allowing the clans to travel, and it gave way to the war chariot."

"She thought of putting a pole through the center of a potter's wheel, but the wheel had already been in use by the dwarfs and Fhrey for hundreds of years. As it happened, there were dwarfs there at the time and they did most of the work, explaining to Roan about axles and bushings and such."

"What about smithing metal?"

"In those days, humans had been smelting copper and tin for centuries. And she learned how to make bronze and iron from the dwarfs in Caric. That was the great talent of hers, the ability to observe in detail and remember, but again, watching and repeating isn't the same as inventing."

"And steel?"

"She used a formula found in Neith, but even with that and an army of assistants—three of whom were dwarfs—it still took her almost a year to work out a process, which she continued to refine for the rest of her life."

"But there were other things, too. What about barrels, shears, and . . ." Amicus struggled to remember. "Oh, yes, ink and glaze."

"She did invent a kind of ink, but barrels were invented by the dwarfs, and shears had been used to remove wool from sheep for generations before she was born. I seem to recall that Roan's version was smaller and had a different grip—more an improvement than anything else. And she didn't invent pottery glaze, merely concocted variations. She also created a leg brace that summer, but it didn't work. Not everything she thought of did."

"And Roan of Rhen was a woman?" Amicus frowned and shook his head, as if this was the most suspect thing of all. "That's not believable. How could a woman—especially in those days—have the capacity to—"

"To think? To observe? To notice that something round rolls? Or realize that if you notched the butt of the drill stick and pulled it against the bow's string, it would fly? Honestly, the part I'm stunned by is why it took so long. I guess it took a person like Roan who had both the curiosity and the time."

Amicus folded his arms, appearing unconvinced.

"Amicus, Roan was my aunt. Not actually my mother's sister, but practically. The woman taught me to read."

Amicus raised a brow.

"Still don't believe me, do you?" Nolyn asked, then shrugged. "Something I've learned about people, both human and Fhrey, is that they hate having long-held beliefs challenged by facts, even about stupid things. Once you get something settled in your head, it becomes comfortable and difficult to dislodge." Nolyn took a sip of beer. The second mouthful tasted better than the first. "No one likes to admit they're wrong, even if they are just agreeing with something someone else told them."

"Hold on . . ." Amicus thought a moment. "Is that what happened between you and Sephryn? Were you stubborn about something stupid?"

Having only recently returned to the world of sun and air from the depths of discomfort, Nolyn's head wasn't as clear as he'd like, and it sounded as if he'd missed something. "What? How did you get there? We were talking about Roan."

"And then you started this whole thing about people being stupid and stubborn. Which made no sense unless it was already on your mind, maybe something you felt guilty about."

"And you settled on my relationship with Sephryn?"

Amicus narrowed his eyes as he studied the prince. "Uh-huh. Riley has a girl in Vernes who's in love with him, but he's not with her; Jerel left his childhood sweetheart to join the legion. Myth brags about having an entire collection of ladies in the wings, and believe it or not, Smirch is married. Even Everett pines for the girl on his neighbor's farm. But in all the years I've served with them, I honestly couldn't tell you the name of any of those women. I've only known you now for eight days, but I've heard you speak of Sephryn so often that I feel like I know her. Only two things can cause that: love and guilt. Given that most of the last eight days have consisted of fighting or running for our lives—not exactly the sort of moments one takes the time to share—I'm guessing it has to be both."

"That's a lot to conclude from the mention of a name."

"It's more than that. It's the tone, the way you talk about her, the look in your eye. My father taught me how to read body language. Damn helpful in a fight." Amicus grinned. "So what happened?"

"What do you mean?" Nolyn gulped the last of the beer and looked at the bottom of the empty cup.

"Between you and this girl."

"Girl?" Nolyn rolled his eyes. "Oh, she'd love that. Sephryn is eight hundred and forty-nine years and four months old. I doubt *girl* suits her."

"See, right there. I can guarantee you that Jerel, Everett, and Riley can't tell me how many years *and months* their women have lived. I doubt Smirch even knows his wife's birthday. So come on, tell me. What happened?"

"Can't you see I'm struggling with seasickness? Did your father also teach you a lack of compassion?"

"Oh . . . that bad, eh? You must have done something truly awful. Did she catch you with another woman?"

"No."

"Another man?" He grinned.

Nolyn looked at his empty cup and frowned as if it had betrayed him. "We had a fight, about a year ago, and I've not seen her since."

"About what?"

"She wanted me to be something I'm not. She's the Director of the Imperial Council. Been trying to improve the lives of humans under my father's rule for generations, but he refuses to listen to the council's suggestions. He promised he would, and supposedly the First Minister forwards their proposals, but so little has changed that she's convinced Nyphron lied. She asked me to talk to my father. Sephryn wanted me to convince him to attend the council meetings. I refused."

"Thought so." Amicus smiled. He was doing a lot of that, and it made Nolyn feel he was losing a contest. Why he thought of their conversation as a competition, he had no idea—except that everything with Amicus felt like combat.

Nolyn lifted his back off the hull to glare at the First Spear. "What do you mean by that?"

"It's just that before, when you mentioned the discussion about the Citizen's Charter, you said the two of you had a lot to drink, as if you later believed it had been a bad idea."

"No, it wasn't that. It's a great idea. Asking me to speak to my father was the problem. What she didn't know—still doesn't—is that my father hates me—always has."

"And you don't want her finding out you're afraid of him, right?"

"You're really sort of a bastard, aren't you?" Nolyn asked.

"I kill people for a living. What do you expect?"

৵

The imperial warship *Stryker* had no private accommodations aboard, not a single bed, hammock, or chest. Personal gear was stuffed into the three-foot gap over the heads of the upper oarsmen. Each night, a heavy rope was used to pull the ship ashore, providing room for the men to sleep. The sailors and one tier of oarsmen did the heavy work of landing the vessel, but the task to secure the beach fell to the soldiers. Along the Estee River, that hadn't been a problem since there were established safe areas with enough depth that the boat could be rowed to shore. But once they reached the sea, the process of beaching the *Stryker* became more difficult. In the open expanse, it was impossible to know what dangers awaited them on shore. Wisdom dictated that a landing had to be deemed safe before the ship maneuvered into the surf. For those tasked to find out, they needed to decide whether to swim with thirty pounds of armor or venture into a potential ambush carrying just a sword.

Fear illuminated the faces of the warship's soldiers as they debated which bits of armor to leave behind. Choosing was a game of chance. Either they drowned from the weight of metal, were slaughtered for lack of it, or nothing at all happened except a harrowing bath.

Amicus relieved them of that burden by volunteering himself, and several members of the Seventh Sik-Aux, for the dangerous detail. He selected Riley Glot, Azuriah Myth, and Jerel DeMardefeld, all of whom opted to swim to shore wearing just their breechcloths and taking only their swords. Amicus opted for a dagger.

"You sure about this?" Nolyn asked as the First Spear stripped.

Amicus grinned. "Are you kidding? This will be fun."

There was a whimsical twinkle in his eyes that was repeated in the faces of those prepping beside him. The members of the Seventh Sik-Aux were not the types to sit idle on deck and watch the coast drift by. That was as much their cup of tea as a cup of tea. These men drank hohura straight from the horn and roared with the burn.

"Will you do me the honor of watching my weapons, sir?" Amicus asked, slipping his dagger into a makeshift wrist sheath. "They are . . . *important* to me."

Nodding, Nolyn noticed a tattoo. Skin markings were not unusual in the legion. Often, they depicted a stylized sword, a fist, a rose, or perhaps thorns wrapping a forearm. The most common was a legion insignia, but Amicus didn't have the Seventh's famous boar symbol. He had but one tattoo, an unbroken ring of runes that circled his body at chest level.

Nolyn was still staring at the tattoo as all four dived off the side of the ship. Only a skeleton crew remained at their posts, keeping the *Stryker* from getting too close to the cresting waves; the rest crowded the gunwale to watch. Four bare backs glistened in the light of the setting sun, breaching the dark blue like dolphins until they reached the frothing whitecaps and rode them in. Watching from the security of the deck, flanked by Smirch and Mirk, Nolyn saw the joy of the swim and regretted not going.

The emperor's son . . . he's one of them now.

He wasn't. By virtue of a birth that gave him near immortality and undeserved prestige, Nolyn could never truly be one of them, but he wished he could. Everyone came into the world with Everett-like innocence, but time burned it out, and his flame had been lit for nearly a millennium. He had loved and lost more friends than he could remember. They came and went with the swift regularity of leaves on trees. He knew he could love these dolphin-men racing one another to the beach, wasting air by calling out taunts even as they approached what could be their deaths. He could love them as he loved life itself because they *were* life—an existence lived as it ought to be: swift and brilliant, careless and courageous. They were shooting stars, sparks from a campfire, a first touch, and a final kiss. Fleeting moments of beauty made all the more wondrous by their brief nature.

Throughout his whole life, there had been but two constants: Sephryn and his father. He saw them as light and dark, good and evil, virtuous and corrupt. But while he had remained loyal to a father he hated, he had turned his back on the brightest star in his life.

Watching the men reach the shore and triumphantly rage against the jungle, challenging any hiding within to combat but seeing not a single leaf quiver in response, he was envious.

What good is it to breathe if I don't live? What value is there in loyalty if it blocks every path? What will I do now?

With the shore claimed in the name of the empyre, or at least the *Stryker* contingent of the Seventh Sikaria Auxiliary, the sailors went to the work of beaching the vessel. Fires were built, and men huddled around the light and warmth, eating from a communal pot of fish soup, a delicacy that was sure to get old long before the supply ran out.

Amicus had dressed but was still scrubbing the wet from his hair when Nolyn approached with the First Spear's three swords. "Unusual weapons you have."

"Heirlooms," Amicus said. "Handed down from father to son."

The rest of the Seventh Sik-Aux were with them at the center of nine driftwood campfires that dotted the sand. The men ate the last of their meals and watched the crackling fire that sent orange sparks aloft on futile quests to join the pale white stars. Demetrius was also there. Pale and shivering, he, too, suffered from Eraphus's Wrath. No one had laid a hand on him since that first day. They didn't even watch him anymore. Initially, the man was too sick to flee, but even though he had improved, he'd be a fool to run now that they were miles from civilization and surrounded by the ghazel-filled Erbon Forest.

Nolyn sat in a gap in the circle that seemed left for him. "Looked refreshing."

"It was!" Myth replied with a huge smile. "Best swimming in the world! Although I was hoping to catch a shark on the way in. Then I could wear its head, the way the Ba Ran do."

"They don't do that," Riley replied. "They just wear necklaces and anklets made from sharks' teeth."

"Even better. Just imagine what they would think if they saw something with the body of a man and the head of a shark coming at them."

"You mean after they stop laughing?" Smirch asked.

"No one laughs at a shark!"

"True, but a man wearing one as a hat?" Amicus chuckled. "C'mon? *That* would be funny."

"None of you knows anything." Myth waved a dismissive hand at the lot. "Although I imagine it would smell horrible—fishy, I suspect."

"Your swords," Nolyn said, staring again at the First Spear's blades, "they have markings on them. The same ones as on your chest. You seem to have a fondness for runes."

Amicus looked up. "My father gave me the tattoo when I was young. Said it was part of my training. Taught me to fight practically from the day I was born. 'Never too early to start the Tesh,' he used to say when dumping me off my cot before the sun was up."

"The Tesh?"

Amicus fidgeted with a buckle to the over-shoulder strap that supported his side sword after looping through his waist belt. Most men would be removing their weapons in preparation for sleep, not attaching them. Nolyn wondered if Amicus would sleep with that big sword strapped on as well. "That's what my father called the first seven schools of combat."

Nolyn smiled. "Forgive me, but I've fought in the legion and with the Instarya for centuries, and I've never heard about any of this. The only Tesh I know comes from the old tales."

Amicus didn't appear surprised. "It isn't well known."

Nolyn looked at the others. "You fight like no one I've ever seen. You're incredible. How is it that such a set of skills could be ignored? I would think everyone would be hounding you for instruction."

Amicus frowned. "The Tesh—it's a family secret."

"But you taught *them*." Nolyn pointed a sweeping arm at the circle of six. "Don't deny it. I've seen them fight."

"Well, I've only really taught Glot, Myth, and DeMardefeld. Been training with them for a few years, and they still aren't through all the schools. Really need to start young to be good at it. I only recently started working with Smirch, and so far, we've gone over little more than footwork and basic—"

"But you have taught them this *family secret?*"

"Sure." Amicus nodded. "They're family."

Nolyn didn't have a reply to that. He'd only been with the group for eight days, and already he felt closer to them than anyone aside from Sephryn or Bran.

"Look, my father's dead. I have no sons, and out here, no one cares who I am. What matters is that I can fight. I teach them because the better they are, the longer I'll live. But not everyone wants to learn. Paladeious and Greig wouldn't listen to a word I said. They were big, and that's all they felt they needed to be. Others came to the Seventh Sik-Aux from different squadrons, or even other legions, and believed they already knew everything. And Everett there"—he pointed at the lad—"just arrived a week before you."

"So you taught four of the five men who, aside from me and yourself, survived the ambush? You don't see that as significant?"

"Honestly?" Amicus said. "I have no idea how Smirch survived."

"I'm like an unsightly mole," the gristly man said. "No matter what you do, you can't get rid of me, bossy."

Everett dragged over another branch of driftwood and added it to the fire. A hive of sparks exploded, flying away toward the overhead half-moon.

"Will you teach me?" Everett asked.

"I'd like to learn, too," Mirk said.

The First Spear sighed. "Sure."

"Be careful what you ask for," Myth said. "The man is a cruel instructor. I was handsome before I became his student. Now, alas, I'm only good-looking."

Riley leaned in toward Myth, studying him, then nodded. "I'm starting to see the wisdom of a shark's head."

Myth threw his bowl at Riley, who caught and stacked it along with his.

"I still don't understand the runes," Nolyn said. "How are *they* part of the training?"

"My father said that they were for defense."

"Against what?"

Amicus lowered his voice as if he didn't want to be heard. "Magic."

"Did you say *magic?*" Myth asked, which surprised Nolyn, as he thought this *family*—this band of brothers—would have covered such a topic earlier. Judging from the interest on the faces of everyone around the central fire, it hadn't come up before.

"There was something called the Orinfar," Nolyn explained. "Dwarven runes that were said to protect against magic. Are you saying that's what those tattoos are?"

"Never heard of an Orinfar, but I do know this"—Amicus pulled his short sword—"is the Sword of Brigham, a relic from my ancestor who fought in the Great War." He tilted the blade so they could all see the markings running down the length of the fuller, or blood-gutter as some called it. "Legend holds that this sword was forged by Roan of Rhen for the Battle of Grandford." He paused to glance knowingly at Nolyn. "And these marks are dwarven symbols. They were put on all the weapons and armor back then as protection from Fhrey sorcerers." He drew out his other, longer blade and revealed the same markings. "This iron one is called the Sword of Wraith, rumored to be the first sword Roan ever forged, and as you can see, it, too, has the same markings." He pulled the one that normally rode on his back from its scabbard. "Now this . . . well, this is what my father said was the holiest of all. He called this blade the Sword of the Word." He held the weapon out to the firelight so everyone could see the markings. These were different. Scratched rather than etched, they were also not runes but phonic symbols. Nolyn could read the markings as Amicus tilted the blade so that it caught the fiery light. Running down the length of the naked metal was the word GILARABRYWN.

"Is that . . ." Nolyn said, stopping himself as his mind replied that it couldn't be. "Are you saying—wait, where did your family get this? Because there was only ever one sword that was known to have had *that* word marked on it."

"You can read it?" Amicus looked shocked.

"Of course I can. You can't?"

Amicus shook his head as he sat up eagerly. "What's it say? I've always wanted to know, and my father couldn't tell me."

"Seriously? You've carried *that* blade around on your back and don't know? Are you familiar with the story of Gronbach?" Everyone around the fire nodded. "Do you recall how at the end of the tale a sword was forged by the dwarfs? One that was enchanted by Suri?"

Jerel asked, "Is she the one that killed the dragon and brought down the mountain?"

Nolyn nodded. "If I'm not mistaken, that's the sword. Never thought it was that big. I suppose they wanted to make certain the thing had enough room to get that long word on the blade. But how did *you* get it?"

"Brigham Killian was the last of the Teshlor Warriors, protégés of Tesh. His mentor had no children, so his stuff went to Brigham, I guess."

"But how did Tesh get it?"

"You tell me. You knew everyone."

Nolyn stared at the ancient sword, amazed. "According to *The Book of Brin*, Suri gave the sword to my mother for the keenig challenge. Persephone gave it to a warrior named Raithe, the hero of the Battle of Grandford, but there was no mention of the blade after that. But that's not odd because *The Book of Brin* ends just after the Battle of Grandford."

Amicus paused, his eyes shifting to the fire in thought. "What's strange is that legends say Tesh used two matching short swords. But only this one is short." He clapped the Sword of Brigham. "And it was Brigham's, not Tesh's, which means neither of these was actually used by Tesh."

"What happened to Tesh's swords?" Mirk asked.

Amicus shrugged. "No one knows—but then no one knows what happened to Tesh, either."

"My mother and her friends said that Tesh went with the party that descended into the underworld, but he didn't come back. That was the story they told us anyway. With them, you never knew what to believe, but . . ." He reached out and touched the dwarf-forged blade. "This *is* real."

Amicus nodded. "So there you have it. My family believed in magic, and my father went so far as to tattoo me with the markings from the swords as a precaution. He said all of the old Teshlors wore these runes, the ones Tesh taught, the soldiers who won the Battle of the Harwood. Without them, they would have died horrible deaths. My father used to say, 'The Tesh can protect you from anything except magic and love. The runes take care of the magic, but nothing works against love.' What can I say? I come from a strange but romantic family."

"Not that strange," Nolyn replied and opened his tunic down the front to reveal a tattoo of runes across his chest.

Everyone stared, none more surprised than Amicus. Everett got up and crossed to the other side of the fire to look at the faded ink markings.

"I suppose you can see now why I was curious," Nolyn said.

"Where'd you get yours?"

"My father."

Amicus raised his brows in surprise.

"It's not like he did it himself."

"But he must have done it to protect you."

Nolyn stared at Amicus, bewildered. Such a thought had never occurred to him.

After his mother died, the day before he was ordered north with the First Legion to kick off the start of the Grenmorian War, his father had ordered him marked. Nolyn wasn't keen on the idea and had refused. His resistance was ignored. He had been stripped, tied to a table, and forced to suffer hours of pain. Forever afterward, he would bear that shameful mark. A ring of tattoos he always associated with the death of his mother and the cruelty of a father who had shown his compassion for a mourning son by torturing him. The next day his father hurled him into peril without so much as a handshake or a farewell slap on the back. Nolyn hadn't known why his father ordered the markings—didn't know what purpose they served. He guessed it was a form of slander, some kind of insult. Criminals were branded not merely as a warning to others but as punishment for their crimes. Nolyn had hidden the tattoo, embarrassed by what it might mean. Never once had he suspected it had been meant to protect him.

But thinking back, there were times . . .

Giants had no magic, but nearly thirty years after the end of the Grenmorian War, Nolyn was sent to fight in the Goblin Wars. During a battle with the Durat Ran ghazel in the caves of the mountains of the Fendal Durat, he and twenty others had encountered a hive of the goblins. That was typical; that they had three oberdaza with them wasn't. Ghazel witch doctors were so rarely encountered that few of the soldiers knew what they were. In an instant, Nolyn's entire squadron was dead. A strange blue fire had burned them, as well as a good number of the goblin warriors, to charred husks. Nolyn survived. He never even felt the heat. Alone in that dark chamber beneath the mountains, Nolyn killed the trio of goblin witches who glared at him in shock, terror, and disbelief. He never knew how he'd managed to survive. He suspected it had something to do with his Fhrey blood, as all the others had been human. His commander told him not to question it, saying sometimes the gods are fickle. He had accepted that explanation, until now.

"Maybe your father doesn't want you as dead as you think he does," Amicus suggested. "These tattoos might be the reason we're still alive. Remember what Lynch said? 'He could burst you like a bladder of blood.'" Amicus made a show of snapping his fingers. "And I thought the emperor hated magic."

"He does." Nolyn frowned as he faced the possibility of being wrong about long-held beliefs. "He outlawed use of the Art across the entire empyre."

"So if it wasn't your father who tried to kill you in the Erbon, who then? I suppose it might not even be a *person*," Amicus said.

Nolyn agreed, "We could be facing a demon, a god, or an old-world spirit like Wogan or Bab. Might even be a crimbal, a tabor, or welo. Well, no, I guess it couldn't be a welo."

"You're a veritable wealth of curiosities, aren't you?" Smirch said. "Anyone ever heard of any of those things?"

Everett nodded. "Crimbals. They're mischievous little creatures, but dangerous, too. My grandmama talked about how she saw them at night—said they looked like little lights bobbing in the field near the forest."

Nolyn shook his head. "Those are leshies. Totally different things." They all stared at him in fascination. "Sorry, I spent my youth in the Mystic Wood. Suri had a thing about forest spirits, talked about them all the time. All I'm saying is that we have no idea what we are dealing with, except . . ."

"Yes?" Amicus said.

"Well, right before the legate exploded, Lynch used the word *he*. 'You're dealing with real power. *He* can destroy you with a snap of his fingers.' Maybe I'm reaching, but I just don't think Lynch would have been so casual if it was a god, nor would anyone refer to a woodland spirit as a *he*. That would point more toward an Artist—a practitioner of magic."

"Whoa. Wait a minute. Did you say Legate Lynch *exploded*?" Riley asked.

"Yeah, I was wondering about that bit myself," Jerel added.

"You said the legate was dead." Smirch scrubbed his stubble. "Didn't say nothing about him exploding."

"Did you actually see it happen?" Mirk asked, his face wrenched in a grimace.

"No," Nolyn said. "Demetrius took off, and we were going after him. But we heard it. Sounded sort of like a pop and a splatter."

"More of a gush, really," Amicus added.

Nolyn shook his head. "No, it was definitely more of a—oh, I know. It sounded just like pulling the cork on a jug of good beer. You know what I mean, don't you? There's that hollow *thug!* Followed by the froth and . . ." Nolyn noticed the expressions of horror on those around the fire. "So, no, we didn't see it, but the noise made us stop."

"We went back in, and Lynch was—all over the place," Amicus explained.

Mirk stood up and started to leave.

"Where you going, Arrow Mouth?" Smirch asked.

"To talk to the sailors," Mirk said. "They're bound to have ink and needles." He stopped and looked back at Amicus. "If they do, would you let me borrow one of those iron swords? The ones with the runes?"

"No problem," Amicus replied. "So long as you return it. Fail, and your first lesson in the Tesh will be extremely short."

The Calynian nodded. "Thanks." Mirk trotted off down the beach.

Riley, Myth, Smirch, Jerel, and Everett exchanged looks; then, as if on cue, they all stood up and followed after Mirk.

CHAPTER TWELVE

Crossroads

Sephryn placed her jug in the fountain. She pushed it below the surface of the circular pool and listened to the gurgle as it filled. She had found the hydria, the one with the broken handle and chipped foot, under the stairs. There had been two, but she couldn't carry both and wasn't relishing the idea of wrestling even the one jug back home. Water was a heavy thing.

"How is Mica?" Adella asked.

The woman was coming Sephryn's way with her own pair of clay pots suspended from a pole. Sephryn frowned in jealousy—she couldn't find her pole. Mica had always fetched their water, and Sephryn had no idea where Nurgya's nursemaid had stashed the carrying stick. Not under the steps, that was certain. She was lucky to find the jugs. Why the pole wasn't with the jugs was—

"I haven't seen her in days. Is she very ill?" Adella, the new young wife of the builder Johefus, wore a worried face that seemed forced and overacted. She put next to no effort into trying to appear sincere.

Mica had never been the friendly sort. The old woman had been quiet, reserved, and more than a little abrasive to everyone. Adella wasn't inquiring out of concern but from curiosity—the same nosiness that fostered scandals even when there wasn't one. Someone from every household in the square came daily to the fountain for water, which made it also a notorious font for gossip. Sephryn couldn't afford chitchat, didn't know how the Voice would respond to rumors leaking, and there had already been some.

Six days had passed since Mica last drew water, and Sephryn suspected that speculation had been running rampant. Routine reigned with these people, who spent each day like the one before. When habits were disturbed, they wanted to know why. They salivated over the change in schedule, and when the reason was mundane, they invented spicier accounts to satisfy their hunger for something different, something new, something exciting. Sephryn had avoided unwanted questions by gathering water at night. But it was only a matter of time before a nosy neighbor came to her door, and she couldn't have that.

"Nadia told me Mica was knocking at death's door. Is that true?"

"Nadia is extremely wise," Sephryn replied, failing to add that Mica had knocked—and the door had opened so violently that not even a body was left.

That part continued to bother Sephryn. Poor Mica had had no funeral, no burial. If any parts of her had remained, Sephryn never saw them. Thinking about it made her sick, and she loved Seymour for helping her clean up such a gruesome mess. The man was a gift. If she had come home alone that night, she didn't know what she would have done.

"Is it that bad?" Adella asked, shocked to discover her fishing line had caught something.

"I'd rather not talk about it right now. I hope you don't mind." Sephryn was being truthful, and that recognition registered on Adella's face, which shifted from curiosity to shame. Adella wasn't a bad sort; none of those she shared the fountain with was more than occasionally rude. They were only bored with the repetition of life. They all sought change and excitement. Never did they give much thought to what gave birth to those things, or how blessed they were to be bored.

"Of course. I'm sorry. Forgive me," Adella verbally retreated.

Sephryn nodded and lifted her jug.

"Is there anything I can do?"

"No," Sephryn replied. "Not yet," she conceded, then sighed. "Right now, all we can do is wait, hope, and pray."

"Of course," Adella said. "Of course."

Sephryn carried the water back to her house. The place was empty and felt hollow. The sun was going down, but Seymour Destone still wasn't back, which wasn't unusual. Every day she escorted him to the Imperial Hall of Records and left him to dig through the stacks, and each night he invariably missed the turn at Ebonydale. She went to the effort of tying a white cloth to a stick and propping it up at the corner for him to see where to make the turn. That experiment had ended in utter disaster when someone took the pole down and Seymour had gotten lost in the city, wandering from the docks to the West End, searching for the white flag. He hadn't made it home until nearly dawn.

She never had any hope of him finding anything. Sephryn had seen the records hall. The place was a mess—more garbage dump than anything else. The thought of him learning about the horn was beyond wishful thinking. She'd sent him there to keep him busy—to keep him safe. Few knew there was such a thing as a palace archive. Appearing like an overbuilt garden shed, the little stone building in the back of the courtyard was ignored by almost everyone. Few people knew its purpose, or what might be inside. No one ever went into the archives, so there was little chance Seymour Destone would accidentally say anything that might get him killed. Her own death she could accept—his was something else entirely. She more than cherished his support—Sephryn needed it. Fearful of endangering anyone, she had deftly avoided friends and associates; those who knew her well, and sensed her suffering, might get her to confess. Even with Seymour, the isolation was horrible.

Without him, Sephryn doubted she could have managed. The idea of facing her torture alone, unable to speak to anyone about it for so long, was impossible to imagine, and yet, she hadn't lost sight of the fact that Seymour's life was endangered because of her.

If in a moment of weakness I hadn't stupidly thought he was Bran, if I hadn't chased after and stopped him in the street, he'd be safe. He'd be shivering under a bridge somewhere, but he'd be okay.

Seymour was but one more life she felt responsible for, another person to save. In the past, she'd done well in that regard. During the famine of the year Two Hundred and Forty-Two, she'd saved the West End by defying imperial restrictions and organizing midnight raids on supplies destined for the wealthy who had more than they needed. In the year Six Hundred and Eighty-One, she had orchestrated the rescue of the aptly named *Lost Horizon*'s crew that wrecked on the shoals of Imperial Bay, and in Seven Thirteen, she'd famously saved the Farington Five — the handful of men wrongly sentenced to death for a crime they didn't commit. These were but highlights, bright points in the night sky of her life that was filled with lesser stars. Lately, her failures had outweighed her successes. Sephryn felt she was riding a wave of bad luck, the shore wasn't getting any closer.

"Sephryn!" Arvis screamed as she beat on the door.

What now? What new problem is knocking?

Sephryn jerked the door open and found the woman leaning on the frame with both hands, breathing hard.

"Arvis, what's wrong?"

"Your friend is hurt!"

"My friend?"

Arvis nodded, struggling to breathe, her makeshift attire soaked with sweat. "The funny-looking guy that's staying with you. The one with the weird bald spot. I think he's dead."

Sephryn felt as if she'd been kicked in the stomach. "Where?" she managed to ask.

"Corner of Grand Mar and Ebonydale."

Sephryn ran out without her shawl. Luckily, she still had her shoes on.

§

"What happened?" Sephryn asked as she ran down Ishim's Way, bracing herself for the expected reply: *There's no sense running. The man is dead. I saw him explode. Blood everywhere. He was talking to someone—a city guard I think—and then he just burst.*

Sephryn was already castigating herself. Without evidence, before even hearing details of the crime, she found herself guilty.

"Stabbed," Arvis replied, struggling to keep up. The woman had obviously run all the way to Sephryn's house, and the race back was a bit more than she could handle.

"Stabbed?" That surprised Sephryn, but then she remembered the ladles and poker.

"Two men. They were robbing him."

"What? Robbing?" It made no sense. "Are you sure? Seymour doesn't have any money."

"And he told them that—I heard him. They said they would take what he had. Some crumbled parchments, I think, only he refused. That's when they stabbed him. He fell, and I came to get you."

Stabbed—by thieves? Sephryn ran faster.

The trip to Ebonydale was only a few blocks, but the sun was already behind the buildings by the time they arrived. Sephryn stopped at the corner where the little street crossed the huge boulevard. She expected a crowd, maybe a wagon brought for the body. The city was quick about such things. Looking around, she saw nothing amiss.

"Where is he?" Sephryn asked.

Arvis raised her hand to point then hesitated, confusion filled her face. She searched the intersection and across the street, then she stared down at her own feet.

"Arvis?"

"I don't know. He was right over there." She pointed at the opposing corner, where a mercer was taking in dress dummies and locking up his shop for the night.

Sephryn waited for a big milk wagon to roll by, then crossed the Grand Mar to the site of the murder. A pair of workmen walked by and offered them pleasant smiles. These were followed by a mother and her two daughters.

"His body was right here," Arvis said. "At least I think it was."

"You think? You *think?*"

Arvis was back to doing that thing with her tongue, her eyes shifting left and right once more. Sephryn wanted to grab and shake her. For days, Sephryn had been on edge. Waiting wasn't something she had a talent for, and she had no idea if Arvis's was having one of her *episodes* or if Seymour really was hurt . . . or dead.

"Excuse me?" Sephryn spoke to the mercer, who was throwing the final bolt across his business's door. "Did you see anything happen here a few minutes ago? A crime?"

The portly but well-dressed man thought only a moment, then nodded. "There was a commotion. I didn't see it, but I heard some loud voices and a cry."

"And you didn't look?"

"Of course I did." The mercer frowned, insulted.

"What did you see?"

"There was a fellow on the ground—poorly dressed, very poorly dressed."

"Did you help him?"

"Didn't need any help. Looked like he just stumbled."

"Are you sure?" Sephryn looked at Arvis and then the mercer.

"Oh, there he is," the man said as he pointed. "You can ask him yourself."

Sephryn turned and saw the little monk coming around the corner not three doors down. "Seymour?" She rushed over. "Are you all right?"

The monk looked a tad bewildered for a moment, then smiled. "I'm fine."

"I was told you were robbed."

Seymour looked at Arvis, who stared back at him as if she were looking at a ghost. "Oh, ah, yes. Actually, I was. Right on the corner here. But fortunately for me, I had nothing of value."

"But you were stabbed!" Arvis shouted.

Sephryn laid a hand on the woman to calm her.

"Oh, well . . . they tried, but I'm skinnier than these robes suggest. I dodged, stumbled, and fell. Hit my head, I think." He rubbed it with his hand. "I guess they ran off."

Sephryn threw her arms around the monk and hugged him. "Oh, thank Mari. I thought . . . I thought . . . oh, never mind what I thought. Can we go home?"

"Ah . . . of course." The monk hesitated and looked around.

"You don't know the way, do you?" Arvis asked.

Seymour didn't answer.

"He never does," Sephryn said to Arvis. "This is the Ebonydale corner. He gets lost here every night."

"Sephryn, I —" Arvis said.

"You scared a century off my life, Arvis. Don't do that again."

Sephryn led the way back across the Grand Marchway. When they reached the door to her home, Seymour went in, and that's when Arvis grabbed Sephryn by the arm and drew her aside. Arvis whispered, "I saw him die."

The walk back had allowed Sephryn to gather her wits again. Being so grateful that Seymour was all right, she could afford to extend some patience to Arvis. "It's okay. I'm sure it looked that way. I'm sorry I was cross with you. It's just that you scared me so. Thank you for coming. If he really had been hurt, doing so might have saved his life."

Arvis looked warily at the open door. As she did, tears filled her eyes.

"What's wrong?"

"I'm getting worse," Arvis replied. "And I think I'm going to die soon. Death is all around me. He even came to visit a few nights ago."

"Who?"

"Death. He was very nice. Really polite. I thought he was coming to take me—"

"You're not going to die, Arvis. Are you hungry? Here." Sephryn gave her a pith. "Get some food—and pay for it this time. Good night."

Arvis looked at the coin in her hand and nodded.

Inside, Seymour stood before the fireplace. Normally the first thing he did was start a fire, but now he merely stood there, waiting for her. "What?" she asked, closing the door.

Seymour said nothing.

"Did . . . did you find something?" Sephryn asked.

The monk grinned, and Sephryn's eyes grew wide.

"I—" he began.

Sephryn waved her hands frantically, then put a finger to her mouth, commanding him to be silent. She followed that by pointing at her head and made a talking action with her hand, all while glaring at him.

Ever since their first conversation about the records office, neither had spoken directly of the matter. All that had been said on the subject was, *"Did you find anything?"* and *"No."* Sephryn just assumed that if Seymour did learn something important, he would find a way to tell her without actually saying it out loud. Clearly, any agreement had only been from her perspective. Any secret communication was impossible, as the Voice appeared to be capable of both hearing and seeing them—at least it had seemed that way when the Voice had threatened Errol. Sephryn felt like she was living with a sleeping monster, and as long as they were quiet, the Voice might not pay attention. Maybe it would only *look* if it heard something. At least she hoped so.

Seymour narrowed his eyes for a moment, then nodded. He turned then and knelt down before the hearth. Sephryn assumed he was resuming his old routine of making a fire, but he pulled out a burnt remnant of a stick and drew symbols on the floor.

She watched, suspecting he was trying to communicate through writing, which she thought might actually work—assuming that the Voice couldn't read—but what Seymour drew were strange symbols that Sephryn thought she'd seen before, though she couldn't recall where. He drew the markings in a circle around them, and when he'd finished, he looked up at her.

"There," he said. "We're safe now. No one can eavesdrop, unless they are literally outside with their ear pressed to the door."

Sephryn knitted her brows and mouthed the word, *What?*

"Here." Seymour reached into a fold of his robe and pulled out a parchment. On it were the same markings as he'd just drawn. "I found this."

"I've seen these," she said. Then she remembered. "They are on the palace walls! The ones Nyphron put up after Suri . . ." Sephryn looked at the circle on the floor. "By Mari! These are the Orinfar runes, aren't they?" she said much too loudly and then self-consciously covered her mouth.

Seymour nodded. "The ones mentioned in *The Book of Brin.* They were used in the Great War to block magic."

"But how can you be sure they really work? How do you know the Voice is even using magic?"

"What else could it be?"

"Really?" She stared incredulously. "You're willing to risk your life on *what else could it be?* What if it's a god or a demon speaking to me? Do you think markings can stop that?"

Seymour started to speak then held back. After a moment he muttered, "I just thought . . . I guess I was just . . ."

The walls! The thought hit her so hard that her hands returned to her mouth. "That's why! Oh, Seymour, you're a genius!"

"I am?"

"The Voice couldn't hear me when I was inside the palace. I tried speaking to it after discovering the horn was locked up, but it couldn't hear me. The instant I stepped outside the walls, it could. You're right. The symbols block the Voice. That also explains why the Voice doesn't just explode everyone in the palace and take the horn himself. So we *can* talk." A worried look crossed her face. "If you drew them right."

She looked at the parchment and compared each symbol with the ones on the floor. They were a perfect match. "Excellent job. How did you . . . oh never mind. I forgot, you spent every day doing exactly this kind of thing, didn't you?"

Seymour smiled.

Sephryn smiled as well. They finally had a tool against the Voice. Her mind lit up with a host of new options. "I could talk to the First Minister and ask to speak to the emperor. I might even be able to find Illim again, but what if they don't believe me? I wish I could go directly to Nyphron. I could tell him that his—" She stopped herself.

"His what?" Seymour asked.

Sephryn sighed. Of all the people in the world, she never would have guessed that someone who had been a stranger a week ago would be the first person she would tell. "Prince Nolyn is Nurgya's father."

"Oh, I see."

"You are the only one who knows this, and I'd appreciate you keeping it to yourself. I want Nolyn to hear it from me."

"You haven't told the prince?"

She shook her head. "Sometimes, he gets a leave from his post in Maranonia. The last time we were together, we had a terrible fight, and I haven't seen him since. That was more than a year ago. The two of us . . . our relationship—well, it was more than just a fight. We didn't separate on good terms. Anyway, if I could get to Nyphron, I could tell him that his grandson has been kidnapped and . . ." She frowned and shook her head. "I haven't been able to get an audience with him in centuries of trying. What are the chances he'll give me one now?"

The game she was playing was for the life of her child. One wrong move and Nurgya was dead. If she went through proper channels, the imperial administration would assume she was once more trying to speak to the emperor about changing laws and he would ignore her. Furthermore, should she try and fail, word might get around about what she was doing, and the Voice would know. Besides, even if she reached the emperor, when she got to the part about a voice that only she could hear who was demanding a horn, it would make her sound just a bit too much like Arvis.

She ticked through a list of everyone she could think of — anyone who could help. She had connections with a few influential citizens — none that regularly dined with Nyphron, though, and painfully few who would believe her. Her father might, but he was so far away, and what could he do? If Suri were alive, Sephryn would have gone to her, but there were no more Artists in the world.

Except the one who talks to me.

The new tool Seymour had found wasn't the solution to their troubles, but it did allow them to talk. For the time being, that was all it did. "I can't bring my case to the emperor; we'll have to continue as planned. You'll need to go back tomorrow and see if you can find anything about the Horn of Gylindora."

"What do you want to know?"

Sephryn smiled at him. "Are you saying you found something? What is it?"

"A holy relic of the Fhrey, a tool they use to determine who rules."

"How is that done with a horn?"

"By blowing the Horn of Gylindora, one of Fhrey blood may challenge for leadership of the Fhrey people."

"That explains a lot. Now we know the Voice plans on challenging Nyphron."

Seymour shook his head. "He can't. The horn can only be blown once every three thousand years, or after the death of the present ruler, a time period known as the Uli Vermar."

"It hasn't even been nine hundred years since Nyphron's reign started."

Seymour nodded. "Apparently, that's how the Great War ended. The two sides were locked in a stalemate. The ruler of the Fhrey died, and a fellow named Mawyndulë—he was the Fhrey ruler's son—blew the horn. Then Nyphron blew it, challenging the prince for control. They fought and Nyphron won."

"So you're saying that this horn can't actually do anything for another two thousand years?"

Seymour again nodded.

"Well, that doesn't sound so bad."

The Voice, as omnipotent as he might be, wasn't all-powerful. There was a time when she thought the source of the Voice might actually be Uberlin, or at least a demon. Now she realized she was dealing with an Artist, someone like Suri. Although that was certainly less terrifying than a god, it wasn't all good news. Suri had been frighteningly powerful. Everyone Sephryn knew treated the mystic as if she were the closest thing to an all-powerful being that still breathed air. Even the emperor of the known world had feared her. The area around Suri's home—the place that became known as the Mystic Wood—was left alone. Nyphron never made any attempt to enter or control it. Even after Suri died, it remained a shrine of sorts.

The idea that Sephryn was dealing with an Artist wasn't much of a relief, but it was something. If nothing else, it meant she was dealing with a mortal being, and that meant he could be fought.

Sephryn looked at the monk squarely. "Seymour?"

"Yes?"

"You should draw these on yourself," she said, indicating the parchment. "If you mark them on your skin like a tattoo, you'll be safe. The Voice won't be able to hurt you."

Seymour looked at the parchment of runes. "Is that what you're going to do?"

"I can't," she said. "We have to keep to the plan and do what the Voice says, and if I use them, he won't be able to speak to me. The moment the Voice can't reach me, he might think I'm dead or up to something. Either way, I'm certain he would kill Nurgya. Now that I think about it . . ." She looked down at the symbols on the floor. "Just being in here for too long is dangerous. Seymour, just do it, put the markings on yourself, then you'll be able to leave and be free of all this."

"Is that what you want? You want me to leave?" He sounded hurt.

"I want you to be safe. At least one of us ought to live through this."

The monk shook his head. "If I disappear, the Voice will be suspicious."

Sephryn considered his words. "But it's not your problem. Nurgya isn't your son."

"But it *is* my *choice.*" With that, he began wiping the charcoal off the floor.

CHAPTER THIRTEEN

Vernes

The crew of the imperial warship *Stryker* cheered when they rounded the point and spotted the jagged peak of Mount Dome. Legend held that the coastal mountain had once been the birthplace of the dwarfs and the roof to the ancient and wondrous city of Neith. Supposedly, the mountain had once been twice as high, but it had been crushed—some might say *dwarfed*—by the mystic Suri, as told through the famous Gronbach story. No one on that ship cared a fish's fin about any of that. What delighted the sailors, oarsmen, and soldiers was that the mountain's appearance meant the port of Vernes was less than two hours away. They would dock by nightfall, their voyage a success, and an evening ashore awaited all.

Nolyn was on deck with the other members of the Seventh Sik-Aux. Each of them was busy tying up whatever gear they had, looking for lost sandals, or hunting for sharpening stones that had been misplaced or loaned out. Nolyn remained amazed at how sea voyages always resulted in missing things. Settling in for long trips was an invitation for scattered items with little hope of finding them again.

"If anyone asks, what do we say we're doing?" Riley threw the question out to the group, most down on their knees struggling with packs.

"What do you mean?" Smirch asked, his head mostly submerged in his cloak bag.

Riley pointed to the boar symbol on his helm. "Just thinking it might not be too smart to admit we're deserters from the Seventh Legion."

"And you decided to wait until now to bring this up?" Jerel asked.

"I didn't know where we were going until this morning," Riley said. "Still don't, actually. Care to fill us in, sir?" He looked at Nolyn, then they all did.

"Well . . ." their commander hesitated, "I've been thinking about the situation, and I'm not certain my father tried to kill us. In fact, the evidence is leaning away from that theory."

"So who did?" Amicus asked.

"I don't know; that's the problem. My life in the salt mine has been pretty quiet over the centuries. As far as I know, I don't have any enemies — certainly none still alive. I mean, I've traveled to other installations because I'm the pre-eminent expert in large-scale mineral excavation. You learn a lot after five hundred years. But there haven't been any trips in the last ten years or so. The only other place I've gone is my furloughs to Percepliquis, but I've not been there for more than a year. So I have to wonder, who have I offended enough that they would want to kill me? I can't think of anyone, let alone someone with enough clout to get me reassigned to the front lines. Lynch was killed before we could find out anything from him. I only suspected Nyphron because he has motive and opportunity."

"What motive?" Amicus asked.

"I thought he was worried about me challenging him for the throne, but that begs the question: Why now? Why not get rid of me after my mother died? So, I started thinking maybe it's someone with a grudge against the empyre. Perhaps an Erivan Artist, a Miralyith, is seeking revenge for losing the war and thought he'd start with Nyphron's son.

Or maybe I have made an enemy that I just don't know about. But the fact still remains that all of us are deserters, and it's possible that at some point Amicus and I are going to be charged with Lynch's death. So I thought we should head inland, strip off these uniforms, shake hands, go our separate ways, and find new lives."

"Not likely, sir," Jerel said.

"No?" Nolyn sighed. "What do you think we ought to do, Jerel?"

"Not a clue, sir. But I know trying to disappear won't happen."

"Because the One said I would be emperor?"

"Absolutely." The man looked as confident as ever. Nolyn hadn't noticed it before, but now he saw what the others had. *His unshakable faith is kind of annoying.*

"Well," Nolyn said, "I suppose we'll have to agree to disagree."

"Taking off the uniforms won't work," Amicus said. "The captain knows who we are. He'll report that you took command of his vessel. And if Lynch's body has been found—"

"I'm not worried about that. Not yet, at least." Nolyn said. "Urlineus doesn't have a rookery yet, does it?"

The others shook their heads.

"Didn't think so. So it's unlikely that news of Lynch's death traveled faster then this ship. The Erbon Forest is filled with ghazel, so no messenger would be sent along that route. We should have plenty of time to disappear. Odds of finding a handful of men who scatter to the far ends of the empyre are slim. But I would strongly suggest that none of us remains in Vernes for too long."

The sun was low as the *Stryker* approached the Vernes wharf.

All the piers had wrapped leather pilings, which protected the ship and the dock. Between them, cleats provided sailors with anchor points to secure their vessels. Those designated with the task waited, poised on the port side and ready to jump as the captain slowly piloted the bireme's approach.

On the pier they were aiming for, a crowd was gathering. More than a hundred people were already jammed on the long jetty. Enraged shouts and raised fists suggested a less-than-welcoming reception. Usually when ships anchored, there was a joyous reunion of loved ones, but the group gathered seemed more like an angry mob.

The *Stryker*'s captain cast repeated and worried looks at Nolyn.

"What do you think is going on?" Nolyn asked the rest.

Riley shook his head. "No idea. But they're civilians, so this has nothing to do with us."

"Maybe they're here for a different ship that is due to come in." Nolyn looked across the deck and out to sea. The ocean was naked of mast or sail.

"Seem pretty intent on this one," Amicus said. "They're all looking at us."

Jerel stepped to the rail and peered down. "Soldiers are coming, twenty or so. City garrison, I think."

A score of men in uniforms and helms pushed and shoved their way through the crowd to the end of the pier. "Back, all of you!" the leader shouted angrily as he struggled to get through.

Jerel reported, "Swords are drawn."

Nolyn threw up his hands. "I honestly would have bet good money that news about Lynch hadn't beaten us here."

Amicus agreed, "I figured he'd lie in that office for days before someone noticed the smell."

"Good point," Nolyn added. "This has to be related to something else."

"But what?" Amicus asked.

"No idea." He looked at Jerel who had a self-satisfied grin. "But I'm guessing we're going to find out."

Nolyn nodded at the captain, who spun the wheel, and called, "Oars up!"

Once the boat slipped into place and the gangplank was dropped, five soldiers charged onto the deck. Blue tunics beneath their light armor verified that they were, indeed, city guards. The blue brush on the foremost one's helmet identified the urban prefect. The officer came directly toward Nolyn, who didn't move. Amicus, Riley, and Jerel, however, stepped forward.

"Forgive me, sir." The prefect slapped his chest in salute. "I am Urban Prefect Tolly, and as you can see, we have a bit of a situation." He scanned the deck. "Are there more below?"

"More what?" Nolyn asked.

"Legionnaires."

"No, just the eight of us."

"Oh." Tolly appeared decidedly disappointed. "Well, I have to applaud your speed, but—so few men, sir. I had hoped for at least half a cohort."

He then spotted the boar insignia on their armor. "Seventh Sikaria . . ." His eyes widened. *"Auxiliary?"* he added, with an impressed tone before straightening up. "That explains it. I do hope your reputation is warranted."

"Leave us alone!" the crowd shouted from below. "We don't need you here!"

"What's going on?" Nolyn asked.

"Didn't they give you a dispatch before you set sail?"

He thinks we were sent here, Nolyn realized. Figuring it would be best to play along he said, "No, there wasn't time. Why don't you fill us in."

"Of course, sir. News has recently arrived that Rhulynia is to have a new governor, an *Instarya* by the name of Advaryn Wyn. Being affluent and on the far side of the Bern and Urum rivers, Vernes has developed an unhealthy desire for more independence. Each year we've had protests and revolts, but they are attracting more attention as of late. That's why the new provincial governor has been appointed—to *correct* the situation. Seeing your warship, the mob mistook your arrival for Advaryn Wyn's."

"So you requested reinforcements?"

Tolly nodded. "Yes, sir. The Second Legion has repeatedly refused to involve itself in the city's unrest. Which makes me wonder why we have them stationed here at all. Keeping the peace has rested entirely on my shoulders, and I simply don't have enough men. I sent word yesterday and thought it would take at least a week for help to arrive. But I was also expecting several hundred men. I never dreamed they'd send so few, even if you are the Sik-Aux."

"How bad is it?" Nolyn asked. "The revolt?"

Tolly made an ugly face. "Worse than I've ever seen, and more widespread than usual. The people are afraid of what the new governor's orders might be, and they're doing more than just voicing their displeasure. They've resorted to taking up arms."

"Prymus? May I have a word?" Demetrius asked. Given how little the man had spoken all trip, the request was strange enough to demand Nolyn's attention.

"Excuse me, prefect," he said and moved to where the palatus stood alone on the starboard bow. "What is it, Demetrius?"

The palatus looked toward the dock. "Those people are revolting against your father's rule. They feel it is unjust because he has created a two-tiered society where humans are little more than slaves who are forced to serve the ruling Instarya elite. And it's getting worse. For this same reason, the Second Legion is slow, perhaps even unwilling, to lend a hand in putting down this insurrection. You see, the legion as a whole has been on the verge of rebellion for years now."

"How do you know this?"

"I am—or was—the palatus to a man who was both a legate and governor. It was my task to read hundreds of dispatches and reports. And I can tell you, the empyre sits on dry tinder. Also . . ." Demetrius paused then said, "You were not wrong about your father trying to kill you."

"What do you mean?"

"I saw the dispatch that Legate Lynch received regarding your assignment. It ordered that you be sent on a mission from which you wouldn't return. And the signature was the emperor's."

Nolyn wasn't shocked at the news, just disappointed. The glimmer of hope he'd had that his father wasn't the bastard he'd long believed was snuffed out. Ever since he learned about the Orinfar tattoos, Nolyn started thinking there must be something more to Nyphron. After all, Persephone had married him for a reason. Perhaps she knew things about his father that Nolyn hadn't seen. The idea that there might be a redeemable aspect to the emperor had been a welcome change. But Demetrius had handed Nolyn the same old man he'd always known.

"Your father wants you dead because he knows he's grown weak. You are the spark that might ignite the flame to his ruin."

"And you're absolutely certain my father ordered me into that ravine?"

Demetrius shook his head. "No. Lynch made that decision, but the order did say that your death must look like a casualty of war. That was the edict."

"And why are you telling me this now?"

The palatus shrugged. "I've watched. I've listened. When you first took me prisoner, I was concerned for my life. I knew nothing about you. But you treated me fairly. The discussions with your men have been honest, and your ideas have merit. I believe that maybe Jerel DeMardefeld's god is right, and you would make a better emperor than your father. I understand what Nyphron has been seeing—that you are the real threat he faces. You can replace your father."

He expects me to start a revolution? Is it possible? A thousand thoughts ran through Nolyn's head. *No, that would take years of preparation. Wouldn't it?* Nolyn spotted the ever-confident Jerel, who insisted the one true god predicted Nolyn's rise, and he thought once again about Sephryn—the guiding star he had failed to follow.

"Prefect Tolly," Nolyn called to the officer, "go down and secure the gangway. We'll be disembarking shortly."

Tolly saluted once more, then led his men off the ship.

"What's going on?" Amicus asked when Nolyn returned to the group.

"Jerel is right. We aren't going our separate ways," Nolyn stated.

"While I'm not sure I'm going to like the answer, I'll bite anyway. Where are we going?"

"To Percepliquis. I'm going to remove my father from power and take the throne."

Ramahanaparus Mirk froze in the middle of tying a knot. Riley Glot held the drawstrings of his food pouch but failed to pull, leaving it dangling between his hands like a puppet. Everett Thatcher stopped chewing whatever he had in his mouth, and Amicus didn't move at all, except to blink several times rapidly.

Smirch was the first to find his tongue. He scratched his bristly chin, limbered up his lips, and said, "I sort of liked the whole disappearing idea."

"Why the change?" Amicus asked.

"As it turns out, it *was* my father who ordered our deaths—well, my death, really. Demetrius saw the dispatch. He's read all the correspondences from the capital, and he says Nyphron has been losing his grip on power and that there is widespread dissent within the ranks." He thought a moment. "Amicus, is it possible that the legion is no longer loyal?"

The First Spear chuckled. "Do you think the legion was *ever* steadfast? Soldiers care about the men next to them, not a ruler sitting in a palace. It's always been that way, and it always will be."

"No," Jerel said defiantly. "It doesn't *have* to be. The One knows that there is another way, a better way."

"Not now, Jerel." Amicus said and then turned back to Nolyn, "No disrespect, sir, but this seems more than a little impulsive."

"And when an unexpected opportunity arises during a battle, are you saying you don't seize it? We've stumbled into a city ripe for revolt. The flame is already lit. Sephryn has always advocated for me to stand up and fight for what is right." Nolyn took a deep breath of sea air. "That argument I had with her, the one I told you about, it wasn't just that I refused to talk to my father. We parted because she had faith that I could make a difference, and I had none. She asked me to advocate for the humans who have been marginalized by Nyphron's prejudices. She said I could be like my mother. But you have to understand, Persephone was a legend. I didn't think I could ever measure up to her. Giving in was so much easier. I let my father dictate my life, or lack thereof. The last time I was in Percepliquis, Sephryn begged me to stay, pleaded for me to defy Nyphron. But I didn't. When my leave was over and I was about to return to the mine, I told her, 'He's the emperor. I have to do what he says.' That was when I saw the light go out of her eyes. I watched her respect die. That was when I knew I had lost her. She wanted me to be a hero, to make the world a better place as Persephone had. But I just didn't believe any of that was possible."

"And now?" Amicus asked.

"I've reached the point where I'm tired of breathing air without actually living. I lost Sephryn because I refused to live up to my mother's legacy. And then there's this guy." He clapped Jerel on the shoulder. "According to him, a god has said that I *am* like my mother. I wouldn't listen to Sephryn, but should I ignore a god?"

"And the plan?" Amicus asked.

"My father rules a rotting throne that sits atop a precarious perch. Demetrius says that many in the legion are less than loyal to the emperor. The Second Legion is based near here, and I suspect they may be sympathetic to this insurrection. Why else would Tolly have to request other legionnaires? If we can harness this popular revolt and gain support of the Second, we could march west and—"

"The First Legion remains in Rhenydd," Riley pointed out. "I suspect that's why the emperor keeps them close. They might have a thing or two to say about your plans."

Nolyn smiled. "I served with the First through the Grenmorian and Goblin Wars. While no one still serving knows me, they know *of* me. If any legion is likely to join our cause, it's them."

"With the First and Second Legions, we could take Percepliquis in an afternoon," Riley said softly. "All they have is the city guard and the palace troops."

"And the Instarya," Nolyn said, pointing a finger at the Second Spear. "Don't forget them. They're tougher than you can imagine."

"Odds of getting the Second to commit treason under the command of a stranger seems more than unlikely. This whole adventure will probably end before it starts," Amicus said.

"You don't have to follow me," Nolyn told him.

"I think you misunderstand," Amicus said. "We aren't against the idea—at least I'm not. This is why we've stayed with you, why I was willing to risk my life and the rest of the squadron. I was hoping this is where you'd lead. I'm just curious to see how you're going to do it."

Nolyn smiled at him. "Me, too."

Nolyn led the way down the ramp that bounced with the harmonic rhythm of their combined strides. Crossing the gangway over the gulf to the dock, they heard the continued clamor and angry shouts of the growing crowd that, if anything, had only gotten louder.

The rest of the city guard, as ordered, had remained at the foot of the ramp in a semicircle. They held back the swell of angry people with shields and the show of naked blades.

Reaching the bottom, the Sik-Aux found themselves surrounded, with no clear way to go. The crowd was full of civilians in street clothes who were armed with an eclectic array of weapons, everything from spears and swords to sticks and rocks. One especially large man, who was front and center, held a barbarian long sword in two hands while he shouted at them, "Go back to the emperor and tell him Vernes will not tolerate Instarya rule!"

Tolly addressed Nolyn, "With your help, we'll disperse this lot, then find and execute the leaders. That will end it, always does."

"I think this time that will be harder to do," Nolyn said.

"Why's that, sir?"

"Because the emperor didn't send us. We aren't your reinforcements." Nolyn looked around. "Find me something to stand on," he told the others.

"Over there," Amicus said, pointing at a stack of crates that were being brought off the ship by a crew eager to be done with their work.

Nolyn climbed on top of one. Not satisfied, he stepped onto a stack of two. From that perch, he could see the whole of the crowd before and below. They spotted him, too.

"Do you think we have come to punish you?"

The mob began to quiet at the sound of his shout.

He waited a moment, then added, "Do you fear retribution for your insurrection?" He made a grand show of shaking his head. "The emperor didn't send me. I am not Advaryn Wyn. I am not here to be your new governor."

The crowd became even quieter.

Nolyn smiled. "To be honest, if my father knew I was here, he'd kill me."

The populace went silent, then one hand punched out above the heads of the others and pointed a finger at him. "That's Nolyn Nyphronian! That's the prince!"

A communal gasp sounded like someone had tossed a wet log on a hot fire.

"How do you know?" someone else asked.

"Came through here just recently on his way to Calynia. I was working the docks when he boarded a ship headed to Urlineus. A bunch of us saw him. The prince shook my friend's hand, he did. That's definitely him."

Prefect Tolly took a step back, his eyes huge as he studied Nolyn anew.

"I'm not here to beat you into submission," Nolyn shouted to the crowd.

"Why *did* you come?" someone asked. He was a large fellow in the front row. The tone was distrustful, violent.

"As I said, the emperor didn't send me, but he did drive me here. He drove me by his arrogance, his injustice and bigotry, and his disdain for humanity."

The murmurs that had sprung forth after hearing his identity quieted. So did the sound of movement as more people stopped to listen.

"My father has protected his brethren at the expense of the people. For too long, the empyre of mankind has been dominated by a handful of Instarya Fhrey. Our cities and towns were built by humans. Our commerce, our roads, our ships, all built by men. Our legions charged with protecting all of it"—he gestured at Amicus and Jerel—"consist entirely of humans, but we are not governed by men. We receive our marching orders from the likes of Nyphron and his brotherhood of *elves.*" At the sound of the word, the crowd gasped anew.

Nolyn continued, "Nowhere in the empyre is a man equal to a Fhrey. The laws work only for them. Kill a Fhrey, and you *and* your family will be executed. But if a Fhrey kills a man? Is the murderer hanged? Is he even imprisoned?"

Several in the crowd were shouting "No!"

"Of course not," Nolyn said. "One doesn't punish a person for killing an animal. And trust me, that's what the emperor considers humans to be."

"But you're his son!" someone shouted. "You're . . ." The next word was swallowed.

"I am *the bridge,*" Nolyn declared. "My mother human, my father Fhrey—I have a foot in both worlds, which grants me judicial neutrality. I alone can be a fair judge, and I tell you now—my father is an ass. He has treated you poorly, subjected you to a two-tiered system.

"For centuries, I have served in the legion." He slapped the chest of his uniform. "I have fought in every war, served side by side with good men, and I have seen firsthand the rewards they receive: humiliation and disregard. Our capital was named after my mother, and I can tell you, she never intended it to be this way. She believed in a world where everyone, Fhrey and human, lived under fair and consistent laws. But Persephone died eight centuries ago, and my father still lives. The world has changed, but the emperor has not. I believe it's time to fix that problem, and *that*, is why I'm here."

"You speak treason," Tolly accused.

Nolyn considered that a moment, then nodded. "Alas, not very well. It's a second language, but I'm learning. We all must do likewise if we want to make this world a better place for our children."

Tolly stepped backward. "You—you would challenge the might of the greatest power the world has ever known?"

Nolyn shrugged. "Why not? My father did, and now he gets to have blueberry tarts every morning." Nolyn had no idea what his father ate for breakfast, but figured no one else did, either. In a loud, calm voice, he addressed the crowd. "A house with a poorly laid foundation will fall—must fall. In its place, a new structure will rise, one that provides shelter to all, not just a few."

"Are you here to join us?" It was the big fellow in the front row again. He'd lowered the long sword but had his lower lip pushed out and a sneer pulling up one end. Nolyn guessed he was either their leader, or at least he wanted to be seen that way.

Nolyn shook his head. "No, not join. But I will lead you." He pointed to the *Stryker*. "You saw this imperial warship as a symbol of tyranny, and you came here as defiant protesters, angry and disorganized. But this ship heralds your passage to a better life. I'm about to make you into true revolutionaries capable of challenging the palace and changing the world."

"The city rabble is one thing, sir," Amicus said. "The Second Legion will be quite another."

They had moved up the street into the Sea Serpent, a public house popular among sailors and legionnaires. The no-frills establishment was little more than a big open room punctuated by thick posts that held up the roof and a simple counter of shipping crates overlaid by decking planks. There were no chairs or tables, nothing that could be busted in a fight.

The remnants of the Seventh Sik-Aux all held wooden cups of beer drawn from the big barrel behind the counter. They sipped slowly. Demetrius declined a drink but stood with them, silent and watchful.

Nolyn nodded. "There are worse places, don't you think?"

"You're crazy. You know that, right?" Amicus said.

"Maybe." Nolyn smiled bitterly. "I'm not sure if I get that from my father or my mother, but I'm certain it runs in the family."

"Do we have a plan?" Riley asked.

Nolyn shook his head. "Tolly will report to the Second's commander that renegade legionnaires are causing trouble near the docks, and that will bring a response of some kind. But beyond that, no. You'd be surprised to discover the officer's handbook doesn't cover starting a rebellion."

"If it did," Myth said, "I don't think it would be smart to follow it."

"The good news is," Nolyn said, swirling his cup, "I don't think there's anything in the handbook detailing how to stop the emperor's son from starting a rebellion, either."

"This handbook sounds downright useless," Smirch said. He leaned one shoulder against the wooden pillar they gathered around, which sported a series of old scars from what had to be sword blades.

"Smirch," Riley said, "you do realize there *is* no such thing as an officer's handbook, right?"

Smirch scowled. "How would I know? I'm not an officer, and I can't read." He grinned as if both were points of pride, then took a sip of beer. "Hope the Second Legion comes soon. This is good stuff. I'd like to get to some serious drinking. Maybe even look around town for a woman. Bet they have some pretty ones here."

"After so many years spent in the Erbon," Myth said, "you'll probably be disappointed not to find a tail to hang on to."

That made each of them laugh except Smirch, who made a halfhearted frown as if he didn't quite understand the joke.

The door to the Sea Serpent opened, and a group of armored men poured into the big room: red tunics, heavy armor—regular legion. They fanned out in proper military formation, lining up to either side of the entrance. A good thirty men were inside when a prymus of the Second Legion and a First Spear finally entered.

The prymus was tall and had that educated superiority about him that suggested he was more appointee than rank-climber. The First Spear was a brute whose uniform looked too small. The most significant thing was that he was freshly shaved. All the men were.

"Are you the group who claims to be the imperial son and his entourage?" the prymus asked.

Nolyn's party had been the only ones in the Sea Serpent for the past hour. Even the owner had fled. Still, Nolyn made a show of looking around. Then he pointed at himself and shook his head. "I'm afraid there has been a mistake. We never claimed anything of the sort."

The prymus nodded and smiled at his First Spear. "See?"

"What I said is that I was here to start a revolution against my father, and I think someone from the crowd recognized I was Nolyn Nyphronian."

The prymus's brows shot up.

The First Spear laughed.

"Arrest him!" the prymus ordered.

Before any of the soldiers moved, Amicus, Riley, Jerel, and Myth dropped their cups and drew their weapons.

"Don't be foolish," the prymus said. "You don't have a chance."

"What do you think?" Amicus asked the Second Legion's First Spear. "Do you think we have a chance?"

The man hesitated.

"I gave you an order, Sikes," the prymus demanded.

"They're wearing the Seventh Sikaria uniforms, sir," the First Spear explained. "*Auxiliary* uniforms, sir."

The prymus narrowed his eyes at Nolyn. "Steal those, did you?"

"Do they look like they don't fit?"

The prymus wasn't at all pleased with his answer. "Why would the Seventh Sik-Aux turn traitor?"

"Didn't, really," Nolyn said. "My father—you know him as the emperor—tried to have me killed, along with these fine gentlemen. As you can see, he failed. It isn't that *we* have become traitors, the *emperor* has—and long before he ordered the sacrifice of the Seventh Sikaria Auxiliary just to make the murder of his only son appear like a casualty of war."

The prymus focused then on Amicus, tilting his head slightly, his mouth hanging open a crack. "I've . . . I've seen you. In Percepliquis. You're Amicus Killian."

The name had a profound effect on everyone hearing it. The ranks of men shifted; some whispered, others nudged. The First Spear, who ought to have barked at them, was himself awestruck at the man before him. "Three swords," he muttered. "There's an imperial bounty on your head."

"Care to claim it?" Amicus asked.

"Prince Nolyn offered to sacrifice himself so that we could escape an ambush set up by his father," Riley said.

Everett spoke up. His youthful sincerity coated every word with emotion. "He saved my life by giving me his horse."

"He wants to make the world a better place for humans. And being a man myself, I find it doesn't make a lot of sense to oppose such an idea. Unless of course"—Amicus took a step toward the prymus—"you're not a man."

Amicus smiled at the officer, who looked ill.

"Let me make this easier," Nolyn said. He clapped his hands, as much to draw their attention as to declare he alone hadn't drawn a blade. "Not only am I the imperial prince, but I hold the rank of prymus and have *much* more seniority than you. So, unless you have orders from my father to the contrary, and until such time as you do, you're duty-bound to follow my commands."

The prymus went from looking sick to appearing lost. He glanced back at his men, perhaps gauging their attitude.

"Ironic, isn't it?" Nolyn said. "Obey me, and you'll stand trial for treason. Disobey and you're guilty of disloyalty. Now, it's true that disloyalty isn't quite as terrible as treason, but since both carry the death penalty"—Nolyn pretended to weigh invisible objects in his hands—"it's really the same thing."

Nolyn crossed the distance between the two of them and casually laid a sympathetic hand on the officer's shoulder. "I think what you have to do is consider what it is you're willing to die for. Is it defending an emperor you've likely never seen and who tells you to risk your life fighting for an empyre that refuses to extend you the same privileges that are lavished on Nyphron's Instarya cronies? Or would you rather help the man in front of you who promises to treat you fairly because he, too, is human?"

A long pause followed.

"There's a really big barrel of excellent beer over there," Nolyn said. "Shall we have a drink and talk some more, or do you want to start killing one another?"

When the prymus still didn't respond, Nolyn took advantage of the lack of resistance to get the ball rolling in his direction. "Everett, pour the Second Legion's prymus and First Spear a drink, and fetch me one as well."

The kid came back with three cups and handed them out.

"To a brighter future," Nolyn said and raised his cup.

The prymus looked at Amicus, then Nolyn. "You're going to have to convince the First Prymus and my legate. You don't outrank them."

"Legate Farnell hates the Instarya," the First Spear said. "And he is a huge fan of the Prophet." He nodded his head at Amicus.

"I didn't say it would be difficult." The prymus looked at Nolyn. "But do you really think you can pull this off?"

"No." Nolyn shook his head, then lifted his cup again. "But I think *we* can." He drank.

The prymus did as well.

❧

Nolyn and Amicus met Legate Farnell in his tent on the heights north of the city. The legate was a career soldier. Nolyn could tell that from his uniform. He wore it in the privacy of his own tent. Not the helmet—the man wasn't crazy—but he was more comfortable in the skirt and plates than in a pallium or tunic. His manner was another indicator. He stood straight, looked them in the eye, and never smiled. If he hadn't spent years leading men in battle, he should have.

"Seventh Sikaria Auxiliary," Farnell said, studying them with dark, shadowed eyes.

"Not anymore," Nolyn replied. "There are only eight of us left, and we deserted, so I don't think we can lay claim to that title any longer."

Farnell nodded. At least Nolyn thought he did. The motion was so slight that he might have imagined it. The others in the command tent said nothing.

Not all legates worked in tents. Prohibited by imperial edict from setting up shop within the limits of any city, some commandeered farmhouses or barns. Nolyn recalled that the legate of the First Legion had once settled into a winery and called it the best headquarters ever. When tents were used, however, they all conformed to the same standards: a large square footprint with red-and-brown canvas walls held up by thick poles. Inside, floors were cushioned by overlapped carpets, and there was always a desk and multiple tables where staff officers worked. In Farnell's case, he had four others in his tent. One was clearly the First Prymus of the legion and another a scribe, who scratched on a parchment, making a sound like a mouse gnawing through wood.

A young man—a runner—dashed in with a small scroll and promptly handed it to the legate. After a hasty salute, he left. Farnell snapped the seal, looked the parchment over, then re-rolled it into a cylinder.

"And you are Amicus Killian." Farnell pointed at him with the end of the scroll.

"Yes, sir." Amicus and Nolyn stood shoulder to shoulder just inside the big tent, holding themselves at attention in front of the big table covered in maps.

"Is that where you've been all this time?" the First Prymus of the Second Legion asked. He'd been introduced as Jareb Tanator, and he stepped forward to receive the scroll from Farnell, which he glanced at and then added it to the pile on the desk that was as covered with scrolls as the table was with maps.

"I joined the legion two days after the fight with Abryll Orphe," Amicus replied.

"You ran away from the emperor?" Jareb asked.

Nolyn didn't detect an insult. Tanator's tone wasn't snide. If anything, it lacked all emotion. Both the legate and the First Prymus were blank walls and would have made excellent card players.

We aren't in chains—that's something, at least.

"There's no precedent for this?" Farnell said, then looked over his shoulder at the scribe working at the little table next to the big desk. His head popped up and quickly shook. "Didn't think so."

Farnell folded his arms. "Had you been anyone else, you'd already have hanged."

"Can't do that, sir," the scribe said. His voice was tinny, like a poorly pitched whistle.

"Yes, I know, Sloot. That's why I said—"

"He's the emperor's son and—"

"I just said I know that, Sloot."

"Sorry, sir."

Farnell shook his head and sighed. "As my scribe is overly eager to point out, I can't put the son of the emperor to death. It would also be *difficult* to order the execution of Amicus Killian—even though you are already under an imperial death sentence. Nor would I win a popularity contest by killing the remaining members of the famed Seventh Sik-Aux. Vernes has been caught up in rebellion fever as of late, and your timing is absolutely awful."

"Or perfect," the First Prymus said.

Farnell gave his officer a disdainful glance. "Nothing is ever perfect, but it's awkward. That declaration you made on the docks has already ripped through my legion. News of it has left the city, spreading out with every merchant trader and itinerant physician. Word will reach Percepliquis in a few days. The emperor will weigh in and instruct me on my duty, which I suspect will be to send the lot of you to the palace for—"

"Entertainment," Amicus said.

The legate looked at him and nodded. "Yes, I suspect as much."

Nolyn held out his arms. "Then why aren't I wearing manacles and chains?"

"You know as well as I do that a commander does not rule by the grace of the gods, but by the submission of his men. I control five thousand trained killers. Fear and respect are what keep my legion in line. Properly evaluating and guiding morale is all that keeps me in this tent and off a pike. Right now, morale is tenuous at best."

"Worse than that I think, sir," the scribe said while not lifting his head or his pen from his work.

"Quiet, Sloot." Farnell glanced at the First Prymus and frowned—career soldiers never smiled, but they did often frown—or what was called the *legionnaire-smile.* "Of course, Nolyn Nyphronian and Amicus Killian are not idiots—are you? You knew all this, or you never would have stood on a stack of crates and declared the start of a revolution."

It was Nolyn and Amicus's turn to show stone faces and wait. In his mind, Nolyn saw Farnell as an open barrel of wine he had kicked, wobbling on the edge of a step. It would either settle and all would be fine, or it would tip, fall, and spill, creating an awful mess.

"But," Farnell said, clasping his hands together thoughtfully, "I wonder if you know about the voices."

Nolyn didn't, and despite his best attempt at holding fast to an expressionless face, he glanced at Amicus, who showed he had no idea, either.

"Didn't think so," Farnell said. The legate crossed the patchwork of overlaid carpets to the entrance of his tent and drew closed the flaps, sealing out the bustle of the camp.

"There are two reasons Vernes is ripe for unrest. The first is that Rhulynia's governor has recently died. The second stems from the emperor's new appointee. Advaryn Wyn is a Fhrey who hails from Merredydd and is known to hate humans. He has vowed to crackdown on the liberal nature of our fair port city. As a result, there has been a general call to launch a rebellion on Founder's Day when the replacement will be official. Most people already thought this year's celebration would be a day of protest, and then you showed up. Now people are taking the whole matter even more seriously.

"The second reason Vernes is on edge is because of the voices." He returned to the desk and leaned on it. "Men—particularly men in the legion—have been hearing disembodied voices in their heads inciting them to revolution."

"Whose voice, sir?" Nolyn asked.

"That's just the thing. No one knows, but those who have experienced it say they believe it's the voice of a god."

"Which one?"

Farnell shrugged. "Doesn't matter. What does is what these voices have been saying. They proclaim the coming of a hero who will save them from the injustice of the emperor."

"You don't mean *me*, do you?"

"Those who report to have heard the voices have explained that this savior will arrive by warship, come out of the east, and be neither human nor Fhrey."

He paused to let the words sink in.

"A god prophesied my coming?"

Farnell nodded. "Impressive, wouldn't you say? And now that you've come, well, what once was a fanciful wish has become a reality. At this point, whatever I order done to you will, in fact, happen to me. That puts me in the unenviable position of either remaining loyal to the emperor and inviting my own men to revolt or embracing the revolution and listen to the voices that say you are destined to challenge your father and change the world for the better."

He pushed off the desk, crossed the carpets, and threw back the tent flap, granting sunlight entry into the darkened interior. "I can hand over command of the Second Legion to you and win the support and affection of the five thousand killers around me. But doing so will also incur the wrath of the emperor. If you win, I become a hero in the eyes of many. If I stay loyal—and survive in the short term—then even if you fail, Advaryn Wyn would most certainly be appointed with a mandate to make an example of Rhulynia and Vernes. I would be ordered to march on the city and kill hundreds of men and women whom I know. People whose only crime is wanting to be treated fairly and equally in their own empyre."

Nolyn realized then that the legate's mind had been made up even before they had entered his tent. "You've heard this voice. Haven't you?"

Legate Farnell didn't answer, but he *legionnaire-smiled.*

CHAPTER FOURTEEN

A Gem of Great Worth

The piece Augustine created was exquisite. He had worked a massive emerald into the exact shape and size of a chicken's egg. Then he netted it with delicate strands of gold, riveted in place by tiny diamonds. The whole thing was set upon a solid-gold pedestal like a one-minute, pickled breakfast for a king. The work of bejeweled art was utterly delightful—and equally useless. Had Augustine created a bracelet, necklace, or armband, there was a chance Nyphron might actually wear it. But an egg? More arrogantly than a peacock it proclaimed its worth, and the size was such that the egg could easily be picked up and pursed if it were foolishly displayed. There was only one home for such an absurd treasure.

"Do you think he'll put it in the safe straightaway?" Sephryn asked Errol.

The thief had once again accompanied her, eager to see more of the Gem Fortress. The three of them sat at a small display table where the gem resided in a beam of sunlight that made the diamonds sparkle.

"Errol?"

He didn't appear to hear her as he sat and stared, captivated by the egg on the table.

"Errol?"

"What?" He blinked. "Oh, ah, of course, what do you expect the emperor to do? Walk around with it? It's perfect. Absolutely perfect. Now we just have to get it into his hands."

They both looked at Augustine with innocent smiles.

Brinkle frowned and leaned back in his office chair, drumming his fingers on the armrest with a sound like a troop of marching mice. "I'm not at all comfortable with making this an official gift from the Belgriclungreians. Such things are matters of public record. I'm not authorized to act independently."

"Is it a crime to give the emperor a gift?" Errol asked.

"Well, no."

"Do you think doing so will start a war or something?"

"Not exactly, but when it's determined what part I had to play in this affair, I—"

"What part?" Errol asked. "You gave the emperor—your host—a gift for Founder's Day. An extremely generous gift. It happened to be an emerald. A lot of people like green gems. Not your fault that it messes with the emperor's safe. You aren't even going to ask him to put it there, are you? Of course not. Sheer coincidence is the culprit. So how does that implicate you in anything?"

"I should mention that it was quite expensive to make." Augustine looked at the egg like a child who is told his new puppy is going to a faraway farm.

"Rain, not Gronbach. Remember?" Sephryn smiled, going so far as to push up the corners of her mouth with her fingers as a show of encouragement. "Trust me. What's at stake is more precious."

Augustine Brinkle sighed. "I shouldn't have let the two of you in. Never should have listened." He shook a finger. "You both owe me."

"The empyre will be in your debt," Sephryn said.

Again, Augustine frowned. "The *empyre* still owes us for the crown we made Nyphron more than eight hundred years ago."

"Sounds like Gronbach-talk to me," Sephryn said. "You need to focus on your legacy and fight those voices in your head."

"I have nothing of the sort."

"Consider yourself lucky."

Sephryn stared at the egg, which was stunning beyond imagination. Although not what she would call beautiful—the gem was far too gaudy for her taste—the artistry required to create it was unmistakable. And the value of the piece, she couldn't even begin to guess. Sephryn was terrified to touch it. Neither she nor Errol tried.

"What about the other gem?" she asked.

Brinkle dug into his pocket and drew forth what looked like a rock. Dull, blemished, reddish in places, purple in others, the uncut crystal was roughly the same size as the egg, but it possessed no beauty at all. "This will do. Just tap it to the safe when Bartholomew is inside, and the lock should release."

"Bartholomew?"

Brinkle looked uncomfortable.

"You *named* the egg?"

Errol reached out, but Brinkle handed the uncut ruby to Sephryn. "I'll want that back, and Bar . . . ah, the emerald. Please remember to take it, along with whatever else you're after, and return it to me."

"And you will see to it that the emperor receives this today?" Sephryn asked.

Brinkle hesitated.

"Sir?" she asked.

The ambassador took a deep breath, pursed his lips, then banged on the arms of his chair with great force. "I want to see you with Audrey," he blurted out.

"Excuse me? You want what?"

"I want to witness the daughter of Moya wield her mother's famous weapon, the bow she named Audrey. I've heard the tales all my life. It would be a dream come true."

"I'm not my mother," Sephryn said sincerely.

Brinkle folded his arms defiantly. "Bartholomew is a gem of great worth dressed up in a suit of splendor, and I made him for you and asked for nothing. I did all this on blind faith. The ruby—even uncut—is worth more than his life." Brinkle pointed at Errol.

"You don't know that for certain," Errol replied, then sighed and shook his head. "Precise—whoever said your kind were punctilious was wrong."

"This is such a *tiny* condition," Brinkle pressed, leaning his hands forward on the table. "If I'm going to risk a fortune, you can show me the bow and give me a demonstration of what you learned from your mother. She was supposed to be so fast that she could loose twenty arrows a minute, and so accurate that she could hit a dove in flight a mile away."

"See!" Sephryn exclaimed. She turned to Errol. "This is what I have to expect. My mother never released more than twelve arrows a minute, and if she did, they wouldn't have been aimed. And for Mari's sake, who would shoot a dove?"

"If you want Bartholomew locked in a box in the palace, then that's my price."

"I'm not that good."

"Still want to see it."

Sephryn looked at the gem. "I suppose you've earned it. Can we make it just the two of us, so I don't make a fool out of myself in front of a crowd? I think it will be hard to live up to a thousand years of hype."

"I'll leash my expectations," he said, but his eyes told a different story. She stood up. "Errol?"

"What?" he replied, his eyes still on the emerald egg.

"We're leaving."

"Of course we are."

"And you stay out of my workshop," Augustine growled at the thief.

"And thank you so much, ambassador," Sephryn said, dragging Errol toward the exit. "Today, you are truly Rain."

"Please, call me Augustine."

❧

"You want me to hold onto the ruby for you?" the thief asked when they were outside.

"Errol, I realize you have about as much respect for me as you might for a turtle, but given that I'm able to walk upright, you must realize I'm not *that* stupid."

"I suppose not," he replied and sighed.

"Now what?" she asked.

"We wait."

"For what?"

He frowned. "Seriously? And you expect more respect than a turtle?" Errol rolled his eyes. "I'll contact you when I know something."

She watched him go. Errol was annoying, but he had been a welcome distraction. Alone, her thoughts returned to Nurgya, and the many things that were likely to go wrong with the plan.

Sephryn headed home, going the long way around to avoid seeing anyone she knew. She headed up the hill past Eagleton's Red Chariots. Eagleton's was a feed merchant that provided most of the animal grain in the city and headed a wealthy and powerful association of farmers, carters, and tradesmen. The company was also the proud sponsor of the famous Red Chariot racing team. There were four major teams in Percepliquis: Red, White, Green, and Blue. Each had sponsors, who often saw sales go up when their teams won.

She had seen her first chariot race with Nolyn almost eight hundred years before. Back then, she had only recently returned to the city after her mother's death. Sephryn had been on her own for the first time. The Grenmorian War was over, the Goblin Wars yet to start, and she, Bran, and Nolyn were in Percepliquis. It was the start of the Wonderful Year when the three were reunited for the last time. On the first day she and Nolyn spent alone together, he took her to the newly built Grand Circus to see his beloved Red Team. Even back then, there had been a Red Team, but Eagleton's wasn't the sponsor; they didn't yet exist. The city was only thirty-four years old and most of the risers in the new arena were empty. At that time, the Red Team was supported by a local bread shop that won fans by offering free loafs at the race.

Nolyn and Sephryn had sat in the stands, chewing their portion of day-old crust and freezing in the blasts of unrelenting late-winter winds. Nolyn had a blanket that they shared, huddled together, arms around each other, heads tilted until they touched. She remembered everything about that day, except who had won the race.

Sephryn paused before the big red sign and looked up at the stylized crimson chariot with bright yellow wheels, ten horses pulling it.

He never met his son, and if I don't get this right, he never will.

Emperor Nyphron, Dragonslayer, Lord of Fhrey and Men, brushed the crumbs of a hastily eaten piece of pecan pie off his tunic as the trumpets sounded, announcing the governor of Merredydd's arrival.

It had been a year since Nyphron last saw Sikar. They met every Founder's Day, out of obligation rather than enjoyment. The two had served together at the fortress of Alon Rhist before the Great War, but Sikar had never been a favorite. A satisfactory warrior and dutiful soldier, Sikar resented that Nyphron had never invited him into the ranks of his elite band of warriors known as the Galantians. Through most of his career, Sikar had been a spear commander, but he had risen to captain of the Rhist just before Nyphron assumed control of it. Truth was, no one liked Sikar. The Fhrey was boring. He didn't get drunk, never disobeyed orders, and had a lousy singing voice. Even Anwir had been more fun. The quiet, knot-obsessed member of the hunter tribe possessed a wicked sense of dark humor. Sikar, however, was a level dirt road without a pothole or bit of gravel to break up the monotony.

Why couldn't Vorath have survived the war? He was a mangy bear, a slob, a drunk, and a dirty fighter, but he was fun. I would also have been happy with Eres or Tek—

Nyphron caught himself. Tekchin *had* survived; he just wasn't the same. Never had there been a more insane Galantian. He had once bet three fingers on his left hand on a single roll of dice. Nyphron couldn't remember what the prize had been; he doubted Tekchin could, either. The jackpot wasn't the point. And the Fhrey was ridiculously lucky, at least until he met Moya.

The big doors to the throne room opened, and Sikar marched up the tiled floor toward the big empty chair. He took four full strides before stopping and looking around. He spotted Nyphron near the balcony window, pouring a glass of wine.

"Hail, Nyphron, Lord of the World," Sikar said with the emotion and sincerity of an obligatory greeting.

"Want a drink?"

"Bit early for me, Your Illustriousness."

Illustriousness? He looked at Sikar and noticed he kept a straight face. *No, not a Galantian.* "The sun is shining, Sikar. How could it be too early for a drink?"

"I just arrived, Your Eminence, and I have a great deal to do before the meeting."

As governor of Merredydd, Sikar and the other province governors were required to attend the Founder's Day Festival and the State of the Empyre Congress that followed. Nyphron had given Sikar the province of Merredydd both to get away from him and to appease the growing protest among the more ardent Fhrey that living with humans made them sick. Nyphron wasn't certain if their assertion was supposed to be a physical illness or a mental state. It likely varied depending on whom you talked to, with some believing that humans carried diseases that weren't native to the Fhrey. Still, Sikar, as could only be expected, took his role as governor seriously. Anyone else — a Galantian, certainly — would use the opportunity to indulge themselves in every possible vice. Tekchin — the old pre-Moya version — would have been dead from excess by now. In contrast, Sikar actually prepared for the meetings. He would have numbers and tallies, export and import lists, and a detailed chart of taxes collected. When facing such an encounter, Nyphron suspected Sikar had been switched at birth with a child from a different tribe. He didn't seem like a warrior.

"How are things at the old fort?"

Sikar allowed a rare smile to reach his lips. "It's a bit more than a fortress now, Your Grandness. Merredydd is a thriving city surrounded by bountiful farms and growing industries. We are a fine example of what can be accomplished without the hindrance of humans." He moved to the window and looked out at Percepliquis. "I see your trees are not experiencing the same level of prosperity."

The throne room looked directly out on the Grand Marchway, where the fruit trees grew down the center of the broad avenue. That year, they struggled to keep pace with the imperial calendar because a cold spring had caused the buds to sleep late. There was still time for them to flower for the holiday, but Sikar appeared to consider their tardiness an indictment of Percepliquis's human population.

"And what of Tekchin? Seen him lately?"

Sikar nodded. "I believe he's coming this year."

"Really?"

"He should be here before long. I invited him to travel with me, but he refused." Sikar shrugged. "I don't know why."

Nyphron did. The two hated each other. Nyphron hadn't been there, but he had heard that Sikar—now famous for his intolerance of humans—had insulted Moya. Sikar was nearly killed in the battle that followed, and he suffered the added indignity of being rescued by Moya. Not that she feared for Sikar's life, but she was concerned for Tekchin's immortal soul if he were to kill another Fhrey.

A faint tap rattled the door. "Pardon me, Your Greatness, but the ambassador of the Belgriclungreians is here to see you."

"I don't recall having an appointment with him today." In truth, Nyphron had nearly forgotten they had a Belgriclungreian ambassador in the city. He hadn't spoken to the dwarf in decades.

"You don't, Great One. He showed up unexpectedly. He says he has a Founder's Day gift."

"Really?"

Hoping it was a bottle of something stronger than the traditional Founder's Day drink of tremble wine, Nyphron nodded. "Fine, let him in."

Nyphron remembered the ambassador the moment he entered. Augustine Brinkle was about as impractical as a person could get and still have all their limbs. He stood little more than three feet tall and had a pudgy face and tiny hands. If not for the beard, most would guess him to be a child.

Is that why all male dwarfs, and even some females, have facial hair?

Augustine entered the throne room and made a show of bowing, which was like watching a dog do a trick. "Great Emperor, Your Imperial Majesty, allow me to extend to you a joyous Founder's Day. And to commemorate our many years of friendship, the people of the Belgriclungreian Empire would like to bestow upon you a token of our appreciation and admiration." He held out a velvet bag tied with a golden cord.

Nyphron took the pouch. Opening it, he withdrew a bejeweled emerald. "An egg?"

"A symbol of the future prosperity yet to be born and shared by our two realms."

"It's an egg," Nyphron said to Sikar, holding it up so he could see.

"Indeed," Sikar said. "The generosity of the Belgriclungreians is legendary."

That was about what he could have expected Sikar to say. He turned back to the ambassador. "What good is an egg? I mean, it's not a real egg, is it?" He tapped the gem on the nearby table hard enough to rattle the surface. At the same time, the ambassador's eyes got so big he thought they might fall out.

"No, Your Imperial Majesty."

"So, again, I ask, what good is an egg?"

"It's ah . . . it's ahh . . . it's incredibly valuable."

"Really?" Nyphron held it up and eyed it skeptically. "Why? A sword I could understand. Even a dagger. But this? It's like that horrible crown your people made for me, but I can't even wear this. I suppose in a sling it would make a fine projectile, but any rock would do just as well—and you say it's expensive?"

"Extremely."

He turned it over and back, then tossed it up in the air and caught it, causing the ambassador to emit a muffled gasp. Nyphron noted the reaction, and while he saw no value in the trinket, he understood that the dwarf did. That alone granted it *some* worth. "Okay, well, thank you."

The ambassador bowed and backed away until he was out of the room.

First the trees, now an egg as a gift. Nyphron sighed. He guessed it wasn't going to be his best Founder's Day.

That night, after Sephryn and Seymour returned from the market with the makings for a pitiful meal, they found Errol sitting by the fireplace. Sephryn frowned, and Seymour admonished, "If you're going to break in, you could at least have the decency to start a fire."

"Didn't *break* anything. No locks. Remember? And it wouldn't do to have me lurking about outside, now would it?"

Sephryn hung up her cape while Seymour unpacked the bags. "I take it you know something?"

"My sources tell me the ambassador delivered the gift this afternoon without incident."

"What does that mean? Is the egg in the safe?"

"I don't know."

"I guess we'll just have to hope," she said. "I've waited far too long already. We'll go tomorrow. We should enter the palace grounds about midday, then hide in the records hall until it's late. Midnight, I suppose."

Errol nodded. "He's not going with us, is he?" The thief glanced at Seymour, who had moved on to working on the fire. "No reason for him to —"

"I'm going," Seymour said. "You might need me."

"For what?" Errol asked.

Sephryn ignored the thief. "If you come, you'll need to stay in the records room. Agreed?"

"I'll be sure to bring a snack, so I'll have something to eat while I wait." Seymour began searching through the woodpile.

"You don't have to go in, either," Sephryn told the thief. "I only need you to unlock the door to the palace."

Errol smiled. "And while I would be ecstatic if that were the case, you know better. What if there are other locked rooms inside? That is why you hired me."

"I didn't hire you. No money. Remember?"

"My life, which you've put in mortal danger I might add, is worth a great deal to me, so I'm in this until you get what the Voice asked for."

Seymour struggled to get the fire started. He stood up and huffed.

"What's wrong?" Sephryn asked.

"I can't find the fireplace poker. Anyone know where it is?"

"In the Urum River," Errol said.

CHAPTER FIFTEEN

Teshlor Nights

Weldon Smirch swung his sword at Everett Thatcher, who countered by raising his own weapon to guard. The blades clanged.

"See? That right there is exactly what every soldier is trained to do," Amicus shouted over both the sound of the sparring and the howl of wind coming down the river valley.

They were once more aboard the imperial warship *Stryker* and riding a river again, but it was the Urum they were rowing up. And they weren't the only warship. Farnell had commandeered five others and loaded them with Second Legionnaires. The rest of the legion, under Jareb Tanator's control, would follow, marching up the riverbank. The ships' task would be to claim the river, securing it as their personal highway and denying the emperor its use.

Everyone was on deck for the training session. Rows of soldiers lined the rails and intently watched as Amicus Killian led a class in combat.

"And it's a terrible response," Amicus explained. "Not only is it a bad counter—all defense and no positioning for attack—but as I said, *everyone* is trained to respond that way. Last night, I could have told you Everett would do that. In a way, it's like seeing the future, and because you know what your opponent will do, that puts you a move ahead. You can use such knowledge to kill him. Everett could have dropped his sword and punched Smirch in the face and obtained better results. At least it would have been unexpected." He waved Jerel DeMardefeld up for a demonstration.

The normally steel-clad soldier had been busy cleaning his armor and was dressed in just his tunic, skirt, and sword belt.

"The Tesh teaches balance: the idea that you need to keep yours while forcing your opponent to lose theirs." Amicus faced Everett. "Attack Jerel."

Jerel hadn't drawn his blade and Everett hesitated.

"Go on," Amicus insisted.

Everett shook his head. "First, tell him to draw his sword."

Jerel smiled. He drew his weapon and promptly tossed it aside. It rang on the wood decking.

"Happy?" Amicus asked.

Everett stared, his mouth open.

"Look, he's unarmed. Just hit him."

"I . . ." Everett stared at Jerel, then looked back at Amicus with a grimace as if he'd been asked to slap his mother.

Amicus smiled. "See?" he told the crowd, "Balance isn't restricted to just the body. Jerel has defeated Everett by his unexpected behavior."

"That's 'cause the lad doesn't want ta hurt his friend," a Second Legionnaire observed. He showed the rank of Third Spear of the first cohort. "If'n a man did that in a real fight, this fella"—he pointed at Jerel—"would be dead."

"Really?" Amicus asked. "Show me."

"How's that?" the man asked.

"Jerel's not your friend, right?"

The man shook his head. "Never seen 'im before."

Amicus nodded. "So go on. Show me."

"You want me to kill him?"

"By all means, yes."

The Third Spear looked at those around him, laughing. "Okay." Still chuckling, he stepped forward and drew his blade. "Am I gonna get in trouble for this?"

"Not if you kill him," Amicus said.

The man looked confused for a moment, then shrugged and looked at Jerel. "You really should pick up the sword."

Jerel looked at his blade. "Just do me a favor, and don't trip on it."

That made the man laugh again. "Your funeral."

The Third Spear shuffled forward and swung. He was an experienced soldier and knew what he was doing. He suspected a trap and didn't fully commit to the attack.

Jerel stepped aside. The stroke went wide.

"So you're quick, I see," the Third Spear said, nodding. His eyes peered at Jerel, recalculating his situation.

"Not really," Jerel replied. "I merely knew what you were going to do."

"Did ya?" The man lunged.

Jerel dodged.

The Second Legionnaire anticipated the move and pivoted, swinging his sword at waist-level. There was no dodging the attack. The blade was too low to duck, too high to jump, and too close to sidestep. Everyone expected an ugly outcome. The stroke wasn't going to cut Jerel in half, but it would slice through his tunic, and there was a real chance it might cut through more than skin. But that didn't happen.

With a quick clap, Jerel slapped the sword down. The tip bit into the deck at his feet. The metal dug in, and before the soldier could withdraw the sword—even before he knew what was happening—Jerel stepped on the blade, jarring the sword from the man's hands. The hilt hammered onto the deck. Then, while the Third Spear was still trying to understand how he'd lost control of the fight, Jerel swung a leg, caught the Second Legionnaire behind the knees, and dropped him to the deck.

"Balance," Jerel said, and, after receiving a nod from Amicus, he returned to working on his armor.

"As you can see," Amicus explained to those watching, "surprise offsets balance."

The Third Spear got back to his feet. Then he waved a hand in the direction of the other former Sik-Aux who stood or sat in a cluster. "Are all of you Teshers, then?"

"Teshers?" Amicus asked.

The man shrugged. "All of you trained in that weird fighting style?"

Amicus laughed. "Let's just say, we're working on it."

"Doing pretty good, I'd say." The man picked up his sword and put it away. "So this is something you picked up in Calynia, then? Some sorta eastern style of combat?"

A bitterness flavored the old soldier's tone. He didn't like being embarrassed in front of a crowd, and Nolyn guessed he sought an excuse that he could use later that night when his fellows chided him. Something along the lines of, *"It wasn't fair! They used this new style of fighting—like ghazel magic, it was! Not right, if you ask me."*

Amicus shook his head, offering nothing to the Third Spear. "It's been around a long time—centuries. The first seven disciplines were developed by a man named Tesh during the Great War as a means of fighting the Fhrey—hence the name, *the Tesh.* Technically, two more disciplines were added later. Those, however, are not part of the Tesh and are generally referred to as the *Lore.*"

"*Lor* in Fhrey means *fast*," Nolyn explained.

Amicus thought a moment, then shrugged. "Makes sense. My father and grandfather told me that practitioners of the Tesh—back in the time of the war—were known as Teshlors. I just thought it was a title, but maybe it does mean 'fast Tesh,' or something like that."

"So you're all Teshlors?" the Third Spear asked.

"*Those* six are." Nolyn gestured at the ex-Seventh. "I'm old-school legion. Everett is new and still learning, and Demetrius is administrative staff."

The man nodded. "But with six Teshlors protecting you, I suppose you don't need a sword."

"I'll teach him, too," Amicus said. "Just takes time."

Nolyn smiled, but after seeing the familiar hills of Rhenydd appearing on the western side of the ship, he doubted time was something he had in great supply anymore.

Having had so little time ashore, Nolyn hadn't lost his sea legs, so he wasn't as affected by the river travel as he'd been on the voyage to Vernes. He felt an inexplicable sense of unease but didn't get sick. He appreciated the reprieve when he walked off the *Stryker* that evening.

Nolyn was greeted by the commanders of both legions and their staffs. Farnell was looking bright with a grand smile on his lips. Beside him, a large man with bushy brows stood. Dressed in spotless armor of silver and gold, he bore the eagle insignia of a legate.

"Legate Hillanus of the First Legion has agreed to join us," Farnell said in greeting.

Both men stood on the pier, grinning. They were within sight of the entrance of Percepliquis, where a great stone bridge crossed the water. Back before the bridge was built, the spot they stood on had been the Havilyn dock, and the ferry was the only way to cross the Urum River. The warships dwarfed the tiny pier that, long ago, Nolyn had frequented with his mother when they traveled on summer visits to the Mystic Wood. He noted with some sadness the missing oak tree that used to grow there. He seemed to recall having a picnic within its shade, and how his mother said it reminded her of Magda, the old oracle tree.

"Indeed," Hillanus confirmed while nodding. He had a broad face and big jowls that jiggled along with his second chin.

"As easy as that?" Nolyn asked Hillanus. Even in his most hopeful fantasies, he'd never imagined the First Legion throwing in with him. "I had no idea I was so loved."

Hillanus chuckled. "With all due respect, Your Highness, this has little to do with you. You're merely the puff of air that was needed to shove the boulder over the cliff. You have no idea how much your father is hated in the ranks. I'm sure it's bad on the frontier, but it's far worse here."

"How's that possible?" Amicus asked. "In Calynia, we sweat in a dank, fly-infested jungle; you get to bask in the sun and drink wine on the banks of a leisurely river."

Farnell shook his head. "In the jungle, you thrive off the pride of your adversity, a brotherhood of hardship. Here, we languish in sight of the privileges the emperor bestows on his kinsmen, who do nothing but lord over us. We are the proverbial dogs on the far side of the fence being taunted by raw meat, and we have the time to complain, speculate, and let our wounds fester."

"Soldiers are built for conquest," Farnell added. "You have ghazel and the jungle to quell. We have only the Instarya to hate."

Hillanus nodded and focused on Nolyn. "Your lineage, mixed blood, and legion experience make you the ideal standard to rally around. Add to that the support of Amicus Killian and the legendary Seventh Sik-Aux, and . . ." He grinned and broke into happy laughter.

"I know," Farnell said, nodding.

"We couldn't have requisitioned a better symbol," Hillanus said.

Symbol. Nolyn noted the term and the fact that Hillanus hadn't offered a salute.

A legate doesn't salute a prymus, Nolyn consoled himself. *But I'm the prince. Still, it might not mean anything.*

"We'll move in tomorrow at dawn," the First Legate declared, assuming command.

Or maybe it does.

With another joyous smile and continued lack of salute, Hillanus and Farnell turned their backs, and, along with their entourage, went off to tents already raised where once an oak tree stood.

"He wants to be emperor," Amicus told Nolyn as the two watched the procession recede. "We'll have to kill Hillanus immediately."

"He's thinking the same of me," Nolyn replied.

The two grabbed their gear and headed down the grassy bank toward where the *Stryker* crew was settling in. The simple weathered tents they pitched, which had seemed luxurious on the beach a week before, now appeared no better than a canvas slum.

They cleared the row of six bobbing warships that blocked their view across the river. The city that marked the center of the world was just on the other side, and as the sun began to set, they found themselves in the city's shadow. White-columned buildings, statues, obelisks, and temples crowned the green-wreathed hillside and seemed to sparkle in the evening light.

"We're dangerously close now," Amicus said as the two walked along the towpath where the river lapped the bank. He might have been referring to the city but more likely was referring to the *point of no return*. The Wooden Crate Speech crossed a line, but an invisible one. Their next action would draw blood, which would be impossible to miss.

The riverbank was alight with campfires as hundreds of soldiers prepared their suppers. Turning his head, Nolyn faced the city of Percepliquis. The tall domes and towers were in silhouette by then, faceless shadows that waited.

"They know we're here," Amicus said, his mouth a grim line. "But we could still turn back."

"You think so?"

"No." He shook his head. "Not really. Just trying to—I don't know. Are you ready for this?"

"Probably not," Nolyn replied. He had always believed that Nyphron hated him, an undeniable fact. Not every son was a source of joy for his father, but the order to have him killed was another matter.

If his father were anyone else, Nolyn still might be able to walk away. But Nyphron was the ruler of the known world, and Nolyn had no hope of evading the emperor's grasp. He must face his father—not as a child but as an equal. With two legions behind him, Nolyn wouldn't need to beg for an audience. He would have the upper hand and could finally end the rivalry that he had never understood, except . . .

Nolyn pressed his hand against his chest, remembering the pain and humiliation he'd suffered when held down and marked with symbols he hadn't understood.

Why'd he do that if he hated me? And if he didn't, why send me away? If he wanted me dead, why not just execute me? Why go to such elaborate lengths?

Nolyn couldn't account for three threads that had weighed on him since setting his feet on the path to revolution. First was the use of magic. His father abhorred the Art in all its forms. The second was that his father had never been shy or subtle. If Nyphron wanted his son dead, Nolyn would have been slaughtered at his post in the salt mine. And last, why go through the trouble of making Nolyn's death look like a casualty of war? That last one bothered him the most because it was a cowardly act, and while Nyphron was many despicable things, gutless wasn't one of them.

Nolyn focused on the outline of Percepliquis—the City of Persephone. Once they passed through the archway, when the legions entered the city, the opportunity for talk would disappear.

It's impossible to hold a civil conversation over the noise of clashing steel.

Nolyn had questions, and he needed answers before those explanations were forever beyond his reach.

"What are you thinking?" Amicus asked. "Something stupid, I suspect."

Nolyn smiled. "You've come to know me all too well, my friend. But telling you would ruin the surprise."

As they neared the *Stryker*'s camp, conversation drifted to them from the newly dubbed Teshlors. They sat in a circle around a fire, much as they had every night since the sand beach after coming off the Estee. Nolyn wondered if they took the same places each night; he couldn't remember but thought they might.

"There should be a clear set of rules," Jerel said.

"There *are*," Riley Glot replied. He poked the coals of the fire with a stick. "The legion has—"

"The legion is governed by corrupt men who act according to their own best interest and pass on that example to their subordinates."

"That's inevitable in any organization," Riley countered.

"But it doesn't have to be." Jerel was sitting straighter than usual. When Nolyn had first met DeMardefeld, he'd felt diminished by the superior quality of the soldier's impeccable armor. Now he knew the mettle of the man wasn't defined just by what he wore. Even in his tunic, Jerel managed to make everyone else appear dull and threadbare. "To say nothing can change because it never has is lazy and self-defeating."

"It's human nature, bossy," Smirch weighed in, as he sat down with a bowl of whatever the cook was serving.

"What would *you* know about human nature?" Myth asked. Unlike the others, the big bear lay full-out on the ground, hands webbed behind his head, feet clapping the grass.

"Ha, ha, ha," Smirch said without mirth. "I know that if given a chance, a man will cheat. And if he's given power, he'll abuse it."

"That's exactly what I'm trying to stop," Jerel said.

"What's he talking about?" Nolyn asked as he and Amicus entered the light of the fire.

Riley sighed. "DeMardefeld is getting a bit ahead of himself. He's growing concerned at the state of the world *after* we are victorious and you're sitting on the imperial throne."

"Gotta love the optimism." Myth chuckled.

"What is the problem?" Nolyn asked.

Jerel went to the trouble of getting to his feet and squaring his shoulders before speaking, as if he were addressing the whole of the world. "You say you want equality throughout the empyre, but how will you achieve that, sir?"

"I'll make a set of laws and write them in stone, make them public."

"And then what? How will you ensure that the governor of Melenina enforces your laws properly? Ervanon is a long way from Percepliquis."

Nolyn shrugged. "I suppose I would send an officer of the legion to be my eyes and ears."

"And what would prevent that officer—so far from home—from becoming corrupt, being bribed, or even getting threatened to ignore crimes he witnesses?"

Nolyn considered the observation. He hadn't done so before, because the chances of such a thing being his problem were infinitesimal. Even if his plan went exactly as he hoped and they reached Percepliquis with two legions willing to fight, Nolyn still had difficulty imagining a victory. Not a good sign. He was marching on the capital with the bravado of confidence, but defeat was in his heart. In too many ways, he felt like a character in a tragic play, unable to turn away from his fate. The present path was his future; it had always been so. "I'm not sure."

"Exactly," Jerel said. "Which is why it's important to discuss it now."

"What are you talking about?" Nolyn asked.

"Jerel wants *us* to do it," Riley explained.

"Us?" Amicus asked, appearing just as baffled as Nolyn.

"Teshlors."

"But we have to have rules," Jerel insisted. "A code of conduct that's taught along with the martial training, preferably from childhood. As representatives of the emperor, we need to be uncompromised examples of virtue."

"You want to be Night Heroes?" Nolyn asked.

Everyone returned blank looks.

"Seriously?" Nolyn said, appalled. "It's from *The Book of Brin?*"

Still no recognition.

"You all seemed to know about Gronbach. I just assumed . . . It's from the Battle of Grandford." Nolyn recited from memory,

"The Night Hero, in armor shining
Did vanquish fear, in truth providing
Hope for all, and silver lining
To a night so dark and uninviting.

"It's about the ride of Gifford the Great when he rode through the Fhrey's camp to . . . oh, never mind."

"No! You're right!" Jerel said. "That's exactly it. We will be Teshlor Night Heroes, agents of the emperor, enforcers of fairness—incorruptible and indomitable. What better use will there be for men such as ourselves in possession of a talent for combat in an age without war?"

"It always frightens me a little," Amicus said, "when I find myself thinking that Jerel isn't entirely insane."

CHAPTER SIXTEEN

Hail, Prymus

Mawyndulë stood in darkness, down near the river and away from the soldiers. He had canceled the weave that granted him the appearance of Demetrius. While not a difficult spell to maintain, it was bothersome, and his only respite came while asleep within a cocoon of wrappings.

The lingering effects of seasickness left him feeling queasy. His legs were weak and his balance off. Like a spoiled child facing adversity for the first time, his stomach couldn't be reasoned with, cursing him equally for eating and abstaining. As with any petulant brat, it needed time to vent its frustration and then take a nap.

Traveling on that wretched boat has been the worst experience of my life, he thought and then cringed at his mistake. *No, not the* worst. Mawyndulë had refused to revisit his *worst* experience, the event that delineated the end of his adolescence and the start of his hate-filled adulthood.

The first thirty years of his life had been fine — good even — although no one could have convinced him of that back then. He had been living the life of a privileged prince in an arboreal paradise, the son of the ruling fane of the Fhrey people. Then the war started, and with it came the inevitable slide—each day worse than the one before. All the intervening years were mere footsteps leading to an inescapable future.

Night had descended along the river, and the legionnaires had settled into their camps. He could hear their sharp sounds cutting the night: crude laughter, the clang of pots, vulgar voices. Mawyndulë wasn't far from the torture device known as the imperial warship *Stryker*. Sitting on the grassy bank among the cattails and rushes, his feet rested on a multitude of smooth stones. The great Urum flowed before him, a broad darkness gilded by moonlight. It reminded Mawyndulë of the Shinara River, that holy stream that meandered past the Fhrey palace. On its banks, he had first touched the love of his life, Makareta.

Dead for more than eight centuries, his last memory of her was fading beyond his reach. Long ago, he'd forgotten the smell of her hair and then the sound of her voice. Now, he was struggling to remember what she had looked like. He had held onto the belief that she wasn't really dead as long as he remembered her. But he'd failed.

Mawyndulë now concluded that he'd had not one but two worst experiences. The first was when his father had killed his one and only lover; the second was when he'd lost his fight and his throne to Nyphron. While each was accompanied by ludicrous levels of pain, one nearly killed him, but the other made him *wish* he were dead.

He might have died if Trilos hadn't picked him up, both physically and emotionally. After losing to Nyphron, Mawyndulë had no incentive to breathe. The activity only prolonged his pain. Trilos had saved his life, and for years, Mawyndulë debated whether that rescue had been a kindness or a curse.

That's what tomorrow will decide.

Mawyndulë straightened his back and peered about. The sky was clear. The moon and stars provided ample light. He was alone.

Time to check in and hope she has good news.

Mawyndulë closed his eyes. He didn't have to but did so anyway—mostly from habit. Ever since Jerydd taught him the weave, he'd gone through the same procedure to make the connection. He drew power from the movement of the water. The current wasn't anything like the Parthaloren Falls, but any sizable current possessed enough strength for his purpose. Tapping into the source, he reached out, concentrating on her mixed blood. For a long time, there had only been two in the entire world. Now he could identify the originals from a distance out of familiarity. The first was just behind him in the nearby camp, having his evening meal with his sweaty band of hounds. The other was in the city only a couple of miles away.

Or should be.

Mawyndulë could always pinpoint her marker with ease. He'd met Sephryn briefly. Nothing significant enough for her to remember, but long enough for him to make a mental stamp so she would stand out from the rest of the city's inhabitants like a lone ladybug in a cluster of flies. At least that was usually the case, but now, Mawyndulë only saw flies.

She's in the palace.

That was the only place he couldn't see her. That was both good and bad. He'd wanted to speak with her before the big day, especially since it had been more than a week since he'd last checked in. The seasickness and the inability to find enough privacy for a long-distance conversation had made reaching out impossible.

Given that Mawyndulë could think of few reasons for Sephryn to be in the palace at night, he hoped she was in the final process of obtaining the horn. There was a certain logic to it. Tomorrow was Founder's Day, and all his plans were in motion. He opened his eyes, stood up, and headed back the way he had come.

A much better way to exact my revenge, he mused while smiling at the river. *Nolyn did me a favor by surviving that ambush in the jungle. If I still believed in the gods, I would have said my new plan was divinely inspired.*

Catching sight of Nolyn near the ship, strapping his helmet on, Mawyndulë's smile faltered.

What's he up to?

෬

Nolyn had never liked hats of any kind, and his military helmet was the worst of them all. Being an officer, he thought it was more important to be seen and heard than to be armored for combat, so he rarely wore one in battle. The stiff horsehair fan of his helm ran from ear to ear as opposed to the front-to-back orientation of lower-ranked soldiers. Why either helmet had that adornment at all was a mystery, as it did nothing but made the helms top-heavy, awkward, and nearly impossible to wear when passing through an average-sized doorway. He wouldn't have bothered with it at all except that the helmet was the primary indicator of his rank, and he might need it to get where he was going. Having retrieved the helm from the *Stryker*, he returned to the riverside where he paused to struggle with its buckle.

"What's with the helmet? The battle isn't until tomorrow, right?" Demetrius asked, coming out of the dark.

"That's yet to be decided. I'll let you know if I return."

"Please tell me you aren't thinking of talking to your father."

The sun had long set, and the moon was well above the tree line, revealing the river with a shimmering white line, as if a luminescent snake were just below the surface.

"I am."

"Don't be a fool. Doing that will get you killed, or worse. The emperor is old and powerful. If given the chance, he'll twist you into thinking up is down. It would be best to stay clear of his influence and kill him quickly. He already wants you dead. You're making it easy for him by walking in there. You ought to wait until tomorrow. Then you can charge in with your army and cut his head off."

"Cut his head off? My father tried to kill me, not you."

Demetrius shrugged and gestured at the legion camps. "Your star appears to be rising. You have two legions who have sworn allegiance to you, and you have the city surrounded. There is a good chance you'll take the throne—assuming you have the wit not to kill yourself. I could do far worse than proving myself valuable to the soon-to-be emperor on the night before his crowning."

"No one has sworn anything to me." Nolyn finally got his helmet buckled. It felt like he had a potted plant strapped to his head. "The legions are loyal to their commanders, not Nolyn Nyphronian. It's likely that the legates will each take this opportunity to try to seize the throne for themselves. Hillanus will win in the short run because he has more men, and he hails from this region, giving him an advantage. But Farnell will keep him off balance, preventing him from consolidating his control by denying him the river, which he will use to choke Hillanus. When the outer legions learn what's happened, they will march on the city. Hillanus will feel the pressure to capitulate to Farnell's demands or be crushed. The two will likely form a temporary pact, but they will be far too late and too weak to stop a long civil war. In the end, there's a good chance that the empyre will be broken up into city-states under the control of each of the seven legions. These legates-turned-warlords will usher in an era of constant warfare that might never end—at least not before the ghazel take advantage of our division."

"You're thinking too much, putting carts before horses. You can worry about Hillanus and Farnell after Nyphron is dead."

"By then it'll be too late. Once blood has been spilled, there is no going back. My father respects strength, and for now, the legions are backing me. So I have to use that advantage while I have it. He'll grant me an audience; hear what I have to say."

"And what do you hope to accomplish with this *talk*?"

Nolyn thought a moment. For over eight hundred years, he'd gone where the wind blew—the wind being his father. He'd only started charting his own course a little over a week ago. He'd always believed himself to be a cautious, calculating person, but now he was making spontaneous decisions—even world-altering ones. Facing his father alone was an idea that had coalesced over only a matter of hours. He didn't want to cause the deaths of thousands if he could avoid it.

What good is it to sit on a throne of blood, ruling a shattered realm?

"The law and his attitude have to change," he told the palatus. "And if that can be done without bloodshed, it's worth a try."

"Have you forgotten he ordered your death?" Demetrius folded his arms roughly, his face scowling.

"No, and that's something else he and I need to discuss."

"He'll simply deny it." Demetrius shifted his weight, his arms still folded as if the man's whole body were a knot.

Nolyn considered the words. "You could come with me. If he denies it, you can testify to what you saw. Would you do that?"

"That depends. Am I still your prisoner?"

"I only forced you to come because I couldn't take the chance of you raising an alarm. You're free to go—have been since we were away from Urlineus. But how often does a man have the chance to shape the future of the world? If you help me, we might do just that."

"I'll go, but I doubt your father will see reason. He might just kill you for leading an army to his shore. You must be prepared to strike him down first. Otherwise, we'll both die."

"Agreed."

"Do you think you can?"

"My father is a legendary warrior, leader of the Galantians. But he hasn't lifted a sword in nearly a thousand years. I'm a veteran of the Grenmorian and the First Goblin War, and I've now fought in our current conflict with the ghazel. If we draw swords, one of us will have an extremely unpleasant Founder's Day."

"No!" Amicus said. "Absolutely not. Are you insane?"

Nolyn frowned.

He had debated heading straight to Percepliquis with Demetrius but realized he had to say farewell to the Seventh first, for their own safety. If Nolyn disappeared, they would come looking, and he couldn't have that. Also, they deserved a proper parting—Nolyn felt he did, too.

"We're on the verge of victory, and you want to—"

"I want a resolution that is a win for *everyone*," Nolyn explained. "The empyre is like a dirty glass. I want to clean it, not shatter it and then try to figure out how, or even if, it's possible to piece it back together again. I've not been all that fond of Percepliquis, but I don't want to see it burned to the ground." He smiled at Mirk. "It would be a shame to ruin your first visit by torching the place."

Mirk smiled back, or tried to, and it wasn't the dual wounds that made the effort difficult.

The group of men were gathered around the fire, which had burned low. Each wore the same shocked expression as they stood, staring.

Amicus scowled. "You showed up on his doorstep with an invading army. He'll kill you."

"Thanks for the vote of confidence." Nolyn frowned. "Look, all my life I've believed my father hated me, but only since Demetrius confirmed the order have I been convinced my father wanted me dead. But . . ."

"But what?"

"Too many things just don't add up. My father wouldn't hire a Miralyith. He hates them too much. And Nyphron isn't shy when it comes to spilling blood. If he wanted me dead, he'd do it himself." He put a hand to his chest. "And then there's the Orinfar. Why go to the trouble of protecting me if he was trying to kill me? I can't ask all these men to fight and possibly die unless I'm positive that's the only way."

Amicus looked unconvinced.

"Look, there's only a few possible outcomes. My father can be reasoned with, which means we don't need to invade. If we battle each other and I win, then the invasion gets a lot easier and fewer men die. Or—"

"Your father kills you on the spot."

"It's definitely a possibility, and if that happens, you need to reassess the situation. So, if by sunrise I don't come back, then assume I'm dead, take command of the Teshlors, and do what you feel is best."

"And here I was just getting used to having you around," Amicus said. "You were really starting to grow on me."

"Really? We faced death twice and traveled half the world in each other's company. You're hard to please."

"I'm discerning."

"You're picky."

"I'm gonna miss you."

Nolyn nodded. "I realized that the moment we met. I eventually have to say goodbye to everyone."

The fire whispered as it died. A faint wind rustled the tall grass along the riverbank. Frogs and crickets filled the quiet gaps.

Nolyn snapped to attention. Lifting his chin, he asked, "How do I look?"

"Like an idiot dressing up for his own funeral." Amicus turned away.

"Don't mind him, sir," Riley said, extending an arm. "Was an honor, sir."

Nolyn ignored the handshake and hugged the man. He did the same for all of them except Jerel, who grabbed his own helmet.

"I'm coming with you, sir," DeMardefeld said.

"I didn't extend an invitation."

"I didn't ask for one, sir."

Nolyn smiled. "Let me be more blunt. I don't want you to come."

"Allow me to reply in kind: I don't care."

"What if I order you to stay?"

Jerel smiled. "God outranks you, sir."

"Is this the same god that was whispering to the legions, telling them I was coming? You left that part out of your prophecy."

Jerel looked hesitant and thoughtful. "I don't think they are the same. The One came to me in person and spoke as a man. The others heard a disembodied voice, and that just doesn't seem . . . I don't know . . . like something he would do."

"Wonderful, now there are two gods who knew I was coming before I arrived. Makes me feel a bit too much like a ball being batted back and forth in a game." Nolyn frowned. "I appreciate your concern, Jerel, but you have to understand I must face my father alone. Anything less will be seen as weakness, and today it's important that he respect me. Surely your god can appreciate that my life is secondary to the goal of a better future for all mankind."

Jerel considered the assertion, then nodded. "Very well. I'll come along but wait at the palace gate. If you need me, just yell."

Nolyn laughed. "If I'm in enough need to yell, do you seriously think you'd be able to reach me trapped in the palace?"

"Yes, sir, I do."

That made Nolyn smile. "Wish me luck," he said to the rest.

"You'll need more than that, bossy," Smirch said. "You'll need a miracle."

"That's why he has me," Jerel said without a trace of humor.

Nolyn had started walking away when Amicus grabbed him by the arm. "Don't you dare get killed, you hear me? I don't want to have come all this way for nothing."

"I'll try not to disappoint."

Amicus gave him a sudden hug. "My father and grandfather always said, 'Never serve the emperor because you'll always be disappointed.' But I want you to know something. I would have served you."

"Me, too," Riley said.

"And me." Myth nodded.

"I usually hate everyone," Smirch said, "but I think I'd make an exception."

Mirk and Everett nodded.

"Hail, prymus!" Amicus shouted, and each offered a salute. "And may good fortune and the blessings of the gods be upon you."

Looking at them, seeing the admiration mingled with fear in their eyes, Nolyn felt the weight of responsibility more acutely than ever before. And perhaps for the first time, he had hope.

CHAPTER SEVENTEEN

Cries in the Dark

The midnight bell rang, waking Arvis.

She thought it strange how she slept worse in warmer weather. With the tolling of the iron bells, it was officially Founder's Day, which was also the start of the planting season, the day when it was believed the nights would never again get cold enough to kill. In winter, Arvis shivered but slept deep. In summer, she tossed. With the ringing of that bell, she couldn't have managed even that.

She lifted her head off the sack of belongings and wiped her eyes. The world hadn't changed.

One day I'll open my eyes, and everything will be different.

She didn't know why she thought that, but she didn't understand the majority of the things that popped into her head. For most people, the world was a mystery, but for Arvis, she was the enigma—a puzzle that even Death had found too tight a knot to unravel.

Something bit her ankle. A spider perhaps, or an ambitious bug that got a jump on the season. The bite itched, and as she reached down to scratch, she heard the sound again. As quiet as the song of butterfly wings, the faint cry of a baby drifted to her.

Arvis stopped moving. Her arm still extended toward her ankle, frozen in place. She held her breath and waited.

It came again and from the same direction as before.

Wasting no time and feeling like she had been granted an unexpected second chance, Arvis burst from her under-the-stairs home and raced down the darkened street through the garment district.

No. Not my second chance; there's no such thing. The other time was to prepare me. Maybe it didn't actually happen. Perhaps I saw a dream or a vision.

Whatever it had been, Arvis was ready. She snatched a torch from the street post at the intersection and ran toward the old milliner's shop.

How can a child live down there? Probably can't for long.

She found the sewer grate in the alley, and without hesitation, she scrambled down. Dropping into the dark netherworld, she paused, holding her breath in anticipation.

Hearing the cry again, she set out, splashing her way without a single concern about the rats or the stench. Reaching a four-way junction, she didn't have to wait for another cry; her previous adventure had left her confident about the path. Then her feet slipped, and she fell into the slop with a spray that splashed the walls. Quick thinking on her part preserved the torch. She held it high, like a military standard on a field of battle.

The cries were loud and crisp as she skidded around another corner, then the echoes stopped. The cry of the baby no longer bounced; it rang clear. No walls lay between her and the source. The baby was . . . the baby was . . .

Please, not in the sludge, not in the water. Please.

That tiny prayer was granted as she found what looked to be the nest of a large animal—no, not an animal, a person. A portion of the sewer wall had collapsed, leaving a hole about four feet off the floor, which was just about the same size as Arvis's sub-stair refuge. There were a few wadded-up blankets, a collapsed water bladder, a handful of small cloths, some chicken bones, and a bucket and brush. The bristles of the brush were dark, and what looked like dried blood stained the sides of the bucket. In the nest, a bundle squirmed, an abandoned swaddled infant. Wrapped tight in dingy cloth, a small, red-faced, tear-soaked child had been tucked between the bucket and the blankets. It looked so small and helpless—no bigger than . . . a loaf of bread.

Beneath, at the base of the wall, an eager audience of rats had gathered. Without a clear way to climb the sheer surface, they were in the process of scaling one another, building a writhing, chattering pillar of hungry rodents that were eager to discover what lodged above them.

Arvis kicked viciously at the mound. She received more than one bite in response, but the pile of rats scattered to unseen holes.

Propping the torch against the wall, Arvis reached into the nest and picked up the baby. The tiny body jerked with cries of pain, fear, confusion—probably all three. But the moment Arvis pulled the child to her chest, the wailing stopped. Her arms surrounded the bundle, one hand cupping the little head to the beating of her heart. Together at last, the two calmed and quieted. Peace settled, and in that horrid place beneath the sleeping world, Arvis's mind returned to her, and she remembered what she'd forgotten.

I had a child.

᪣

Time, Arvis knew, was a slippery thing that all too often escaped her when she failed to pay attention. Holding the child, feeling the warmth they shared and listening to the peace that reigned outside and within, Arvis refused to step out of that perfect moment. She had brought serenity not only to the child but herself as well. She and the baby were at once whole, and so long as time didn't move and the world failed to notice, these two undeserving hearts found joy.

For the first time in as long as she could remember, Arvis didn't hate the world—or herself. The gods who had tormented her for so many years had apparently gotten bored and nodded off. She feared waking them, so she held the baby tight and prayed that her one singular moment of joy wouldn't end.

Most people don't realize the best time of their lives until long after it's over. But not me. I know—I know because I'm living it!

How long she stayed in that place she would never be able to remember. To her, it felt both an instant and an eternity. The world, however, wouldn't be denied, and the gods only took short naps.

The torch, which wasn't all that grand to begin with, was growing short and with it, so was time. She didn't want to be caught down there without light. Taking care with the child, she cradled it in one arm and picked up the torch. Arvis looked forward and back, unsure which way was out. One of the rats she'd kicked was dead, or at least it lay unmoving. She vaguely recalled kicking it in the opposite direction from where she had come and guessed that back was the other way. Holding tight to both baby and the dwindling torch, she set off in search of an open sewer hole.

Coming to an intersection, she was absolutely positive she had no idea which way to go. She couldn't even remember the junction. She also couldn't recall having encountered a crossroad.

I'm lost, her mind reported as it reluctantly took control. *That's the problem with the heart; it drives the cart into the ditch and then walks away with an innocent, "Oops."*

"All roads lead somewhere," she whispered. Talking to herself was one of the batty things she did, and she knew it. But this time . . . she shook her head. "No, not to myself. I said that to you," she told the child and smiled. "You make me not crazy."

The baby didn't deny a single word, having already fallen asleep.

The rats kept their distance, as if news of the kicking madwoman had circulated throughout rodent town. She was grateful for that. Despite being more than prepared to wage war on behalf of her new charge, she preferred a clear path.

"To all the rats, spiders, beetles, and everything else that crawls in the night, beware!" she shouted, her voice echoing, gaining volume and depth as it bounced down the tunnels so that she sounded like a god herself. "With Elan as my witness and Eton as my judge, I'll thrash you to the edge of existence should you threaten this child!"

That was no idle boast. Arvis had already held hands with Death himself. What more could Life throw at her?

She got a clue when she stumbled on the first dead body. A man, floating in the water, was bumping against the wall. The second was only a few feet farther away. Both were difficult to see because of the writhing mass of rats eating them. Armed with both feet, Arvis shooed the rodents away. In many ways, doing so was a mistake. The view below the rats wasn't a pretty one, and she retreated, whispering to the sleeping baby, "You don't need to see that."

I didn't come this way.

She took a different corridor, and that was when she heard it. Initially, she thought it was the scratching of rats. She revised that notion as she grew closer, and the sound grew in volume.

There was a clacking, a scraping, and a banging. In between, far more disturbing noises made her stop. Guttural sounds, deep-throated utterances issued up the passage in a language she'd never heard before. That area, she noticed, was devoid of rats. She spotted a pickax leaning against the wall, a queer, twisted tool made from some sort of gray wood and dark metal.

Life was going out of its way to prove who was the boss of her; for at that moment, as she stood in the passage contemplating the sounds and the tool, the torch flickered one last time and died. In the dark, she heard clicking, chattering, and digging.

Big rats, she thought.

"You don't want to go that way," a voice told her.

Spinning and thrusting out her dead torch as if it were a dagger, Arvis spotted a woman coming out of the dark. Wrapped in a shawl, she held a small lantern in one hand and a heavy sack in the other.

Step, lurch, step, lurch. The woman moved slowly, slogging through ankle-deep water. "That way is . . . bad. The children of Uberlin are coming. Ferrol has invited them for Founder's Day."

Step, lurch, step, lurch. She inched closer.

Arvis watched her approach with growing dread.

"You found the baby, didn't you?" the woman accused. "Right down here. You took it, isn't that right?"

Arvis retreated a step, pulling the baby tighter to her chest.

Step, lurch, step, lurch. "It isn't yours. That baby is—"

"Yes, it is!" Arvis snapped, as the fire of rage that had toppled a pillar of rats reignited. "I didn't steal anything. The Bakers took her from me!"

The woman stopped and appeared confused. "Her? The child in your arms is a boy," the woman said.

Arvis hesitated as unwanted memories descended on her with a force heavy enough to crush. "No . . . wait . . . that's not right . . . they didn't take her. I . . . I . . ."

Step, lurch, step, lurch.

"I didn't have food for her. I couldn't feed either of us."

Step, lurch, step, lurch.

"Don't you see?" Arvis pleaded with the woman.

Step, lurch, step, lurch.

"She would have died. We both would have. I did the best—the only thing—I could for my beautiful baby girl. They wanted a child and couldn't have one. They promised to keep her safe and feed her well. And they said they would give me free bread for the rest of my life. But . . . but they didn't. Not after I forgot."

Step, lurch, step, lurch.

"That was after *he* beat me—beat me real bad—and my head." Arvis pointed to the scar as best she could while holding the torch. "I couldn't remember things after that. But I didn't forget the bread—the innocent little loaf that I had traded." She looked at the bundle in the crook of her arm.

"This baby isn't that one. It's Sephryn's. The great god Ferrol came—he chose me! I witnessed wonders—and miracles. He needed my help, and I gave of myself freely. He told me to splatter the nursery in pig's blood, and paint strange markings on the wall, then he asked me to take Nurgya and keep him alive until Founder's Day. He said that was when *they* would bestow our salvation. And they are coming. You can hear them, can't you? They clack and clatter."

"I know you," Arvis said. "You're Mica DeBrus. You live with Sephryn."

The old woman, who by then had moved up close to Arvis, showed a sad smile. "Not anymore."

Arvis didn't see the knife until it was too late.

Step, lurch, step, lurch.

CHAPTER EIGHTEEN

Six Toes In

"How old is this stuff?" Errol asked, picking up a scroll, looking it over, then tossing it back into a cubbyhole. A tiny puff of motes issued forth and fell through the single shaft of moonlight like fairy dust.

"Can't you stop fidgeting? And you put that back in the wrong spot. It belongs in the container right below," the monk said sternly, as if they were in his home and those were his things the thief was poking through.

"Oh, good thing you told me, Seymour. I'm sure the people who never come here will be filled with worry when they can't find that rotting piece of parchment they don't know exists."

Sephryn, Errol, and Seymour were holed up in the records hall and had been since sunset. The moon was full—as it was each Founder's Day eve—because the holiday was designated as the day immediately following the first full moon of spring. Although the moonlight wasn't bright enough to read by, the beams managed to spill through the open door and down the steps, providing enough illumination so they could just make out the stacks, steps, and dust.

The monk sat quietly in the pool of light at the bottom of the stairs, whereas Errol wandered the shadows of the stacks, peering into nooks that overflowed with boxes, barrels, and what appeared to be a wine rack. The stacks themselves were crammed with scrolls and loose sheets. Sephryn perched near the door, resting a small bag on her lap. From her seat on the top step, she watched the course of moonlight track across the courtyard and waited for the signal that would call them to action—the midnight bell.

"Perhaps you should take up reading," Seymour said. "These are ancient records dating back to the early days of the empyre. You'd be amazed by what you can discover in old books. They're really quite enlightening."

Errol continued to slink about, peeking into the various nooks and cubbyholes with a miserable grimace. "I don't have the slightest interest."

Seymour looked at the thief and frowned while shaking his head. "Which puts you on par with most of the simpletons living today."

"Really?" Errol turned with a smirk of surprised amusement. "You think I'm the dumb one?" He laughed. "Given the present membership of our intrepid band, I don't think I'm the one lacking intelligence. What do you know about anything?"

"Oh, you have no idea."

Errol, apparently bored with Seymour, turned back to his exploration with the grim fascination one might find on the face of a child poking a dead frog with a stick.

While the men bickered, Sephryn worried about her son and wondered whether she could have handled the situation better. She hadn't demanded evidence that Nurgya was still alive, because it wasn't as if she were negotiating with a thief in a dark alley. Only recently had Sephryn determined she was dealing with a Miralyith rather than a god. While better than facing a divine being, she knew little about the Fhrey Artists.

During the Great War, the Miralyith were the ruling tribe that fought against Nyphron and Persephone. That was why the emperor hated magic. Artists had always been his enemies. After the war, Nyphron decreed a death sentence for anyone who crossed the forbidden river that divided the Fhrey homeland from the rest of the empyre, so whoever kidnapped Nurgya took a big risk crossing over — *but why?*

The answer seemed almost too obvious.

"Most of this is pointless tallies and useless reports," Errol said. "Inventory from a hundred years ago. What value could you possibly expect to find in here?"

"Writing, as we know it," Seymour replied, "was invented before the empyre was founded. This room could contain some of the earliest records."

The first toll of the bell rang out, hollow and haunting.

"It's midnight," Sephryn declared, her voice sounding ominous even to herself. "It's Founder's Day."

"You *are* aware that not *everyone* is fast asleep by the late bell?" Errol said. "I'm sure *you* normally are." Errol tilted his head at the monk. "Him, too. But it's a common fallacy to imagine all people are just like yourself. Easy mistake to make. I, for one, can testify to the fact that many sleep most of the day and have their first meal as the sun sets. For them, this is like your midday."

"I doubt anyone living in the palace keeps to a thief's schedule," Sephryn said.

"But what are the hours of an emperor? Do you know?"

Sephryn admitted, if only to herself, that she had no idea. "Do you have a point? Are you suggesting we wait longer?"

Errol considered the question, looking around as if his present circumstance had a bearing on the subject. "No. For all the gods' sake, let's be done with this before I go mad."

Sephryn placed her hands on Seymour's shoulders. "Remember, you wait here. Do nothing. The Voice won't be able to harm you within these walls — won't even be able to find you. If everything goes well, I'll return. If things go badly — please, cover yourself in the Orinfar and disappear. Go back to Dibben or wherever, and never speak about this to anyone.

You've risked far too much already for a person you barely know. If this is the manner of all monks, I pray your brotherhood spreads." She kissed him on the cheek. "Thank you."

As far as Sephryn knew, there was only one guard stationed inside the courtyard. He had no designated post and simply wandered the grounds. In a hundred years, no one had ever caused trouble in the palace. The guards, wall, and gate had grown into decorations like the ivy, but the men still carried swords, and she guessed they knew how to use them.

Sephryn followed Errol along the flagstones to the pillared porch and up the steps to the front door of the emperor's home. Not nearly as grand as the Aguanon or even the Gem Fortress, the palace was rumored to have been a rushed job, cut short because of Nyphron's desire to move in. Another story insisted that Persephone—being a simple country girl—disdained grandeur and insisted their home be humble. Sephryn knew Persephone had grown up in a dahl more modest than any present-day farm, but the whole country-girl mystique was more than absurd—it was insulting. The woman had been a clan chieftain, and later the keenig who ruled every human soul. Whatever the reason, the palace was as humble as a two-winged, four-story, white-marble-pillared building could be.

Errol had stopped at the door. While crouching to examine the lock, the door opened and hit him full in the face.

A young woman with a bucket stared at him. "What are you doing?" she asked, with the distinct note of an accusation in her tone.

Errol sprang up, one hand to his head. He opened his mouth, but for once, Sephryn managed to speak first. "Opella, how are you?"

The wash-girl looked over and spotted Sephryn. The moment she did, suspicion shifted to confusion. "Oh—your ladyship! I—" She looked back at Errol, who remained frozen like a soldier halted at attention. "Is *he* with you?" she asked quietly as if Errol wouldn't be able to hear.

Errol looked at her, and for the first time, she saw that arrogant mask melt into concern.

"Yes," Sephryn replied, cheerfully. "This is Mathias Hagger." She pulled the name from the deep recesses of her memory. Someone her mother used to know. "He's doing some work for me. He was buckling his boot, and you nearly took him out with the door."

"Oh! Sorry. I didn't mean—"

"That's all right, dear," Sephryn soothed. "You didn't happen to see my beige scarf when you were cleaning up, did you? I'm sure I left it in my office. I just can't sleep till I find it. It was a gift."

"Oh, of course!" Any lingering lines of befuddlement faded from the girl's face, and she smiled. "Prince Nolyn gave it to you, didn't he? And I can see why you can't be without it tonight, but I didn't see it when I was up there." Opella moved around Errol to dump her dirty water.

"That's all right," Sephryn said, puzzled, but not about to chitchat. "I think I know where it is."

"Okay, but be careful. I just washed the floor, and it's still wet. It gets slick."

They entered the palace. The entrance hall looked entirely different at night. Sconce lamps illuminated the chamber, while the tall windows were black. Opella returned, then waited. Clearly, she intended to follow them.

Sephryn stared at Errol, giving him a firm and—she hoped—telling look. The thief had always suggested he was intelligent, and she hoped it hadn't all been a swindler's act. "Opella?" Errol said. His hand still cupped to his forehead. "You hit me awfully hard with that door."

"I'm so sorry. I didn't mean—"

"It's just . . . I mean . . . I'm feeling faint, and I think I might be bleeding. Is there somewhere I could sit or lie down? I—" Errol staggered, put his back against the wall, and slid down until he was sitting on the floor.

"Oh, dear!" Opella said. "Let me go get someone who—"

"No—no, that won't be necessary. I'm just a bit—I merely need a moment. And perhaps if it isn't too much trouble, could I have a cup of water?"

"You're certain you're all right?"

"Just a chair and a glass of water, please."

"Oh, yes. Right away." Opella rushed off.

Errol glared at Sephryn. "I warned you not to make assumptions about others."

"Who knew we had to account for wash-girl hours."

"Make it quick and don't forget to grab Bartholomew."

No lights burned upstairs, leaving the residence a geometric painting of elongated moonlight on marble. She kept to the shadows and was cautious with her movements. Sephryn clutched the rolled-up bag in her fist, her heart picking up speed. She'd never stolen anything but a kiss, and even that hadn't gone well. The only law she'd ever broken was when she protested the treatment of humans—an act in which she'd felt justified and proud to be caught doing. She didn't feel that way now. What she was about to do was nothing less than a simple, ugly theft. She wasn't just crossing a line; she was performing a running jump. If caught, she could lose her hands, or since she was stealing from the palace even her head. Sephryn had often wondered at those who faced such severe punishments. She didn't understand how they could risk such high stakes, until now.

"It's a common fallacy to imagine all people are just like yourself."

Errol, she determined, had been wrong. Everyone was the same and only the situation made a difference. What good were her hands, or even her life, if she allowed her child to die?

Moving across the tile flooring and up the marble steps, she didn't make a sound.

Sephryn was good at being quiet. Mica had complained that Sephryn had a nasty habit of startling her *one-foot-and-six-toes-into-*

the-grave on numerous occasions after putting Nurgya to bed. Sephryn apologized, but it still happened. After one jolt too many, Mica threatened to leave and went to the extravagant length of packing her things. The old woman had nowhere to go and not much to put in her single canvas bag. After that, Sephryn promised to stop and she had. Yet as Sephryn crept along, she realized she had done Mica no favors, and the bag Sephryn held in her hands—the one in which she hoped to conceal the horn—had been Mica's.

Sephryn reached the door where she'd once encountered Illim. She stared at it, holding her breath. She looked up the corridor and then down. No light, no sound. She was alone. When she raised the latch, the door drifted in a bit under its own weight. Sephryn gave it a light push, and it swung farther. She peered inside. The interior was illuminated by a light, but it burned in a room far down a corridor.

"But what are the hours of an emperor?"

She waited, listening. No sound, not even heavy breathing.

Then Sephryn grimaced at another possibility: the awkwardness of interrupting the emperor if he wasn't alone in his bed. Fhrey were known to be less traditional in their intimate habits, but also to have less interest in carnal relations—their long lives caused them to outgrow its pleasures the same way adults lost interest in leapfrog and somersaults. Still, given he shared his chambers with Illim, finding them together wasn't impossible. An accidental interruption, and the subsequent embarrassment, might be fatal.

He'll execute me for certain, no ceremony necessary. Nyphron will exercise his judgment and punishment right here, then haul my body out with the rest of the palace trash.

She moved slowly and more silently than a cat toward the stone imperfection that she hoped was the gemlocked vault. She knelt down and let her fingers run over the surface, top to bottom, learning absolutely nothing. Then she glanced back over her shoulder toward the faint light coming from deeper in.

The reason I so deftly managed to scare Mica six-toes-in was partly because of my Fhrey heritage. Not every hound was a born hunter, but all of them had keen noses, the same basic traits. A similar observation could be made regarding Fhrey. Agility, keen eyesight, and acute hearing were dominant traits just like her ability to move silently. Being a full-blooded Fhrey, Nyphron had to be even better, so he could appear without warning at any minute. She pictured the emperor of the world with bed-hair, wearing only an untied robe and a scowl.

She reached into her purse, which was tied to her belt. An ever-present part of her attire, the small leather pouch with the drawstring contained her life savings and an ugly, rough-cut ruby the size of an egg. She pulled on the strings, but the mouth remained stubbornly closed. *Of all the times to be annoying!* She untangled the string, repeatedly looking over her shoulder. Then she opened the bag and drew out the stone.

Here goes.

Sephryn held the ruby out to the wall.

Nothing happened.

With her other hand, she pressed on the area where there was a faint depression.

Nothing.

She began to move the stone about, sliding it along the surface.

The emperor never put Bartholomew in the box! An avalanche of doubt followed, including the idea that Brinkle had made a mistake, and the vault wasn't a gemlocked box after all. *Why did we even think that? Or did Brinkle lie? If the dwarf went to Nyphron and told him the whole thing, then any minute now—*

Click.

The sound was muffled and indistinct, and yet, she heard it.

Oh, please, let that be it!

Her hands were shaking.

Once more, Sephryn looked back toward the distant flickering glow, as if it were the den of a dragon. She had marked the extent of the light's reach and watched to see if it changed, if it had moved. It hadn't, and there was no sound from the bowels of the residence.

Again, she pressed the wall, and it popped open and moved as if on hinges. The interior looked like a cupboard, but in place of dishes was a medley of oddities. A black-bladed sword etched with symbols; a simple golden cup; a beaded mask; an old, battered helmet; a dark bottle; a pair of gloves; a green, jewel-encrusted egg; and an old ram's horn.

Sephryn carefully drew out the horn. She expected it to be heavy but found it as light as a hollow gourd. Stuffing it into Mica's bag, she cinched it closed and clutched the bundle to her chest. Then she removed the egg and put it and the ruby into her purse.

Footsteps.

Sephryn's heart stopped.

The steps came quickly, as if someone was moving at a trot—not from inside, but out.

Sephryn closed the vault and, as fast as she could, found and threw the bolt on the inside of the chamber door, locking it.

From outside came the sound of feet sliding to a stop and then a knock. The noise was so loud that she jumped. She turned and faced the illuminated corridor behind her and froze. The knock came again, even louder. Sephryn's heart skipped as she waited for the emperor or Illim to appear. She imagined one or both marching down the hallway, angry at the late intrusion, then spotting her just stupidly standing there.

At her feet, light leaked under the hallway door from whatever lantern the visitor held. Twin shadows of feet shifted back and forth nervously. Then the latch jiggled, and Sephryn stopped breathing.

She was too scared to think, too terrified to even pray.

It's over. This is it. I'm dead, and so is Nurgya.

"The emperor isn't in his chambers," a distant voice said from outside.

"Do you know where he is?" someone just on the other side of the door replied.

"In the war room. What's this about?"

She heard more footsteps but couldn't tell if they were coming or going.

"The emperor's son is at the gate, and he insists on seeing his father immediately."

Nolyn? Nolyn is here?

"Escort him to the waiting room. I'll notify Nyphron."

The footsteps faded.

Nolyn is here?

Returning to the entrance hall, Sephryn had imagined finding scores, no, hundreds of soldiers armed and waiting. Instead, she found Errol seated comfortably on a cushioned chair with a drink in hand. Opella was nowhere to be seen. Errol put the glass down, hopped to his feet, and without a word, the two darted for the courtyard.

Sephryn was shaking and kept looking back.

"Stop doing that," Errol whispered.

They walked quickly across the courtyard to the records room where Seymour waited.

"Well?" the monk asked.

"Yes—well?" Errol repeated.

"I got it." She held up Mica's bag.

"And the emerald?" Errol asked.

She tapped her purse.

"Everything worked perfectly. Here, take it." Sephryn shoved Mica's bag into Seymour's hands.

The monk looked at it, surprised.

"Why give it to him?" Errol asked.

"I'm going to demand that the Voice returns Nurgya first. I think the Voice is a Fhrey Miralyith, and he plans on using the horn to make himself ruler of the Fhrey. I'm not exactly sure how. It shouldn't work until several thousand years in the future, but maybe we're missing some of the details. Once Nurgya is safe, or I learn that he's . . . well . . . I intend to go to the palace and tell Nyphron everything."

"*Everything* everything?" Errol asked.

She frowned. "I think I can leave both of you out of it."

"So what do you want me to do with this?" Seymour asked.

"Just keep it here. If by sunset tomorrow I don't come back, take the horn to the emperor and give it to him. Tell him you had nothing to do with the theft because, of course, you didn't. Blame me because that's the truth. Okay? Will you do that for me, Seymour?"

The monk nodded.

"Thank you." She gave him a hug.

"What about me?" Errol said. "I took a door to the head and endured the profuse apologies of a servant."

Sephryn approached and looked at his head. He actually had an ugly bump there.

"Thank you, too."

Errol held out his arms. "Arvis said you'd sleep with me as payment . . ."

Sephryn's eyes went wide.

He smiled. "But I'll settle for a hug."

Sephryn left the records room with Errol. Together they walked to the gate, where the guard smiled. "Late night, I see. Nothing wrong, I hope?"

"We'll see," she replied.

"Farewell, nice working with you." Errol gave a wave and trotted off.

Sephryn paused, looking at two men just outside the gate who appeared to be waiting. One was tall and dressed in mirror-like armor. The other, much smaller, man wore robes of the state.

A strange time to be standing outside the palace.

She indicated the two. "Did they arrive with the prince?"

Andrule nodded. "Something important, I guess."

Sephryn had long begged Nolyn to confront Nyphron, and he had always refused. Father and son hadn't spoken face-to-face in centuries. She had no idea why Nolyn was demanding an audience in the middle of the night before Founder's Day, but she knew it wasn't because of something trivial. She looked back at the palace and hesitated, wondering if she ought to go back in and . . .

. . . *and what? Tell him the son he never knew existed was kidnapped, and I just robbed the palace in an attempt to save him? "C'mon, honey. Forget whatever you're doing here in the middle of the night, and let's go talk to a disembodied voice and hope that the son I just told you about is still alive."*

How did my life become such a mess?

Aunt Suri would have said that his return wasn't a coincidence, that having him show up on the same night she was stealing a horn to save their son couldn't be the result of random chance. Despite doubting most of what her mother and aunts had told her, Sephryn still felt a powerful urge to suspect something more was going on. Everything at that moment felt connected and purposeful, as if the world was aligning itself, tilting toward some immense event, and she, Sephryn, daughter of Tekchin and Moya, stood remarkably close to the center. But Sephryn also knew that ordinary things could feel filled with portent when it was dark. And just now she was standing under late-night stars.

She was a block down the Grand Mar before noticing that her purse was missing.

CHAPTER NINETEEN

Father and Son

The steward that escorted Nolyn through the palace was human. Nolyn was certain of that. He had round ears and dark eyes; he walked with a fumbling, uncertain gait, and his hair was black. Despite all that evidence, Nolyn could have sworn he had followed the same attendant when his mother was alive.

Perhaps this is Malcolm, he speculated.

His mother and aunts had all spoken of a person by that name who wasn't human, dwarf, or Fhrey. When pressed on the question of what he was, they often changed the subject, making Nolyn believe they didn't know. In the many outlandish stories they told, Malcolm was a minor character who appeared on the margins. Little was ever said about him, yet Nolyn always found stories that included Malcolm to be the most interesting. He was present at pivotal moments, guiding important decisions, and of course, he didn't age. He was said to have visited Persephone on the day of her death to say goodbye. Similar rumors surrounded the passing of Roan and Gifford of Rhen and Aunt Suri.

In each tale, Malcolm was reported to have *not aged a day*. Before long, Nolyn spotted the trend and began looking for Malcolm even in the stories where he didn't appear, believing his hand to be there somewhere, perhaps in disguise.

Given the potentially momentous, and possibly cataclysmic, nature of the meeting with his father, Nolyn could imagine it would be an event where Malcolm would attend. He'd heard the stories from a young age, and his child's imagination cultivated the image of Malcolm as a mischievous gremlin who tampered with the lives of otherwise normal folk, exchanging their fortunes for more amusing fates.

As Nolyn walked the stone corridors of the palace following the little man in his stuffy, long-coated uniform, he hoped the steward was, indeed, Malcolm. At least then something good might be wrung from the encounter, and it would be proof that his life had some meaning. If not, he saw his time on Elan as a mistake, a dead end, a long branch that never managed to grow leaves, much less bear fruit.

He recalled the story his mother once told him of how Raithe went out the gate of Dahl Rhen to confront the Fhrey gods and prepared to engage in a losing fight with Nyphron of the Galantians. Nolyn always pictured it sunny and heroic. His own encounter would be the night before Founder's Day in a cold, moonlit palace.

The steward guided him to a comfortable room, then left.

So much for him being Malcolm.

The room held a hearth with a burning fire. Curtains framed tall windows that in the dark of night acted as nothing but black mirrors reflecting his image—one that was quite unimpressive. Shields and swords hung on the walls. *We won't lack for armaments in this fight.* Two high-backed chairs faced each other on either end of a small table decorated with a vase of early blooming lilies. Nolyn was standing behind one of the chairs when the door opened, and his father entered.

At first glance, Nolyn was surprised. His father had always seemed huge and frightening. Yet the person walking in was slightly shorter than himself, a bit overweight, and dressed in a simple, rumpled, pullover tunic cinched with a wide embroidered belt. But the most striking thing was that he was smiling. Nolyn never remembered his father doing that. In his few fleeting memories, the emperor was a stern, cold ruler and distant father. He never went to the Hawthorn Glen with the family and would have appeared out of place if he had. *"A pine tree in an apple orchard,"* his Aunt Suri might have said. She had a thing about trees.

"Will you look at that," Nyphron began. "You've grown up. I still remember you best as that kid with the runny nose in your mother's tent in the High Spear Valley. Do you remember that? Probably not. Now look at you. A warrior, a soldier in uniform . . . but only a prymus? Eight centuries and that's as far as you've come? That's disappointing. I also see you wear your sword. Do you know it's not permitted to come into the presence of the emperor wearing a blade?"

"Your steward didn't say a word."

"If my steward were replaced with a well-trained dog, I'd likely get better service." As if to demonstrate the fact, Nyphron looked around, scowled, then moved to the decanter of wine and pulled the top off. "I suspect he anticipated that, as my son, you would refuse to relinquish your weapon. I certainly would, and he likely assumed you're just like me."

"He would be wrong." Nolyn gripped the ears of the high-backed chair in front of him like a lectern. "I'm nothing like my father."

That made Nyphron smile again. "No? So, you *would* have given up your sword, then?"

Nolyn wanted to say he would, except that would be a lie.

"Yes, I see," Nyphron said. "Completely unlike your father."

The emperor moved to a cabinet and picked up two golden cups. He carried them and the decanter to the little table before the flickering hearth.

"I don't think a drink is appropriate," Nolyn said.

"Because you're on duty or because you're here to kill me? I do hope it's the latter. Otherwise, I'll be sorely disappointed. Making just prymus in eight hundred years of service is one thing, but refusing to drink because of regulations is unforgivable. After all, you're the son of a Galantian. Besides, this is really good wine."

Nolyn didn't move or speak.

Nyphron poured wine into one of the cups and smiled. "Don't look so shocked. You've assumed command of my First and Second legions and used five warships to take control of the Urum River. And you've arrived the night before Founder's Day wearing your sword—which is also the anniversary of your mother's death. What else could you be planning? A surprise party?"

Nolyn was the one surprised. An instant later, he realized he shouldn't have been. *A fleet of warships is a hard secret to keep.*

"You shouldn't have tried to kill me," Nolyn admonished, trying to sound superior.

"Kill you?" Nyphron paused in his pouring of the first drink to stare at his son, confused. "What are you talking about?"

They weren't swinging swords yet, but it felt that way, and his father was battering him off-balance with ease. Nolyn hadn't expected a denial. His father wasn't the subtle type. If nothing else, Nyphron had always been forthright. The Fhrey had no shame, didn't know the meaning of the word. "You ordered me into an ambush. Palatus Demetrius of Urlineus is waiting at the palace gate, and he will testify about the dispatch you personally sent to Legate Lynch that instructed him to make my death look like a casualty of war."

That not only made his father smile but also laugh aloud. "Why in Elan would I . . . I mean, seriously, Nolyn, I'm both your father *and* the emperor. If I wanted you dead, that's what you'd be. And I wouldn't delegate that duty to a corrupt legate in Calynia. Do you think me such a delicate flower that I would shrink from an unpleasant task? I made you, Nolyn. I'd be perfectly capable of eliminating you. But why would I?"

"Because you see me as a threat."

"Really? What sort?" Nyphron picked up his cup and made a swirling motion toward the dark windows. "Are you referring to the legions you stole? The ones who are about to march on this city and crown you emperor?"

The way he said it made Nolyn realize he'd been outmaneuvered. *He's had time. Not much, but enough for the legendary Nyphron to outwit my spur-of-the-moment rebellion. My father is a military genius.*

"My legions are corrupt, blighted to the core, but there are certain advantages in rotten apples. They are easily squeezed. You might think that an army of humans would be a weakness for a Fhrey ruler because humans are organizationally weak, but I don't rule them merely from above, but also from within. Corruption works both ways, and as it turns out, no one can outbid the emperor."

Sephryn made the turn onto Ebonydale and ducked under the eaves of the Imperial Masquerade Emporium, the exact spot where she had once placed a flag to help Seymour find his way home. The streets were empty, ghostly, and the moonlight bounced off the cobbles and bathed the tarps and awnings in a light glow. She'd never liked the mask shop. The gruesome faces that hung from the porch as samples always unnerved her. All those grinning visages looked evil, and she often wondered about the people who carved such awful things and what kind of nightmares they suffered. The pale light and deep shadows only enhanced the ghastly impact of the masks, and yet it felt more than appropriate — it felt staged.

The gods are watching, and I'm tonight's entertainment.

Sephryn expected to hear from the Voice the moment she stepped outside the palace gate, but there she was, all the way to the Masquerade Emporium and the Voice hadn't so much as whispered in her ear. She was far enough away now, and the streets were empty. Sephryn was alone in the night.

"Hello?" she ventured softly.

No response.

"I stole the horn like you wanted. Are you there?" she asked. *Probably doesn't believe me. Even I didn't think it would be possible, and yet, it wasn't all that difficult.*

That, too, bothered her. Inside the palace, she hadn't encountered a single guard, and the room with the vault wasn't even locked. She considered the other items stored there. None struck her as particularly valuable—the horn least of all. The safe seemed more like a curio cabinet than a treasure hoard. The most valuable item in it was Bartholomew.

She waited for the Voice's response, but all she heard was an annoying clicking sound. Usually, the night noises of peeping frogs and chirping crickets didn't penetrate so far into the city. The lack of ponds and the presence of only a few grassy areas meant there wasn't adequate housing for a proper musical troupe. But then again, the clicking didn't sound like frogs or crickets. Sephryn considered the possibility of cicadas or locusts because the noise was high-pitched, rapid, and coming from everywhere at once. But it was still early spring, too soon for either of those. The clicking was louder, sharper, and more defined. Sephryn had seen shows where southeastern dancers clapped little metal disks in time to music. The instruments were called zills, and they were strapped to the very top of the women's fingers. The sound she heard now was like that—as if there were thousands of invisible zill-equipped performers competing to see who was the most dexterous.

Sephryn took a step and peered down the alley that ran between the masquerade shop and an alchemist. The noise was louder down that way. As she looked, Sephryn spotted movement. She was quite gifted at seeing in the dark, and the full moon helped. Even so, the alley was shrouded in overlapping shadows. All she could make out were dark shapes that writhed and undulated in an unpleasant rhythm.

Maggots. The thought came to her instantly. Sephryn wasn't squeamish about much, but the pale-white larvae bothered her. The way they moved—squirming over one another to form a writhing, mindless mass—made her skin crawl. That's what the shapes in the darkness reminded her of as they rocked and shifted.

Disgusted yet fascinated, she took a step in their direction.

"Do you have it?" the Voice said in her head.

Sephryn stopped. Not knowing who or what was in the alley, or if it could hear and understand speech, she turned away and quickly walked down the street. "Yes, but I'm not going to give it to you until I see my son. I want to know he's alive." She held her breath. She'd never made a demand of the Voice before and didn't know what to expect. At the very least, she anticipated outrage. Sephryn cringed in anticipation.

"Fine. But before that can happen, I'll require one additional task from you."

"What?" Sephryn was pleased she was alone on the street because she said the word far louder than intended. "We had a deal. I already did what you asked."

"Be that as it may, events have occurred, and changes must be made."

There was something strange about the Voice. Something off, something different. The tone was deeper, and the demeanor was more . . . polite.

Perhaps that was a good sign. An indication that things would work out. He had agreed to let her see Nurgya, which meant her son was still alive. She couldn't turn back now. "What is it?"

"I want you to get your mother's bow, find a place with a good view of the fountain in front of the palace gates, and when Emperor Nyphron comes out into the square, I want you to kill him."

Nolyn rested a hand on the pommel of his sword and waited.

Amicus and Demetrius were right. Coming here had been a bad idea.

I should have known better. My father didn't become emperor of the world by inheriting the title.

Nolyn glanced at the doors to the little chamber that was freakishly pleasant, even cheerful, with its bouquet of lilies in a white porcelain vase. None of the doors opened, and Nolyn heard no stomping of boots.

"Sure you don't want that drink now?" Nyphron asked, walking to a chair with his cup and plopping himself down.

"I'm fine," Nolyn lied. He felt as he always did just before combat. Every sense on alert, his heart beating at double time, a faint sheen of sweat rising on his skin. If he didn't think he needed every advantage possible, he would have guzzled every drop from the decanter.

"Fine? Really? I doubt that." Nyphron grinned and threw his legs up over the arm of the chair, letting his feet dangle. "Tell me, did you enjoy fighting the gobs in the Durat?"

"What?" Nolyn asked, confused.

"When I was with the Galantians, we had the time of our lives up there in the mountains. Every crack, crevasse, and fissure held adventure. Of course, most of them also contained ghazel." He sighed, reflectively. There was a look on his father's face and a tone in his voice that Nolyn had never experienced before: affable, ironic, wit-laced, and filled with a dark humor, this sort of exchange was usually reserved for the ranks of bonded warriors. "There's just something so exhilarating about that cold mountain air and the way goblin blood steams off a wet blade, I just—"

"Are you seriously reminiscing about the good old days?"

Nyphron raised his cup of wine. "Absolutely. Here's to those glory days of grand hazards and life-affirming risks. You've heard your mother's stories dozens of times, but you've never heard mine. And my tales are far more exciting. Like the time when—"

"Stop it!" Nolyn demanded. "I didn't come here for stories."

His father lost his grin and went back to swirling his drink. "No? Why not? I haven't seen you in centuries. Seems about time we got caught up, don't you think?"

"No." Nolyn was surprised at his own frustration, which bloomed into full-on anger. "We are not friends."

"But we could be."

"No, we can't. It's impossible because you're a self-centered, egotistical bastard who always hated me and my mother. You drove her to an early grave and ordered my death."

"Back to that, are we?" Nyphron's brows knitted, and his lips pulled into a sidelong frown. "Where'd you get this from, anyway? And incidentally, I'm the legitimate and recognized son of Zephyron, so I can't actually be a bastard. And for the record, I never hated either of you."

"You're lying." Nolyn waved his arms at the walls. "Look at this place. It was built in two parts. A wing for me and Persephone and separate quarters for you. That's not the way married people live."

Nyphron took a sip of wine. "Your mother and I didn't have *that* kind of relationship."

"What kind?"

"Romantic."

"Then what sort did you have?"

"One of mutual respect and admiration and devotion to an ideal — the notion that we were perfectly suited to make the world a better place."

Nolyn let out an exasperated, half-choked, bitter laugh.

"Don't believe me, eh?" Nyphron looked into his cup as he continued to swirl it. "Tell me, then, why would a self-centered, egotistical bastard like myself name this city after a woman I supposedly hated?"

"Malcolm made you do it." Nolyn used the name like a magic talisman, and like all magical items, he had no idea how it worked or what it might do.

"Malcolm?" Nyphron grinned. "Now there's an echo from the past."

"He visited Mother just before she died, eight hundred and thirty-three years ago. Right after that, you dedicated the city in her name."

Nyphron responded with a smug smile. "If he was here that day, I didn't see him. He and I haven't talked since . . . well, since before I became emperor. Besides, Malcolm never ordered me to do anything. He knew better than that. I don't respond well to *orders*."

"In the Battle of Grandford, he ordered you to shroud the archers. And later, he forced you to become fane even though you wanted to slaughter all the Erivan Fhrey."

"He didn't order me, or even so much as demand. He asked and was quite polite with his *requests*. And"—Nyphron nodded—"he was right on both occasions. He told me I would see it his way eventually. So I suppose he was right about that. But I named the city after your mother because she deserved it. She lived a long time, for a human, but not long enough. I didn't want her memory to be lost to history. She was already overlooked by many, her accomplishments forgotten. Persephone made this city possible as much as I did. She was the one who picked the spot. In your mother's day, this was just a grassy bluff overlooking the Urum, an exposed cliff of flint shards, which were used as knives and to start fires. She considered it a place where dreams could be realized, a spot we could build something lasting. The dwarfs disagreed. They complained about the site, said the ground was bad. Apparently, it's hollow. The city sits above limestone caverns and an underground river or lake. I forget the specifics, but your mother wouldn't be deterred. She insisted on building here, and she would have no other." He nodded again. "This is her city. She'd always said it was the people's, but she's the one who made it rise and deserved the recognition. That's why I named it after her. Persephone's City—in the Fhrey: *Percepliquis*."

"And me?" Nolyn asked.

"What about you?"

"You hardly spoke to me when I was a child."

Nyphron shrugged. "I'm not good with kids. Fhrey have so few. We aren't accustomed to them. I left you to your mother because she was the expert. That's how we did things, she and I—each to our own strengths. And we were honest with each other . . . as I'm being with you now."

"Uh-huh," Nolyn said dismissively. "And when she died, do you remember how you consoled me? Allow me to refresh your memory. You ordered me stripped, forced me to be tattooed, then sent me north with the First Legion to fight and nearly die in the Grenmorian War."

"Exactly." Nyphron dropped his feet to the floor, leaned forward, and nodded proudly. "Nothing is better for grief than killing. I knew you'd be devastated by her loss. Nothing I could say—nothing anyone could say—would make it better. You were going to be raging with anger and hate. What you needed was a way to let that out. Slaying giants was the answer. And you did well."

Nolyn had been more than angry; he wanted to fight, desired blood. It took a whole year to exorcise his demons, to drown them in lakes of giants' blood.

"And after? You also sent me to the Durat to fight the goblins," Nolyn accused.

"Sure," Nyphron grinned. "Figured you earned a reward."

"A reward? How is that a reward?"

Nyphron's eyes brightened in memory. "Best days of my life were spent killing goblins in the Durat." Nyphron smiled broadly as he looked up at the ceiling. "Gods, those were fine times: basking in the sun at the top of the world, butchering the little buggers in their holes, fighting desperate battles against overwhelming odds, drinking ourselves stupid at night and roaring like animals at the moon. Never since have I felt as alive or as free. And you can only do that when you're young, unattached, unfettered, and unencumbered by the truths that come later—the weight that anchors you to the ground. Only the carefree can fly. That was my gift to you, a youth well lived."

"I nearly died."

"Great, wasn't it?" His father pointed at him with the hand that held the cup.

At that moment, Nolyn hated his father more than ever. Not because Nyphron was wrong, but because the emperor might be right. Those years had always been poisoned by the belief that his father had sentenced him to war as punishment for crimes he never committed. A blanket of resentment had smothered the joy out of every achievement, every friendship, every starry night spent on a ledge observing the glory of the world. Fear, misery, death, loss, and regret had scarred him, but he had also known beauty, kindness, love, and wonder. The lows were deep, but the highs dizzying. Life after the Durat continued with pinnacles and valleys, but the range was muted, dulled to a hazy, vague boredom. Accepting his father's excuse threatened to leave Nolyn with a hole where his hate used to be.

"And the salt mines? Was that also a reward?"

"No, but by then I felt it was time for you to do real work."

"How was that *real* work?"

Nyphron stared at him, stunned. "Are you not aware how vital salt is to the empyre? All the gold, diamonds, and silver are nothing compared with a constant flow of salt. We can't live without it. Air, water, food, and salt are the basics everyone needs to survive. A growing empyre needs a lot, and there's not much to be had. When I assigned you to that post, we had just acquired rights to that quarry from the Kingdom of Belgreig. When Rain was king, I could trust them, but the rulers since then have grown increasingly deceitful. I anticipated problems, and I sent you to guard this empyre's greatest treasure."

"Is that why I spent more than five hundred years as the *assistant* administrator of the mine?"

"That was genius, if I do say so myself." Nyphron smiled. "No one would bribe or try to blackmail an assistant who is also the emperor's son. No advantage in that. You didn't have the power to make decisions, but you could ruin a businessman's day if you reported anything to me. No administrator would dare accept a bribe or engage in shady dealings with the son of the emperor watching his every move. And no one was stupid enough to try to kill you after your performance in two separate wars. Your tenure at that mine kept the empyre safe."

Nolyn stared at his father, unsure what to think. He was angry, and afraid that if given time to reflect, he might lose that edge. He glanced at the doors again. "You talk a good game, but I can't trust anything you say. So, are you going to have me executed for treason? Or are we going to fight?"

His father smiled again and shrugged. "I suppose that's what we're deciding, isn't it?"

CHAPTER TWENTY

Children of Legends

Sephryn stepped into her house. Closing the door behind her, she fell against it and slid to the floor. She was shaking, and she pulled her knees up to her chin. She started to rock.

Oh, dear Mother of All, what am I going to do?

Stealing an old horn had been one thing, but murdering Nyphron was unthinkable.

I can't kill the emperor.

The very notion was insane. Not only was it horribly wrong, it was also completely impossible.

He's a living legend for two different races.

The universe would never allow someone like her to destroy someone like him, even if she wanted to—which she didn't. Nyphron was a renowned warrior and a full-blooded Fhrey, the leader of the famous Galantians. One of three things would happen: He would swat her attack away like a bug, his armor would deflect the arrow, or most likely, he'd catch the projectile and laugh.

I can't kill the emperor.

Sephryn began to repeat the words in her head in an attempt to chase away any other ideas that might seek to enter. Citizens of Percepliquis did something similar on New Year's Day. The entire population of the city came out and rang bells and hammered pots to frighten demons away. Sephryn's fiend was already planted in her head, and she couldn't let it take root.

I can't kill the emperor. I can't kill the emperor. I can't kill the emperor.

The words became a chant, a magic shield to ward off evil. Words, however, were a weak defense against thoughts that had so many places in which to seep in.

The Voice knows about the bow. Has he known about my legacy all along? Was this part of his plan from the start, or was he listening when Errol and I spoke to Augustine Brinkle?

Sephryn thought she had sensed something, but that might have been her imagination. And yet, it was absurd to think that the Voice wouldn't have been present for that conversation.

Maybe he knew, maybe he didn't. Does it matter?

Her gaze started to rise toward the hearth, and she forced her sight back to the floor.

No! I can't kill the emperor. I can't kill the emperor. I can't kill the emperor.

She heard the sound of a baby crying, muffled and distant. The chugging, huffing, desperate whimper of an infant in discomfort filtered through her chants.

Am I hearing that through my ears, or is it in my head? Is it outside, or is it Nurgya?

Rocking her back hard against the door, she couldn't tell. The Voice might be allowing Nurgya's cries to reach her through whatever conduit he used to speak to her. It also might be a fake, an imitation, or even another child used to prod her into action. And there was a good chance it was just a nearby baby awake in the night and crying to be fed.

Sephryn slapped her palms to her ears and held her head as she rocked in torment.

I'm losing my mind. I'm losing my mind. I'm losing my mind. But I'm not going to kill the emperor. Not going to kill the emperor. Not going to kill the emperor.

Her hands muffled the sound, but she couldn't snuff it out. As if in response, the child's cries grew more urgent. The huffing whimpers shifted to louder, frantic wails.

"Nurgya," she sobbed. "I'm so sorry, baby. Please don't cry."

I need a new thought—a new thought—a new thought.

One came to her.

Why is Nolyn back? Does he know about his son? How could he?

Sephryn was exhausted. She'd been up nearly a full day and night, and she hadn't been sleeping well before that. The anxiety of the robbery had kept her awake. Sleep deprived, she found it difficult to think, to judge.

Not going to kill the emperor. Not going to kill the emperor.

With each chant, her back hit the door. It clapped against the frame, adding a *ka-thap, ka-thap* to the repeating rhythm of her thoughts. *Ka-thap. Not going to kill the emperor. Ka-thap. Not going to kill the emperor.*

The sound of the crying child grew more desperate. Sephryn crushed her ears with her hands but couldn't silence the wails.

Ka-thap. Not going to kill the emperor. Ka-thap. Not going to kill the emperor.

The floor was cold, and her back hurt from being slammed against the door.

"Can you do it?" Augustine Brinkle had asked her. *"Can you shoot like your mother?"*

Ka-thap. Not going to kill the emperor. Ka-thap. Not going to kill the emperor.

Sephryn dug her nails into the sides of her head, squeezing the flat of her palms as hard as she could against her ears.

"I bet you can. I'm sure you're incredible."

The baby was shrieking by then, screaming in the night. *Why won't anyone help that poor kid? What's wrong with its mother? Doesn't she care? Doesn't she hear?*

Sephryn realized she was looking across the room at the fireplace. She focused on the stack of wood, at the hearth utensils, and the space where the poker used to be. She couldn't stop herself; her sight drifted up. She saw the mantel, and just above it was . . .

"The daughter of Moya the Magnificent, who is also endowed with the Fhrey blood of an Instarya father, would be amazing."

Audrey.

The bow was long and made from the dark wood of Magda, the oracle tree of Dahl Rhen that had told Persephone how to save mankind. The ancient tree had been killed by lightning sent by the Miralyith, splitting it wide. Roan of Rhen took the heart of Magda and fashioned it into the first bow, a thing believed at the time to be magic. Moya had named the bow Audrey, after her own mother.

"I bet you can. I'm sure you're incredible."

The bow had no string, merely an elegant curve and a stunning grain pattern that had deepened with age and the oil and sweat from her mother's hands.

The baby is crying. Am I going to just sit here? I must do something. If I don't, Nurgya will die. And that can't happen, not while . . .

Shadows lost their grip on the room as dawn broke. A hazy light entered the open windows, highlighting the elegant, curved wood of the bow. That weapon was just as much a legend as Nyphron. It had destroyed Balgargarath, securing weapons so that a desperate race of people could rise against their oppressors. It had killed Udgar, clearing the path for Persephone's rule and the salvation of every man, woman, and child on the face of Elan.

Sephryn recalled Kendel, the man who had died on the street, and the words of his grieving mother. *"Why can't you stop this? You've been our hope. We've believed in you. Trusted you."*

"I want to see them punished when he's crowned," Arvis had said.

"But I don't think you'll get the chance. Emperor Nyphron is just a little over seventeen hundred. He'll likely live another five hundred years."

Sephryn had stopped slamming against the door, and the room grew quiet. Even the baby had stopped crying. Silence—eerie and tense—filled her room.

The emperor was Fhrey. He was from another time, a different reality, an age when humans were Rhunes and Fhrey were gods. Nyphron would never change the laws. Under his rule, men and women would forever be second class. Sephryn's mother had fought to free her race from the yoke of the Fhrey, but Moya's war had been left unfinished. The Fhrey still ruled and would do so forever. Unless . . .

"Why can't you stop this?"

Moya's bow had killed so many Fhrey.

"I bet you can."

With the death of just one more, everything would change.

"I'm sure you're incredible."

With Nolyn on the throne, she could help him bring about Persephone's vision for true peace between men and Fhrey.

"The daughter of Moya the Magnificent, who is also endowed with the Fhrey blood of an Instarya father, would be amazing."

"I understand," Nyphron told Nolyn after taking a sip of wine. "I felt much the same way about my father. Zephyron was the commander of all of Avrlyn, the head of the Instarya, but I received no benefit from being his son. Quite the opposite. He treated me like an unwelcome dog. Gave me the worst assignments. I thought he hated me. I wasn't the only one. The entire garrison at Alon Rhist witnessed his ill treatment and sympathized." Nyphron sighed, grimaced, and then in a whisper he said, "I was forced to rake out animal pens, and I did it regularly. No one did that—no Instarya, at least. That was the task of slaves. But when I was young, I actually shoveled manure. I stood ankle-deep in filth, and I cursed Zephyron until the pigs blushed. Couldn't understand it. I didn't know what I'd done to deserve such treatment."

Nolyn continued to stand, feeling oddly restrained, trapped by his own intent, forced to follow his father to whatever absurd end they were headed to. At that moment, he had no idea where that would be. And for all his nonchalance and casual indifference, Nolyn didn't think his father knew, either.

"I was certain it was punishment for something, but I was wrong. It was a gift. Couldn't have convinced me of it at the time, but that's what it was. By suffering more than everyone else, I grew strong, and because I didn't complain, I gained the respect of my peers. My father forever gagged those who would point fingers and say I had it easy or that I was weak because I was born privileged. His poor treatment made me their equal. Instead of servants, my father gave me brothers. Instead of resentment, I was gifted respect. In place of doubt, I had earned confidence in myself and in the eyes of those around me. In my ignorance, what I had believed to be unwarranted cruelty was love—at least the sort showed by an Instarya to a son."

Nolyn wasn't certain what to say to that. If words were blows, Nolyn would have been down on his back with his wind knocked out.

This isn't at all what I expected.

"You're not like me, of course," Nyphron went on. "At least that's what you want to think. You're a different sort altogether, aren't you? You would never treat *your* son the way I treated you, never treat your wife the way I treated mine, and you certainly wouldn't rule the empyre the way I have."

"That's mostly why I'm here." Nolyn thought he could get in a few jabs of his own in and turn the tide of the battle in his favor.

His father was quicker. "Of course it is. You came to implement change because you know you're my opposite. You are nothing at all like me, and as such, you're perfectly suited to enact the changes necessary to fix the world, right?" His father smiled wryly. "*I* certainly would never have led a rebellion against the ruler of *my* people the way *you're* doing now. Oh, wait. I did, didn't I? Well, be that as it may, I hear you've gathered a group of exceptional warriors, each of whom is renowned for combat skill—seven of them, correct? Did you know there were exactly that many Galantians—one of whom was considered to be the greatest warrior in the world? You don't have anyone like that in your little squad, do you? Someone quiet, someone else who's loud, perhaps someone from a different culture but who fits in just fine?"

Nyphron took another sip of wine.

Nolyn didn't know which to be more concerned about: his father's intimate knowledge of his activities or the obvious connections he was making.

For a moment, Nolyn suspected the emperor had planted a spy in his midst, but he quickly discounted the idea. He didn't need a spy. More than a hundred men had witnessed his activities since landing at Vernes. He'd hardly made his presence or intent a secret. He would also know about Amicus—the rest might even be guesses.

Nolyn had had enough of letting his father swing away. *My turn.* "Over ninety percent of the people in this empyre are human. Yet of the eleven provinces, only two are governed by men. One is a temporary appointment, and the other is about to be replaced by a Fhrey. Not a single human has a position of genuine authority here at the palace. The same is nearly true for the provinces. The treasurers, city tribunes, censors, nearly all the legates, most of the prymuses, the judges, advocates, prefects, and lawyers are Instarya. The ten biggest corporations, including the gladiator schools and chariot teams, are also run by Fhrey. And then, of course, there's the emperor himself. For an empyre born from a war to end the tyranny of Fhrey dominance, this is pretty messed up."

Nyphron rolled the cup between his two open palms. "When you put it that way, it sounds quite unfair."

"And how would you describe it?"

"Necessary."

Nolyn wondered if it was a simple bluff, or if his father really had a reason. "How so?"

"The Instarya are in charge because they must be."

Not a reason. That was exactly what he expected his father to say. So blinded by pure prejudice he—

"Humans, you may have noticed, have the life span of gnats," his father went on. "They learn a job, just become proficient at it, and then they die. Reliability comes with age. To run an empyre this size, I need stable leaders, not power-hungry, short-lived humans. That way invites disaster. It's all quite romantic, this notion of a people having a say in how they are ruled, but the reality is that humans are not capable of long-term thinking. It's not their fault. Their short existence reduces the distance of their vision. They focus only on today, or tomorrow, and frequently fixate on yesterday. That's no way to guide an empyre. When the fate of the world is in your hands, gambling is an unaffordable luxury, and idealism is often burned on the altar of reality. Longevity grants knowledge and experience that humans couldn't possibly obtain in their half a century. When choosing who should fill a position, emotion—or a sense of social justice—should never have a say. The choice must be determined by who can do the job the best. You wouldn't send your worst soldiers into battle to defend your home just because they feel left out. When the future is at stake, you send your best and brightest, the elite of your society. That is what the Instarya are. Your mistake is seeing us as different. You're focusing on race instead of common sense. Your time among the rank and file has caused you to see the Instarya as something other than equal members of the empyre."

He's accusing me of intolerance? Absurd *just received a new definition.*

"But they *aren't equal*," Nolyn protested. "They're privileged. Instarya aren't even tried in the same courts as humans."

"*Equal* doesn't mean 'the same.' Humans are equal to one another, and yet, no two are identical. The members of your squad are superior to other members of the legion. Among humans, they are the elite. And yes, being the best affords certain privileges. They are called rewards. Without them, there is little incentive to be the best, and no one wants a society of mediocrity. Also, it would be a travesty of justice for Fhrey to be judged by a court of humans. People—even Fhrey—tend to resent their superiors, and such a thing would only invite spiteful attacks."

The way he spoke, the manner in which he said things, the sheer magnitude of his confidence made every word sound true.

But it isn't.

Nolyn countered, "Being emperor doesn't make you right. It only means you *should* be right, and in this I know you're wrong. The Fhrey's longevity *and* their privilege cause them to believe they are better than those they govern. They can't help but lose empathy for humans, to see them as a lower class, as animals that don't need to be treated with dignity. And while you may be right about the shortsighted nature of humans, I know of no one who would prefer the enlightened rule of a foreign race over poor self-rule. That's why you rebelled against Lothian."

Nyphron looked confused. "He and I were of the same race."

"Yes, but you didn't see it that way, did you? To you, he wasn't merely Fhrey. He was of a different tribe, so unlike yours that they were almost a different race. He was Miralyith, and you were Instarya. The Miralyith told you they were the elite, didn't they? Both of you were Fhrey but of two lines that had split long ago into different cultures with divergent values. He lived on the far side of the Nidwalden in luxury and refinement while members of your tribe were forced to scrape by in the wilderness. That galled you, drove you to rebel against its rule. And if I were speaking to Lothian right now, he would make the same argument you just did. That the Miralyith are better suited to rule because of their indisputable advantage of magic. Don't you see? It's the same thing, and the humans want just what you did—a voice." Nolyn took a half step forward. "Have you ever considered that you might believe the Instarya to be superior merely because you *are* one? That you see your own strengths clearly but are blind to your faults? How can a member of only one of two competing groups fairly evaluate people and accurately assign the titles of *elite* and *superior*? You would need someone capable of fairly representing both groups."

Nyphron chuckled. "Let me guess . . . you?"

❧

Sephryn reached up and took down the long bow. It came off the hooks easily, and she held it in one hand. The old weapon was as airy as a hollow bone—lighter than she remembered. Her fingers wrapped around the grip, and memories returned.

"You're overthinking," Moya had said as she tutored Sephryn so many centuries ago.

Sephryn was holding the bow straight out with her arm locked, the string pulled back as far as she was able, an arrow nocked. She had her left eye closed, her right eye open, looking down the length of the shaft.

"What are you doing?" Moya asked, hands on hips, an eternal scowl of disapproval on her face.

"I'm aiming." Sephryn struggled to hold the bow steady. Audrey wasn't weak, and Sephryn didn't have the strength to bend her fully. Pulling the string as far as she did, Sephryn's arm grew tired and began to shake.

"Aiming? What do you mean, aiming?"

Her mother knew exactly what Sephryn meant. Moya's feigned ignorance was being used to belittle her daughter. By treating Sephryn's actions as ridiculous, as so unthinkable as to warrant a dumbfounded question, her mother drove her disapproval home. There was no reason to be so insulting, so dramatic, so condescending, and little things like that increasingly irritated Sephryn. Perhaps her mother had always been demeaning. Maybe Sephryn never noticed before because she was too young to see; back then, it was all she noticed. Sephryn was twelve, just starting to make the turn from child to woman, and in that transition, Moya's rule by ridicule had risen to the next level.

Sephryn let the arrow fly. It missed the acorn by a foot.

"What do you want from me? I have to aim. How can I hit a Tetlin acorn the size of a—"

"Watch your mouth."

"Watch my . . . are you serious?" It was Sephryn's turn to pretend ignorance and ask a question that wasn't actually an inquiry. Only twelve, but she was old enough to realize she had mimicked the exact action she had seen as a fault with her mother.

I might not be able to hit the acorn, but the nut hasn't fallen very far. That unpleasant recognition, the horrible truth that she might be a reflection of her mother, sparked a need to lash out, to fight against the inevitable. At the time, she hadn't realized her reaction was more proof of how much of Moya there was in Sephryn. She even went to the unconscious effort of placing her free hand on her hip. "You curse like the Tetlin whore herself and—"

That's when Moya hit her. Not hard, merely a slap, but it hurt, and the sting to her cheek was the least of it.

Sephryn didn't want to cry—not in front of Moya. She wouldn't give her mother the satisfaction. Sephryn clenched her teeth, willing her emotions to stay down. The effort made her shake just as the bow had.

"Don't you ever swear by that name again," Moya ordered. "Do you hear me?"

Sephryn did nothing more than blink.

"I don't know where you get such language," her mother continued, shaking her head.

Where I get it! Sephryn had been furious, sucking air in and out of her nose so forcefully it made her nostrils flare.

"Take another arrow," Moya ordered. "And this time don't think. Don't aim. It's like throwing a ball, a single fluid motion. Draw down. Pull to your cheek. Arch your back, press your shoulder blades toward each other. Don't think—feel. Let your body take over. Arch like the wood, then release the tension and fly."

Fuming, teeth still clenched in mute rage, Sephryn loaded the arrow. She wasn't thinking about the acorn a hundred feet away; she was fixated on her mother and the tingling heat on her cheek. She wanted the lesson to end.

Sephryn drew Audrey. In her anger, she found the power to pull the string deeper than ever before. Without pause, she loosed the arrow. She did so without thought, without care, without overthinking.

The acorn split in half.

For an instant, Sephryn couldn't believe it. She'd tried to hit that thing for days. Only once had she gotten close. That time the arrow hit dead center, and the nut was cut into perfect halves.

"See?" Moya said. That single word, bathed and dressed in coarse condescension, shattered Sephryn's moment of triumph.

Moya ruined everything.

"And she's still at it," Sephryn said to herself as she ran her fingers along the carved wood. She hadn't touched the weapon in a long time. Now, she stood in the growing light of morning before a dead hearth, remembering the day when she was twelve and her mother had slapped her.

Sephryn's fingers continued along the upper limb and down to the grip. That bow had been such an important part of her mother's life that it felt as if she might still be in there somewhere, the weapon haunted by Moya's spirit.

Why did she hit me?

Centuries later, Sephryn still didn't know. Moya was famous for her crude language and behavior. Maybe it was a case of *do as I say, not as I do,* but Sephryn had cursed in front of her mother before and never heard a peep about it. Thinking harder, Sephryn couldn't recall a time when Moya had cursed by the name of the Tetlin Witch, even though almost everyone else did. The phrase had become so common it had lost its power and fallen out of favor. By the time of that archery lesson, the term was considered too tame for most. Why Moya had taken such offense must have been because of her mother's tall tales.

Supposedly, Moya had met the witch. The incident was one of her mother's most outlandish stories—the one where she died and had tea and cakes with the gods and every famous person who had ever lived. The chronicle ended with Moya's return to the land of the living just in time to witness the birth of the empyre. Sephryn suspected that story started as a myth, an ancient yarn Moya had heard around the lodge fire in her youth and into which she'd inserted her own name and those of her friends.

But a more likely explanation was that Moya had been drinking the day of that archery lesson. Sephryn's mother hadn't cared much for wine or beer, but that spring, the year in which Persephone died, she'd discovered a fondness for both.

Moya took the empress's death hard, but the serious drinking occurred thirteen years later when Roan passed. By then, Moya was in her sixties. Sephryn had grown strong enough to pull Audrey deep, and she was consistently hitting acorns at *five* hundred feet, but her mother's eyes were too weak by then to see. Wrinkled and stripped of her ability to shoot, Moya had begun her campaign of epic tirades against Sephryn's eternally youthful father. The drinking added bite to her bitterness. That's when things went bad. The last fourteen years of her life, Moya had put the Tetlin Witch's notoriety to shame.

The original string and arrows are upstairs.

Sephryn had squirreled them away under floorboards shortly after moving in, back when she rented the middle floor. She'd only just returned to Percepliquis after Moya's death. Her father had insisted she take the bow, said it hurt him too much to see it. The sight of Audrey was painful for Sephryn, too, and she would have stuffed it under the floorboards, but the gap between the support beams wasn't large enough to accommodate Audrey. Substituting new arrows and string, she had used the bow when angry to release her frustration. The last time was after her argument with Nolyn. After that, the bow had lived in a corner of the room, wrapped in a cloth. Sephryn couldn't recall how it got above the mantel. She must have put it there at some point but couldn't remember when or why.

For her current undertaking, Sephryn felt the need to use the old arrows.

After eight hundred years, the quiver and string might have turned to dust. She headed toward the stairs. *Only one way to find out.*

Sephryn hadn't been to the second floor since the murder-kidnapping. Ascending the stairs was something she did slowly. She heard the creak of each loose step. The sun was growing brighter, morning well on its way. She didn't know how long it would take to pry the arrows and string out, and if they hadn't survived the years, she wasn't sure what she would do. She had plenty of practice arrows, which would likely do the job, but they weren't designed to kill. The ones under the floor already had. She also wanted a bit of practice to warm up. Then she would need to locate a good spot to shoot from such as a rooftop near the Imperial Plaza. There was so much left to do. Sephryn had an emperor to assassinate.

Light was coming in the window of the palace, faint and hazy, but the sun was on its way. Given his father's admissions, Nolyn didn't expect an attack anytime soon. He'd lost his bid to take the throne without striking a single blow.

"So it's not ambition but self-righteousness that drives your bid for power?" Nyphron said in a form of conclusion. "Not sure how I feel about that. Must have gotten that kind of mindset from your mother. She was that way."

Standing before his father in the light of a brightening Founder's Day, a quick calculation left Nolyn with equally poor choices.

"So what now?" Nolyn asked.

"You're the one who barged into my house. You tell me."

Nolyn wished he could. There was an outside chance that if he killed his father, he might be capable of persuading the legions to back him. That hope was slim, though, since serving an emperor wasn't nearly as enticing as *being* emperor. Against their superior numbers, Nolyn had little chance of prevailing. There was also a possibility that his father would forgive him. Lastly, Nyphron could be bluffing. He obviously knew about the rebellion, but he might be lying about the successful bribes.

Nolyn laid a hand to his sword.

"Hold on," Nyphron said. "You've already made one ridiculous error. Allow me to prevent you from making a bigger one."

"If what you say is true, I don't see what I have to lose. If I fight you and fail, I'll die. But if I do nothing, I'll be executed. If I fight and win, I *might* have to contend with Farnell and Hillanus, but if they can be bribed by you, I could offer them similar compensation. Granted, there's only a slightly smaller chance of that happening, but it's better than the alternatives."

Nyphron shook his head. "This is what comes from being raised by your mother. You think too much but don't understand the basics. As a result, you have it all backward. Killing me is actually your worst-case scenario. Any other outcome is better."

Nyphron was delaying him. His father didn't want to fight.

Maybe he is bluffing. Can he be afraid of fighting me? No. Nyphron knows no fear. Can it be he doesn't want to kill his own son?

Nolyn found it impossible to believe that his father had feelings for him, but perhaps such an action would harm the emperor's image as a virtuous ruler and father.

"I don't agree." Nolyn pulled his sword.

Nyphron did not. "You're my son."

"I'm surprised you're willing to admit that. To be honest, I was starting to wonder if you doubted that."

"So much of your mother in you."

"That's a good thing—for you—or I would have struck already. Get one of those pretty swords off the wall. I'll wait."

Nyphron smiled. "But some of me is in there, too, I see. That's the problem. As my son—you're also a Fhrey."

"Half-and-half, actually."

"Doesn't matter. Even a drop of Fhrey blood is enough. You can't kill another Fhrey. If you do, you'll sacrifice your immortal spirit. You'll be barred from entering Phyre. You'll also lose your claim to the throne, and *that* won't just affect you. It will ruin the world."

Nolyn grew tired of hearing him talk. He grabbed a sword off the wall and tossed it to his father. Nyphron let it fall on the floor.

"Pick it up!" Nolyn shouted.

He wanted it to be over. One way or another, he needed their conflict to end. Over eight hundred years of festering hatred felt like a loose tooth that refused to come free. Nolyn was determined to yank it out. He knew it would hurt, but the endless torment was worse. It had to end here. It had to end now.

"No," Nyphron said.

The emperor turned his back on his son and walked to the decanter to refill his cup. "This really is fantastic wine. Just got it. Comes from over the sea. An insane sailor named Captain Elon Morrissy sailed out beyond the sight of land. Was gone nearly a year. He crossed the Blue Sea to the west and returned with it. Said he found a vineyard in the foothills of a mountain that he understandably named after himself." He took a sip and sighed contentedly. "Bastard won't tell anyone where it is."

"Pick up the sword, or I'll kill you where you stand."

Nyphron turned back to face him and showed an amused smile. "No, you won't."

He returned to the chair and sat once more. He put his feet up in the spot that Nolyn had left vacant. "Once upon a time, I knew a son who actually *did* kill his father. He wanted his father's throne for many of the same reasons you want mine. They were Fhrey, so the son paid a terrible price."

"And what makes you think I won't—"

"There is a fundamental difference between you and Mawyndulë. The prince of Erivan was raised in the traditional Fhrey manner. He never knew his mother. Even if he had, his mother wasn't Persephone. Yours was." Nyphron swirled his wine. "You may think you're *half-and-half,* as you said, but she made you more human than Fhrey. She taught you compassion, empathy, and an unwavering sense of right and wrong.

She's been dead for centuries, and still you're standing there wondering what she'd think, what she'd want you to do. Mawyndulë didn't have that. You do. And we both know what your mother would say if she were here, and it wouldn't be, 'Kill your father, son. End the old bugger and take his throne.'" Nyphron looked down at his cup. "If I'm wrong, have at it. Prove once and for all whether you're her son . . . or mine."

CHAPTER TWENTY-ONE

A Cup of Wine

Amicus was up before the sun. He took special care to ensure that each buckle was properly fastened, each hook correctly closed. More than eight years had passed since he had set foot in Percepliquis. Back then, he had just won the overly hyped *Battle of the Century* by defeating the Instarya warrior Abryll Orphe. Hours later, the imperial guard was dispatched to arrest him. Turned out he wasn't supposed to win. Amicus refused their invitation to the palace prison by killing them instead. Then he ran. No one in the Erbon Forest had ever heard of Amicus Killian, and he faded into the foliage like so many other soldiers.

Now he was back. He stood staring at the city as if it were a living thing. One great beast into whose mouth Nolyn Nyphronian had walked.

"Don't listen to them," Amicus's father had said, his grandfather nodding in agreement. "The emperor, the leaders of the legion, don't even hear them out. It's always the same thing. To win their battles, they need us to fight. Brigham helped during the Great War. His reward was to fight the Grenmorians. When he was too old, they insisted his son

Ingram go to the Goblin Wars. What was his reward? Was it riches? A fine house? Respect? No, it was the privilege of having his son fight in the same war. And so on, and so on. So don't listen to them and never serve the emperor."

Amicus wouldn't—he knew that for sure—especially with Nyphron on the throne. As he stared at the complicated contours of the city slowly revealed by the growing morning light, Amicus understood. The difference was simple. His forefathers had all expected a reward for their efforts and sacrifices, but Amicus wanted nothing from Nolyn. He was done serving emperors; he was worried about a friend.

Riley roused the others. As usual, Smirch required a kick to get him started. They were halfway through their meal when Amicus noticed a lack of preparation in the other camps.

The First and Second were up, but the camps were quiet. No officers barked orders; no meals were cooked. The sun was nearly above the hills, but no line of men had formed.

"Awfully casual for the first day of a war," Amicus said.

Myth looked up from his bowl. "Lack of experience. Most likely haven't seen combat. Probably think it won't get going until midday and that there'll be a break for a catered meal."

"Hillanus did say they would attack at dawn, right?" Riley asked.

"Let's find out." Amicus grabbed his big sword, slung it over his shoulder, and set off up the bank toward the big tent.

Legates rarely suffered a stay in a tent, but when they did, it was an elaborate affair. Hillanus's quarters was the size of a barn, with several other fringe-endowed, brightly colored canvas mansions circling it. These were the hardship quarters of the legate's personal retinue: his scribes, palatus, First Prymus, and other staff officers and their servants. They formed a tiny community of isolated leadership.

Out in front of the big tent was planted the sacred legion standard: a great raging bear made of gold. It rose up on hind legs and stood above the blue-and-gold silken banner.

"I'm here to see Legate Hillanus," Amicus explained as a pair of guards thrust out spears that crossed his path.

"He's still sleeping," one of the guards said.

"Is he?" Amicus nodded. "Well, we're about to attack the city in just a few minutes. So maybe you ought to wake him?"

That made the soldiers chuckle. "If you want to speak to the legate, come back later. I would suggest past midday, after he's had his wine."

"What's going on?" Riley asked, jingling up behind Amicus with the rest of the Seventh. That was one of the differences between the eastern and western legions. The western left their gear in tents when they marched to battle. The eastern carried everything everywhere they went.

"I don't know," Amicus said. "But I have a feeling we were lied to."

"They're not going to attack?" Everett asked, his gaze shifting back and forth between Amicus and the guards still holding crossed spears before the tent. "But Prince Nolyn is already in the city."

Amicus looked at the sun peeking over the hills. "And it's dawn."

"If by sunrise I don't come back, then assume I'm dead, take command of the Teshlors, and do what you feel is best."

The word *best* had never before felt so vague.

"Amicus Killian." The tent flap flew back and Hillanus stepped out, yawning. He wore a blue robe over a white nightshirt, his face red and blotchy on one side, eyes squinting from the light of day. He scowled at the rising sun. "My lords, how early is it?"

"Sorry to wake you, but we have a revolution to start, sir," Amicus reported.

"You're right. We could do that." Hillanus nodded and wiped a crust of dry drool from the corner of his mouth. "And technically, I'm supposed to let you go in—you and your little group. I think the emperor wants to personally see all of you, but I'm reminded that there is a bounty on your head, Amicus. I could let you walk in, but if I bring you into the city in chains, I can make the argument that I deserve the reward. The emperor might not agree, but there is a chance he may." He raised an arm over his head and made a casual come-here motion with his fingers.

More soldiers raced up. These had weapons drawn, and they settled in between Amicus and the legate. Behind him, Amicus heard the Seventh drawing metal.

"Do what you feel is best."

The influx of infantry already outnumbered them, but the soldiers made no move to attack. Instead, they adhered to the "dog-distance"—the term derived from the gap left between rival canines seeking to intimidate but not yet ready to fight. They watched Hillanus, who waited for more to arrive. While that might be a sign he understood what he was up against, it could be that the legate wanted a sufficient show of force to ensure surrender. He stood a better chance at the reward with live criminals than corpses.

While Amicus didn't know what Hillanus was thinking, he knew he and his men were in a strategically bad spot. Backing away, he was pleased to see Hillanus's men giving ground. He retraced his path to the river.

"Don't let them get near the ships," Hillanus shouted, his voice growing distant. "We'll have a lousy time fetching them out. Probably have to burn the damn things, and that won't do."

More legionnaires appeared, jogging in and driving the Sik-Aux north, away from the ships and toward the bridge.

"We can't fight all of them," Myth said. "I mean, we could, but it would be a terrible battle."

"We've already lost," Amicus said as they reached the bridge, the only strategic place to make a stand and anything but ideal. The span was majestically wide. All of them in a line couldn't block it, and any force coming from the city would strike at their backs.

"What about the city?" Riley asked, pointing at the great archway behind them. It lacked a wall. The arched gateway that marked the entrance was ornamental—an overgrown trellis.

"I remember it has a lot of narrow streets, too," Smirch added. "Maybe we can lose them."

"While dressed in uniforms?" Myth asked.

Seeing them near the city, Hillanus must have felt his chance at the reward dwindling.

"Take them!" he shouted. "Kill them if you have to, but stop them now!"

"He certainly doesn't want us going in," Riley said.

The camps were awake now. The ships had deposited six hundred soldiers on the bank, and some of those who were on foot arrived during the night to bolster that force. Amicus guessed the number of men facing them across the bridge—those presently charging—to be only fifty. Many more would follow.

With a miserable resignation, Amicus knew he and the Sik-Aux would lose. They were incredibly outnumbered and caught on a battlefield with no strategic advantage. But neither of those reasons was the real problem. Their cause of death would be because they were facing legionnaires rather than ghazel. Not that men were better at combat. On average, the ghazel were more formidable than a typical soldier. What would kill them was the reservations he saw in the eyes of his men. They didn't want to fight. Their hearts weren't in it. Killing goblins was one thing; killing fellow soldiers wearing the same uniform was soul crushing.

What was left of the Seventh Sik-Aux continued retreating until they reached the entrance of the still-sleeping city. Amicus took position at the center of the line, under the great stone blocks of the massive Grand Arch that marked the formal entrance to the city, and waited.

It's better this way, he thought, *better than dying of the pox, at least.*

৵

Nolyn saw relief break on the face of Jerel DeMardefeld the moment he returned to the palace gate. Pain-filled tension melted away, thawing into an undeniable grin. Jerel was a concerned father seeing his son emerge from the dust of battle.

"You had me worried, sir," Jerel said as Nolyn walked out. "You might not have noticed, but it's dawn."

Nolyn was well aware of the time. The sun was up. Many of the streets were shrouded in shadows, the alleys caves. The plaza was still waking, ghostly cart merchants rushing to find ideal locations for Founder's Day.

"How did it go, sir?"

"You and your god are right, Jerel. I'm my mother's son."

"What does that mean?" Demetrius asked. The moment they were far enough away from the gate guard, he added, "Is he dead?"

"No. We just talked. Turns out I was wrong about him—mostly. He didn't try to kill me—knew nothing about it, and I believe him. The rest was a series of misunderstandings."

Nolyn led them into the plaza that formed the terminus of the Grand Marchway. The large square was paved in flat stones, and a fountain at its center depicted four horses bursting out of frothing waters. The plaza gave birth to the Grand Marchway that ran straight as an arrow in front of the palace. Every Founder's Day that Nolyn had spent in the city that boulevard had been lined with flowering trees. But during this spring, cold weather had delayed the opening of buds. The weather hadn't daunted the citizenry. The traditional blue-and-green flags were already out, hanging from balconies, flying over homes and shops.

"What about your plan for making laws fair for everyone?"

Nolyn nodded. "He's a bit set in his ways, and quite smart, but he had no answer when I compared him to the Miralyith. I think there's a foothold there, a foundation on which we might be able to build something."

Jerel looked up. "The sun is rising. We ought to get back or—"

Nolyn shook his head. "The legions won't be attacking."

Demetrius stopped walking and shook his head. "You were supposed to kill the emperor!" he fumed, his hands clenched in fists.

Nolyn glanced around, pleased to find most of the square empty. They were alone. "Relax. It's not happening. It's over."

"Why didn't you kill him?"

"Because doing so would be wrong. Some things are that simple. And I now believe I can work with him. I got a toe in the door, if you will. And a greater understanding was reached for both of us. I think I can help my father see that he has been perpetrating the same injustices on humans that drove him to war with the Miralyith. He's not an idiot or a tyrant, just flawed."

Demetrius continued to shake his head, looking baffled and incredibly disappointed. "I was certain you would go through with it." He looked at his feet, or maybe at the paving stones. "The symmetry was just so perfect. Now you've ruined everything."

"What are you talking about?" Nolyn asked.

Demetrius sighed. "It doesn't matter anymore." The man looked thoroughly disgusted. "I worked so hard, planned everything so precisely. Don't you get it?" Demetrius spun, his hands outstretched, presenting the city. "It's Founder's Day—*Founder's Day*! And you, his son, would have killed the emperor, not even caring about the loss of your soul. That's why I waited and didn't end you myself when you returned from the jungle. I wanted you to lose the afterlife just like I did. It would have been so grand. Your entire line would have been eliminated, both your father and your son, and you'd have no claim to the throne. I'd get my second chance, and I would be unopposed. This time the decision of who rules wouldn't come down to a duel. There wouldn't be anyone to challenge me—no one of any consequence, at least."

"My son?" Nolyn asked. "You're not making any sense. I have no child, living or dead."

"Demetrius," Jerel said, "are you feeling all right?"

"Oh, stop calling me that. My name isn't Demetrius."

"I don't understand any of—" Nolyn started to say when he heard a familiar sound. Cocking his head, he spun and peered into the shadowed streets behind them.

"What is it?" Jerel asked.

"Oh, by the blood of Mari!" Nolyn cursed. He stared at Demetrius, stunned. "What have you done?"

"A whole lot of digging," Demetrius replied. "Fortunately, this city is built on limestone caverns. I didn't have to go far. They have come."

"Who?" Jerel asked.

Nolyn continued to search for the source of the clicking sound. "Ghazel."

❧

Amicus drew two of his swords and set his feet. To either side, the others took up positions to block the passage as fifty legionnaires barreled toward them. When they were only a few feet away, Amicus identified his first five targets. He didn't calculate the necessary moves. Such things had been relegated to muscle memory, a fact that hampered his ability to train others. Decades of practice took over and he —

The first few legionnaires stopped while still ten feet away.

They didn't stop, Amicus realized. *They slammed into something.*

With a set of rapid grunts, the three coming at him halted as abruptly as if they had run headlong into a stone wall and then fell. The one in the center lay on the ground, his nose busted.

All along the line, man after man cried out as they hammered into nothing at all and collapsed on the cobblestone roadway.

"What's happening?" Mirk asked.

"Dunno," Riley replied, fascinated by the bizarre sight of men ramming into nothing. Some even bounced back several feet.

Amicus reached out ahead of him, feeling into the space where the men had stopped. Nothing was there. He took a step forward, and then a few more. Reaching out, he touched the boot of an unconscious Third Spear. "There's nothing between us."

The latecomers to the fight saw the pile and stopped. They reached out with swords. Everyone heard the *tink* when the metal blade struck something hard. Wary of Amicus and his men, they used their hands to feel what their eyes couldn't see. Amicus watched as spread palms pressed against what looked to be glass, a barrier clear enough to be invisible.

"Sorcery!" someone on the far side declared. "Find a way around."

The soldiers spread out but found no breach. The archway was sealed. They moved beyond it.

"Circle!" Amicus ordered, concerned their opponents would loop around behind them. None of them were able to, so the bewildered soldiers returned.

"It can't be like that for the whole city!" a voice said. The white brushed helmet of First Prymus Jareb Tanator appeared, pushing through the turmoil and confusion. He was pointing at Amicus. "You did this!"

"Are you insane? I'm no sorcerer."

Tanator didn't look convinced. His eyes shifted around, trying to see the invisible barrier. He reached up and his fingers touched it. He jerked his hand back in shock. "Not a sorcerer, eh? This is awfully convenient, then."

"I have no idea what's going on. But it's not us."

"Amicus!" Riley called. "Listen!"

From the city streets behind them, a distinct high-speed whine rose. They knew what it was, or at least all of the men who had who had slept in the dark beneath the canopy of the Erbon Forest did. That's when their nightmares usually came out. Like the jungle cats and flying foxes, ghazel preferred to hunt in the night.

"Not so convenient after all, I think," Amicus told Tanator. "You're on the safe side."

The sound grew louder. Nolyn grabbed his sword and pulled, but the blade stayed stuck in its scabbard. Jerel reached for his own weapon, and it, too, was frozen in its sheath.

"Your swords," Demetrius said, "aren't covered in the Orinfar, and I prefer not being stabbed. It's a shame DeMardefeld got the tattoos. I would have enjoyed popping him right in front of you."

"Who are you?" Nolyn stepped away from the palatus.

"Well, I'm certainly not *Demetrius*."

The palatus's face turned sinister, and a horrible chill ran up Nolyn's spine.

"We need to get back to the others and rally the legions," Jerel said.

Demetrius chuckled. "I wouldn't expect much help from them. They can't get in."

"You're an Artist, a wielder of magic," Nolyn said. "You're doing this."

The palatus shook his head. "Mostly, but not all." He jerked his head toward the growing sound of clicking claws coming from the creatures still hidden in the shadows. "The Blind Ones have the Art. Terribly crude, you understand, although they're much better at it now. I had to teach them proper techniques other than using those disgusting leaves they usually burn." He shuddered. "Doing so was part of their price — as was this city. I mean, it's not like they're going to work for free, after all."

Demetrius pointed at the sky, where clouds turned morning into dusk. "They did that. They love being able to make the sun disappear. And they sealed the city. No one can come in, and no one can leave. And every Rhune, Fhrey, and Dherg trapped inside will die. Nyphron isn't the only one who can yoke a civilization to do his bidding — to fight his war for him. Oh, look, here are some now."

A score of ghazel entered the square. Nolyn pulled again on his sword, then on his dagger. Neither came free. "They're going to kill you, too, you know."

"Don't think so," Demetrius said, and with a wave of his hand, he transformed from a prim palatus into a Ba Ran ghazel.

Nyphron set down his cup of wine when he heard the sound of bells in the city and rushing feet coming down the corridor.

"Your Eminence," Plymerath said, bursting into the room, "we're under attack."

"The legions?" Nyphron asked, surprised.

For a moment, he wondered if he'd underestimated his son. Perhaps Nolyn had outplayed him after all. In that instant, he discovered a strange sense of pride.

"No, sir," Plymerath said. "Ghazel."

"What?" The very idea was absurd, and he began to laugh. "Are you serious?"

"Yes, sir. Reports say they are coming up out of the sewers, wells, bathhouses, and city gutters."

"Amazing," Nyphron said. "And really bad timing for them as we just happen to have two full legions waiting outside. Order them into the city and have—"

"Can't, sir. There's a barrier, an invisible wall keeping us in and them out. Several people have reported seeing a ring of dancing ghazel in the Imperial Arena."

"Oberdaza."

Plymerath nodded. "We're on our own, sir, and . . . we are seriously outnumbered. The city guard is fighting in the streets, mostly along the Grand Mar, and losing ground block by block. Outside, the palace guard is forming, but so are the ghazel. The guard won't win. The ghazel seem to be headed this way."

Plymerath looked at the cup of wine on the table.

Nyphron also noticed it. He had placed it near the edge—precariously so. "Order the Instarya to arms. Have my armor brought here. It's time to clean off the dust."

Plymerath hesitated, still staring at the cup. "Maybe you'd like to set that cup a bit—"

"I'm not planning a blaze of glory, Plym. You said there's a ring of oberdaza in the arena. We just need to get to them. If we break that ring, the legions will do the rest. It'll be like old times. I have a feeling this will be the best Founder's Day ever."

CHAPTER TWENTY-TWO

Founder's Day

Sephryn didn't want to run into anyone who might ask what she was up to, so she approached Imperial Square taking backstreets but avoiding alleys. The alleys had worried her ever since hearing the sounds near the masquerade shop that left her feeling something wasn't right, and she wasn't going anywhere near those sounds.

Avoiding unexpected encounters with neighbors was important because in one hand Sephryn carried a bundle of arrows, while in the other she held the long bow her mother had named Audrey. The bow had needed a new string, and she found one—a good one—at the East Market where merchants were already putting the finishing touches on their Founder's Day decorations. Missing her purse, Sephryn traded her shoes for the string. They had been good, reliable shoes; she hoped the string was, too. She got arrows as well, a score of bodkins on credit from the same fletcher who now owned her shoes. There were only four of the old arrows, and she might need additional tries. Blackened from age, The Four had burned-in symbols carved on their shafts that created a word Sephryn couldn't pronounce. Moya never shot The Four in Sephryn's presence and wouldn't even let her daughter touch them. Her mother had kept the set in an elaborate mahogany case, like holy relics. According to Moya, these weren't *old arrows*. These were supposedly *The Original Arrows*—or as her mother called them the *a . . . rows*. Why she pronounced the word that way wasn't ever explained. Whenever Sephryn asked, her mother would only smile. Moya had said these were the first arrows ever made. Crafted by Roan of Rhen, these had been the ones Sephryn's mother had used to destroy Balgargarath, the demon beneath the dwarven city of Neith. Of course, her mother never called it a *dwarven* city; she'd always said *Dherg* city. But Moya wasn't known for being polite.

"That's what we called them back then. Everyone called them that. Don't roll your eyes at me, young lady! You don't know everything and—you can trust me on this—you don't want to, either."

Walking as fast as she could—running would draw too much attention—Sephryn realized the latent wisdom in those words. She already knew too much: like where she was going and what she was about to do. Some people bit their tongues to stop themselves from talking; Sephryn remembered her mother to prevent herself from thinking.

One of "The Four" had been the arrow that was used to kill Udgar, the Gula chieftain who had challenged Persephone for the right to rule the Ten Clans. Sephryn believed that story because Persephone herself had confirmed it, and Sephryn never had trouble trusting her namesake. Maybe that faith was due to Persephone being the empress or because she didn't use offensive slurs like *Dherg*. But most likely, it was because Persephone had never slapped her child when drunk.

Sephryn's bare feet began to hurt from the hard impact of her rapid heel-toe race on the brick street. She followed the northwestern thoroughfare, Morton Whipple Way, toward Imperial Square, then turned at Lipton Street, weaving through the deserted maze of buildings closed for the holiday, and finally worked her way across Ferry Street, aiming for the back side of the Aguanon.

I'm about to use my mother's bow and her a . . . rows to kill the emperor. The infinite levels of wrongness in the act were making Sephryn sick. She could feel her stomach cramp, and there was the faint kiss of nausea lingering in the background, like a suitor waiting to ask her to dance. *My mother was Persephone's Shield, the old-fashioned term for bodyguard, and now I'm about to murder my namesake's husband.* She glanced up at the sky. *If the gods don't want me to kill him, they'll find a way to stop me.*

Overhead, clouds were rolling in, one on another: a bed of blankets like a winter storm. Sephryn had never seen clouds like these before. They traveled fast, exploding in volume and density, and they were darker than any she could remember. Morning had arrived, but she could hardly tell. The city lay beneath a vast shadow, the promise of dawn snuffed out in favor of a continuing night.

Maybe they will stop me.

She moved through the little garden and hopped the wall behind the Aguanon—Percepliquis's Temple of Ferrol. The building with its grand dome stood on the east side of Imperial Square. In the center of the square was the great Ulurium Fountain; beyond it to the west, the palace gate lay. The plaza-side roof of the temple at the base of the dome provided a grand view of the entire square. Long ago, she'd found a hiding space—a little crook formed by a gable that provided access to the exterior base of the dome. It had always been her deserted island surrounded by the ocean that was the city, Sephryn's secret place, a refuge that was hers alone. Only once had she ever shared it. Nolyn didn't know it at the time, but taking him there had been a declaration of Sephryn's love.

But this is Founder's Day. People always swarm the plaza and dangle from balconies. Someone might go up there to watch the parade. What will I do then?

Worry about that if it happens—I have too much on my shoulders right now. Let's not add more!

She approached the temple from the back. Slinging the bow and sack of arrows over her shoulder, she entered the garden and climbed the old poplar tree. That had been the third yellow poplar to be planted there since Sephryn had begun using them to access the roof. The first one had been perfect; its branches extended directly to the eaves of the temple. The second had been the worst; its limbs were too short, making a dangerous jump necessary. The current one was better, but not great. Sephryn had to balance on a branch and stretch a long way to grab hold of the iron ornamentation. Lifting herself onto the sloping slate shingles, she climbed to the dome.

Nothing had changed.

She'd come there the day Persephone had died, and again when Suri passed. She had wanted to come after her mother's death, but that time had been "between trees," and the little sapling wasn't up to the task. Everything had felt like it was dying back then, and she was exiled from her secret shelter. Later, that same sapling had grown tall enough so that she was able to find solace again after Nolyn left for the Goblin Wars. The last time she'd climbed that tree was the day she and Nolyn argued—the last time she'd seen him. Sephryn had since vowed never to return. She was going to become a mother. Having a child meant she couldn't run away from problems anymore, even for a little while. She had to put away childish things, and a secret place to hide from the world was most certainly one of those—at least until it became the ideal place from which to assassinate the emperor.

No one was there. Even the broken tile from her last visit was still cracked.

If only this was then, I would climb down and tell Nolyn about his son and say I was sorry. Maybe then—maybe if I had done that—none of this would have happened.

She settled in. Her body knew where to go, all of it so familiar. Her refuge from storms didn't conjure fond memories. Like the intended comfort from the fragrance of flowers at a funeral, the familiarity welcomed her back with centuries of grief. Today was no exception. In many ways, Sephryn felt her entire life had been leading to this moment, this act.

What if there are demands for my execution? The Fhrey of Merredydd will likely demand my head on a platter. For Nolyn to prove himself to be a fair and just ruler, he'll have to ensure that justice is handed down. It's good that he's here. I'll have time to make sure our son is safe in his care before I die. Nolyn will come to see me. Yes, he will do that. I can tell him then. Even if he doesn't, Seymour will make sure he finds out. Meeting that monk has been a blessing. I'll leave the house to him. He can use it to start his . . . whatever.

But first I have to save Nurgya.

She bent the bow and tried to hook the new string. It didn't go easily. Audrey fought her. In the end, Sephryn braced the wood between her thighs and threw her full weight into the task. Finally, the loop took hold, and the string held.

Out in front and down below, the dark plaza was coming alive. Being Founder's Day morning, the plaza would soon fill with crowds of celebrants. Sephryn could see movement and hear a multitude approaching the square.

Sephryn picked up a bodkin. She looked at it, then set it down.

Why else had The Four been preserved if not for this?

Sephryn picked up one of the blackened shafts. The thing was crude. It had three feathers, but there had been a fourth that was torn off.

This is the one Moya used to kill the demon.

Sephryn fitted the nock in the string. She imagined her mother so long ago. Sephryn could see her trapped in the cave at the bottom of the world holding Audrey and that arrow as the giant demon charged. Steadfast and courageous, a woman in her prime.

Sephryn didn't feel like any of those things.

From her height at the base of the dome, she could see over the palace wall as Emperor Nyphron, dressed in bronze armor, stepped out. As she watched, he crossed the courtyard and then paused just inside the wall at the gate, looking out at Imperial Square. There were others with him, all of whom seemed to be preparing for some sort of holiday event.

If he gets anywhere near the fountain . . .

"I bet you can. I'm sure you're incredible."

A shaft of light broke through the thick clouds, and the metal breastplate shone just like it did in that painting depicting him slaying the beast—armor that she knew the *a . . . row* couldn't punch through.

ॐ

Dressed in his old armor, Nyphron stood at the gate, looking out at Imperial Plaza. The chest plate still fit, but the girdle was a bit tight. He remembered the suit being more comfortable. In ages past, he'd made a habit of sleeping in his gear.

How did I do that? Why did I do that?

Around him, Instarya warriors gathered, each checking their own armor and weapons. Battle was something none of them had played at in centuries, and their old toys seemed unfamiliar. Most of the faces were foreign to him as well. These were the sons and grandsons of those few Instarya who had populated the four frontier outposts: Alon Rhist, Seon Hall, Ervanon, and Merredydd. Most, like Sikar and Tekchin, had settled in Merredydd to avoid the rising sea of humans. Nyphron knew only a few of these warriors. Illim stood beside him. Plymerath and his grandson stood beside Anyval's son Vigish, and Elysan's son Milyion. Sikar was also nearby, and around him was his court: all young—young and pale. This generation of Instarya had not lived in the field; they hadn't grown up using sword and dagger daily. One was trying to put his breastplate on backward. Another had his sword on the wrong hip.

What has become of the Instarya?

Two more showed up late and without armor. These wore pallium robes, which resembled asicas. The young reveled in the old Erivan culture: the eastern rhetoric, the religion, political systems, and love of leisure—and the hatred of humans.

Perhaps Nolyn is right. Maybe too much of the old world has seeped into the new. These Fhrey have spent centuries in comfort, lounging within villas and wine bottles. I fought to save them from the depravity of the Miralyith, and now they have become something even more useless—all the decadence, none of the Art.

The clicking chatter of the ghazel wafted into the plaza, the sound preceding their arrival. The inexperienced thought the sound was a form of language—that the goblins were like crickets or crows. In truth, the Blind Ones were rattlesnakes. The loud whine was their version of hammering hilt against shield. That was their way of boosting morale and intimidating their enemy. And they certainly excelled at invoking terror. Their painted masks and armor made them look like beasts from nightmares. But underneath, the ghazel weren't much different from humans, Fhrey, or Dherg.

Nyphron reflected upon the virtues of each race: Fhrey were blessed with cunning, beauty, and grace; Dherg had skill and determination; humans could overwhelm their enemies with vast numbers. But the ghazel had no merits of their own. Instead, these bastards of the lot stole their advantages. Ghazel possessed the cunning of the Fhrey, the tenacity of the Dherg, and the proliferation of the humans. With each of these strengths, they made formidable foes.

Nyphron knew that the infestations of ghazel in Avrlyn and Calynia were advanced invaders. The real strength of the Blind Ones—the creatures called moklins by the Fhrey—lay to the far east in the ancient lands, where it was rumored that they ruled a powerful empyre.

One day they will win. But not today.

Nyphron led the others to the gate. He wished Tekchin had come with Sikar. He would have liked having his old comrade in arms beside him. These new kids were Instarya in name only. Where were his Galantians? Where was Eres, Medak, Grygor, Vorath, Anwir, and of course, Sebek? Dead, centuries ago—victims to the Great War that had given Nyphron his crown. Surrounded by a host of armored Fhrey, Nyphron felt alone.

"Nolyn!" Nyphron shouted as he spotted his son running across the city's plaza toward him.

"Father," his son said, and stopped just short of the gate to offer the legion salute. "I thought you might need another sword."

Nyphron couldn't help beaming with pride.

Perhaps there is one last Galantian, after all.

❧

Nyphron was framed by the gate, just across the plaza—approximately seven hundred feet away. Back when Sephryn used to train every day, she could reliably hit her mark at five hundred. Even though Nyphron was much bigger than an acorn, shooting him where he stood was unlikely. She needed him to come forward.

Anywhere near the fountain. Don't think. Don't aim. It's like throwing a ball.

Sephryn pulled back on Audrey, testing her. Then she checked the placement of her feet. Everything had to go perfectly. It wasn't like throwing a ball and nothing like anything she'd done before. When Sephryn let go, someone would die. At that moment, it hardly mattered that it was Nyphron—that it was the emperor.

That queasiness in her stomach was growing. Sephryn struggled to breathe as the memory of the Voice crept into her thoughts. *"That's not how this works . . . I guess I'll just have to kill him. Is that what you want?"*

She pulled air into her lungs, clenched her teeth, and swallowed down the rising bile.

"That's better, but don't take too long. I don't think little Nurgya likes it here, and you wouldn't want to scar him for life, would you? So do hurry, for his sake."

Sephryn checked her grip on Audrey. When she looked back, she spotted Nolyn running to his father.

❧

"We need to cut our way to the oberdaza ring," Nyphron told his son. "Reports say they are in the arena down in the West End. If we can reach them and disrupt their enchantment, the legions can enter and finish off the rest." Nyphron looked at his son and thought a moment. "It might be best if you hold the line here, while I lead a handful of the others to the arena. Just in case."

Nolyn shook his head. "Today, I fight at my father's side."

Nyphron couldn't hold back his grin. "In that case, I feel sorry for the ghazel."

Ahead of them, the goblin horde rushed up the Grand Marchway and poured into the plaza, flooding the far side of the great square. Nyphron drew his sword, as did Nolyn and the rest of the Instarya. Together father and son led the attack, rushing forward into the square, meeting the fray halfway.

The clicking whine stopped the moment the two sides crashed.

Centuries of idleness blew away as little more than dust the moment Nyphron came against his first foe. His heart pounded; his arms felt their old grace and balance; his feet remembered the steps. Ghazel blood was his reward as two of the creatures lost their heads to his blade. He expected to see Nolyn fighting at his side, but his son was missing.

Concerned that his boy had been wounded, Nyphron stopped his push and turned. His mind had nothing to do with his next action; there was no thought nor purposeful intention. Pure reflex saved the emperor's life as his sword deflected his son's. Nolyn had tried to stab him in the back, thrusting his weapon at a gap beneath his breastplate. Nyphron was stunned, not so much that Nolyn had tried to murder him, but that he did so in such a cowardly way.

Plymerath was there in an instant, driving forward against the ghazel, filling the gap Nyphron's pause had left. There, beside the Ulurium Fountain, in the eye of the hurricane that swelled around them, father and son faced each other.

"You're not my son!" The idea came to Nyphron with such perfect clarity that it freed him. He struck out with the pommel of his sword, hitting Nolyn in the face.

The boy fell at Nyphron's feet. As he did, the illusion flickered and Nyphron caught a glimpse of the Miralyith on the ground.

Mawyndulë?

"You!" Nyphron shouted. "This is all your doing! All of it. I should have killed you centuries ago. Time to fix my mistake."

Nyphron raised his blade.

Mawyndulë hastily moved his hands, weaving a spell, something to defend himself. Nyphron had seen the gesture before. It wouldn't work. Nyphron's blade was etched with the Orinfar, his whole body tattooed. The Miralyith's magic was useless.

Sephryn watched as Nyphron and Nolyn charged out into the square, father and son defending the city, or maybe the entire empyre, against a raging horde of—of what? They were undoubtedly the imagined maggots she'd heard in the alleys, but these strange and terrifying creatures wore armor, held curved swords, and possessed massive claws and mouths filled with sharp teeth.

That wasn't what she'd expected. Nothing about that day made sense.

Being Founder's Day, there were supposed to be speeches, music, and a parade. Instead, there were . . .

Goblins?

Nolyn had told her about them, but those monsters were distant threats on the periphery of the empyre. Centuries ago, he had been sent to fight them, and Nolyn had—

Nolyn! Is that why he's here? Did the goblins break through? How is that possible?

She hadn't heard any rumors of an attack. No warning that the new war was going badly. There hadn't been any refugees. So how could goblins be in the city—and in such large numbers? Lost in ignorance and confusion, Sephryn was baffled.

What am I going to believe? Common sense or my eyes? And why today? Why now?

The coincidences were too numerous to ignore: the Voice, a goblin invasion, the order for her to retrieve the horn, her missing son, Nolyn's arrival, and the demand for her to kill the emperor. Everything was linked, all part of a bigger picture. A plan of some kind.

But whose?

Sephryn's stomach did a backflip. She knew in her heart—felt it with unquestionable certainty—that the Voice had lied. "My son is dead, isn't he?" she called out. "You killed him. He's been dead all along, hasn't he? Hasn't he?"

Silence.

"Answer me!"

The Voice wasn't talking. It didn't have to. Her baby had been killed on the day he was taken.

Sephryn put down the arrows, her body losing strength. "I don't know what you're doing, but I won't be part of your plan. I'm not killing anyone."

"Yes, you will," the Voice finally spoke.

"My son is dead. So you can kiss my culling ass, you *brideeth eyn mer!* And if I—"

"Your son still lives, but Nolyn's life hangs by a string. It's up to you to save him."

Down in the square, she watched as the emperor, Nolyn, and the Instarya charged into the plaza and attacked the goblins.

"You can see him, can't you? In the square with Nyphron?"

The Instarya advanced in a formation like the flight of geese. The emperor formed the point as they crashed into the sea of goblins. Fewer than two dozen Fhrey, and Nolyn, fought against hundreds.

Where are the legions?

Sephryn nocked her arrow again.

Only twenty-four arrows and there must be nearly five hundred goblins.

"I don't have to kill him. The emperor is going to die anyway."

"Keep watching."

Sephryn stood up and placed one bare foot on the iron rail that decorated the base of the dome. She loaded five arrows in her draw hand—the way her mother had always done. The act felt natural.

"The daughter of Moya the Magnificent, who is also endowed with the Fhrey blood of an Instarya father, would be amazing."

Nyphron slew the first four goblins in his path. The rest pulled back.

Nolyn and the Instarya followed behind his father. They were in a tight pack, pressed in from all sides.

Sephryn looked toward the river and the Grand Arch.

Where are the legions?

When she looked back, Sephryn saw Nyphron turn around and strike Nolyn in the face with the butt of his sword.

Nolyn went down, lost within the sea of Fhrey and goblins. Over the roar of battle, she distinctly heard Nyphron say, "You're not my son!"

With Nolyn lying somewhere on the ground, Nyphron raised his sword, and proclaimed, "This is all your doing! All of it. I should have killed you centuries ago. Time to fix my mistake."

"Nolyn!" Sephryn cried out.

Don't think—feel. Let your body take over. Arch like the wood, then release the tension and fly.

It wasn't until she saw the arrow hurtling toward the emperor that Sephryn realized she'd launched it.

CHAPTER TWENTY-THREE
Miralyith

Still unable to draw their weapons, Nolyn and Jerel had bolted for the docks. Demetrius—or whoever he or it was—had run off in the opposite direction, working his way upstream as the ghazel horde descended. The two men ran past white limestone columns and pale granite walls. In the past, Nolyn had always thought of Percepliquis as locked in an eternal winter—stark and cold. That morning, as the monotonous pallor blurred by, he saw it as a tomb, a monumental sepulcher to the folly of man and Fhrey.

Nolyn didn't understand exactly what had happened, but magic was involved. Of that he had no doubt. Someone, or something, had disguised its true form, and the city was being overrun by ghazel—a plan worked out well in advance.

Is Demetrius a goblin warlord? Or maybe a Ba Ran ghazel chieftain trying to end the war in one bold stroke?

That would make sense, except . . .

"The Blind Ones have the Art. Terribly crude, you understand. Although they're much better at it now; I had to teach them proper techniques."

Whoever was pretending to be Demetrius wasn't a ghazel. That left only a student of his aunt Suri or a Miralyith.

Nyphron's words came to his mind. *"Once upon a time, I knew a son who actually did kill his father. He wanted his father's throne for many of the same reasons you want mine. They were Fhrey, so the son paid a terrible price."*

Nolyn had been so young when the Great War ended. But everyone from that time knew about the one-on-one battle between Nyphron and the former Prince of Erivan.

"Demetrius is Mawyndulë!" Nolyn shouted to Jerel as they ran. Whether his fellow soldier knew that name and what it meant was impossible to tell.

The Grand Arch came into view, and both of them stopped running. The race was over, and they had lost. Blocking the way, a crude line of ghazel warriors stood.

"Back to the palace?" Jerel asked, panting for air.

Behind them, a dozen goblins closed in.

Nolyn tried again to pull his sword but found it still frozen in its scabbard. Whatever enchantment Mawyndulë had used was still in effect. "We'll never make it."

Jerel and Nolyn shifted to stand back-to-back.

In response, ghazel closed in from both sides. They didn't rush. The two teams fanned out like hunters working to secure their trap. The white marble colonnades outside the Imperial Baths stood on either side of the broad way, offering possible refuge but no escape. Nolyn considered running inside, then rejected the idea. If the two of them had access to their weapons, perhaps that would work. But running for cover would only delay their deaths. Hope, both for them and the city, lay in reaching the river and the legions, then finding a way to break the enchantment. Mawyndulë wasn't the one keeping the others out. There had to be oberdaza somewhere, and with any luck, the witch doctors were nearby.

But luck hadn't been with Nolyn that morning, and he had no reason to suspect that would change. He had no hope of reaching the river.

It's Founder's Day. Normally, the city would be filled with people, even at such an early hour, but no minstrels filled the air with music; no drums announced the parade; not a single tremble stand had been set up to sell the sweet, seasonal drink. *What a sad holiday this is.*

The ghazel that approached held spears and shields. Not often had Nolyn seen them use weapons. Usually, blades and armor were reserved for elite troops; these did seem bigger, but it was difficult to tell with ghazel. They had a habit of bloating themselves, inflating their size like grouse or howler monkeys. Their glowing eyes flashed brightly at the sight of their prey.

"This god of yours," Nolyn said to Jerel, "did he mention this?"

"Sadly, he was light on specifics."

"They always are, aren't they?"

As the ghazel closed the distance, his mind flew to Sephryn. Nolyn remembered the way she braided her hair back in four lines; how to most she hadn't appeared to age, but he had noticed that her face became longer and thinner over the centuries. It had lost its youthful fullness, allowing a more mature definition that he preferred. In summer, her cheeks were dappled with faint freckles — so un-Fhrey-like. So was her one crooked tooth. Most never noticed that, either; Sephryn agonized over it.

She was so close, likely still asleep in that little house of hers on Ishim's Way. If the route had been clear, he could have run there in less than ten minutes.

I don't have ten minutes.

Nolyn wished he could see her one last time, but also wished she was a hundred miles away.

Maybe she is. Maybe she's visiting her father in Merredydd.

As the ghazel neared, Nolyn formed the only weapons he had left, clenching his hands into fists.

This city is a tomb.

The piercing clang turned everyone's heads, even those of the ghazel, who pivoted toward the river like a flock of pigeons caught off guard. Another clang and then a shriek. Not a human sound—the scream came from a ghazel.

Everything about the goblins disturbed Nolyn. The inhuman way they moved, the clicking, the leathery look of their lips and the forest of teeth they framed—all of it was unnerving. Their death cries were no different. When stabbed, they wailed like demons, a soul-shaking shriek. That is why he aimed for decapitation when possible. At that moment, however, Nolyn found himself elated with the sound.

He was even more pleased with the next shout.

"Nolyn! Jerel! This way!" Amicus yelled from the river side of the piazza.

The Sik-Aux! They're here!

"Go, sir!" Jerel shouted as he put himself between Nolyn and the onrush of goblins.

The bravery of the man was undeniable, and Loyalty itself could learn a thing or two from Jerel. Nolyn thought about staying, but only for a moment. He would best serve Jerel by running. His hesitation, so as not to appear a coward, would only prove to kill them both.

Seeing the Sik-Aux, Nolyn had hoped Mawyndulë had lied, and that he would also find the full contingent of legions pouring into the city. Instead, he found only a small band of Teshlors wound up in a ball, battling an angry hive of goblins.

Seeing Nolyn, Amicus broke free, stripped himself of caution, and ran toward his commander. Three ghazel tried to stop him. Two died. The last one lost an arm and, with it, his will to fight.

One ghazel remained between Nolyn and the First Spear. Guessing correctly that Nolyn was the easier kill, the ghazel set his feet.

Nolyn accepted as fact that the Prophet saw into the future. His only question was whether Amicus had determined his next move before starting his run.

Two swords were thrown into the air.

The first was the Sword of Brigham, which was thrown with such perfect accuracy that its handle practically landed in Nolyn's hand. He caught the sword an instant before the goblin impaled himself on its tip. The second, the Sword of Wraith, was hurled with more strength, passing high over Nolyn's head.

Seeing Amicus barehanded, the nearby ghazel swarmed him—but not before the big blade came off his back. The Sword of the Word rang out with a mournful whistle as it cut through the air, but that sound was soon drowned out by soul-shaking shrieks.

Catching movement from the corner of his eye, Nolyn spun, his blade raised. What he found was Jerel, holding the Wraith. The bloodstained blade indicated it had arrived similarly gift-wrapped.

The other Teshlors made their way to Nolyn, Amicus, and Jerel, cutting a hole through the ghazel's ranks. Where once there had been thirty goblins hunting two unarmed men, now seventeen of the creatures faced eight swords. The odds were still in the ghazel's favor, but recent history suggested the tide had turned. They stayed back.

"Welcome home, sir!" Mirk greeted him with a great grin, punctuated at the corners by his wounds.

"How'd it go with Daddy?" Smirch asked as the Teshlors formed a circle defense.

"Perplexing," Nolyn admitted, feeling the weight and balance of the sword in his hands. He hated fighting with an unknown weapon, even if it was a legendary heirloom. "Family holidays are never comfortable or, in this case, what you'd expect."

"You're alive."

"Like I said, never what you expect." Nolyn gave his new blade a quick practice swing, then nodded toward Amicus. "Thanks for the sword. Ours aren't working today."

"Figured as much," Amicus said. "But remember, it's just a loan. There are generations of Killians who'd haunt me if I lost them."

"Where'd you find the ghazel, sir?" Myth asked Nolyn as he took a moment to wipe the sweat from his hands on his chest.

Before he could answer, Riley said, "Strange, I'm seeing a surprising number of Urgvarian Ba Ran, the smaller ones without claws. They are seafaring goblins, unlike the Ankor warriors we've been fighting in the Erbon. Don't see them much around here. They're usually on the Green Sea."

"That explains it," Myth said. "These are cheap imported imitations. Must be on sale. Buy one, get one free, no doubt."

"What are they doing here?" Smirch asked. The air was morning-cool, and the clouds blocked any direct sun, but Smirch also took advantage of the pause to clean his hands and wipe his brow.

"I think they were invited," Nolyn said.

"By who?" Amicus asked.

"Mawyndulë."

"Who's that?"

"Someone bad," Nolyn replied, "A Miralyith prince with a grudge against my father, and apparently me as well."

"Is he the one keeping the legions out?" Riley asked.

From the ranks of the nearby goblins, a horn sounded—a long, lone, high-pitched note.

Nolyn shook his head. "Oberdaza are somewhere in the city. Quite a few, I suspect, to manage this."

"And that's not entirely a bad thing," Myth said. "We don't want them."

"Really?" Nolyn said. "Bravado is one thing, but—"

"Oh, it's not that, sir. The legion wants to kill us," Riley explained. "That's how we got here—running from them."

"Oh," Nolyn replied. He didn't know what else to say. What could be said when trapped between two armies united by a common desire for their deaths?

Answering the call of the horn, more than a hundred ghazel from the center of the city joined the horde, surrounding the Teshlors.

Amicus sighed. "At first, I thought the legion's inability to reach us was a good thing. Now, I'm not so sure."

෬

The moment Sephryn let go of the string, she knew the flight of the arrow was perfect. It traveled with a predestined precision, as if gods guided it home. For all her protests, Augustine Brinkle had the right of it. Sephryn was better than her mother at archery. She could have aimed for a thigh, or shoulder—even the hand holding the sword. She didn't. Fear, compressed into a split-second decision, had demanded a deadly blow. Sephryn had been in love with Nolyn since the age of thirteen, and there was never any doubt she would die for him. Until that moment, however, Sephryn had no idea she would also kill.

The arrow pierced the one bit of exposed flesh, lodging halfway through Nyphron's throat. The emperor continued to stand for only a scattered dash of seconds, then crumpled to the stone pavement. At first, no one noticed. His fellow Instarya continued to fight, pressing the attack. A cry went up, first from the Fhrey, then from the ghazel. The disciplined advance was replaced by wild fury. The line between sides shattered.

In a blind rage, each Instarya slaughtered a dozen or more ghazel. They became clear circles in the ocean of goblins, but those circles drifted apart until they appeared as isolated islands upon which unrelenting waves crashed. Then the islands were overwhelmed, one after another.

Sephryn nocked another arrow, seeking a glimpse of Nolyn and ready to kill any threat. But with the death of the last Instarya, a horn sounded, and the goblins moved off. They flowed out of the central square, dividing into small groups. From the top of the Aguanon, it was like seeing a sink drain. That's when she saw him. Nolyn lay on the ground beside his father, left for dead by the receding goblin horde.

Sephryn grabbed her satchel of arrows and leapt for the branches of the poplar tree. She was nearly to the bottom when she discovered two remarkable things. The first was that she hadn't instantly killed Nyphron. The emperor must have lingered because the second realization arrived when she reached the base of the tree and discovered that Ferrol's Law wasn't a myth.

Sephryn felt her soul leave with the suddenness of a snapping bowstring, a sharp recoil. With its departure came the cold. Unlike anything she'd felt before, it issued from within. The sensation was so sudden and powerful that she missed her footing and fell to the tree's roots, hitting her knee and cutting her cheek on the last branch. She lay there, gasping for more than merely air. Part of her had slipped away. She struggled to suck it back in, but no amount of effort could draw back what she'd lost.

The scene of Kendel's death flashed in her mind.

"Don't forget Ferrol's Law. You can't kill another Fhrey."

"But she's —"

"Even a single drop of Fhrey blood is enough. It's not worth sacrificing your immortal spirit. You'll be forever barred from entering the afterlife."

Dearest Mari, what have I done? That thought was instantly replaced by another. *Nolyn!*

Pushing to her feet, Sephryn grabbed the bow and sack of arrows before running as best she could toward the corner of the building and the plaza beyond. The Temple of Ferrol, which had been a refuge to hide in during the worst moments of her life, was now seen through different eyes. She felt hollow and abandoned by a god she had never worshiped.

With blood tearing down her cheek and limping from her bashed knee, Sephryn crossed the now-empty, body-strewn plaza. Nolyn had a black bruise forming on his cheek, but . . . *he's still alive!*

"Nolyn!" she cried.

Dropping the bow and arrows, she reached out to embrace him.

Shuddering and pushing away, his eyes shot open. Glaring at her with a cruel, vicious expression, he shouted, "Don't touch me!"

She stopped with arms still out. "Nolyn, I'm sorry." She glanced at Nyphron's body, the arrow still in his throat. "He was going to kill you."

He blinked several times, then shook his head as if clearing his thoughts. Nolyn looked at his father, then the arrow and, finally, at the bow she had dropped. "Yes . . . yes, he was. So it was you, then? You saved my life?"

"Yes." The word fell from her mouth.

Nolyn reached out and touched his father's cheek. "He really is dead, isn't he?"

Sephryn put a palm to her own chest that felt like a wind-whistling cavern. "Yes," she said again. The bitterness of the word grew worse with each utterance.

"I did it. I succeeded. Trilos was right. I got my revenge." Nolyn looked at her. A smile bloomed across his face. "Where is the horn?"

"What? How do you know about . . ." Sephryn stared at him.

"You went to get it last night. So where is it?"

No. No, it's not possible. Nolyn isn't the Voice.

Sephryn looked at Nolyn's wrist where he had always worn the braided bracelet she'd given him; it was bare. Even after their last terrible fight, he wouldn't have taken it off. "You're not Nolyn. You're the Voice from inside my head!"

"Doesn't take a genius, does it?" As he spoke, the visage of Nolyn faded and another person sat before her. A Fhrey—a bald one. He looked to be near her own age and had thin lips, cold eyes, and the bruise was now swelling one eye. "Yes, it was me. I tried to get Nolyn to kill his father because that would have been *so* perfect. But when he refused, I had to take matters into my own hands." He looked at Nyphron's body once more. "I suppose I should thank you, but killing him isn't what I asked of you. Now that he's dead, I *need* that horn. Where is it?"

Sephryn couldn't speak, couldn't move. The shock and the devastation was too overwhelming.

No. No, it's not possible. I killed the emperor to save Nolyn. I didn't sacrifice my soul for—

"Did you steal it or not?" The Fhrey stood, dusting off his hands. He surveyed the square and the bodies that lay scattered like the floor of the fish market after a net drop. Again, he smiled and added what looked like a self-satisfied nod. "Well?"

"I—yes. But you can't have it, not yet. I told you."

"Told me what?"

"That I have to see my son first."

"You never made any such demand."

"I did!" she yelled at him, causing the Fhrey to flinch. "When you told me to kill Nyphron." She stopped. Sephryn was emptied of her soul, but anger was rapidly filling that void.

The Fhrey looked confused and asked, "When I told you *what?*" Then recognition spread across his face, and he muttered, "Trilos." He spoke the word as if it solved a complicated mystery or held great meaning, but the name meant nothing to her.

The Fhrey smiled. "The horn isn't in the sack, is it? Of course not. You came here to kill the emperor and expected to be caught. You couldn't risk having the horn taken. So where did you put it? I doubt you would stash it in a cupboard. You left it with someone—a person you trusted—just in case you died."

"If you want it, then prove my son is alive," she growled through clenched teeth.

The Fhrey ignored her and continued on, "My old mentor is involved. He's the one who convinced you to kill Nyphron. But why? He's never aided my plans before, always seemed indifferent to them. I'm not complaining but . . . why did he help me this time?" The Fhrey's eyes widened. "The Invisible Hand. Of course! Trilos is trying to lure his brother into the open. That makes sense. He wasn't trying to help me at all. He used me *and* my plan. All he cares about is that I'm a catalyst for chaos. He wanted me to . . . to . . . what is that phrase he's always using? Oh yes, *make the world wobble.* But why kill Nyphron? And why use you?"

He looked at Sephryn, as if she would provide him an answer. She had none and didn't even know what he was blathering about. All she wanted was for him to take her to Nurgya.

The Fhrey clapped his hands together. "I've got it!" he said excitedly. "Trilos is using the horn as bait. He's betting Turin—that's his estranged brother—will come out of hiding to protect the horn and keep me from blowing it. That's logical, especially considering he's done that exact same thing before. If Nyphron still lived, the horn would be useless, and Turin would have no reason to butt in. Trilos knew that the emperor's death had to happen." The bald Fhrey grinned. "So, that means Trilos's brother has inserted himself in exactly the right place, at precisely the right time. You unknowingly gave the horn to him, the Invisible Hand. That's how Trilos will find him!"

"I don't know anyone named *Turin*," Sephryn snapped. "And I don't care about any culling horn, the loss of my soul, or that Nyphron is dead. The only thing that matters is my son. Now tell me. Is he—"

"Oh, well, I don't know Turin, either, but Trilos goes on and on about him all the time. He's been hunting his brother for centuries. If Turin actually exists, he's a canny fellow. He goes by different names. The most recent was Malcolm."

"Malcolm? Ancient Malcolm?" she asked out of reflex.

*He's trying to confuse me, so I'll reveal something—probably the whereabouts of—*Sephryn stopped herself. *Can the Voice hear my thoughts? Can Miralyith do that?*

"He's probably going by a new name. Who did you give the horn to? Not many options, are there? You couldn't talk to anyone new." He tapped a finger to his head. "You never know who might be watching, am I right? So, let's see. Was it Errol?" He shook his naked head. "No, too risky. You can't trust him. Arvis? No, she's not responsible enough. So that leaves—that monk!" The Fhrey clapped his hands together again. "How did I not see that?" He grinned in triumph.

"I didn't give it to anyone," Sephryn declared. "I hid it."

The Fhrey laughed. "You're lying. First murder, now dishonesty. You're falling down that slippery slope, aren't you? But knowing who has it isn't nearly as important as where they are. I suppose there's only one logical place. Somewhere that magic can't enter, isn't that right?"

"I'll get it for you, I promise. But you must take me to Nurgya. Right now!" she shouted, then reached for the bow.

"Can't."

The single word landed like a weapon's blow.

"Why not?" The words escaped her lips barely above a whisper.

"I don't know where the body is. It's likely there isn't one. Not anymore."

Sephryn's mind spun. "What are you saying?"

"The kid is dead. Mica was instructed to keep him alive until today, just in case you demanded to see him. Dawn on Founder's Day was the deadline I gave her. This invasion was planned months in advance." He rolled his eyes. "Oh, the trouble I went through. When Mica told me that Nurgya was Nolyn's son—" He paused, watching her reaction. "What? You thought she didn't know? That old woman wasn't stupid, just extremely willing to believe she'd been singled out by the god she worshiped. A few demonstrations of the Art sealed the deal. But you shouldn't judge her too harshly. After all, it wasn't so long ago that all humans believed in the divinity of my kind. But I'm off topic, aren't I? Anyway, since Nurgya is an heir of Nyphron's, he had to die. If any seed from Nyphron exists, then they inherit the throne, and I can only challenge. But if everyone from the Nyphronian line is dead, I can blow the horn and ascend to the throne unopposed. You see, the Fhrey have come to learn that opposing a Miralyith isn't such a smart idea. And thanks to Nyphron, all of the others in my clan are on the far side of the Nidwalden, and none of them can arrive in time."

Sephryn had barely heard any of the words after the first. Her head spun. She didn't know where she found the breath to speak but she had to ask. "Are you sure he's dead? You said you didn't see his body, so there's a chance that—"

The Miralyith shook his head. "No, there's not. Mica follows my instructions with an understandably exuberant zeal. But on the off chance she couldn't follow through, I had a contingency plan. There's a reason I set Mica's deadline for today. Her little hidey-hole is in the sewers. And the ghazel would have discovered it as they made their way here. For them, the youngest of your kind is considered a great delicacy.

For his sake, I hope Mica found enough courage because my instructions would make your son's death quick and relatively painless. Hers . . . not so much."

The Miralyith got up, smoothed out his rumpled asica, and said, "Now, since our business is concluded, I need to get going. While I doubt Trilos would deny me the horn, I think it's best that I get to it first." With that, he turned his back to her and walked in the direction of the palace.

Sephryn pulled an arrow from the sack.

Without turning, the Fhrey snapped his fingers, and Audrey's string broke.

CHAPTER TWENTY-FOUR
The Horn

Just like the city streets, the palace grounds were empty. All the little humans were cowering in their homes, behind their feeble wooden doors. Mawyndulë was surprised so few had poked their noses out. Granted, it was still early, and being Founder's Day, many might be sleeping in, having breakfast, or taking time to dress in their best. He didn't especially care. The fates of the human race as well as of the ghazel were on his list, but near the bottom. Once the city was taken, the ghazel would loot and torch it. While it burned, they would slip back down the sewers and into the ancient caverns beneath the city. Returning to their ships, which waited on the underground sea, they would set sail for their homeland. That was the plan, and a fine one, Mawyndulë thought.

Nyphron and Nurgya were dead, and by now Nolyn would be, too. All that remained was getting the horn. Percepliquis and the ghazel were but bit players in a grander performance. He was the main character in the tale of snatching triumph from tragedy. He would finally have his day in the sun—he looked up—or thick clouds, at least.

Mawyndulë honestly had no idea if a frenzied army of goblins would think twice about killing a bald Fhrey, should they see him. In his dealings with Zula Bar, Mawyndulë had taken the form of a ghazel oberdaza. That had been more than a nightmare. Urlineus was a resort when compared with the ghazel stronghold of Aoz Hilus. Just being there was dangerous. Mawyndulë had maintained the illusion for weeks, canceling it only when he slept in a tiny crevice of a dark cave. The weave wasn't particularly difficult — a task he relegated to the back of his mind — but it was a pretense he couldn't afford to drop.

He could, and would, resume the ghazel disguise to escape Percepliquis's impending inferno, but no spells were possible within the walls of the palace grounds, so his timing was important.

Approaching the gates, Mawyndulë knew what was coming, and he dreaded it the same way he would hate jumping into a lake of cold water. Even when prepared, passing through the entrance was a terrifying experience. Crossing the threshold, the runes stripped away his access to the Art, cutting him off from the world.

Mawyndulë had experienced something similar when a rogue wave flipped a boat that he had been riding in. He went completely underwater, and the capsized vessel blocked the sunlight. The moment he sensed there was something solid between him and the surface, he panicked. Being trapped and unable to reach air was beyond horrifying. He felt isolated, stripped of power, and vulnerable. Inside the walls of the palace, he felt as desperate as he had under the boat. Despite knowing that the sensation of drowning was all in his head, Mawyndulë still struggled to breathe.

Mawyndulë paused just inside, trying to determine which way to go. He began wandering around the gardens of the courtyard. His first inclination was to look for it in the palace proper. He entered and looked around, but then he recalled a conversation he had heard between Sephryn and Seymour. He had often used the Art to eavesdrop on Sephryn, at least until his sea voyage on the *Stryker*. While aboard that cursed ship, he had been sick beyond imagining and couldn't have cared less what she was up to. But in the beginning, he had listened to her for hours. For most of his time in Urlineus, he had been waiting for news of Nolyn's death to arrive. During that period, Mawyndulë made himself appear like a legion officer—what rank exactly, he hadn't a clue; he wasn't that interested. He mainly hid in the cool of a storeroom, his bunkmates barrels of wine. Lost in the shadows, he focused on Sephryn and listened in on her life in Percepliquis.

Most of it was dreadfully dull. Sephryn didn't live a grand existence. He wasn't listening for anything in particular, just gathering information and guessing he might hear something important, or at least useful. Standing inside the gate of the palace, he puzzled out where to go.

"If you could search through the parchments at the records office and write down anything you find about the horn, that would help."

"Where is that?"

"At the palace. There's a little building just inside the gate to the left of the entrance. I can show you tomorrow."

Mawyndulë discovered there were actually several small buildings. He focused on a tiny stone structure that was round like a tower but too short to be called one. A narrow door hung open, revealing steps that went down instead of up. Mawyndulë guessed it had been built as a storage pit—a root cellar perhaps. The muted light of that morning's impotent sun drizzled down the steps, fading into darkness. He had to be in the right place.

He's in there: Seymour, the all-too-convenient monk.

Despite his need to return to the surface and escape the rune-covered walls, Mawyndulë moved closer to the door, gaining a straight view down the dark staircase. Then he stopped. The entrance didn't look inviting. It seemed dangerous.

"You'll succeed," Trilos had told him. *"You'll have your revenge, at least."* Why had he added "at least"?

Mawyndulë stared ahead into darkness. What lay through the doorway was a mystery. Although what he had told Sephryn about the monk being Turin made perfect sense, he didn't actually know for certain. Now that he faced the possibility of meeting the one waiting down there, he paused.

Mawyndulë's master plan had called for a clean sweep. When the smoke of a ruined Percepliquis cleared, all the Instarya—anyone with Fhrey blood—would be dead. A Fhrey from Merredydd might arrive in time to put forth a challenge, but no Miralyith lived there. And if the challenger was young, which was the most likely scenario, he wouldn't have tattoos—only veterans of the Great War would have remembered that important trick.

Sephryn knows.

He stopped to consider if she could be a source of any true threat.

I should have killed her. I was planning to. But she did *save my life, and that stayed my hand. Was that moment of weakness a fatal mistake?*

Cut off from the Art, Mawyndulë felt both blind and deaf. Defenseless as he was, it would be easy for Sephryn to sneak up on him. Mawyndulë spun around, expecting to see the half-Fhrey stabbing at his face with a fistful of arrows.

She wasn't there.

He studied the open spaces surrounding him but didn't see her. Oddly, everyone seemed to have disappeared. The palace courtyard was as empty as Imperial Square had been. The ghazel were no doubt off looting and feasting. Mawyndulë stood in the center of the most populous city in the world and was utterly alone.

Eerie, he thought.

He looked back at the entrance to the records hall, at that small doorway that led to the future he had worked so hard for. Someone calling themselves "Seymour" was down there.

Did Turin select that name as a joke? "See more" was a bit too on the nose, wasn't it?

But if Turin was half as powerful as his old mentor had implied, then such a being could afford to be brash. Trilos repeatedly referred to his brother as *pure evil.*

How awful does something have to be for a demon to use that label? I'm inside. I'm underwater. Helpless and alone.

Surrounded by the Orinfar, the palace was a perfect place to trap a Miralyith.

Maybe I should wait for Trilos to show up. He will. Now is his big chance to catch his brother.

After so many centuries of planning, Mawyndulë was mere inches from his goal, but fear made him hesitate.

Who is Turin, really? What kind of being frightens a demon like Trilos? I should have asked more questions when I had the chance. But I never cared until now. All I wanted was revenge and to get back the crown that was stolen from my hands.

After Mawyndulë had killed his father, after he broke Ferrol's Law, nothing had been "right." Food didn't taste as good. Sunsets weren't as colorful. And all the water on the face of Elan couldn't slake his thirst. It had been more than eight hundred years since he'd lost his soul, and still that feeling of emptiness remained.

Once I blow the horn, I'll get it all back.

Then a new thought walked in, a wonderfully amazing revelation.

What if Trilos is wrong? He's been chasing his brother for longer than I've been alive and hasn't even come close. What if Seymour really is just an ordinary monk?

All he had to do was walk down those steps, take the horn, and blow it.

How hard is that? One short toot and everything will reset. I'll become invincible—at least for a day. Then once the time of challenge has passed, I'll cross the Nidwalden and enact revenge on every Fhrey who betrayed me. After that, I'll resume the war and erase the Rhunes.

Realizing his trip down the stairs was his destiny, Mawyndulë stopped putting it off. He walked forward, ducked his head, and went down.

The monk was right where he ought to be, seated on the bottom step, using the faint light to read an old parchment. Mawyndulë couldn't see much else. The morning light was so dim that even his Fhrey eyes failed to detect much more than the vague shapes of clutter at the base.

Mawyndulë was less than five feet away when Seymour sensed his presence and looked up. As he did, Mawyndulë spotted the bag at his side. "Give me the horn," he said with as much menace as he could muster.

Mawyndulë didn't like the monk's response. He should have jumped and cowered.

Instead, Seymour smiled. "About time you got here."

Mawyndulë froze. *It's true. Trilos wasn't wrong! Curse it all!* "You're the Invisible Hand!"

"I'm not Turin, you idiot."

"Trilos?" Mawyndulë stared at the slender figure in the battered frock. Over the centuries, Mawyndulë had been forced to play the game of *Find the Trilos;* he never knew when the demon might turn up in a new body. The *exact* reason for each jump was often difficult to figure out. Some bodies were worn for decades while others were kept for less than a year. They didn't seem to decay, so that wasn't the reason. Sometimes, Trilos left a body because it became damaged or ill. Mawyndulë's mentor seemed unwilling to suffer through something as mild as a head cold. A few times, a corpse was abandoned merely because its muscles were sore. Most of the time, Mawyndulë assumed a switch was done to provide variety because everyone liked a new outfit now and again.

"Have you . . . were you in this body all along?"

The monk shook his head. "No, just the last few days."

"But you've been here? Watching how things played out?"

"Yes."

"You were right," Mawyndulë told him. "The plan worked."

"No, it didn't."

"What do you mean? Nyphron and his heirs are dead, and we have the horn!"

"The only reason the emperor died is because I intervened; had I not, then *you'd* be dead. I was so sure that Turin would stop Sephryn. But he didn't bother to raise a finger to save that poor woman from losing her soul. I should have known better. His cruelty knows no bounds. Turin is a heartless bastard."

Now that the fear of facing an unknown evil had passed, Mawyndulë discovered he was irritated. "You could have told me what you were planning. If I had known—I mean, I didn't need to be here at all. I nearly died while trying to stab Nyphron."

"I couldn't. I needed to wait until the last moment to act."

"Why is that?"

"Because there could be another reason Turin didn't stop Sephryn. And if it proves to be true, then we may have learned something very important today."

"Such as?"

"Perhaps Turin can't predict what I will do. Maybe he can only witness the effects of my actions after they occur. Like a blind spider, he might not be able to see me, and he only knows I'm nearby after feeling the vibration of the web as I move through it. *That* would be a very important piece of information to have at my disposal. And it should be easy to test such a hypothesis."

"If you say so. But don't count on me to help. I already have a lot on my plate. I just need the horn," Mawyndulë said and held out his hand.

Trilos tossed the bag to Mawyndulë. "Here. But it won't help you. It's a fake."

"What?" Mawyndulë flung the pack open. Inside, was a ram's horn, old and cracked. "How is this possible?"

"Because even if Turin can't see me, you are as easy to spot as a black bear after a heavy winter snow. Nyphron knew you'd be coming for it. Turin did, too. My brother likely saw what you were going to do centuries before you were strong enough to make an attempt. Maybe even before you were born. Knowing it was safe meant there was no reason for him to make an appearance."

"No!" Mawyndulë shouted and threw the horn against the steps where it bounced three times, rattling its way to the bottom.

"Don't make such a fuss. You're closer to your goal than you were last night. Nurgya is dead, right?"

Mawyndulë nodded, although his face sported a full-on scowl. "Either by Mica's hand or eaten by the ghazel."

"Two down. What about Nolyn?"

Mawyndulë looked up the steps at the still-hazy light. "By now, he's probably dead, too, or soon will be. I sealed his sword in its scabbard, and a horde of goblins was after him. In a few hours, there won't be anyone but ghazel alive in this city."

Trilos nodded. "Good. In that case, you might yet get your chance. When the news spreads that the emperor is dead and he has no living heirs, some ambitious Fhrey on this side of the Nidwalden will demand that the horn be presented. When it isn't, he'll petition to rule. That means notifying the non-Imperial Fhrey, the ones restricted by the Ryin Contita. Turin's fragile peace between the two races will dissolve; the Nyphronian empyre will fall, and humanity will be reduced to cowering in hunted pockets. Endless skirmishes will leave everyone weak and ripe for the ghazel." He made a *tsk-tsk* sound. "So much of my brother's hard work will fall apart. Perhaps that's enough cause for him to show himself. Either way is fine by me."

"But it does me no good," Mawyndulë retorted. "I need to blow that horn when I'm farther than a day's journey from any other Miralyith. If Nyphron's prohibition against travel across the Nidwalden ends, that'll be difficult to do, even if I can locate the real horn."

"You're young. There's still plenty of time." Trilos, dressed in his shoddy monk's frock, nodded and smiled. "We haven't yet won the war, but today has brought some victories our way. That's enough for now. How about some breakfast? This body is starved."

Mawyndulë dropped the bag in disgust. He didn't get the victory he wanted, but he was alive, and Nyphron was dead. He had that much, at least. "I don't want to eat here. This place is going to be a bloody mess."

"Oh, that's right," Trilos said. "I can't exactly walk through a mob of goblins like this."

"There are plenty of ghazel corpses in the square."

CHAPTER TWENTY-FIVE
The Invisible Hand Moves

Sephryn cried over the body of Nyphron. She did so for her son, for Nolyn, and for the emperor she had just killed. Lack of a soul did nothing to armor her against guilt and sorrow. She was jolted out of her grief when something fell at her side. It looked vaguely like a snake. Wiping her eyes, she saw a piece of string—a bowstring.

"I hope you'll excuse the intrusion, but I thought you might need this."

A blurry glance revealed a man in a common off-white tunic and tattered hood. He was tall, slender, and had a kind face.

She glanced at the string, then looked toward the palace. The Miralyith who killed her son was inside, but if she hurried, she could—

"Don't waste your time. Seymour is already dead, and Mawyndulë isn't a major concern."

"What?" She pushed herself up.

"I'm sorry." The man grimaced. "That was terribly blunt, wasn't it? I just didn't want you to run off to . . . oh, never mind."

She took a staggered step backward. "That Miralyith killed Seymour?"

"No. He actually died several days ago. Arvis was right about the incident on Ebonydale. Someone has been using your friend's body ever since. He's the one who tricked you into killing Nyphron."

"You know about that?" Sephryn wiped her eyes and stared at the man. He wasn't a complete stranger. She had seen him before. He was . . . she struggled to remember. "You were in the market. The person who bought the bread for Arvis."

"Yes. And I'm here now, Sephryn, to tell you that none of what's happened is your fault."

"You're wrong! You have no idea. Oh, Grand Mother of All." Sephryn plunged her face into her hands, then ran them through her hair, pulling hard on the strands. "I ruined everything—everything." She looked at the blood-soaked stones of the plaza. "I couldn't save my son. And I . . . I . . ." Her sight shifted to the fallen body of the emperor, lying with his back leg twisted unnaturally, his left cheek resting on the ground, eyes still open. "I've killed Nyphron!"

"Yes—yes, you did. You've had to pay the price for my own failings, but I want to do what I can to ease your pain. And I *can* do that, but you must listen and do as I say. And that means you can't tell anyone what you did. In fact—" The man stepped forward, and unceremoniously jerked the arrow from Nyphron's neck. The emperor's head flopped back to its other cheek. "I'll get rid of this, so no one will know."

"What difference could that make? Do you think I care if I'm executed? I deserve what's coming. I don't even have a soul anymore! Do you know that? You don't, do you? You can't. You're a human, but I have Fhrey blood and broke Ferrol's Law. I thought that was just an invented legend. But it's real, and . . . now I'm empty inside."

"I'm sorry about that, too. I didn't see what was coming until it was too late to do anything." The man looked guilty as he tapped the tips of his fingers together awkwardly. "I failed you. I can't see my brother, and I didn't know what he was planning until he spoke to you. By then, too many plans were in motion, converging all at once, and I had so little time to react. You're a good person, Sephryn. Your mother would have been proud of the woman you've become. You don't deserve the fate that's befallen you."

He looked toward the palace gate. "You have to understand that an impromptu interference can have disastrous repercussions. Even speaking to you now is a risk—a huge one. He's probably in that courtyard, which means we don't have much time. But I must do what I can so the world doesn't fly apart. I owe that to Nyphron, and Persephone, and Raithe, as well as, well . . . so many people, both living and dead."

He smiled, and his face softened. "You were forced to do evil today, and while I can't restore your soul—for there are tallies that cannot be erased—I can still reward you for such a great sacrifice."

"I don't want anything!" Sephryn blurted out. She felt sick. The nausea had returned. A general weakness was spreading throughout her body, which may or may not have been related to the loss of her soul. Tears, however, were in ample supply. They slipped forth once more as if from some inexhaustible well. "Nurgya died because I failed. I lost my soul because I've killed. Why would anyone *reward* me? And what could you possibly give me that I care about?"

"I know that you think your life is over, and that the eternity to follow will be worse, but it doesn't have to be. If you listen to me now, if you can hold on for just a while longer, you'll find redemption. Your life can be wondrous, and you'll receive everything you always wanted. Everything that you dared to hope for. Everything you deserve after so many years of striving to bring about a better future—not for yourself, but for everyone else."

"I don't understand."

"You will. Nolyn is here."

"No . . ." She shook her head. "That's an impostor. I saw him change."

"Yes, you're right about that. But the *real* Nolyn is also here. At this moment, he's fighting for his life at the Grand Arch." The man tilted his head to the east. "A call for reinforcements has been sounded. So that's where most of the ghazel are heading. They'll kill him unless you act quickly."

Sephryn discovered that heartbreak, when severe enough, allows for a belief in miracles. She didn't need proof of what the man said. "Tell me what I need to do. Please!"

"Two things. The first I already mentioned. You must make a solemn vow that you'll never tell anyone that it was you who killed Nyphron. Not even Nolyn. If you keep this pledge and do the other thing that I'm about to ask of you, then you'll not only save the emperor's son, but the empyre as well. And doing that will move the world one step closer to becoming what it's meant to be."

"I swear. Now, tell me. What is the second request?"

The man smiled. "The same one I gave your mother at the Battle of Grandford, and you'll be even more amazing than she was."

Sephryn ran through the city, not to the east but north. She raced up Reglan Road, across Reanna Boulevard, to where it intersected with Maeve Avenue. She made her turn at the moneylender's stone house with the signboard out front in the shape of two imperial coins. A wagon was parked out front. Underneath the cart, two dogs cowered. Sephryn imagined their master did the same inside his stone fortress. The city that had been poised to celebrate held its collective breath. She had seen few people on the streets. Most looked frightened, or at least confused. The rest were dead or in hiding. Bodies lay scattered. Sephryn ran past a woman in a nightgown who lay in front of her home, a ruby smear streaked across the door. A man and his three children formed a bloody puddle in the middle of Maeve Avenue. These were the early risers, the ones who had been off to stake out good seats for the day's events. If the goblins didn't kill everyone, the lazy would be rewarded for sleeping in.

Racing past the pottery shop Sephryn found a dead horse whose throat had been torn out. Then she heard a woman scream.

Without pause, Sephryn pulled three arrows from the sack that clapped her thigh. She trapped the feathered ends between the knuckles of her draw hand. Then she grabbed one more and held it between her thumb and forefinger. These were the newer arrows. She could feel the bone-reinforced nock, and unlike the hawk quills in the originals, these used common cock feathers.

Rounding the pottery shop, Sephryn spotted three women leading a line of hand-linked children. All were dressed in their holiday finest. In colorful tunics and whimsical hats, they had set off for a day of celebration, oblivious to the attack. *Likely thought all the shouts were from riotous merrymakers.* Each of the children held tiny green-and-blue flags on miniature flagpole sticks, waving them earnestly.

Two ghazel ran at them, teeth bared, claws clicking.

Sephryn had never seen a goblin before that day, but she had asked Nolyn about them. He never said much. *"I'd prefer that you didn't suffer sleepless nights as I do,"* was his only comment. He was adept at changing the subject whenever his years spent in the Durat came up. Nolyn had, however, mentioned the claws, teeth, and glowing yellow eyes. In her mind, Sephryn had imagined them as tiny badger-like beasts that snarled and snapped.

These were nothing like badgers. The goblins were brutes as big as, and in some cases bigger than, men: hunchbacked, thick-necked, oily-skinned fiends with massive arms and monstrous clawed hands. They shambled rather than ran. Their limbs quivered inhumanly, their movements unnatural.

The solo scream became a chorus as all the women and children took up the shrill song. Their happy hand-clasped line collapsed into a tight group. And as the ghazel came close, hands let go of each other as they were raised in a feeble defense.

Sephryn didn't think. She felt. And it was fluid, like throwing a ball.

Two ghazel crumpled, slapping the pavement without so much as a grunt. The third one—the goblin that the little parade of children and their guardians hadn't even seen because it crept up from behind—made a little cry as an arrow entered its eye.

"We're under attack! Find shelter! Stay indoors!" Sephryn barked at the little troupe as she took the time to stop and reclaim the shafts.

With her three arrows back in hand, Sephryn was off again. *How long does Nolyn have?*

❧

"No sense in waiting, is there?" Nolyn asked, tilting his head at the remaining ghazel that surrounded them.

With the legions powerless outside, Amicus ordered the Teshlors into a semicircle defense with himself at the center, just as they had done in the Erbon Forest. Behind them, men of the First Legion spread out in a line along the edge of the invisible barrier to watch like spectators at an arena contest. The remaining eighteen ghazel—who had broken off from fighting with the Teshlors—were content to wait for overwhelming odds by the addition of their brethren.

The ghazel fidgeted as they waited. Some licked their lips; others sneered and growled like dogs. Nolyn was looking into the eyes of his own death once more—a bad habit to get into. *But this time is different. In so many unpleasant ways, this is clearly a trap.* A noose was tightening. Inevitability, when it arrived on such sturdy feet, brought with it a sense of freedom and comfort. With no way to win, he didn't have to worry about losing.

"You're right," Amicus said. "I'm tired of being on the defensive. Let's have at them for a change."

As usual, Amicus led the way. Driving forward, he charged the ghazel. Using his great sword, he spun, and before anyone else had time to close the distance, he'd killed four. Riley was up next. Using sword and shield, he backed up Amicus, coming into the battle on his weaker left side, becoming the man's shield—but a deadly one as he laid out a pair of ghazel. Myth took up residence on Amicus's right and killed two more. Nolyn took down his own with a quick thrust. Jerel, who tethered himself to the prince's side, killed the one next to him. Mirk, Smirch, and Everett never got their chance to engage. In an instant, the immediate battle had been reduced to even odds. The remaining ghazel didn't care for the math and retreated to the safety of the onrushing swarm that came out of the city streets like an ocean wave rolling toward them.

"Back to the arch," Amicus ordered, and the eight of them shifted position.

They lined up once more shoulder to shoulder in the familiar half-moon formation with the legions behind them.

"Astounding," someone beyond the barrier said. "Did you see that?"

"It really is Amicus Killian, and the others . . ."

"They fight like he does."

"Amazing."

"Such bravery!"

Nolyn glanced behind him and spotted Jareb Tanator, shaking his head in disbelief.

He wasn't the only one. Legionnaires were now ten-deep, all watching as if pressed against a pane of glass.

"Watch out. They're coming!" Tanator shouted.

He needn't have warned them. His shout was a trifle compared with the roar of charging goblin feet that was powerful enough to make the pavement jump. The soldiers outside drew back, apparently no longer confident that the invisible barrier would hold. In the face of the stampeding horde, which poured down the tiers of the city like a dark wave, the bulk of the empyre's forces flinched. But standing before them, eight men stood their ground.

Leaving the narrow corridors behind, Sephryn sprinted the span of the Mirtrelyn Garden. The park, decorated with trees and statues, surrounded the Imperial Arena. Normally filled with crowds bustling into or out of the amphitheater, the place was empty that morning.

Sephryn killed a pair of ghazel guards clustered in a shadow near the south entrance before they knew she existed. Retrieving the arrows, she climbed the stairs to the high terrace. These were the cheap seats: too high up to see the action clearly, too far away to hear the grunts or feel the spray of blood. But the spot was perfect for Sephryn, who sought elevation and an unobstructed view.

She could hear them. The rhythmic sound echoed through the stone arches, rising and falling in a communal chant, "Unza hafa, zala hafa, unza hafa, zala hafa . . ."

As she rushed up the narrow steps, Sephryn held an arrow ready but knew it wouldn't help if she met a ghazel in such a tight place. She listened carefully for the hint of something above but heard nothing. Soon she was on the terrace, an open ring that circled the top of the arena wall. Carefully, her chest heaving for air, she crept to the railing. She realized she needn't be concerned. The top floor of the arena was empty, and the group of oberdaza who danced and chanted in the center of the field far below were oblivious to everything but their magic.

"Unza hafa, zala hafa, unza hafa, zala hafa . . ."

Sephryn knew the story—everyone did. The Battle of Grandford was the highlight, the apex, the shining moment in the history of the empyre. The conflict at Alon Rhist had all the ingredients of legend: underdog humans facing an overwhelming foe, a final stand in a crumbling fortress, noble heroes facing evil villains, tragedy and victory, prophecies and magic. There had even been a dragon. And Sephryn's mother had played a pivotal role. She had led her archery corps out onto the field of battle and rained death from above onto the hill called Wolf's Head, where Fhrey Miralyith conjured their magic. Just like the oberdaza who were now below Sephryn, the undefended, armorless Miralyith of old had chanted and swayed in a circle and wreaked havoc on the human defenders. Moya had been the one who stopped them.

Sephryn set down the bow, dumped all the arrows out of her sack, and lined them up against the rail. Her palms were moist, and without the three-fingered glove she had used in her youth, she worried the sweat could impair her string release. She might slip or roll the cord.

"I never needed a glove," her mother had repeated every time Sephryn put it on.

"I'm not you," Sephryn always answered.

"There's more of me in you than you think."

"Mother, for both our sakes, let's hope that's not true."

At that point in their ritual verse and refrain, Moya would scowl, and Sephryn would smirk. But her mother wasn't there.

Below, she counted six chanting ghazel. The number of arrows wasn't a problem. Nor was the fear of missing. The oberdaza were much closer than Nyphron had been. Sephryn could see the dust they kicked up from the clay floor of the battlefield, the colorful feathers around their waists, and their necklaces made of human teeth. She was confident that she could drop each one. The issue to deal with revolved around the fact that as soon as the first one died, the others would notice her. The stories of the Great War and the tale of Suri at Neith taught Sephryn that even one wielder of the Art possessed enough power to destroy an entire army. Five of them could definitely ruin Sephryn's day. She couldn't afford that, nor could Nolyn. For that matter, the city couldn't, either.

The key to success, then, was to kill each of the six at the same instant.

"I bet you can. I'm sure you're incredible."

Sephryn began taking deep breaths.

"They say Moya was the best ever because she invented archery and used a magic bow carved from the famous oracle tree of the Mystic Wood."

Sephryn picked up Audrey. She felt the old bow in her hand. There was an indentation, a furrow, and a trough in which her fingers and the clutch of her palm fit perfectly. A knot protruded just a hair above the bend of her thumb. Sephryn had no idea if the spot on the grip had been carved by Roan of Rhen or whether it was merely worn down by decades of use. But what she did know was that Moya had held the bow exactly the same way when she faced the Miralyith on Wolf's Head.

"But the Fhrey have a dexterity that humans and Belgriclungreians lack."

Forcefully inhaling through her nose and out through her mouth, Sephryn pumped air into her lungs. She was still on short supply after the run, but anxiety also shortened her breath. She had to calm down, needed to relax and clear her mind. Sephryn vaguely recalled how Suri had long ago taught her students to hum as a means of tapping into the natural world and its power. Sephryn did that now. She wasn't an Artist, but she felt the method to be similar. And perhaps she was making the same sort of link. Maybe that's what everyone did when they prepared for something monumental—searched for the rhythm of Elan.

"You can thrash your way upstream," Suri had once said, *"or you can enter the current and let Elan lend a helping hand."*

Sephryn gripped six arrows in her draw hand, index markers all facing to the right. Below her, the oberdaza danced and sang their violent melody.

"The real Nolyn is also here. At this moment, he's fighting for his life at the Grand Arch."

"Unza hafa, zala hafa, unza hafa, zala hafa . . ."

"A call for reinforcements has been sounded. So that's where most of the ghazel are heading."

"Unza hafa, zala hafa, unza hafa, zala hafa . . ."

Sephryn slowly stood up. She nocked the first arrow.

"They'll kill him unless you act quickly."

"Unza hafa, zala hafa, unza hafa, zala hafa . . ."

Rather than directly aiming at the ghazel, she aimed high. One last inhale, then she let her breath out slowly and released. As fast as possible, she nocked, pulled, and released arrow after arrow, starting high, then reducing the arc of each shot.

"In archery . . . the daughter of Moya the Magnificent—who is also endowed with the Fhrey blood of an Instarya father—"

The arrows didn't hit their targets at exactly the same time. The little guy on the right died half a heartbeat later than the three on his left, and the remaining two went down a whole three beats behind the rest.

Blood filled Nolyn's eyes, making it difficult to see. His face, chest, arms, and legs were soaked. He could taste the iron in his mouth. The blood shower was so intense, he wondered if perhaps it was raining from the sky. His hands were slick where they held the sword; fearful he could lose his grip, he used both hands, sweeping the blade right and left faster then he'd ever done before. The most amazing thing about the blood storm was that it wasn't his. As far as he could tell, none of it was human; all the gore was ghazel-born.

The unstoppable stampede of the goblin horde slammed into the unmovable Teshlor wall and fared as well as meat encountering a grinder. Whatever lessons the ghazel learned in that box canyon in the Erbon Forest had not spread to these monsters. Nolyn and his fellows faced neither arrows nor oberdaza magic, and the result was a brutal killing field.

The ghazel were forced to drag back their dead to create paths to their enemy. Out of growing frustration, a group of more than a dozen charged forward weaponless, running full tilt and trying to knock them down. Without discussion, the Teshlors dodged, letting them through their line. The invisible barrier proved as impenetrable to them as it was to the legions, and the ghazel slammed against it with so much force that a few fell unconscious. The others were easily dispatched.

Behind them, the legions cheered, "SIK-AUX! SIK-AUX!" But before long, that chant was overwhelmed by, "TESH-LOR! TESH-LOR!"

Perhaps the spectators were beginning to hope that the intrepid band of eight would pull off a miracle and win the day. Nolyn knew different. He was getting tired. The others were, too. Blood-covered as they were, fatigue showed in their eyes. Exhaustion was setting in, and although they'd already killed many, hundreds more waited in their wake.

"Why are they here?" Amicus asked as the ghazel once more took time to draw away their dead and wounded. The onetime First Spear stood with drooping shoulders, wiping blood from his face with his forearm, panting for air. "Why waste their time with us?"

"Where's the Instarya?" Smirch asked, doubled over, breathing hard. He used his sleeve to mop the blood tears from his face. The sleeve, soaked through, only smeared the gore around. "And the city guard? They were always around when I didn't need them."

"Just a guess," Riley said, "but if this many ghazel are here, they've probably already dealt with the city guard and the Instarya."

Nolyn agreed. "They're fixated on us because we're all that's left. With the legions locked out, the ghazel only need to kill us to own the city."

"How'd we get in?" Everett asked. The boy looked pale and scared, but he held his panic in check, giving it no foothold.

"Maybe the barrier came up the moment we entered?" Riley offered.

"That's crazy convenient," Myth said.

"The Orinfar. Those symbols block magic."

"We all got the tattoos," Riley said. "That's how we . . . wait a minute, wouldn't that mean . . ."

"Are you kidding me?" Smirch asked.

"Can we all just walk out?" Amicus asked.

Just then, the wall of teeth, claws, spears, and sword clashed once more.

Combat, as it was happening, wasn't something Nolyn could focus on. His mind didn't freeze up; on the contrary, his body reacted at a speed beyond conscious thought, freeing his mind to the point of wandering. In a real sense, Nolyn felt like an observer watching himself fight. He emotionally cringed in anticipation of a mistake and cheered when he escaped unscathed. He was his own audience, just as invested and emotional as the most ardent fan, but still just a spectator to the event. He wasn't deciding when to swing or how. His movements were dictated by reflex, the accumulated result of centuries of experience, much of which he couldn't put into words. Instead, when trying to explain it to new recruits, he used vague terms like *dancing* or *rhythms in music*. Hearing himself describe it, he was certain no one—except those who already knew—could understand.

Careful! There's one coming up on the left. Be ready!

He gave himself advice like an onlooker certain the participant was unaware of the hidden threat.

He's going to swing high!

Nolyn ducked and stabbed; he felt the blade sink in.

Pull it out! Pull it out! Another one! There's another on your right. You're too late!

Jerel's blade saved him.

The shiny warrior always managed to know when to step in.

It's the Teshlor training. They see the future; all of them are forecasters of the fight, clairvoyants of combat. Or is it true? Is there one god, and did—

"Fall back!" Amicus shouted, perhaps hoping they could, indeed, pass through the barrier and that the legions outside may have changed their minds about killing them.

Nolyn's foot slipped. Blood on the stone was slick as ice. His balance faltered. The next blow was blocked, but it sent him farther off-center. He was far from down, but the fall was predestined. Even Nolyn, who lacked Teshlor training, knew that.

Look out! Look out! his mind screamed. *Oh, no! You're going down!*

Facing the end, Nolyn managed to notice a cry from the right.

Everett's voice. Got him, too. This is it. It's over.

Another strike caught by his blade sent Nolyn backward. His remaining foot went out, and he felt the fall.

Jerel's blade blocked, blocked again, and then . . . there was a cheer followed by a roar.

As Nolyn's back hit the pavement and his head slapped the stone, he heard a sound like an ocean wave crashing. Loud and close, the roar rumbled over Nolyn as he watched legs running past on both sides. Several leapt over him.

The barrier was down. The legions had entered.

CHAPTER TWENTY-SIX

Telling the Truth

All of the oberdaza were dead.

Sephryn had checked. She'd gone down to the arena floor, bow nocked. Then while aiming the razor tip of a brand-new bodkin at each face, she kicked each ghazel one by one. They were either dead or *really* good at pretending. She relaxed the bow and started pulling arrows. Four came out just fine. One had somehow managed to splinter as if it had hit stone, and the last one wouldn't pull free no matter how hard she tried.

She calculated her supply of arrows as she departed the arena: *twenty-one left.* By the time she reached Maeve Avenue, Sephryn was hot, and when she passed the double-coin signage of the moneylender, she needed to wipe perspiration from her brow or risk getting it in her eyes. A blind archer was a dead archer. Still, she didn't want to take a hand away from the bow even for an instant. Sephryn saw movement in the narrow corridors between the shops and homes — shadows that lurked.

When did it get so hot? She glared up at the bright sun that swam in a vast blue sky.

What happened to the clouds?

Like startled grouse, a cluster of ghazel burst out from between an herbalist and a weaver's shop. Sephryn turned and launched six arrows between three heartbeats. Each shot entered a goblin's eye. She hadn't planned it that way—hadn't thought at all. But in retrospect, she realized that all those years of acorn splitting had paid off. More footfalls approached, and she nocked again, but the new arrivals weren't ghazel.

Five legionnaires sprinted onto Reglan Road, swords in hand. They stopped, looked down at the staggered line of fallen ghazel, then at Sephryn. Laughing, they offered a salute. One said, "Pardon the interruption, dear lady. We thought these were getting away."

As the soldier spoke, Sephryn spotted another group of five ghazel far down the street jumping over a stone wall beside the fuller's shop. Six other legionnaires were in close pursuit, shouting profanities and grunting as they hopped the masonry wall. The soldiers saw it, too. "Have to go, ma'am! Got a lot of cleaning to do!"

"Wait!" Sephryn called as they bolted like hounds, joining the chase over the wall. "Is Prince Nolyn alive?"

Maybe they didn't know or hadn't heard, or perhaps, like hounds after a scent, they were too single-minded to answer. Either way, Sephryn was once more alone on the street. After that, she jogged rather than ran. The heat from the sun, the stress from the arena, and the sense that the danger was waning started to take hold.

She slowed to a walk and realized she was more than tired. Sephryn was reluctant to reach her goal, afraid to face what she was starting to believe to be the truth.

"At this moment, he's fighting for his life at the Grand Arch."

I took too long. He's dead. I know it.

Sephryn remembered the sight of hundreds of ghazel. *Was there ever really a chance?*

To reach the Grand Arch, she had to pass back through Imperial Plaza, which was still a bloody mess. Bodies lay on top of one another, a fresh coat of blood sprayed over older stains. The rings of slaughtered ghazel were laid out like flower petals, with dead Instarya at the center of each. Their bodies were still there. All of them surrounding the big circle in the middle where—

Sephryn stopped in shock.

At the center of the plaza where Nyphron lay, a solitary legionnaire stood. He appeared to have been dyed red. They saw each other at the same instant. His face, coated in sadness and blood, washed with relief as their eyes met. Dropping his sword, he ran to her. For a moment, Sephryn worried it might be the bald Fhrey in disguise again, but then she noticed the wristband. She'd made the bracelet long ago when she was so poor that she had to cut strips of leather from her sandals. The thing was ugly—Sephryn was no artisan—but it had been made with love. At that moment, it was beautiful because it was still on his wrist. The impostor hadn't had that hideous, poorly crafted, and yet absolutely wonderful leather bracelet.

Nolyn!

He embraced her. She was off the ground, swinging in a circle as he whirled her about. His arms squeezed her so tightly she could hardly breathe. She didn't care. She didn't need breath, not anymore. *He's alive! He's alive!*

"You're safe!" he shouted, setting her down, tears making clean lines down his cheeks.

"So are you," she managed to get out.

"I'm so sorry," he told her. "I should have done what you asked. I shouldn't have left you. I should have gone to my—"

"No, no, no." She stopped him. "I was wrong. I always am."

"No, you're not." He squeezed even tighter and whispered in her ear, "And I love you. I always have."

Then he drew back, his hands running down the length of her arms, moving toward hers.

"Nolyn, I—"

"You have your mother's bow," Nolyn said.

"What? Oh, yes. There were ghazel dancing and chanting in the arena. There aren't anymore."

"It was you! You saved us."

"She saved everyone," the man behind Nolyn said.

Only then did Sephryn realize they were not alone in the world. Imperial Square was full of soldiers. The shabbiest and bloodiest stood just behind Nolyn. The one who had spoken, the man in a First Spear uniform, she recognized. "Amicus Killian?"

"How in Rel can you remember names like that?" Nolyn smiled at her. His hand came up and cupped her cheek. His eyes locked on hers.

He doesn't want to look away. Doesn't want to see what's right beside him.

Eventually, as the soldiers gathered around, he had to. Sephryn watched the happiness fade as Nolyn looked down at the body of his father.

The emperor's eyes were still open, one leg twisted in an undignified manner. Nolyn knelt and straightened it, then closed the emperor's eyes.

"Nolyn . . ." she began but then faltered. She had to tell him. How could she not? "Nolyn, I—"

"I misjudged him." He continued to look at his father, and his voice grew heavy. "I thought he hated me. He didn't. I thought he tried to kill me, but it wasn't him. I thought he'd sent me away after my mother's death out of cruelty, but—at least in his mind—it was out of kindness. I thought the tattoos were meant to humiliate me, but they were for my protection." Nolyn placed a hand on the emperor's head. "He wasn't the father I wanted, but I think he may have been the father I needed."

His words hurt. Sephryn knelt beside Nolyn and took his hand, pulling it to her chest. She had to tell him the truth. It felt so wrong not to. She'd been forced to promise a stranger she'd keep silent, and other strangers had forced her to steal a horn and kill the emperor. She was done letting others control her. While terrified that the news would end their relationship and create an uncrossable chasm between them, keeping the truth from Nolyn would be cowardly. She knew nothing about the man who'd given her the bowstring or why he wanted her to stay silent.

How could remaining a coward save the empyre, much less the world? She wanted his words to be true, but wanting didn't make it so. "Nolyn, I have to tell you something. Something terrible. Something unspeakable, and I have to say it now, or I won't ever be able to. I did an awful thing. A horrible thing. You're going to hate me."

Nolyn looked at her. "I could never do that."

Such a wonderful thing to say, but reality often made short work of pretty words. "You don't yet know what I did. I—"

"Sephryn!" a woman's voice called. "Sephryn!" The soldiers moved apart to let the woman through. It was Arvis, and in her arms, she carried a bundle. "I saved the bread, Sephryn."

Sephryn shook her head violently. "Not now, Arvis. For Mari's sake, not now!"

"But . . . I saved the bread." Arvis began crying. Tears ran down her cheeks. "I'm sorry. I had to kill Mica to do it. I didn't have a choice. She came at me with a knife—was gonna kill both of us. Don't be mad—please don't be angry. I couldn't let her take the bread—not this time. But this isn't my bread, Sephryn. I know that—I mean, I didn't, but I do now. Mica told me. And that's when it all came back. You see, the Bakers took mine. Rodney and his wife, Gerty the Turdy. They took my daughter, Alina. It was years ago, but that's what happened. Oh, no, that's not right. They didn't *take* her. I couldn't feed Alina, so I gave her up. I gave my daughter to the Bakers. That doesn't matter, but this does because this bread isn't mine. It's yours. Don't you see?"

"Arvis, what are you—"

The bundle in Arvis's arms moved, and a baby cried.

Sephryn's heart leaped at that sound; she knew that cry. "Nurgya?"

Arvis nodded. "I saved the bread, Sephryn. But it's not my loaf. It's yours."

"The bread . . ." Sephryn broke from Nolyn and, reaching out, took the child. Her arms shook until her baby filled them.

"You were in the market. The person who bought the bread for Arvis."

"You were forced to do evil today, and while I can't restore your soul—for there are tallies that cannot be erased—I can still reward you for such a great sacrifice."

"And what could you possibly give me that I care about?"

She looked at her son's rosy face, then up at Nolyn. "This . . . this is the awful thing I did," she lied. "I didn't tell you about your son. Here he is." She cooed at the baby, then added, "Nurgya, this is your father."

CHAPTER TWENTY-SEVEN

The Last Galantian

For the first time in eight hundred and thirty-three years, Founder's Day had been skipped. Some saw an ill omen in Nyphron's death occurring on the anniversary of the city's founding. But everyone agreed that the emperor, who had died while defending his people from an invading ghazel army, was a hero to the end. Everyone also agreed that his son, Nolyn, and a handful of elite soldiers known as Teshlors had fought a courageous battle at the Grand Arch. Their bravery and skill had confounded the ghazel horde until Sephryn, daughter of Moya the Magnificent, used her famous mother's bow to break the magic spell on the city. Together Nolyn, Sephryn, and the Teshlors had saved Percepliquis from destruction — and rescued its citizens from a gruesome death.

Emperor Nyphron was laid in a golden coffin on a satin-covered catafalque that was placed in the center of Imperial Plaza. He was dressed in his full set of armor, which had been polished until it shone as bright as the sun. The population of the city filed past the body for three days.

On the third day, as the bundles of flowers began to wilt, he was laid to rest in an alabaster sarcophagus. Lacking a proper tomb—no one had thought the emperor would need one for centuries—the sarcophagus was placed in the palace.

Over those same three days, the city had been cleaned. Blood had been mopped and stones scrubbed, but it soon became obvious that a faint, unsightly stain would forever remain. Every dark corner of the city had been searched for hiding ghazel, and large sections of the sewers had been filled with concrete. Despite all such efforts, rumors of goblins lying in wait persisted, and for a long time, mothers had little trouble ensuring their children would be home before dark.

"You could have spaced it out a bit," Smirch said, struggling with his uniform. "That's all I'm saying."

"Actually, he can't." Amicus adjusted Nolyn's ceremonial sword belt. "You can bet Hillanus and Farnell are plotting as we speak. Right now, everyone sees us as heroes. Only an idiot would raise an objection. Hillanus would be killed by his own men if he tried. We need to get that crown on Nolyn's head while the wave is still cresting."

"Besides, I prefer to get everything over with at once." Nolyn scowled at the gaudy, full-length mirror that revealed a vision of himself in golden robes and an ermine mantle. "No sense having to get dressed like this twice."

"Just seems such a waste." Smirch pulled on his buckle. "Why have only one party when you can have two?"

The Teshlors and the soon-to-be emperor were holed up in the echoing Grand Hall. They gathered at one end, near the single high window that cast a lone shaft of white light on the tile floor. Nolyn's father had been placed in the emperor's private quarters until a final resting place could be constructed, and Nolyn didn't feel comfortable dressing in the same space as a huge alabaster sarcophagus. In truth, Nolyn didn't feel comfortable anywhere in the palace, his father's private quarters least of all.

I don't think I can live here. Maybe Seph and I can just run away? Oh, and Nurgya, of course. Can't forget him. By Mari, I'm a father!

Nolyn didn't feel like a father. There had been none of the pomp and ceremony that usually accompanied a royal birth, and he hadn't had enough time to become acquainted with the idea. The kid was just there, waiting. Nolyn had hoped that the moment he looked at his son he would feel something. He had imagined some magic enchantment would overwhelm his heart, and he would instantly fall in love with the boy. It hadn't—at least not yet.

Have I inherited my father's indifference? Nolyn stared at himself in the mirror and physically shook at the vision of an emperor staring back. *By the eyes of Eton, I look like him.*

"Seriously, *Your Eminence.*" Amicus emphasized the new title they were all still getting used to. "You were less nervous in the Erbon Forest."

Nolyn scowled. "That's because I wasn't about to become a husband, father, and emperor of the known world. Things were easy way back then. I was only waiting to die."

"Way back then?" Riley questioned as he checked over the dress uniforms of the Teshlors. "That was just two weeks ago, sir."

They all looked at him.

"Are you sure?" Amicus asked. "You know it's a crime to lie to the emperor."

"I'm not the emperor yet," Nolyn said. "Lie all you want, Riley."

Riley straightened Everett's collar and noted the deep cut on his forehead, the blow that had nearly killed him. "Put your helm on."

Everett did so. The helmet had an ugly dent where the blade that caused the cut had creased it.

"Never mind. You're a lost cause," Riley said, and turned to inspect Jerel.

"Well?" Jerel asked and smiled.

Riley rolled his eyes and moved on to Smirch, who had his belt buckle on the wrong hip and wore a two-day growth of beard. Riley shook his head. "Honestly, man. It's the coronation."

"I'm not ready for this," Nolyn said. "I mean . . . look at me!" He turned to face them, holding out his arms and turning around slowly. "This isn't right."

"Well," Amicus said, "it's got to be a better job than assistant administrator in a salt mine."

"You're not getting out of this, you know." Nolyn wagged a finger first at Amicus and then at the rest of them. "I'm going to do what Jerel wanted." He said it as a threat and pointed at DeMardefeld, who shone like a mirror.

"We're going to be bodyguards, right?" Mirk asked, with a hopeful rise in his voice. Mirk and Everett were delighted to be in the city at the center of the world, to be all dressed up in gleaming metal. For them, the terrors of the past were forgotten and the dangers of the future yet to be realized.

"No!" Nolyn shouted, then reconsidered. "Well, yes, but not in the way you think. You're going to be bodyguards, but the body you'll be protecting is the empyre. The empyre will be your family now, Amicus. I want you to train an elite corps of troops that will be unequaled in combat."

"For war?" Amicus asked suspiciously.

"No, for peace," Nolyn replied. "Your Teshlors—my Teshlors—will protect the empyre, eliminate corruption and cruelty, and uphold my laws and the new charter of rights."

Amicus laughed. "I'm not a god. I can only teach them how to fight."

"That's where Jerel comes in. He will turn these warriors into Night Heroes by instilling in each the modesty, goodness, and truth that Gifford of Rhen embodied when he courageously rode out to face single-handedly the army of the fane. The rest of you will assist them. Through all of you, by the power and honor of the Teshlor Nights, we will make the empyre not merely great, but noble. In other words, if I have to be emperor, all of you are going to suffer with me."

The entire place had been meticulously cleaned for the celebrations. Sephryn watched Nurgya playing on the floor of the bedchamber that had once belonged to Empress Persephone, but since her death, it had become more like a shrine than a home. The room hadn't been occupied in centuries except by a lonely ghost, if the tales of the cleaners were to be believed. No members of Nyphron's staff had ever entered the old bedroom.

The palace servants were a bit giddy at the prospect of a living empress once more inhabiting the palace. The great canopy bed was covered in a quilt that depicted the history of Clan Rhen. Rumors reported it had been crafted by Brin. The gorgeous rug had been a present from the ancient warrior Menahan. The fired clay cups and bowls on the glass-encased shelving, which had been made by Gifford of Rhen, were all washed and dusted. With so much memorabilia, the place felt more like a museum than a bedroom.

As much as Sephryn had loved her namesake, who had become a vague memory of light and goodness over the years, she found it difficult to imagine sleeping in Persephone's bed. Emperor and empress would be expected to live in the palace, but it didn't feel like a home, much less *her* home. At the same time, Sephryn couldn't imagine returning to the empty house on Ishim's Way. Even though Mica hadn't been murdered there, Sephryn couldn't forget the blood-covered walls.

Nurgya was her salvation. He appeared to take after Nyphron's side of the family, his hair so blond that it looked nearly white. His eyes, however, were as green as Nolyn's and Sephryn's—a shade darker, perhaps. And he was perfect. Sephryn had checked her son over a dozen times. Not a mark was on him. As best she could determine, the Miralyith likely never touched Nurgya. Mica had staged her own death and, after stealing Sephryn's son, the two of them had hidden in the sewers.

How could she do it? Mica had always cared for Nurgya like her own child. And then she took him because a voice in her head told her to? A voice she believed was a god.

Sephryn wanted to hate Mica but found it difficult.

I did the same thing, didn't I?

Sephryn tried to draw a distinction between what she had done and Mica's actions, rationalizing that not only had Nurgya's life been at stake, but so had the future of the empyre. Sephryn truly believed that the world would benefit if Nolyn or Nurgya became emperor, so her decisions hadn't *just* been because of a voice.

But what if Mica had felt she had equally good reasons for what she did? What if she had been just as convinced that Nurgya would be a horrible emperor? And what might the Miralyith have promised her? Perhaps Mica also thought the weight of the world rested on her actions.

Since the attack, many people were calling her a hero. The citizenry's praise just made her feel worse. The wrestling match Sephryn had held with her conscience through the days of mourning had made her wedding feel less celebratory. Nurgya's return, however, made everything bearable. She was overjoyed that he appeared none the worse for wear, but even more important than that, his survival spoke to a greater truth. The stranger's promise—that had seemed so preposterous—was now inexplicably plausible because of the miracle of her son's life.

Was it really Malcolm? And did he have a hand in getting Arvis to save Nurgya?

"Your life can be wondrous, and you'll receive everything you always wanted."

While no one knew the life span of a dual-heritage descendant, Sephryn didn't feel old, and she, Nurgya, and Nolyn would likely have centuries together. Like Persephone before her, Sephryn would finally be able to make real changes, helping to unite humans and Fhrey. These improvements would outlive her, so she would have a lasting impact on the world. Sephryn's soul wasn't lost so much as spent. Her eternity had paid for the future happiness of millions. Barred from the afterlife, she had just one regret. She would never be able to apologize to Nolyn, Nyphron, or her mother.

The wedding would take place first, and then the coronation would immediately follow so that Nolyn and Sephryn could be presented to the city as emperor and empress. Neither ceremony would be performed in the Temple of Ferrol. Old traditions were being swept away, a sign that humans and Fhrey stood on even footing. A sentence was added to the official ceremonial text: "These two *bridges* will unite the empyre's races." Sephryn had suggested the idea, and Nolyn had agreed.

The final touches were being applied to Sephryn's stunning dual-purpose wedding and coronation garment. Her son was alive, safe, and happily playing on the floor with his three nursemaids. And Arvis, who was now the child's official bodyguard, watched them. Sephryn stood because sitting was impossible in the elaborate construction that the imperial tailor had referred to as a *dress*. She waited for the bell that would summon her to the ceremonies that, until then, had always seemed like an impossible dream. The day was bright, the sky blue. Birds sang, and trees flowered. After three days of official mourning, and having been cheated of their Founder's Day festivities, the people of the city were ready to celebrate.

A knock on the door made Sephryn jump.

Arvis opened it.

"Is she decent?" Sephryn heard the familiar voice of her father, and she wanted to rush forward. The dress restrained her.

"Who's asking?" Arvis replied, not the least bit intimidated, although she should have been.

Tekchin, now the last of the Galantians still walking the face of Elan, was a different sort of being. An Instarya of the old order, he was the last of those said to have died, entered the underworld, and returned to tell the tale. Normal rules didn't apply to him; to hear her father talk, they never had. He knew it, and so did everyone else — except Arvis. She stood her ground and fixed him with a threatening stare, but the woman could no more stop Tekchin than she could halt time.

Dressed in a loose shirt and traveling cloak, he strode in and hugged his daughter. He lifted Sephryn up and carried her around like she was ten. "Look at you, my little star!"

It had been centuries since he had called her that. "You're here!" she cried.

"Would have been here sooner, but . . ." He paused.

"What?"

Tekchin put her down and shook his head with a disbelieving grin. "There was this fella in the middle of the road halfway here. He waved me down and asked if I was Tekchin. Never saw him before, but when he confirmed who I was, he said I had to give him a ride back to Merredydd."

"A ride? You came by horse? But you hate horses."

"Not this one. His name is Feranza. He has a great temperament. Anyway, I told him I couldn't because I was heading to Percepliquis for Founder's Day and to visit my daughter and meet my new grandson."

"Oh! You got my message?"

"I did."

"Couldn't have come a month ago?"

"Can I get back to my story?"

She folded her arms and frowned, but then she nodded.

"Well, this guy said he normally wouldn't care about my plans, but . . . and this is where the story gets odd . . . he said a guy paid him good money, and would give him even more, if he could convince a Fhrey named Tekchin to give him a ride to Merredydd."

"And you did?" Sephryn narrowed her eyes. She knew her father, and only one thing had ever deterred him from a goal, and Moya was dead. "Why?"

"Because when I asked who the guy was, he said his name was . . . Malcolm."

"Really? You mean as in — *the* Malcolm? The *mystery man* that you and Mother always talked about?"

"I was wondering the same, so I asked what this Malcolm guy looked like, and he described him as a tall, gangly man without a beard who had a long nose, sharp cheeks, clever eyes, and a kind face."

"Did he say what he was wearing? Was it a simple off-white tunic and a tattered hood?"

Tekchin's brows rose. "You've seen him, too?"

Sephryn started to speak but closed her mouth. There was too much to say, and too much she couldn't.

Tekchin stared at her a moment, and when she didn't say any more, he went on. "So, I dropped Keenan—that was the fella's name—in Merredydd, thinking Malcolm might be there. To be honest, I was a bit apprehensive."

"Because Malcolm visits old friends just before they die?"

Her father touched the tip of her nose with a finger. "Exactly. But Malcolm wasn't there. I looked around, found nothing, and so I climbed back on Feranza and came here. Turns out I missed a few momentous events, but . . ." He took a step back, appraising the dress. "I got here in time for this. Your mother would torment me for all eternity if I hadn't."

Looking toward Nurgya, Tekchin smiled. "Is this my grandson? He looks—" He crossed to the child, lifted him up with one hand, and nestled him in the crook of his arm when the child appeared frozen in fear.

Sephryn started to cry.

"What's wrong?"

Sephryn shook her head. "I'm just . . ." She wiped away a tear. "A lot has happened. Nyphron is dead."

"I've heard." He returned to Sephryn and wiped her tears. "The thing to keep in mind is that there was no better way for Nyphron to die. He was Instarya and a Galantian. We should never die in a bed."

"It wasn't just him," she said. "A lot of people died, many of the Instarya. Sikar survived, but Illim and Plymerath were killed."

Tekchin nodded. "I heard that, too. I spoke to Sikar on the way in. Looks like he'll recover. Hard to kill Sikar, but they came close. Best as I can figure, that was why Keenan was standing on the road. Otherwise, I would have been in that square. Not sure if I'm pleased or upset about that. On the one hand, it would have been a grand way to go, but on the other . . ." He hefted the boy in the air. "I'd have missed meeting this little guy. So why the tears? Were you that close to Nyphron?"

"Not really, but a close friend of mine, Seymour Destone, was killed. He reminded me a lot of Bran, who won't be at my wedding. And now, neither will Seymour."

He wiped her tears again.

"You know, it's strange, but you look so much like your mother right now."

"It's just because I'm older."

"Don't think so. Even now, I only remember your mother the way she was back in Dahl Rhen." His eyes smiled. "Pretty and smart, with those big doe eyes of hers."

"*Doe eyes?* Seriously?"

"See!" He grinned and pointed at her. "There you are, just like her. I know you don't think that's a compliment, but you should." He played with Nurgya, who wanted to grab his finger. "You'll see. When you meet her again, when you're sitting in Mideon's great hall, you two will chat, and you'll learn the truth and understand everything."

Tears ran down her cheeks. "We don't need to talk; I already know."

"There's something else, isn't there?" Tekchin handed the child to Arvis.

Where's the damn bell? Sephryn was terrified he might be able to see — notice that there was nothing inside. She had to say something, needed to distract her father for fear he'd draw out the truth and cause her to ruin everything. "How much do you know about what happened here?"

"The city was attacked by ghazel; Nyphron and the Instarya defended the palace; Sikar was nearly killed and most of the Instarya died; magic was keeping the legions out, and you used your mother's bow to kill the oberdaza who were casting the spell." He smiled. "Oh, and Nolyn and a band of soldiers, who interestingly call themselves Teshlors, kept the city from destruction until the legions could enter."

"You didn't mention that the ghazel were invited in."

"Really? By whom?"

"A Miralyith named Mawyndulë, who was seeking revenge. He kidnapped my son." She pointed at Nurgya. Arvis, who was looking up at them, nodded. "To get Nurgya back, I had to bring him a relic called the Horn of Gylindora. Do you know what that is?"

Tekchin hesitated.

"I'll take that as a yes."

Tekchin smiled at Arvis. "What's your name?"

"Arvis," she said suspiciously.

"Arvis, why don't you and these other ladies take Nurgya out for a stroll or something? I'd like a word alone with my daughter before I give her away forever."

"Well?" she asked after Arvis and the nursemaids had slipped out the door.

Tekchin continued to stare at his daughter. "What do *you* know about the horn?"

"Not a lot. Just that it's old and was used to determine who rules the Fhrey. And that it can only be blown once every three thousand years or after the death of a ruler—a period known as the Uli Vermar." She had no idea if she'd pronounced that correctly, or if Seymour had, or even if it had been him who'd told her. So much of the last few days was still whirling in her head.

Tekchin nodded, suggesting she was close enough. "That's how the Great War ended, and Nyphron became emperor. Nyphron blew it, and Mawyndulë challenged him. Nyphron spared the Fhrey prince's life. Not sure why." His tone lacked the normal Galantian exuberance and bravado. He practically whispered.

Tekchin's taciturn response left Sephryn with a growing unease. "The reason I brought the subject up is because Mawyndulë has the horn. Is that a problem?"

"It would be if he really had it."

Sephryn frowned and hung her head. "Unfortunately, he does. I'm the one who stole it from Nyphron's vault and gave it to him."

"Nyphron wasn't a fool. The Horn of Gylindora was never in his vault. That was a fake, put there for exactly this reason. The real horn is safe and sound."

"Oh, good," she said, and placed a hand to her chest letting out a sigh. "That's a relief. I thought there might be a problem."

"There is." Tekchin turned away and began walking around the room, looking at his feet. Unless drunk, her father was never comfortable sitting or even standing in one place. Moving, she suspected, was a comfort to a person who'd spent centuries fighting one thing or another. It also suggested he was uncomfortable. Something was wrong, something bad enough to concern a two-thousand-year-old Fhrey who'd faced the afterlife and returned to tell the tale. "I didn't think about it until I bumped into Sikar. We got to talking and realized that now that Nyphron is dead, the Erivan Fhrey are no longer obligated to obey the empyre."

"But Nolyn is the new emperor."

"Of men. But he's not the *fane*—that's what the Fhrey call their leader."

"So, does that mean Nolyn needs to blow the horn?"

"No. He can't challenge himself. As Nyphron's heir, he's already a contender. But his Ferrol-given powers as fane won't kick in unless the ritual is completed. Sikar and I discussed the prospect of one of us sounding the horn. A challenge doesn't have to end in a fight. We could yield, and that would satisfy the requirements. That's how most of the transitions used to go."

From her father's demeanor, Sephryn had been expecting more. "So what's the problem then?"

"If the horn is blown, all Fhrey will hear it. Even those in Erivan. They will know Nyphron is dead. The only reason the war stopped is because Nyphron became fane; our side would have lost otherwise. Without him, the war will start again, and this time the non-imperial Fhrey across the Nidwalden will *win*."

Tekchin was prone to exaggeration. His stories weren't just tall—they soared. Only she saw no hint of a smile, no wink. Her father wasn't joking. He was serious.

"But we aren't a band of tribal villages anymore. We have trained legions and—"

"The empyre is not as strong or as united as you'd think," he said sharply as if revisiting an old wound. "Look at the revolution that Nolyn harnessed. The nine provinces are little more than wild dogs that Nyphron kept on a short leash for good reasons." He stopped himself and took a breath, his face softening. "Sorry. The sad truth is that after the wedding and coronation, you'll receive an education in the unpleasant complexities of rule. Humans are, well, like your mother: high-strung, emotional, and independent. But full-blooded Fhrey are more inclined to be constrained by rules, myself and Nyphron excluded, of course." He winked. "Sephryn, you must understand that humans have never liked anyone telling them what to do. But sometimes, most of the time, that's absolutely necessary. You and Nolyn have quite the challenge ahead. If you're able to keep the provinces from breaking away, that will be a feat in itself. You don't want to add facing the might of Erivan to that mix. Also, and perhaps even more important, you must keep in mind that during the Great War the use of gilarabrywns turned the tide. The Erivan Miralyith still know how to create those winged monstrosities, but with the passing of Suri, we don't."

"But you can still do that yield thing, right? Then Nolyn would be fane just like his father."

Tekchin resumed his circling stroll, rubbing his chin where the faint shadow of a beard was emerging. "We could, but . . . I'm not an Umalyn priest, and I know there's a bunch of stuff that goes into who gets the chance to blow the horn. Sikar didn't know any more about it than I do, and we'd hate to find out we missed something. If we screw up, then Nolyn would have to fight. He'd end up battling a Miralyith and likely to the death. They won't yield. And Nyphron's trick of tattooing himself with the Orinfar to negate Mawyndulë's advantage is well-known and won't work twice. So it's absolutely essential that no one on the other side of the river learns of Nyphron's death. I suspect it's the reason he set up the Ryin Contita in the first place." Tekchin paused and looked out the narrow window at a blue sky that Sephryn had previously hoped heralded a beautiful day. "Also, the horn has to be kept a secret from everyone. I don't even know how you found out so much about it. Does Nolyn know? Have you discussed this with him?"

"No."

"Keep it that way."

"You want me to lie?"

"Just don't volunteer information that all humans, and a good number of imperial Fhrey, have forgotten about." He crossed the room and took her hands in his. "Look, we both know the type of person Nolyn is. If he learns he's required by Fhrey law to present the horn, he'll want to do what he believes is right, even if that means putting his own life in jeopardy. And to be honest, if it was only *his life*, I'd tell him to go right ahead. I've done exactly that on hundreds of occasions. But it's not, is it?" He held her sight with his. "The decision he makes could undo nearly a millennium of Fhrey and humans living side by side."

He let go of her and walked back toward the window, halting when the sunlight filled his face. "I'll admit that Nyphron didn't do the best job integrating the races. But that's not where his strength lay. Persephone and Moya knew there was a better way. They just didn't live long enough to see it through." He turned to face her again. "Now their children have a chance to change that. What do you think is a better use of Nolyn's time? Working on fixing that problem, or letting his sense of decency cause him to gamble with his own life and possibly all mankind as well? Given that, do you really want him to know?"

Sephryn didn't answer. Like her father, she had a strong suspicion Nolyn would face the challenge. "But what about Mawyndulë? He knows Nyphron is dead. His plan was to eliminate Nolyn and Nurgya as well. And even though he didn't accomplish that, if the danger to Nolyn is as great as you say, wouldn't he try to force the issue?"

"Mawyndulë won't tell anyone, certainly not those in Erivan. He's an outcast from there. They would kill him on sight."

"What if he finds the real horn?"

"He won't."

"So you know where it is?"

Tekchin nodded.

"But you won't tell me?"

"Someday, I will."

"Why not now?"

The bell began to ring, calling the ceremony to its official start. Half a dozen servants poked their heads in, each smiling with excitement. "It's time, Your Greatness."

"After I become empress, I can order you to tell me."

"Yes, of course, after the ceremony." Tekchin grinned at her. "Your mother would have been so proud. You look wonderful, by the way."

CHAPTER TWENTY-EIGHT

Finding the Way Home

The twin ceremonies had taken forever, but they were over faster then Nolyn expected. Forever, he discovered, was brief when measured against eternity. The plodding coronation ritual, invented on the spot with no handbook for such a thing, ended and launched the rest of Nolyn's life. The moment the crown was placed on his head and the presiding official shouted to the masses, "All hail Emperor Nolyn Nyphronian, Ruler of the World," he knew he was at the dividing moment bisecting the two halves of his existence. What came before and what followed would be as different as an acorn was from an oak.

Standing on the platform before the multitude, he saw his years to come spreading out before him. As with any view of one's own future, it was hazy, lacking detail, but the slope of the landscape was clear enough. He would trade the real for the imaginary. His foes would be ideas, movements, misunderstandings, and lies. His sufferings, no longer physical, would be frustration, regret, and boredom. He felt as if a door had been locked, and he imagined hearing a snicker before the person with the key tiptoed away. In an instant—which a moment before he'd perceived as "forever"—not only had the world changed, but so had he. As emperor, he had been robbed of his birthright to complain. From now on, he would be the hook upon which people hung their grievances. With the revelation, Nolyn felt his first stab of remorse, as if by some miracle or evil curse, wearing the crown had allowed him to start to understand his father better. He witnessed his own ignorance, and he saw his former self as childish, arrogant, and stupid.

"When the fate of the world is in your hands, gambling is an unaffordable luxury, and idealism is often burned on the altar of reality." Nyphron's words were true. And Nolyn realized they applied equally to becoming emperor and to just growing up.

Eight hundred and fifty-five years old, and only now am I becoming an adult.

Feeling the impact of the roaring crowd, Nolyn took comfort in two things. The first was a distant, dreamlike memory of his mother on a snowy morning when Suri had introduced him to a white wolf.

"This is Minna. Minna, this is Nolyn."

"Does he bite?" Nolyn asked, concerned.

"Only if you call her a *he*," Suri replied.

"Can I—can I pet her?" he asked.

"That's up to Minna."

"Is it safe?"

Suri shook her head. "Nothing is safe. Nothing worthwhile, that is. Minna will either let you or eat you."

"Life is full of risk, Nolyn," his mother said. "But you should never let that hold you back. You can't let fear stop you from living. Just make certain the chances you take are worth the peril."

He had reached out, put a tentative hand on Minna's head, and rubbed. She nuzzled him, and he had grinned from ear to ear.

Nolyn wasn't certain why that fleeting fragment of memory made him feel better, but it did. He took even more comfort from the woman beside him, whose hand he squeezed as if it were his last fingerhold on a cliff's edge. She had been the one constant in his life. Together they were a unique pair, marooned in that world from another reality, providing reassurance to each other that neither was insane.

They moved through the crowd, lost in a sea of people who reached out to touch them, drowning among the waves. In the future, those oceans of hands would be reaching out for another reason, looking for an audience so their petitions could be heard.

The two managed to reach the palace gate and the sanctuary of the courtyard. And while not nearly as crowded, it, too, was filled with well-wishers—these being the more influential and affluent sort. Nolyn recognized the First Minister, the imperial treasurer, several provincial governors, even Ronelle Sikaria—son of the still-bedridden governor of Merredydd. Nolyn also spotted one surprisingly small, well-dressed Belgriclungreian anxious to speak to Sephryn. She didn't appear quite so pleased to see him.

"I'm sorry about . . . ah, Bartholomew," Sephryn said. "Errol—"

The dwarf raised a hand, stopping her. "Consider it a wedding present. I really just wanted to offer congratulations and to say that I saw you."

"You what?"

"The Belgriclungreian Empire had plans to enter a chariot team in the Founder's Day Grand Circus Event for the first time this year. I was in the West End around dawn on Founder's Day, checking on last-minute details, when I saw you run into the arena with Audrey. I thought you might be going in there to practice. I couldn't help myself. I chased after you, but I don't have your long legs and never managed to catch up. Still, I was on the third-floor rail when your arrows flew." The dwarf grinned. "You, Your Most Esteemed and Serene Imperial Eminence, are a wonder of modesty." With that, he bowed and kissed her hand. "You are, in a word—incredible."

"Who was that?" Nolyn asked.

"Belgriclungreian ambassador," she replied.

"He probably wants something."

"I don't think so. He's already received the only thing he wanted."

When they reached the entrance hall, they started up the stairs toward the residence, but Sephryn paused to search the crowd below. They were toasting the newlyweds.

"Looking for someone?" Nolyn asked.

"I'm surprised my father isn't here."

"It's likely the Teshlors have cornered him somewhere. I know Amicus would love to talk with him. He has a lot of questions about Tesh, Brigham, and the rest."

Waving good night to the crowd and feeling rather drained, the two slipped free of their admiring guests.

They were in the residence of the palace, alone together for the first time as husband and wife and as emperor and empress.

"Hello!" Sephryn called out, hearing her voice echo in the vast stone chamber that was the first room of the imperial residence. She presented an awkward, sarcastic smile. "I like a place that talks back. Makes it seem so . . . *cozy.*" She looked up at the vaulted ceiling. "I hear that Persephone roams the corridors at night. It's wonderful imagining your mother-in-law keeping watch over your wedding bed."

"Let's not forget my father's sarcophagus in the next room. That adds a special touch."

"Oh, it's in there?" Sephryn's smile became more forced. "How . . . nice to have family around."

Nolyn noted the stands of armor, swords, and shields lining the massive marble walls. "Not exactly homey, is it?"

"It's . . . okay," she said.

Nolyn had seen cats cough up hairballs with less effort. "You don't like it here, do you?"

She shrugged. "What's not to like? I've always wanted my own—" She pointed at a weapon mounted on the wall. "What is that?"

"An ule-da-var. A traditional Fhrey weapon from around a billion years ago."

"Oh, well, then sure, we need one. I'll bet all the best families have these, right?"

Nolyn frowned at her. "I'm sorry."

"For what?"

"For chaining you to my nightmare."

She stopped looking at the walls and ceiling and focused on him. "It's a nice chain."

He smiled back. "Still, this place is horrible. It's what happens when you cross arrogance with insecurity."

"The Belgriclungreian builders?"

"No—my father."

She held a finger to her lips and jerked her head to the side, and whispered, "He can probably hear you."

Nolyn smiled, but he realized it was funny because, on some uncomfortable level, it felt true. Except for that first *hello!* of Sephryn's, they had spoken in soft, quiet, indoor voices. They didn't feel alone or welcome.

"We don't have to stay here." Sephryn gave him a playful smirk. "I'm pretty certain I heard someone say you were emperor now. Doesn't that position come with—I don't know—unlimited power or something?"

Nolyn took the crown off his head and held it to the lamplight. "Huh. I thought this was just a crappy party hat. You're right. I am the emperor. That has to have some perks, right?" He glanced at the door, grinning and hoisting his brows with a wickedness he was certain was unbecoming for an emperor. "Wanna get out of here?"

"Although consummating our love under the gaze of your mother's ghost sounds hard to pass up, what did you have in mind? I mean, it's not like we have a lot of choices. I don't like this festively decorated mausoleum of cold stone and weapons, but it's not like we can get a room at the local public house, right?"

"It's warm tonight. Do you recall how we used to chase spring fireflies in the Hawthorn Glen?"

"I remember lying on the grass next to you, looking up through that gap in the leaves at the endless stars."

"Ever make a wish on one that fell?"

"I did."

"Was it this?" He waved a finger at the stone around them.

She smiled. "It was *this*." She leaned in and kissed him.

Although not officially the first of their married life—they had engaged in a proper peck at the conclusion of their wedding vows—this kiss was different. The press of soft lips, moist and welcoming, caused his problems to fade, and Nolyn was reminded that he was lucky to be alive. If Sephryn was with him, being the ruler of the world might not be so awful.

"Follow me," he told her with a mischievous grin and pulled her along by the hand.

They went into a servant's dormitory and plundered a few wardrobes. Nolyn stole a ridiculously large tunic with a hood that he raised. Sephryn traded her ornate dress for a baggy white palla whose size didn't matter because of how it wrapped and hooked with brass pins. Or maybe she just looked beautiful in everything she wore.

"Should we leave them a note or something?" Sephryn asked.

"Doubt they can read."

Sephryn shrugged. "I just don't want to be accused of stealing."

Nolyn laughed, then stopped. She hadn't laughed with him, and there was an earnest look on her face.

She's not kidding.

"I mean . . ." she began with a self-conscious rise of shoulders, downturn of eyes, and a bobbing head. "I know you're the ruler of the world and all, but it's still theft, right?"

Dear Mari, I love this woman.

"I'm pretty sure the palace provides clothing to those who work here, which means we already sort of own these."

She thought on that a moment. "We haven't been rulers for more than an hour, and already we're taking liberties with our people."

"I honestly can't imagine anyone will be upset, but if you want to spend the night here—"

"No! By every god, no. You're right. I just want to be sure we are always aware—constantly conscious—of how we wield power. I think that the longer the pole you hold the more care you need to use when swinging it."

"Quit it," he scolded her with a smile. "You're ruining this awful day by reminding me how much I love you."

"Sorry." She straightened up, bowing her head in mock shame.

"C'mon." He grabbed her hand and led her out the back of the palace.

The celebration outside was ongoing and would likely continue until dawn. The plaza was a sea of people in colorful clothes, dancing in currents around bands of wandering minstrels. Nolyn and Sephryn each had a wooden cup shoved into their hand as they passed by a group of men handing them out from a tray set on a barrel, as if the men were high priests and it was a sin for a reveler not to have one. The newlyweds sang along with the rest in between swallows of tremble wine. Nolyn pulled his hood lower as a few celebrants peered at them suspiciously. When they found a gap in the crowd, the two dashed around a set of carts loaded with more barrels and disappeared into the city streets. With fermented tremble spilling over their hands, they ran down one road and then another until they came to a masquerade shop, where Nolyn stopped.

"We need masks!" Nolyn grinned at her and panted for air. He reached for a purse that wasn't there. "We have no money. A fine state. I should raise taxes."

It didn't matter. The mask shop was closed.

Nolyn took a sip of tremble. The drink was just as sweet as ever. As a kid, the once-a-year treat was amazing; as an adult, he could hardly bear it.

"Where are we, anyway?" he asked. "This is Ebonydale, right? I always get turned around here." He looked back toward the plaza. He couldn't see it, but the sound of singing, laughter, and cheers still reached them. "The bad news is that we have to go back at some point. Although I suppose we can always build another palace." He said it as a joke but realized it might not be. "Unfortunately, the best place would be on the north side of Imperial Square, except that's where Nyphron's tomb is slated to be built. Everyone agreed that was the best spot. They want to create a whole shrine where people can go to pay respects for years to come. You should see the drawings. They want to put up this massive gold dome, bigger than the top of the Aguanon. I suppose our dream house will have to wait, but maybe we can build something outside the city. What do you think, Seph? Seph?"

She was crying.

"What's wrong? Are you hurt?" He looked at her hand where he had pulled her along, thinking he must have been too rough.

She shook her head. "I'm fine. I'm sorry. It's just . . ."

"What?"

"This is . . ." She looked at the mask shop. "This is the corner where Seymour Destone . . . where he . . . well, this is where he always got lost on his way back from the records hall."

"The fella that reminded you of Bran?"

She nodded. "He was no one, just a kind man who believed in the written word, and who comforted me when I needed someone the most. Now he's dead, and no one even knows his name." She set her cup down and wiped her face with both hands. "He got lost here every night because he always missed the turn. I tried putting a flag up for him once, but someone took it down. He wasn't buried with a stone, and now . . . now I'm afraid Seymour will remain lost forever. I fear he'll never find his way home."

She began to sob into her palms.

Nolyn pulled her close, cradling her head. "He won't get lost. And people will remember him. I'll see to that."

"How?"

Nolyn studied the intersection. "This is a big crossroad. I'll have a pillar placed here, a big stone ten feet high, so no one can miss it. And

380 · *Nolyn by Michael J. Sullivan*

it'll be so heavy that no one can ever move it. We'll name it Destone's Pillar, and there will be a directional arrow so your friend can forever see which way to go." Nolyn looked left then right. "Which way should it point?"

Sephryn nodded toward Ishim's Way. "West. Toward home."

"Consider it done."

"I'm starting to like this empress thing. Am I going to get everything I want?"

"Knowing you . . . probably."

She smiled.

Nolyn looked around to get his bearings and heard more crying. "Seph, are you still—" But it wasn't his wife. The sound came from the side of the mask shop. They both approached and found a little girl huddled in a niche between the emporium and the alchemist store. She couldn't have been more than five or six.

"What's wrong?" Sephryn asked.

The girl said nothing.

"Where are your parents?"

Something in his wife's tone mirrored the same dread Nolyn felt.

"Dead," the girl said. "Killed."

"Oh, you poor thing." Sephryn reached out and hugged the girl. "How long have you been here?"

The girl shrugged. "When those creatures came, a tall, thin man told me to hide over there." She pointed. "Our house is gone—burned down—so I stayed here. Don't know what else to do."

"You did fine. That was very smart. What's your name?"

"Alina Baker."

Sephryn gasped and stared wide-eyed at Nolyn.

"What?" the new emperor asked.

Sephryn didn't answer. Instead, she held out her hand to the child. "You need to come with us, Alina. We're going to help you. You see, there is someone—a very special someone—you need to meet. A woman you used to know, a mother who loves you and has been searching for the child she lost for so long it nearly made her crazy."

The girl took her hand with an expression that was hopeful but bewildered.

Turning to Nolyn, Sephryn spoke so softly that he almost missed it. "Malcolm did it again."

"Did what?"

"A miracle."

"I don't understand. What's going on?"

She smiled at him. "We found the bread—Arvis's lost loaf."

✢ THE END ✢

Farilane Sneak Peek

We hope you have enjoyed *Nolyn*, the first book in the *New York Times* bestselling trilogy The Rise and Fall. Below is the first chapter for the next book in the series, *Farilane*, which has been regarded by many as the best book I've written. Please check it out.

CHAPTER ONE

The Twelfth Night

Another series of bright-white explosions erupted where sea met shore as Farilane stood on the rocky coast and scanned the darkening sky for the star that would guide them to the treasure. That was the hope. Being that this was the twelfth night she'd stood at the same spot, Farilane had her doubts.

On the first three evenings, it had rained. The next two, while dry, were frustratingly overcast. The sixth day dawned blue, but by late afternoon, the clouds had returned as if they'd forgotten something. Poor weather continued throughout the seventh and eighth days. The three after that were literal washouts, forcing a retreat to her field camp or risk being rinsed into the sea. Trapped in her leaky tent, Farilane had reread her notebooks, verifying the calculations for the hundredth time. She'd missed nothing. That shelf of stone partway down a rocky cliff was the correct place. Everything except the weather was perfect, but time was running out. She couldn't bear to wait for another year.

Then on the twelfth night, she caught a break. A star appeared.

"Is that it?" Kolby asked, pointing at the singular pinprick of light on the darkening horizon. There was hope in his voice.

"Tell you in a minute." Farilane took out her astrolabe and positioned it directly over the staff she'd placed days before. She struggled to align the device's rule with one hand while dangling the delicate instrument with the other. "Be a dear and hold this for me, will you?" She offered the ring at the top of the disk to him.

Kolby took the brass apparatus of movable plates with his left hand. Farilane had known he'd use his left before she had offered the instrument. His choice wasn't arbitrary; nothing about Kolby ever was. He always reserved his right hand for his sword.

"What is this thing?" he asked, his eyes studying the device, his nose turned up as if the metal reeked.

"You're holding the entire universe in your hands." She smiled. "So don't drop it."

Kolby narrowed his eyes, first at her and then at the device, his concern turning to skepticism. He held the large ring at the full extent of his arm so that the bottom barely touched the top of the measurement staff, leaving the disk to hang like a lantern.

A lantern. Farilane smiled at the idea. *Yes, that's exactly what it is, a tool to illuminate the world.*

"Now hold still," she commanded.

"How still?" he asked.

Typical Kolby: precise, exacting, and literal. A byproduct of the training, no doubt. All Teshlors were that way to a degree—more than a bit inhuman, until you saw them drunk or angry. That didn't happen often. She suspected that controlling one's rage was also part of the training. If it wasn't, it ought to be. An enraged Kolby topped Farilane's list of the scariest things she'd ever seen.

"Like you're about to loose an arrow for a very important shot, one you can't afford to miss."

Kolby nodded, took a deep breath, then held it. The astrolabe hung from his fist as if nailed to a tree.

Farilane resumed lining up the rule with the star. As she did, Virgil stirred. The philosopher woke with an unhappy moan. He had been napping on the cold rock for the last two hours.

Wiping his eyes, he got to his feet. Snow-white hair, long beard, and a dark cloak flew about him like living things. As he stretched his arms and neck, a grimace relented to the demands of a wide yawn.

How can he sleep on the eve of such an auspicious discovery, not to mention on such a narrow ledge?

The old philosopher was such a sound sleeper that he could doze on the back of a cow caught in a stampede during a thunderstorm. He'd always been that way and had gotten better at it with age. "Well?" he asked.

"Give me a second," Farilane said. She rotated the astrolabe's rete to the proper position, realigned the rule with the star, then read the face of the disk. "That's the Eye of the Bear, the brightest star in the constellation Grin the Brown—first evening star of early spring."

"Are you done? Can I move now?" Kolby asked.

"No. Keep holding that bow steady, soldier." Farilane offered him a grin, then moved around to the other side of the astrolabe and peered through the same sight holes on the rule. "There!" she yelled, pointing down near the foaming water at a dark gap in the honeycombed cliff.

"What's she pointing at?" Kolby asked Cedric, a note of concern in his voice. The younger soldier instantly advanced, and after taking a look, he shrugged.

Farilane had nearly forgotten Cedric was with them. Although physically larger than Kolby, he seemed smaller. She attributed this conflicting phenomenon to personality. Kolby had a presence, but

Farilane couldn't remember having heard Cedric speak. She had supposed he might be mute but felt it would be impolite to ask. "Relax," she told the pair. "We aren't in any danger of being attacked."

"You always say that," Kolby grumbled.

"What are you worried about?" She looked up at the rapidly fading, orange- cast sky, where a handful of seabirds soared. "Man-eating seagulls?"

"Goblins," Virgil said. "They didn't name this the Goblin Sea because it's shaped like one."

"The Ba Ran are seafarers," Farilane pointed out. "We'd see their ships if any were near."

"Not necessarily," Virgil added. "This area is littered with coves and caves. They could hide their vessels in any of them. That happens all the time. Haven't you heard about that poor little village of Tur? It's been ravaged over and over."

"That's all the way down on the southern tip of Belgreig. And goblins aren't raiding that coast. Pirates are."

"Perhaps, but let's not forget that a thousand years ago, *goblins* came from out here and used a network of underground waterways to attack Percepliquis and kill Emperor Nyphron."

"That's only one theory," Farilane qualified. "We both know there are several contradictory accounts of the first emperor's death. And for the record, he died one thousand twenty-nine years, eleven months, and two weeks ago."

They all stared at her as if she'd belched.

"How many hours?" Virgil asked and then chuckled.

Confused as to why the scholar was laughing, she replied, "Sixteen and a half." She glanced at the astrolabe. "Give or take a minute or two."

Virgil stopped laughing, and they all stared at her, dumbfounded.

"What?" she asked. "How precise do you need me to be?"

His expression changed from amusement to shock. "Ah no. That's . . . that's fine."

"Are you sure? Or would you prefer to discuss the ramifications of the Belgric War for a few hours before getting back to why I practically screamed *There!* twenty minutes ago?"

No one said anything.

"Good. Because I was pointing out the cave entrance we're looking for. I found it. It's that one down below us." She took the astrolabe back from Kolby and carefully stowed it in her pack. "Shall we, gentlemen?"

"You can't be serious," Virgil said. "It's nearly night. Now that we know which hole to explore, can't this wait until morning?"

Farilane pointed at a hazy gray curtain of rain sweeping across the Goblin Sea. "Wind is blowing our way. The last storm trapped us for days, and we're running low on food. Besides, all these crevasses look the same, and if we come back in the morning, I doubt I'll be able to identify the right one."

The old man frowned as he looked down the slick, jagged face of the cliff. "Allow me to rephrase. You don't expect *me* to climb over slippery stone in the *dark*, do you?"

"Why not?"

The old man replied with a dangling jaw.

When she didn't respond, he explained, "I'm not a limber young woman. I'm sixty-eight years old, and even in my prime no one would have described me as athletic." He took a step forward for a better look, then grimaced. "One slip and your man-eating seagulls will be pecking flesh off my shattered bones."

"Virgil," she began, placing her hands on his shoulders, "life is a gamble, my friend. The trick is to wager wisely, balancing risk against reward. At your age, nothing is too perilous. Working for a wedge of cheese at a leper colony wouldn't be out of the question. And the reward waiting in that cave is so much better than a bit of cheese."

"You can't know that. The book you're searching for has been intentionally hidden for centuries. I have to think there's a reason. Perhaps you should reconsider the implications of unleashing such a thing upon the world."

"I seek the truth, and the truth is always a good and noble goal."

"Is it?"

"Yes." She nodded sharply. "For example, earlier you said you weren't a limber *young woman*. This was meant to suggest the contrast between the two of us. But Cedric might interpret the comment to verify the all-too-vocal and false rumor that the imperial family *is* human. It's possible Cedric could repeat the comment, erroneously describing me to his friends as *a young woman,* and thus further the misconception. If repeated enough times, that inaccuracy could be believed by millions. So, what began as an innocent joke between friends might become a distorted reality for future generations." She hoisted her pack to her shoulder and turned to the younger knight. "For the record, I'm old enough to be Virgil's great- great-great-grandmother, and I'm not a *woman.*"

Cedric eyed the princess suspiciously.

Farilane frowned as she considered the myriad of things the young knight could be thinking. "What I meant is that I'm only *part* human. My father is descended from Nyphron who was elven—or *Fhrey* as they used to call themselves." She paused to calculate. "Since all the emperors except Nolyn took human wives—and because both Nolyn and his wife, Sephryn, were half-elven, which resulted in no bloodline dilution—that makes me only one thirty-second elven. Arguably, I am more human than elf, but it's still not technically accurate to call me *a woman.*"

"It's truly a wonder why you aren't married." Virgil shook his head. "You knew what I meant."

"*I* did. *He* didn't. Facts are important. They are the notches we cut in trees as we explore reality—lose them, and we might never find our way."

The old man shook his head again. "The point I was making is that I can't climb as easily as the three of you can."

"What do you want from me, Virgil?" Farilane slapped her sides. "The knights aren't allowed to abandon me even to assist my tutor, and you can't climb back up the rope by yourself. I can't leave you here on the side of this cliff. You'd fall asleep, roll off, and die. Either we climb down now or give up, and I'm not willing to quit—not after so many decades of searching—not when we're this close." She took a breath, then added, "Look, it will be okay. I promise. And when we get back to camp, you can have pie."

"Oh really? Pie? Well, that's a completely different argument, now, isn't it?" Virgil peered below at the violent war being waged between sea and coast. "And you're right." He sighed. "I'm not risking much, am I?"

Kolby found the nearest thing to a path and led them down in single file over algae-and-lichen-covered rocks to the mouth of the cave. The sea continued to battle the cliff. Waves churned and exploded in geysers, each accompanied by an impressive *boom!* Blasted by the constant ocean wind and drenched by the salty spray, the four shivered with cold. Farilane pulled tight the front of her cloak and drew up the saturated hood. She attempted to wipe her face with a sleeve, only to discover that it, too, was soaked.

Kolby and Cedric entered the sea-slicked cave first. The younger man paused just inside and dropped his pack next to a small tidal pool. He drew forth one of three lanterns and set to lighting it as evening faded into night.

"All the caves on this coast are reputed to be haunted. Did you know that?" Virgil asked while struggling to keep up. "People in the village said so."

"Every town has ghost stories." Farilane adjusted her pack, which had been cutting into her neck. Satisfied that the strap was in a better place, at least for the time being, she glanced back at Virgil. "And since when do you believe in ghosts?"

"Always have."

Farilane smirked, to no effect. The man was going blind and likely couldn't see her face beneath the hood. "Next you'll be telling me you believe in the gods."

"I *do.*"

"Really?" she scoffed.

"We've discussed this on many occasions!"

Farilane frowned. "I'd hoped you were just going through a phase. I mean, how can you still believe in deities? You're the most educated man I know."

Virgil shook salt water off his cloak. "The more we know, my dear, the more we understand how little we understand."

"Sounds like you're stuttering in whole words." She smirked again, only to remember he still couldn't see her expression.

"No one knows everything, and you could benefit from listening to me once in a while."

"Uh-huh. Okay, old wise one, tell me this: Do gods grant wishes to their faithful?"

Virgil considered this a moment, then shook his head. "Not usually, no." "Then what's the point of having them?"

"Wishes or gods?"

She smiled. "Cute. Gods, of course."

"That's like asking what's the point of air, trees, or rain. You can't—"

Farilane used her fingers to tick off each of the three in order. "To breathe, for lumber and fuel, and to drink."

"Okay, bad examples."

"Not at all. They illustrate my assertion perfectly. Everything has a purpose, except the gods. So why have them?"

"But we don't *have them.* They exist by their own right."

"Oh, really? Can you name a single person who has seen a god?"

"There are several stories where—"

"Those are myths. The question is, have *you,* or anyone you've personally met, encountered a god?" "No, but—"

"Neither have I, and I'm nearly two hundred years old and have a social circle that includes people who have lived to be more than a thousand. Tell me, Virgil, have you ever seen a tree being blown around in a rainstorm? Of course you have. Everyone has. Air, trees, rain, all accounted for. But the gods—well, they never seem to show up, do they? Strange, don't you think? Given how vain they're reported to be, you'd expect them to pop up all the time to demand praise, propagate fear, or inspire awe. Instead . . . nothing. If you got rid of all the people, the trees, rain, and air will still be here. But the gods? Could it be because we invented the whole lot, and they only exist in stories?"

"Such an insane notion could only be conceived by you."

"Yeah, well, we both know I'm odd. So tell me, Virgil—O Believer in All Things Divine—which member of the grand pantheon managed to provide the crucial bit of evidence that kept you faithful? Are you a follower of Eton, the god of the sky? Eraphus, the god of the sea? He'd be really handy right now, don't you think? Or is it Arkum, that bright fellow who supposedly rides a chariot overhead each day, then takes a nap before doing the same thing the next morning, and oddly never tires of the routine? Or are you devoted to that stodgy old elven relic, Ferrol, who is still somehow the official imperial god? Oh, wait—no—don't tell me you're a convert to the new cult, the one that insists Nyphron was a god. Or is it a demigod? I always forget."

"You're being purposely obtuse just to annoy me." "Of course I am." "Why?"

"It's fun. Where is your sense of humor?" She threw back her hood, this time to reveal a grin. "You know how easily I get bored. You just have the misfortune of being around when it happens."

Virgil shook his head. "Kolby is always with you, too. You never speak to him like this."

Farilane glanced at the two men who worked single-mindedly to light the lantern. "Oh, he'd just smile and nod. There's no fun in that." She inched closer to the philosopher and whispered, "Besides, if he actually comprehended my supposition, Kolby would kill me."

Virgil raised both eyebrows. "The man is sworn to protect you with his life."

"His oath to a distant emperor and an ancient creed is hardly a shield against momentary rage coupled with a razor-sharp sword. The man is a walking death trap. A vicious lion held by a string leash."

"You don't honestly believe Kolby would ever hurt you?"

Farilane shook her head. "Of course not."

"But then why did you—"

"Oh, please!" Farilane threw up her hands. "You *really* don't understand the meaning of the word *fun*, do you?" Once more, she grinned, and Virgil sighed as if a noisy expulsion of air was a remarkably convincing argument.

Virgil folded his arms, locking them in a show of frustration. "We're on the outskirts of the empire, beyond the civilized world, literally at land's end, and venturing into a complicated labyrinth of sea-soaked tunnels—at night! I'm cold, wet, and quite frankly, more than a little frightened. We have no idea what lies ahead. Could be anything. This is incredibly dangerous—no joke. Anyone who went to such great lengths to hide a book down here didn't want it found. They likely took precautions to protect their treasure. Every step we take is a risk."

"Oh . . ." Farilane said, surprised. "I apologize and stand corrected. You *do* know the meaning of fun."

The lantern caught fire, and the glow illuminated a natural tunnel that twisted and turned.

"I'll take that." Farilane stepped forward and reached for the light.

Kolby snatched it away. "I'm going first." Then he dutifully added, "Your Highness."

Farilane frowned. "I could order you to stay here." "Think that would do it, do you?"

Farilane looked to Virgil.

"Kolby Fiske!" the philosopher snapped in a reprimanding tone that was designed to quash the self-confidence of pride-filled students. "You're honor bound to obey her."

"Sort of," Kolby replied.

"Come again? What do you mean by *sort of?*"

Kolby shrugged. "We serve to protect the emperor and his family— even *from* the emperor and his family. It's part of our code."

Virgil eyed the knight with the concentration of a cat prior to a pounce. The philosopher knew the Knight's Creed as well as anyone, and he was a skilled orator who had used rhetoric to win debates in the Imperial Council. "Where exactly is that written?"

Kolby grinned. "In the section that says, 'Don't be an idiot.'"

Farilane snickered. And when she saw Virgil's appalled expression, she laughed harder.

"The two of you . . ." Virgil huffed and shook his head. "It's like being trapped with children, and I'm tired of being the only adult."

"I'm sorry," Farilane said, and she took the philosopher's hands in hers. "But you're just so good at it. You have that whole frowny-face thing going for you, and that marvelous sigh, which really lets me know how disappointed you are with my behavior."

"Yet it does no good, now does it? We were almost crushed to death by that giant near Fairington and nearly drowned in the headwaters of the Urum River. Then there was the . . . *Dwarf Incident* in Haston five years ago. Don't think I've forgotten. Believe me, I've tried. I still have nightmares. And I don't know how we escaped without starting a war."

"Would have been a really short war," Cedric muttered.

They all paused and looked at the knight. Then the joke landed. Not the cleverest of jests but given how little he'd said up to that point, it made even Virgil laugh. "We have *two* comedians now, I see."

Farilane and Kolby looked at each other, puzzled and a little disappointed.

"All right—" Virgil relented. "*Three.* You're all clowns. Does that make you feel better?"

Farilane nodded. "Much. Now, shall we proceed?"

"I'm still getting pie, aren't I?"

"We didn't bring any, Virgil. The pie is a lie. You know that, right?"

The philosopher sighed but nodded. "Then by all means, lead us to our deaths."

Farilane turned to Kolby and made a welcoming gesture toward the tunnel as if the cave were her home. "After you, light-bearer."

The knight held the lantern as if it were an astrolabe and began the descent. Cedric followed at the rear. The route was uncomfortably tight at first, and the knights struggled to squeeze armor-plated shoulders through the narrow space. Certain noises were painful to Farilane's ears, and metal scraping stone was near the top of her list. The tunnel widened but never allowed for more than a single file march. They hadn't gone far when Kolby stopped. "That's not good."

"What's wrong?" Farilane asked, unable to see past him. His silhouette, outlined in the glow of the lantern, filled the tunnel, but she heard a constant rushing sound, a roar of water that echoed loud enough to suggest the corridor had opened considerably.

"See for yourself." He stepped aside, granting her access while holding the lantern higher. The tunnel stopped at the edge of a cliff—a massive vertical shaft with no visible ceiling or floor. A waterfall spilled from high above, its spray illuminated by the lantern. "Passage ends here."

"No, it doesn't." Farilane pointed across the chasm. "The tunnel continues on the far side."

"You can see a far side?"

"Yes. About thirty feet, maybe less. What I can't make out is a way to cross." "Might not be any," Virgil said. "There may have once been a bridge, which time and that waterfall destroyed. Or perhaps the means of access was intentionally removed."

Farilane shook her head. "I don't think so. There are no signs of erosion, and while the book has been buried to keep it safe for future generations, the monks would have needed a means to retrieve it." Farilane looked up at the waterfall that issued from darkness and plummeted to more of the same. There was a bottom. She couldn't see it but heard the splash from far below. "Why do you suppose that waterfall is here?" she asked.

"Because water has to go somewhere? And usually that direction is down." "But why here?"

"You know, Your Highness, sometimes there isn't a reason." Virgil leaned on the stone wall of the tunnel and took off one of his sandals. "You need to accept that some things just are. The gods are. That waterfall is. The world doesn't manifest itself merely for your entertainment."

"And yet, that hasn't been my experience."

Virgil rubbed the heel of his bare foot. "Growing up in a palace could have something to do with that."

"Don't confuse me with my brother. He's the one who wears silk pajamas and has a gold crown waiting. I'm . . . well . . ." She gestured at her skirt and leather tunic. Except for the dragon pendant in the center of her chest, she looked like a youthful legion scout on his first deployment. "Let's just say the sun doesn't shine on my ass because I want it to."

She caught Kolby and Cedric smiling and wondered why. They might see her as the quintessential spoiled brat who got whatever she wished, but the pair of grins could have been an expression of solidarity. She hoped for the latter but cautioned herself against seeing only what she wanted. Farilane spent more time in their company than her brother's, and while a princess, she felt more at home with the knights than the imperial family.

No one spoke after that, which returned her attention to the sound of falling water. "Why *is* that waterfall here?" Farilane looked at each of them. She didn't expect an answer. It wasn't a real question, at least not for them. This was merely her process, the way she solved puzzles. She addressed the riddle and waited for it to answer. In this case, the waterfall was being pigheaded, refusing to give any clues. "No, I'm certain that waterfall doesn't just *happen* to be here."

Kolby reached out his free hand, wetted his fingers, and tasted. "Fresh."

"Fabulous," Virgil said. "Good to know we won't die of thirst. One less item on the lengthy list of potential causes of our demise."

"Hmm," Cedric uttered. Unlike the others, he wasn't looking into the shaft, but rather at the floor beneath their feet. This caused each of them to do likewise. "Hmm, indeed," Farilane agreed. "Kolby, if I promise not to jump into the abyss, can I borrow the lantern?"

He held it out to her. The princess backed away from the edge, bent over, and examined the floor.

"Writing?" Virgil asked.

"Looks like it." Farilane set the lantern down and brushed aside dust and dirt until the engraved markings were clearly visible.

"Can you read it?"

Farilane exhaled a disapproving puff of air. "So, you found your sense of humor after all. Was it lost at the bottom of your pack or something?" Farilane held up the lantern to get a better view and then read, "But by the name of god will you enter here."

"How wonderful," Virgil said, delighted. "It is so rare for irony to be on my side."

The princess set the lantern on the floor once more. "This doesn't mean gods exist, merely that another person has been equally duped."

"And yet what is existence, but that which we believe it to be?"

Farilane scrubbed her palms together to clean off the dirt. "I'm astounded that *you* were appointed to be *my* teacher."

"It may appear that I've been a poor tutor. After forty years, I wonder if you've learned anything from me, but is that the fault of the instructor or the student?"

Their conversation was abruptly interrupted by Kolby shouting, "Ferrol!"

Turning, they saw him with hands cupped on either side of his mouth, yelling into the darkness. He looked surprised when nothing happened.

"He's so cute," the princess said to Virgil.

"What?" the knight asked. "God's name is Ferrol."

"You're right," Virgil told the princess. "He wouldn't have comprehended the supposition."

"I don't understand," Kolby said.

"Exactly," the philosopher replied, and having rubbed life back into his heel, he put his sandal on.

Kolby frowned and hooked a thumb in his sword belt the way he usually did when annoyed. "Would you care to explain whatever it is I'm apparently missing?" "Certainly," Virgil said. "My role is to educate, after all, and since the princess refuses to allow me to improve her mind, I might as well help you. First, there are hundreds, perhaps thousands, of gods. Everybody has their favorite. Second, Ferrol is the elven god, and the people who built this vault were definitely not elven. They were, or are, a sect of humans known as *monks*, a word derived from the elvish *monakus*, meaning *solitary*. This is a bit of a misnomer, as these men always dwell in groups. You saw one of their little habitats outside the village of Roch—that ruined stone building next to the domed temple. They call buildings like that *monasteries*, which also absurdly means *to live alone.*"

"Or *apart*," the princess inserted. "The monks were outlawed by the empire during the reign of Nyphron for spreading subversive lies. They were driven into hiding in remote places like this. They were hunted, practically for sport."

"Why?" Kolby asked.

"Nyphron didn't like the monks' practice of writing things down," Virgil explained. "He sought to erase their slanderous lies by destroying their records, hoping that memories would, in time, grow fuzzy and fade into non-existence. The monks countered by hiding their most important texts in secret vaults like this." "So we're here to destroy this book you keep speaking about?" Cedric asked.

Farilane shook her head. "No. We're here to learn the truth."

Virgil coughed most insincerely.

"My pedagogue disagrees," Farilane said. "He is willing to accept the official imperial dogma just the way it is, all whitewashed and tidy with no inconvenient questions like: If Persephone insisted on having the capital built on the site of her childhood home, and Nyphron obliged her out of his intense love, why was Percepliquis built on the wrong side of the Urum and Bern rivers, since every known record describes Dahl Rhen as being just south of the ruins of Alon Rhist, placing it in western Rhulynia?"

"A mapping error," Virgil said.

"Not likely. Percepliquis is located in the Imperial Province of Rhenydd, which is clearly elvish for *New Rhen*. Can't have a *new* Rhen without an *old* Rhen, right? And do you honestly think Nyphron betrayed his own people—led a war against them—for the love of a woman whom he'd just met?"

"As you already mentioned, there are many who believe Nyphron wasn't an elf at all, and his real name was Novron. To some, he was purely human, or even a god, depending on who you talk to."

Farilane's brows rose. "Oh my! So the cultists *have* gotten to you."

Virgil smiled, and a glint of mischief was in his eyes. "I thought you knew the meaning of *fun.*"

"Ha ha." The princess pretended to laugh and added three slow claps of make-believe applause. "Isn't it about time you stowed that sense of humor back in your pack?"

"So I still don't understand," Kolby said. "What did the monks call their god?"

"That's easy." Farilane bent down, and placing her face close to the floor, she blew what remained of the dirt and dust away from the markings.

BUT BY THE NAME OF GOD WILL YOU ENTER HERE

A quick check proved all the necessary letters were present. Placing her thumb on the "M" in the word *name,* she pressed. The stone on which the letter was engraved dropped slightly into the floor. Then she moved to the "A" and did the same.

"They're levers of some sort," Kolby said, then looked around for the effects of her actions, but nothing had changed.

"Fifteen hundred years ago or so, "Virgil began in his lecturer's voice, "the early monks enjoyed a friendly relationship with the Belgric Kingdom. Those dwarfs likely showed them all manner of insidious mechanisms."

Farilane depressed the first "R," then the "I," then the first "B."

"I can't read," Cedric admitted as he studied Farilane's movements. "What is the name she is using?"

"The monks believe the god of humankind is named Maribor," Farilane said, as she finished by depressing "O" in *of* and the second "R." "Maribor, Ferrol, and Drome—the three sons of Erebus, father of the gods."

An instant later, they felt the ground shake—not really a tremor, more of a short-lived jarring as if a massive hammer had hit the floor. Nothing else happened. For a long moment, no one said a word. Heads turned side to side, all of them looking into the shadows beyond the lantern light.

Farilane got up and brushed off her knees. "Something is different."

"What?" Kolby asked.

"The waterfall. Don't you hear it? The sound has changed. The tone of the splash is hollow." The princess moved past Kolby to the edge and peered down. "The shaft is filling up."

Both knights moved to the edge and looked down.

"Is that a good thing?" Virgil asked.

"If the water rises high enough, we can swim across," Kolby said.

Virgil looked back up the narrow corridor. "And if it goes too high, we might drown."

"Won't need to swim," Farilane announced. "There's a bridge floating on the surface of the water."

"There is?" Kolby held the lantern out over the drop. "I don't see— oh, there t took surprisingly little time for the shaft to fill and the bridge to appear, bobbing like a long dock.

"This corridor will fill up," Virgil warned. He glanced back.

Kolby looked concerned, first at the rising water and then at Farilane. He was calculating when he would need to grab her and run for it. The princess's life was his responsibility, his sole concern. Kolby wouldn't waste an instant on the survival of either Cedric or Virgil. When events crossed a certain line, no force on Elan would stay his actions.

The moment the bridge became level with the passage, Kolby took a step toward Farilane, then stopped after hearing a rapid series of snaps.

Virgil pointed at the writing on the floor. "The markings have popped up."

"The bridge is going back down!" Farilane shouted. Without hesitation, she ran onto it.

"Damn it!" Kolby cursed. He handed over the lantern to Cedric. "Stay here in case we need you to punch that name in again."

Cedric shook his head. "Not a monk. Can't read. Can't spell."

"I can do it," Virgil said. "I'll stay with Cedric. Go with her!"

Farilane had leapt out as far as she could onto the bridge, guessing correctly that it was an unstable raft, and her weight—dumped too close to one side—might capsize the whole thing. Seeing the rate of descent, and the far passage rapidly rising beyond her reach, she scrambled through the cold shower of falling water until her weight began to tip the scale. The moment Kolby jumped onto the bridge, his impact nearly catapulted Farilane off. Only a fast drop to her knees and a quick grab of the planks saved her from a swim.

"Stop!" she shouted, holding a palm out toward Kolby as the knight worked his way toward her. "You'll tip us."

With his weight as a counterbalance, Farilane reached the opposite end. Whatever had corked the shaft and lifted the bridge had come unplugged and the discharge far outmatched the inflow. Already the passage on the far side was more than five feet above the bridge. By the time she got there, the opening to the tunnel was too high to reach.

"Go back!" she shouted and waved at Kolby. "Use your weight to raise this end!"

"I need to come with you!"

"You can't! I need you to lift me! Do it! Do it now!"

With a frustrated growl, the knight shuffled backward. His weight, far more than hers, lifted Farilane's end until she could almost grab the ledge. "Jump!" she shouted over the rush of the falls crashing on the center of the bridge.

She didn't look to see if he heard her. Farilane turned her back on him and positioned herself on the edge of the bridge-raft like a diver on a board, her toes hanging off the end, her knees bent, and her arms out. The bridge went down briefly, then lurched up.

Farilane jumped.

Her fingers caught the ledge of the far passage. The wooden platform fell away, leaving the princess to dangle, legs swinging. Her body slammed against the rock wall as the bridge, Kolby, and the water plummeted beneath her.

This probably wasn't a good idea.

She heard Kolby gasp and grunt as he dealt with what she imagined to be an unruly raft reacting poorly to her exit. He sounded disturbingly far away.

Fingers can't last! she mentally yelled at herself. *Up! Climb! Up!*

She got her chin onto the ledge. Gritting her teeth, she used her jaw as a third hook, just enough to find an improved grip with her left hand.

"Farilane!" Kolby shouted, his voice a gasp from far away. "Are you all right?"

Can't talk right now—I'm hanging on by my chin!

Once she had her elbows up, life improved immensely. Pressing both down, she bent at the waist, lifting her hips and swinging a leg up. After that, she rolled onto her side and lay panting for air. Her heart raced and muscles burned.

"Princess!" This time it was Virgil.

"You're missing all the *fun,* my friend," she shouted back.

"Oh, I'm certain of that. Are you okay?"

Farilane sat up. Looking across the chasm, she spotted the glow of Kolby's lantern. "Nothing broken, and I'm on the far side. Kolby, how are you?" "I'm fine, but I'm at the bottom."

"We'll need to raise the water level again," Virgil said.

"Not yet. Hold on. Let me light a lamp."

Farilane pulled off her pack and took out her old clay pot. Working by feel, as she had many times before, she filled it with oil from the little bottle. Stuffing the wick in, she made certain to drench it. Finally, she fished around for her char cloth, flint, and the striker that was shaped like a little flat metal dragon with a long, curved tail. A few good sparks, some deep breaths and solid blows, and Farilane had the lamp lit.

Ahead of her was more tunnel. Rough-hewn, poorly chiseled rock displayed an impoverished work ethic by its narrowness. These monks got by with the least amount of effort, leaving her a tight passage and an easy decision. "Okay, everyone stay where you are," she shouted. "I'll be right back."

Virgil asked, "Where are you going?"

"I'm certain it's just ahead, and it looks perfectly safe."

All of this was a lie, but she felt going unaccompanied was for the best. If the choice had been hers, she would have taken the entire trip alone. But the Princess of House Nyphron was an imperial treasure too valuable to leave to her own devices. She had been forced to accept not just one but *two* Teshlors and Virgil—whom she could only guess was there to talk some sense into her. Farilane's greatest fear was the possibility of getting someone in her party killed. Virgil had been correct in his evaluation that this venture was perilous. The ancient monks were clever beyond normal men. Armed with literature, they had a collective repository of information that stretched back thousands of years. Each monk possessed the knowledge of all those that had come before. They documented centuries of problems and the solutions that worked, as well as those that didn't. Even the ancient elves couldn't rival their knowledge. So long as the monks had their books, they forgot nothing.

"I'm sure it'll only take a few minutes."

"That's what you said in Fairington right before the giant attacked," Virgil shouted. "Just let me raise the bridge so Kolby can join you."

"You can't do that."

"Of course I can. I'll just repeat what you did."

"This crossing was designed to be used by a team. For Kolby to get to me, Cedric would need to join him on the bridge, putting Cedric at the bottom. And since we need you to operate the controls to reverse the process, I don't think it's a good idea to leave you alone. What if the goblins that you're so afraid of turning up come to investigate the light of your lantern shining out of this cave? If something happens to you, the rest of us would be trapped."

No one replied. The only sound was that of the waterfall.

Farilane continued to shout, "I'm fine. Kolby's fine, and you're protected by Cedric. I'm just going to grab the book and come back. It can't be far. The Monks of Maribor are human, not dwarven, so they couldn't have dug too deep. Just sit tight."

Everything she said made perfect sense, her logic impeccable, but still, she was worried.

"I've got this." She spoke too quietly for them to hear over the splash of the waterfall. That didn't matter. She'd said it mostly to herself.

Afterword

Hey, all, it's me, Robin. I'm Michael's wife and "helper bee." You probably don't know me or what I do, but I see myself as having two primary roles. First, I'm here to take as much of the administrative burden off Michael's plate so we can get more stories. To that end, I manage the Kickstarters, organize and run the beta and gamma reader programs, and I also coordinate with . . . well . . . everyone: agents, copyeditors, printers, narrators, designers, and distribution partners. Second, I'm Michael's alpha reader, which means I get to read the book before anyone else—one of the perks of being married to the author! Hopefully, I've made the story better through my early feedback and the editing support I've provided throughout the creation process.

For people who have read my other afterwords, you know this is where I get to "dish" about my favorite (and sometimes disliked) parts of the book, so let's dig in.

Michael often teaches new authors that writing a book is similar to flying a plane. By that I mean that the most critical times are the takeoff and landing. I couldn't agree more, and I think he nailed it in this one. It's not easy starting a new series. There is so much to convey, and you want to do so efficiently while still being entertaining. For me, I felt a connection to Nolyn right from the start. But the best part of the opening was watching the unspoken communication between Jerel and Amicus that had me gleefully anticipating when I would find out what they knew that I didn't.

Oh, and before I go any further, let me state for the record how much I enjoyed the masterful way that Michael spun the tale. Yes, dear, I said masterful, but don't get a swollen head. What I'm referring to are the early mentions of (a) Audrey, (b) losing your soul if you break Ferrol's Law, and (c) how important it is for the dead to reach Phyre. It wasn't until I re-read the book that I noticed how these things come full circle. I tip my hat to you, dear husband. I knew I was wise to snatch you up when I did.

Okay, other likes. I adored every scene where we were inside Arvis Dyer's head. The way her scrambled mind thought, the bravery she exhibited when Death pays a visit, and her courage to fend off the foes in the sewers to save Nurgya were all favorites of mine. Please do me a favor, go back and reread the first two paragraphs of chapter ten. The opening of the scene is beautiful and heartbreaking.

Another favorite aspect of mine was the camaraderie of the men-at-arms that are the Seventh Sik-Aux. Jerel's unrestrained devotion to Nolyn, Amicus's initially skeptical view of his new commander that bloomed into shared respect, and even the comic relief of Smirch made me look forward to the scenes when we returned to this band of brothers.

And then there were the surprises! To be honest, I didn't expect to see Malcolm. And I completely missed all the clues during the scene with the bakers. In fact, when Mawyndulë first mentioned that Seymour's name was obvious—I, too, was taken in. I thought to myself, *Why didn't I suspect this all-too-convenient monk.* And then I was proven wrong when Malcolm dropped the bow string to Sephryn.

While it may seem odd, one of my favorite parts of this book is that things didn't go the way Malcolm planned. I'm a massive fan of the old television show *Quantum Leap*, where Sam Becket is "striving to put right what once went wrong," and that is Malcolm in a nutshell. If everything always worked out for him, this series wouldn't be nearly as interesting. But Michael upped his game in this book by showing us that even Malcolm can trip and fall. And my husband broke my heart by making Sephryn pay the price for Malcolm's shortcomings.

Speaking of which, I know from my interactions with the beta readers that Sephryn's fate is a disappointment to some. But I have a different perspective. First, I think she, Nolyn, and Nurgya will have hundreds of bliss-filled years together. Also, Sephryn is like me in that we are happiest when we have goals to strive toward and positive results come from our efforts. I see a lot of potential for that in her new role as empress, so that gives me hope. But I also know that Michael is a "happily ever after" kind of guy, and I'm confident he has some tricks up his sleeve. And, no, this isn't a carrot I'm dangling because of things I know about privately. It's just that after forty-two years, I know how Michael thinks, and we are both romantics at heart. But even if I'm wrong about that, another book of Michael's has taught me that people who have broken Ferrol's law can still have a happy existence filled with purpose and fulfillment even if that means finding it on the face of Elan rather than in Phyre.

While we are on the subject of Sephryn, I should mention that just because I'm not singing her praises doesn't mean I didn't like her. On the contrary, I enjoyed her quite a bit. But as I already mentioned, we are a lot alike, so it's awkward for me to say too much about her.

Now for my one gripe: Moya. The first time I met her in *Age of Myth*, I wasn't impressed. To me, she was a "pretty girl with a cheeky mouth," who I had seen before. In many ways, I thought of her as a throwaway character. But then came *Age of Swords*, and Michael changed my entire perspective (something he has done on multiple occasions, so I shouldn't have been surprised). Anyway, after one particular scene, she became one of my favorites of all time. Because of my love for Moya, I wanted her and Sephryn to be close. In many ways, they are, but not how I wanted them to be. I wasn't fond of how Michael portrayed my beloved Moya in this book, and even though what we saw was "Moya as seen through Sephryn's eyes," I hope new readers don't get the wrong impression. From a story perspective, I know why Michael made the choices he did, but I still wish I could have convinced him for some changes.

While I wasn't able to influence the book in that particular case, there are places where my feedback did result in alterations. One of the cool things about writing an afterword is providing a behind-the-scenes peek into the creative process, so I'd like to share one of those now. In the original version, Trilos was in Seymour's body from page one. When I discovered this, it "tainted" my early impressions of the monk. What I saw as a genuine and sincere person turned out to be a deceptive and manipulative cretin, and that didn't sit well with me. After much debate, Michael conceded that I could have my well-loved monk and that Trilos would take over "at some point," but he left the time of transition vague and untold. As a reader's advocate, I thought some would feel they had been the victim of a bait and switch, so Michael eventually added the scene where we see Trilos step in.

That illustrates just one of the thousands of decisions made during the creation process. Ultimately, how much you enjoy a book depends on how often you agree with the author's choices, and I hope that in the case of Nolyn, it's more often than not.

Well, my time is up. I sincerely hope you'll return to Elan for the release of Farilane in the summer of 2022. It's one of Michael's favorite books and for many valid reasons. For now, I'll bid my adieu by saying thank you for the continued fantastic support. Michael and I will keep working hard to provide you with the best stories we can.

Robin Sullivan

Acknowledgments

Even though it's my name on the cover, many people are responsible for making *Nolyn* possible through their time and talents. Robin and I would like to thank the following professionals: Marc Simonetti for his always unique artwork, Shawn T. King, for his cover design skills, Laura Jorstad and Linda Branam for their copyediting eagle eyes, Shawn Speakman for his work with distribution and promotion, and of course, Tim Gerard Reynolds for his exceptional narration.

We would also like to thank the incredible pool of beta and gamma readers that volunteered their time to make this book shine. Some of the people who contributed include the following: Tammy Abma • Anna Abraham • Jaslyn Adams • Sam Adams • Samantha Adams • Garrett Aikens • Robert S. Aldrich II • Blaise Ancona • M.H. Armour • Dee Austring • Michael Bailey • Richard Bennett • Clif Bergmann • Hugo Bresson • Amy Lesniak Briggs • Jude Brown • Sara Brunson • Michael Jay Brunt • Courtney Cabaniss • Jeffrey Carr • Tim Challener • Timothy Challener • Julia Charlow • Charlotte Choo • Greg Clinton • Brandon Cole • Beverly Collie • Ramon Crawford • Tim Cross • Felicia D. Culbertson • Buffy Curtis • Joanna Davis • Michael Dayan • Zach Dixon • Stéphane Dufresne • Elysia • Angie Engelbert • Gabe Erwin • Gabe Erwin • Morgan B. Ewers • Louise Faering • Mazyar Fallah • Lynette Floyd • Cathy Fox • Michael Fox • G. Miles Frankum • Rohan Gandhi • John Geisen-Kisch • Sheri L. Gestring • Stephen Ginnetty • Bhavik Gordhan • Joshua Eli Gossett • Christopher Griffin • Nicole Guay •

Audrey Hammer • Lesley Hanly • Ryan M. Hart • Ryan Michael Hart • Chris Haught • Espen Agøy Hegge • Ted Herman • Sarah Hersman • Andrew Hogg • Angela Marie Howe • Austin Hughey • Rebecca Hunt • Justin Isbell • Craig T. Jackson • Raven N. Jones • Katrina May Jordan • Steve Kafkas • Marty Kagan • Pulkit Kansal • William G. Keaton • Evelyn Keeley • Nelli Khamraeva • Nathaniel & Sarah Kidd • Amanda K. King • Danielle Knight • John Koehler • Tony Kuehn • Joan Labbe • M. R. Landers • Hannah Langendoerfer • Mark Larsen • Scott Latter • Youko Leclerc • Benjamin Lee • Chris Lee • Christiaan Lennaerts • Amy Lesniak • David Liesez • Linnea Lindstrom • Jonas Lodewyckx • Sasha Luthra • Richard Martin • Charli Maxwell • Debbie McCoy • Jamie McCullough • Chris "Gunner" McGrath • Melanie • Alex Ryckman Mellnik • April Mendis • Michaela • Anders Mikkelsen • Adam D. Miller • Alex Miller • Erin Millner • Kali Montecalvo • Corrie Moran • Kim Morgan • Peter Morrison • Cheryl S. Moss • Mrbill2705 • Kellyn Neumann • Charles Norton • Dr. Charles E. Norton III • Elizabeth Ocskay • Megan Odom • Ganesh Olekar • Nathaniel Patton • J. Peretz • Christina Pilkington • James A. Plotts • Calvin Post • Steve Rainsford • Amanda Ramsey • Jo Randall • Sarah Retza • Kristen Roskob • Beth Rosser • Jen Ruth • Sarah S. • Dillon Sabo • Zach Sallese • Pamela Sanford • Mini Saraswati • Steven Schmelling • Catherine Schmidt • Doug Schneider • Mitchell Schuster • Jeffrey Schwarz • Brett Shand • Rohit Shankar • Heather Sinke • Elakkiya Sivakumaran • Shawn Robert Smith • Andrew Sprow • Stefan Randolf Statlander • Jennifer Strohschein • Noah K. Sturdevant • Genevieve Stutz • Ian Sutherland • Richelle Trivedi • Rachel Dee Turner • Dani van Ommeren • Harsh Varia • Richard D. Vogel • Joshua M. Wallace • David Walters • Sarah Webb • Adam "Swiff" Weller • Deana Covel Whitney • Dick Wilkin • Bob Williamson • David Winter • Joshua Woolnough • WooPigFoodie • Rob Wootton • Allison Yablonski

About the Author

MICHAEL J. SULLIVAN is a New York Times, USA Today, and Washington Post bestselling author who has been nominated for nine Goodreads Choice Awards and has received six Amazon Editor's Picks. His first novel, The Crown Conspiracy was released by Aspirations Media Inc. in October of 2008. Michael has been published by the fantasy imprints of Penguin Random House (Del Rey) and Hachette Book Group (Orbit). He has also been a pioneer in the indie publishing movement. As of 2023, Michael has released twenty novels (nineteen set in his fictional world of Elan, and one standalone sci-fi thriller (Hollow World). His series include:

- The Riyria Revelations (6 books - released as three omnibuses)
- The Riyria Chronicles (4 books)
- The Legends of the First Empire (6 books)
- The Rise and Fall (3 books)

Today, Michael has returned to his indie roots while still providing his novels through retail bookstores. Each novel is launched via Kickstarter (eleven books and counting), where his campaigns are among the most-backed and highest-funded fiction projects of all time. Doing so provides his most-ardent fans with unparalleled author access, deluxe limited-edition hardcovers, exclusive perks, and the ability to read the story months before its official release.

Michael always enjoyed hearing from readers, and you can email him at michael@michael-j-sullivan.com.

About the Type

This book was set in Caslon, a typeface named for the English designer William Caslon (1692–1766). Caslon worked in the tradition of what is now called old-style serif letter design, which produced letters with a relatively organic structure resembling handwriting with a pen. His work was influenced by the imported Dutch Baroque typefaces, which previously had not been common in London.

Caslon's typefaces established a strong reputation for their quality and their attractive appearance, suitable for extended passages of text. The typefaces he created were popular in his lifetime and beyond After a brief period of eclipse in the early nineteenth century, they returned to popularity, particularly for setting printed body text and books.